Praise for *New York Times* bestselling author Diana Palmer

"Palmer proves that love and passion can be found even in the most dangerous situations."
—*Publishers Weekly* on *Untamed*

"You just can't do better than a Diana Palmer story to make your heart lighter and smile brighter."
—*Fresh Fiction* on *Wyoming Rugged*

"Diana Palmer is a mesmerizing storyteller who captures the essence of what a romance should be."
—*Affaire de Coeur*

"The popular Palmer has penned another winning novel, a perfect blend of romance and suspense."
—*Booklist* on *Lawman*

"Diana Palmer's characters leap off the page. She captures their emotions and scars beautifully and makes them come alive for readers."
—*RT Book Reviews* on *Lawless*

Dear Reader,

I can't believe that it has been thirty years since my first Long, Tall Texans book, *Calhoun*, debuted! The series was suggested by my former editor, Tara Gavin, who asked if I might like to set stories in a fictional town of my own design. Would I! And the rest is history.

As the years went by, I found more and more sexy ranchers and cowboys to add to the collection. My readers (especially Amy!) found time to gift me with a notebook listing every single one of them, wives and kids and connections to other families in my own Texas town of Jacobsville. Eventually the town got a little too big for me, so I added another smaller town called Comanche Wells and began to fill it up, too.

You can't imagine how much pleasure this series has given me. I continue to add to the population of Jacobs County, Texas, and I have no plans to stop. Ever.

I hope all of you enjoy reading the Long, Tall Texans as much as I enjoy writing them. Thank you all for your kindness and loyalty and friendship. I am your biggest fan!

Love,

Diana Palmer

NEW YORK TIMES BESTSELLING AUTHOR

DIANA PALMER

ROPING THE TEXAN

2 Heartfelt Stories
Tyler and *Calhoun*

HARLEQUIN SPECIAL RELEASE

HARLEQUIN® SPECIAL RELEASE

PLEASE RECYCLE · THIS PRODUCT IS RECYCLABLE

Recycling programs for this product may not exist in your area.

ISBN-13: 978-1-335-44849-1

Roping the Texan

Copyright © 2022 by Harlequin Enterprises ULC

Tyler
First published in 1988. This edition published in 2022.
Copyright © 1988 by Diana Palmer

Calhoun
First published in 1988. This edition published in 2022.
Copyright © 1988 by Diana Palmer

For questions and comments about the quality of this book, please contact us at CustomerService@Harlequin.com.

Harlequin Enterprises ULC
22 Adelaide St. West, 41st Floor
Toronto, Ontario M5H 4E3, Canada
www.Harlequin.com

Printed in U.S.A.

CONTENTS

A prolific author of more than one hundred books, **Diana Palmer** got her start as a newspaper reporter. A *New York Times* bestselling author and voted one of the top ten romance writers in America, she has a gift for telling the most sensual tales with charm and humor. Diana lives with her family in Cornelia, Georgia. Visit her website at www.dianapalmer.com.

Books by Diana Palmer

Long, Tall Texans

Fearless
Heartless
Dangerous
Merciless
Courageous
Protector
Invincible
Untamed
Defender
Undaunted

The Wyoming Men

Wyoming Tough
Wyoming Fierce
Wyoming Bold
Wyoming Strong
Wyoming Rugged
Wyoming Brave

Visit the Author Profile page
at Harlequin.com for more titles.

TYLER

CHAPTER ONE

To TYLER JACOBS, the hot arid southeastern Arizona landscape still seemed about as welcoming as Mars, even after six weeks of working on the Double R dude ranch near Tombstone.

He was restless and vaguely depressed. He'd taken a day off to fly to Jacobsville for his sister, Shelby's, wedding to Justin Ballenger, a man she'd refused to marry years ago. Tyler was still puzzled by the courtship. They hadn't looked the picture of a happy couple, and he knew that Justin had been bitter toward Shelby for breaking their earlier engagement.

But it wasn't any of his business; he had to keep that in mind. And better to see Shelby married to Justin, who was old-fashioned enough to keep his marriage vows, than to see her mixed up with the local playboy attorney she worked for. Maybe things would work out for them. If the way Shelby had looked at Justin was any indication, they had to work out. She was obviously still deeply in love with him.

Abby and Calhoun had been at the wedding, too, and Tyler was relieved to find that his brief infatuation with Abby was over. He'd been ready to settle down and was unconsciously looking for the right kind of woman. Abby had fit the bill in every respect, but he wasn't nursing a broken heart. His eyes narrowed in thought. He wondered if he was capable of loving a woman. Sometimes he felt that he was impervious to anything more than surface interest. Of course, there was always the woman who could hit a man hard before he knew it. A woman like Nell Regan, with her unexpected vulnerabilities and compassion...

Even as the unwelcome thought touched his mind, his pale green eyes narrowed on a rider approaching from the direction of the ranch house.

He sighed, glaring through the endless creosote bushes. They dominated the landscape all the way to the Dragoon Mountains, one of Cochise's old strongholds back in the mid-1800s. The "monsoon season" had almost passed. Today it was on the verge of a hundred degrees, and damn what they said about the dry heat not being hot. Sweat was pouring down his dark olive complexion from the sweatband of his gray Stetson, soaking his Western-cut chambray shirt. He took his hat from his jet-black hair and drew his forearm over the wetness while he got his bearings. Out here one stretch of valley looked much like any other, and the mountain ranges went on forever. If elbow room was what a man wanted, he could sure get it in Arizona.

He'd been out in the brush trying to round up some stray Hereford calves, while his worn leather chaps were treated to the double jeopardy of cholla and prickly pear cactus where the creosote wasn't so thick. Nothing grew around creosote. Having smelled the green bush, especially in the rain, he could understand why.

Before the rider got much closer, Tyler realized that it was Nell. And something was wrong, because she usually kept the length of the ranch between them. Their relationship had become strained unexpectedly, and that saddened him. It had seemed as though he and Nell would be friends at their first meeting, when she'd picked him up at the Tucson airport. But all too soon something had sent Nell running from him.

Perhaps that was for the best. He was earning a living, but not much more, and all his wealth was gone. He had nothing to offer a woman like Nell. All the same, he felt guilty if he'd hurt her, even inadvertently. She didn't talk about the past, and neither did anyone else. But Tyler knew that something had happened to make her wary and distrustful of men. She deliberately downplayed the few attractions she had, as if she was determined not to do anything that would catch a man's eye. Tyler had gotten close to her at first, because he'd thought of her as a cute little kid. She'd been so anxious to make him comfortable, sneaking him feather pillows and all kinds of little things from the house to make him feel at home. He'd flirted with her gently, teased her, delighted in her shy company. And then, like lightning, the housekeeper had made him see that the child he was playing with was really a twenty-four-year-old woman who was misinterpreting his teasing. From that night on, he and Nell had somehow become strangers. She avoided him, except at the obligatory square dance with guests twice a month.

Nell did seem to find him useful in one respect. She still hid behind him at those every-other-Saturday-night barn dances. The way she clung to him was the only crumb left of their easy first acquaintance. But it was vaguely insulting, too. She didn't consider him a threat in any sexual way, or she'd have run screaming from his presence. He'd made some hard remarks about Nell to his sister, Shelby, but he hadn't really meant them.

He hadn't wanted anyone to realize how Nell was getting to him.

He sighed, watching her approach. Well, she wasn't dressed to fan a man's ardor, in those baggy jeans and blouse and slouch hat, and that was a good thing. He found her shyness and his odd sense of empathy for her disturbing enough without the added complication of an exquisite figure. He frowned, wondering what she looked like under that baggy camouflage. As if he'd ever find out, he thought, laughing bitterly. He'd already scared her off.

He wasn't a conceited man, but he was used to women. His money had always attracted the beautiful ones, and whatever he wanted, he got. And so, being snubbed by the stone girl stung his pride.

"Have you found those strays yet?" Nell asked with faint nervousness as she reined in beside him.

"I've only gone through five thousand miles," he murmured with soft antagonism. "Wherever they are, they're probably enjoying the luxury of enough water to drink. God knows, except in the monsoon season, they'd need a divining rod or second sight in this barren wasteland to find any."

Nell searched his hard face quietly. "You don't like Arizona, do you?"

"It's foreign." He turned his gaze toward the horizon, where jagged mountains seemed to change color as the sun shifted, first dark, then mauve, then orange. "This takes some getting used to, and I've only been out here a few weeks."

"I grew up here," she remarked. "I love it. It only looks barren. If you see it up close, there's all kinds of life."

"Horny toads, rattlesnakes, Gila monsters..." he agreed dryly.

"Red-winged blackbirds, cactus wrens, roadrunners, owls, deer," she corrected. "Not to mention wildflowers by the score. Even the cacti bloom," she added, and there was a sudden softness in her dark eyes, a warmth in her voice that was usually missing.

He bent his head to light a cigarette. "It looks like desert to me. How's your trail ride coming?"

"I left the guests with Chappy," she said with a sigh. "Mr. Howes looked as if one more bounce would put him on the ground. I hope he makes it back to the ranch."

Tyler smiled slightly as he glanced at her rigid figure in the saddle. "If he falls off, we'll need a crane to get him back on."

Nell grinned without meaning to. He wouldn't know it, but he was the first man in years who'd been able to make her smile. She was a somber, quiet woman most of the time, except when Tyler was around. Then she'd found out what he really thought of her....

"Tyler, could you take over the campout for me?" she asked unexpectedly. "Marguerite and the boys are coming for the weekend, and I have to go into Tucson and get them."

"I can handle it, if you'll persuade Crowbait to cook," he agreed. "I'm not making biscuits again. I'll quit first."

"Crowbait isn't so bad," she defended. "He's—" her dark eyes narrowed as she searched for a word "—unique."

"He has the temperament of a cougar, the tongue of

a cobra and the manners of a bull in heat," Tyler said shortly.

She nodded. "Exactly! He's unique."

He chuckled and took another draw from his cigarette. "Well, boss lady, I'd better get those strays before somebody with an itchy trigger finger has beef for supper. I won't be long."

"The boys want to go looking for Apache arrowheads while they're here," she added hesitantly. "I told them I'd ask you."

"Your nephews are nice kids," he said unexpectedly. "They need a firmer hand than they get, though."

"Marguerite isn't the ideal parent for two high-strung boys," Nell said defensively. "And since Ted died, it's been worse. My brother could handle them."

"Marguerite needs a husband." He smiled at the thought of Marguerite. She was like the life he'd been used to—sophisticated and uncomplicated and pretty. He liked her because she brought back sweet memories. She was, in fact, all the things Nell wasn't. "But a dish like Margie shouldn't have much trouble finding one."

Nell knew her sister-in-law was beautiful, but it hurt somewhere deep inside to hear Tyler acknowledge Margie's good looks. Nell was only too aware of her own limitations, of her round face and big eyes and high cheekbones. She nodded, though, and forced a smile to her unlipsticked mouth. She never wore makeup. She never did anything to draw attention to her...until recently. She'd tried to attract Tyler, but Bella's comments had killed the notion. Tyler's subsequent behavior had buried it.

Now Nell knew better than to make eyes at Tyler.

Besides, Margie was just his style, she thought bitterly. And Margie was interested, too.

"I'll go into Tucson, then, if you're sure about the campout. And if you can't find those strays by five, come back in and we'll let your Texas friends look for them in the morning," she added, referring to two of the older hands who shared a Texas background with Tyler and had become fast friends of his in the six weeks he'd been in residence.

"I'll find them," he said carelessly. "All I have to do is look for a puddle of water, and they'll be standing on their heads in it."

"You already know not to sit in any dips or washes," she murmured. "Out here is even worse than in Texas. It can be raining twenty miles away and the sky can be clear, and before you know it, you're in a floodplain."

"We have flash floods where I come from," he reminded her. "I know the dangers."

"I was just reminding you," she said, and hated the concern that she'd unwittingly betrayed.

His eyes narrowed and he smiled unpleasantly, stung by her condescending attitude. "When I need a nurse-maid, honey, I'll advertise," he said in a pronounced Texas drawl.

Nell steeled herself not to react to what was blatantly an insult. "If you have a chance tomorrow, I'd like you to speak to Marlowe about his language. One of the guests complained that she was getting tired of hearing him swear every time he saddled a horse for her."

"Why can't you tell him?"

She swallowed. "You're the foreman. Isn't keeping the men in line your job?"

"If you say so, ma'am." He tipped his hat with faint

insolence, and she wheeled her mount too quickly, almost unseating herself in the process when she pulled
on the bit too hard. She urged the horse into a trot and
soothed him, stroking his mane as she apologized. She
knew Tyler had seen that betraying action, and she felt
even worse. She was the last person on the ranch who'd
ever hurt a horse voluntarily, but Tyler had a talent for
stoking her temper.

He watched her go, his cigarette smoking, forgotten, in his lean, tanned fingers. Nell was a puzzle. She
wasn't like any woman he'd ever known, and she had
quirks that intrigued him. He was sorry they'd become
antagonists. Even when she was pleasant, there was always the reserve, the bitter holding back. She seemed
to become rigid when she had to talk to him.

He sighed. He didn't have time for daydreaming.
He had to find six little red-and-white-coated calves
before dark. He turned his horse and moved into the
thick brush.

Nell dawdled on her way back to the adobe ranch
house. She wasn't anxious to have Marguerite around,
but she hadn't been able to find an excuse to keep the
redhead away. Tyler's remark about her sister-in-law
still rankled. He found Marguerite attractive, and it
wasn't because of Nell that Marguerite was finding rea-
sons to spend time on the dude ranch. She wanted Tyler.
She'd made it obvious with her flirting.

Marguerite was beautiful, all right. She was red-
headed, green eyed, and blessed with a figure that
looked good in anything. She and Nell got along fairly
well, as long as neither of them looked back nine years.
It had been Marguerite who'd helped put the scars on

Nell's young emotions. Nell had never been able to forget what had happened.

On the other hand, it wasn't until Tyler came that Nell really noticed how often Marguerite used her. She was impulsive and thought nothing of inviting her friends out to the ranch for horseback rides or of leaving her two young sons in Nell's care.

Those actions had never bothered Nell very much until lately. Recently, Nell had been feeling oddly restless and stubborn. She didn't like the idea of Marguerite coming for two weekends in the same month. She should have said so. Giving in to her sister-in-law had become a habit, the way of least resistance. But not anymore. She'd already given Marguerite some unmistakable signals that little Nell wasn't going to be walked over anymore.

Margie only came out to see the Texan, Nell was sure of it. She felt a sense of regret for what she might have felt for Tyler if he hadn't made his lack of interest so apparent. But that was just as well. Margie had made it obvious that she liked Tyler, and Nell knew she was no competition for the older woman. On the other hand, she was pretty tired of letting Margie use her for a doormat. It was time to say so.

HER SISTER-IN-LAW and her nephews, Jess and Curt, were already packed and waiting when Nell parked the Ford Tempo at the steps of their apartment. The boys, red-headed and green-eyed like their mother, made a bee-line for her. At seven, Jess was the oldest. Curt was five and already a contender for a talking marathon.

"Hi, Aunt Nell, how about taking us to hunt lizards?"

Curt asked as he clambered into the backseat a jump ahead of his taller brother.

"Never mind lizards, nerd," Jess muttered, "I want to look for arrowheads. Tyler said he'd show me where to look."

"I reminded him," Nell assured the older boy. "I'll go lizard hunting with Curt."

"Lizards make my skin crawl," Marguerite said. She wasn't quite as tall as Nell, but she was equally slender. She was wearing a green-and-white striped dress that looked as expensive as the diamond studs in her ears and the ruby ring on her right hand. She'd stopped wearing her wedding band recently—just since Tyler came to the ranch, in fact.

"Well, if I get a lizard, he can live with me," Curt told his mother belligerently.

Nell laughed, seeing her brother in the small boy's firm jaw and jutting chin. It made her a little sad, but it had been two years since Ted had died, and the worst of the grief had worn off. "Can he, now?"

"Not in my house," Marguerite said firmly. After her husband had died, Margie had taken her share of the ranch in cash and moved to the city. Margie had never really liked ranch life.

"Then he can live with Aunt Nell, so there."

"Stop talking back, you little terror." Marguerite yawned. "I do hope all the air conditioners are working this time, Nell. I hate the heat. And you'd better have Bella stock up on Perrier—there's no way I'm drinking water out of that well."

Nell got in under the wheel without any comment. Marguerite always sounded like a conquering army. It was annoying and sometimes frankly embarrassing to have Margie ordering her around and taking things for granted. Nell had taken it for a long time, out of loyalty to her late brother, and because the boys would suffer if she didn't. But it was hard going, and until just recently she'd taken a lot from Marguerite. It was only when Marguerite began making a dead set at Tyler that Nell had started talking back. And now that she'd gotten the hang of it, she rather liked not being talked down to and told what to do. She stared at her sister-in-law coldly while the boys argued in the backseat about who got the middle and who got a window seat.

"The ranch is mine," she reminded Marguerite quietly. "Uncle Ted is in charge until I turn twenty-five, but after that, I'm sole owner. Remember the terms of my father's will—my brother got half and I got half. Uncle Ted was executor. Then when my brother died, you got his share of the ranch in cash. As executor, Uncle Ted keeps control until I come of age. You don't give orders to me, and you don't get special consideration just because you're an in-law."

Marguerite stared. It wasn't like Nell to fight back so fiercely. "Nell, I didn't mean to sound like that," she began hesitantly.

"I haven't forgotten what happened nine years ago, even if you're trying to," Nell added quietly.

The older woman actually went bloodred. She looked away. "I'm sorry. I know you don't believe that, but I really am. I've had to live with it, too. Ted despised me for it, you know. Things were never the same between us after I had that party. I still miss him, very much," she added in a soft, conciliatory tone, with a glance in Nell's direction.

"Sure you do," Nell agreed as she started the car.

"That's why you're dressed to the teeth and finding excuses to suffer the heat at the ranch. Because you miss Ted so much, and you want to console yourself with my hired help."

Marguerite gasped, but Nell ignored the sound. She pulled out into traffic and started telling the boys about the new calves, which kept the older woman quiet during the drive home.

As usual, when Bella saw Marguerite coming in the front door, the buxom housekeeper went out the back door on the pretense of carrying an apple pie over to the bunkhouse. On the way there she ran into Tyler, who looked tired and dusty and half out of humor.

"What are you doing out here?" he asked, grinning at the older woman with her black scowl.

"Hiding out," Bella said grumpily, pushing back strands of salt-and-pepper hair while her black eyes glittered. "She's back," she added icily.

"She?"

"Her Majesty. Lady Leisure." She shifted the pie. "Just what Nell needs, more people to take care of. That lazy redhead hasn't lifted a finger since poor Ted drowned in a dry wash. And if you knew what that flighty ex-model had done to Nell..." She flushed as she remembered who she was talking to. She cleared her throat. "I baked the men a pie."

"You baked me a pie," Nell muttered, glaring at her housekeeper as she came out of the back door. "And now you're giving it away because my sister-in-law is here. The boys like pie, too, you know. And Margie won't spoil her figure with sweets, anyway."

"She'll spoil my day," Bella shot back. "Wanting this, wanting that, make the bed, bring her a towel, cook her an omelet… She can't be bothered to pick up a shoe or carry a cup of coffee, no, not her. She's too good to work."

"Don't air the dirty linen out here," Nell said shortly, glancing at Tyler.

Bella lifted her small chin. "He's not blind," she said. "He knows what goes on here."

"Take my pie back in the house," Nell told her.

Bella glared at her. "She's not getting a bite of it."

"Tell her."

The older woman nodded curtly. "Don't think I won't." She glanced at Tyler and grinned. "You can have a slice, though."

He took off his hat and bowed. "I'll eat every crumb twice."

She laughed gleefully and went back inside.

"Aren't you late for the campout?" Nell asked curiously.

"We canceled it," he replied. "Mr. Curtis fell into a cactus and Mrs. Sims got sick on the chili we had at lunch and had to go to bed. The rest figured they'd rather watch television."

Nell smiled faintly. "Oh, well. The best-laid plans… We'll try it again on the weekend."

Tyler studied her quietly, his eyes narrowed in thought. "About this afternoon…" he began, holding Nell's surprised gaze.

But before he could say another word, the door behind Nell swung open.

"Why, Tyler, how nice to see you again," Marguerite said laughingly, pausing in the doorway.

"Nice to see you again, Mrs. Regan," he replied dryly, and there was a world of knowledge in the pale green eyes that swept lazily down her slender body. Marguerite couldn't take him in with that strategic pose. He knew too much. But it was amusing to watch her try.

Nell wanted to throw herself down in the dust and cry, but that wouldn't have done any good. She went back inside, giving up without a struggle.

Marguerite gave her a curious glance, but Nell didn't even look at her. If she wanted Tyler, she was welcome to him, Nell thought miserably. After all, she had nothing to give him herself.

Supper was a quiet affair, except for the boys squabbling over everything from milk to beans.

"Tyler is taking me riding tomorrow," Marguerite said, giving Nell an apprehensive glance. "You'll mind the boys, won't you?"

Nell looked up. She felt rebellious. Restless. "As a matter of fact, I can't," she said with a faint smile. "Take them with you. Tyler's already said he wouldn't mind helping them find arrowheads."

"Sure!" Jess burst out. "I'd love to go."

"I'll go, too," Curt said.

Marguerite looked annoyed. "I don't want you along."

"You don't love us," Jess wailed.

"You never did," Curt seconded, and he started to cry.

Marguerite threw up her hands. "See what you've done now!" she accused Nell.

"I haven't done anything except refuse to be your doormat." Nell finished her potatoes. "I don't remember inviting you here," she replied coolly. "Don't expect me to entertain you or babysit for you."

"You always have before," Marguerite reminded her.

"That was before," Nell replied. "I'm not doing it anymore. You'll have to take care of yourself."

"Who's been talking to you?" Marguerite asked, fascinated.

"Nobody has," Nell replied. "I'm just tired of holding up the world. Why don't you get a job?"

Marguerite's gasp was audible, but Nell had gotten up and left the table before she had time for any outbursts.

TYLER TOOK MARGUERITE and the boys riding the next morning. Marguerite did look good in a riding habit, Nell had to concede, but the redhead was obviously out of sorts at having the boys along. Tyler hadn't fussed about taking the boys, either. He liked children. Nell smiled. She liked them, too, but it was Marguerite's job to be their mother, not Nell's.

She wandered out to the kitchen and picked up a biscuit, having refused breakfast because she hadn't wanted to hear Margie raising Cain about the boys going along on her romantic ride.

"And what's eating you, as if I didn't know?" Bella asked.

Nell laughed. "Nothing at all."

"You've got Margie running for cover. Imagine, you talking back to her and refusing to be pushed around. Are you sick or something?" she added, her keen old eyes probing.

Nell bit into the biscuit. "Not at all. I'm just tired of being worked to death, I guess."

"And watching Margie flirt with Tyler, I've no doubt."

Nell glared at the older woman. "Stop that. You know I don't like him."

"You like him. Maybe it's my fault that things never got going between you," Bella confessed gently. "I was trying to spare you more heartache, or I'd never have said anything when you put on that pretty dress…."

Nell turned away. She didn't like being reminded of that day. "He isn't my type," she said gruffly. "He's Margie's type."

"That's what you think," Bella murmured dryly. She put her towel down and stood staring at the other woman. "I've wanted to tell you for years that most men are nice critters. Some of them are even domesticated. All men aren't like Darren McAnders," she added, watching Nell's face go pale. "And he wasn't even that bad except when he was pushed into getting drunk. He loved Margie."

"And I loved him," Nell said coldly. "He flirted with me and teased me, just like Tyler did at first. And then he did…he did that to me, and it wasn't even because he was attracted to me. It was just to make Margie jealous!"

"It was despicable," Bella agreed. "But it was worse for you because you cared about him, and you felt betrayed and used. It was a good thing I happened upstairs when I did."

"Yes," Nell said tautly. The memories hurt.

"But it wasn't as bad as you've always made it out to be, either," Bella said firmly, ignoring the shocked look she got from Nell. "It wasn't," she added. "If you'd ever gone out with boys or had a date, you'd understand what happened a lot better. You hadn't even been kissed—"

"Stop it," Nell muttered miserably. She stuck her

hands in her jeans and shifted. "It doesn't matter, anyway. I'm plain and countrified and no man is ever going to want me, no matter what I do. And I heard what Tyler said that night," she added with a cold glare. "I heard every word. He said he didn't want a 'lovesick tomboy hanging on to his boots.'"

Bella sighed. "So you did hear him. I was afraid that's why he was getting the deep-freeze treatment lately."

"It doesn't matter, you know," Nell said with deliberate carelessness. "It's just as well I found out early that I was annoying him. I've been careful not to bother him since."

Bella started to say something, but obviously thought better of it. "How long is Her Highness here for?"

"Just until tomorrow afternoon, thank God." Nell sighed. "I'd better get cracking. We're going riding, and then this afternoon I've got a busload of shoppers to take into town. I thought I'd run them over to the El Con mall. They might like to get some real Western gear at Cooper's."

"The silversmiths are over near San Xavier," she was reminded. "And they could have some Papago fry bread for refreshments."

"Tohono o'odham," Nell corrected automatically. "That's a real Papago word, meaning 'people of the desert.' They changed it because they got tired of being called 'bean people' in Zuni."

"I can't say that," Bella muttered.

"Sure you can. *Tohono o'odham.* Anyway, the fry bread is a good idea if we have any time left from the shopping."

"Are any of the husbands tagging along?" Bella asked.

Nell pursed her lips. "Do you think I'd look this cheerful if the men were coming with us?"

"Stupid question," Bella said with a sigh. "I'd better get started on chow, or is Chappy laying on a barbecue tonight before the square dance? He never asks me, he just goes ahead with whatever he wants to do."

"Chappy did say something about a barbecue. Why don't you make a bowl of potato salad and some home-made rolls and a few pies to go with it?" She put an arm around Bella's formidable girth. "That will save you some work, too, won't it? Actually, I think Chappy's kind of sweet on you."

Bella flushed and glared at Nell. "He ain't, neither! Now get out of here and let me get busy."

"Yes, ma'am." Nell grinned and curtsied before she darted out the back door.

Nell went down to the stables to check on the mounts for the morning ride. Chappy Staples was alone there, and after all these years, Nell was still a little in awe of him. He was older than most of the men, but he could outride the best of them. He'd never said a thing out of the way to Nell, but she couldn't help her remoteness. It was the same with all the men, except Tyler.

"How is the mare this morning?" she asked the wiry man with the pale blue eyes, referring to a horse with a bad shoe.

"I had the farrier come over and take a look at her. He replaced the shoe, but she's still restless this morn-ing. I wouldn't take her out if I were you."

She sighed. "That will leave us one mount short,"

she murmured. "Margie's gone riding with Tyler and the boys."

"If you can handle it alone, I'll keep Marlowe here and let him help me work the colt, and one of the guests can have his horse," Chappy said. "How about it?"

"That sounds great." She sighed, thanking her lucky stars that the foulmouthed Marlowe was being kept clear of her guests. If he kept it up, he'd have to go, and that would leave them a man short. Nell didn't like the idea of adding on new men. It had taken her long enough to get used to the ones she already had on the place.

"We'll start at ten," she told Chappy. "And we have to be back in time for lunch. I'm taking the ladies shopping about one-thirty."

"No problem, ma'am." He tipped his hat and returned to work.

Nell wandered back toward the house, deep in thought, almost running head-on into Tyler because she didn't see him until he rounded the corner of the house.

She gasped, stepping back. "Sorry," she said, faltering. "I didn't see you."

He glared down at her. "I was about to head off riding with Margie and the boys when I heard that I'm escorting Margie to the square dance tonight."

"Are you?" she asked, all at sea.

He lifted an eyebrow. "That's what Margie tells me. She said it was your idea," he added in an exaggerated Texas drawl that could have skinned a cactus at close range.

"I guess you wouldn't believe me if I told you I haven't said a word to her about it," she said resignedly.

"You throw her at me every time she comes out here, don't you?" he asked with a mocking smile.

She lowered her eyes and turned away. "I did once or twice, sure. I thought you might enjoy her company," she said in a subdued tone. "She's like you. Sophisticated and classy and upper crust. But if you'd rather she went with someone else, I'll see what I can do."

He caught her arm, noticing the way she tensed and froze. "All right. You don't have to make a federal case out of it. I just don't like having myself volunteered for guest escort services. I like Margie, but I don't need a matchmaker."

"No, you wouldn't," she said more sadly than she realized. "Will you let go of my arm, please?"

"You can't bear to be touched, can you?" he asked speculatively. "That was one of the first things I noticed about you. Why?"

Her heart went wild. He couldn't know that it was his touch lancing through her like white-hot pleasure that made her tremble, not a dislike of being touched by him. And that surprised her. "My private life is none of your business," she said firmly.

"No. You've made that very clear lately," he replied. He let her go as if her arm burned his fingers. "Okay, honey. Have it your own way. As for Margie, I'll work things out with her."

He sounded vaguely exasperated, but Nell was far too nervous to wonder about his tone of voice. A quick getaway was on her mind. When she was alone with him, it took all her willpower not to throw herself into his arms, despite all her inhibitions.

"Okay," she said, and shrugged, as if what he did were of no consequence to her. She went around him and into the house without looking back, unaware of his quiet gaze following her every step of the way.

CHAPTER TWO

NELL AVOIDED TYLER for the rest of the day, and she didn't go to the square dance that night. She excused herself right after the barbecue and went up to her room. She was being a coward, she thought miserably, but at least she wouldn't have to watch Margie flirt with Tyler.

But memories of Tyler wouldn't be put out of her mind. Her thoughts drifted relentlessly back to the very beginning, to his first few days at the ranch. From the moment she'd met him at the airport, he'd been gentle and kind to her, putting her at ease, making himself right at home in her company.

And not only with Nell—he'd won over the men and Bella just as quickly. Nell had warmed to him as she never had to any man, with the exception of Darren McAnders. But even though Darren had left deep scars on her emotions, Nell knew instinctively that Tyler wouldn't harm her. Before she realized what was happening to her, she was following him around like a puppy.

She grimaced, remembering. She'd alternated between sighing over him and trying to find ways to make him more comfortable. She didn't realize how her eagerness to please him might seem to other people... or even to Tyler. She was in awe of him, the wound of McAnders's long-ago rejection forgotten.

There was a square dance the second week he was in residence. Nell hadn't put on a dress, but she did make sure her long hair was clean and neatly brushed, and she didn't wear her slouch hat. As usual when there were strangers around, especially male ones, she drew into herself. Tyler made a convenient hiding place, and she got behind him and stayed there.

"Scared?" he'd teased gently, not minding her shy company. She was a little sunflower, a child to cosset. He hadn't asked her age, but he assumed she hadn't made it out of her teens yet. She didn't threaten him in any way, and he could afford to be kind to her.

"I don't mix well," she confessed, smiling. "And I don't really trust men very much. Some of the guests... well, they're older men and their wives aren't interested in them. I guess any young woman, even one like me, is fair game to them. I don't want trouble, so mostly I stay away from dances." Her dark eyes sought his. "You don't mind if I stick back here with you?"

"Of course not." He leaned against one of the posts that supported the loft and busied his fingers braiding three strands of rawhide he'd found. "I haven't been to a barn dance in a long time. Is this an ongoing ritual here?"

"Every other Saturday night," she confided. "We even invite the kids, so everybody gets to join in. The band—" she indicated the four-man band "—is a local group. We pay them forty dollars for the evening. They aren't famous, but we think they're pretty good."

"They are," he agreed with a smile. He glanced down at her, wondering what she'd think of the kind of party he was used to, where the women wore designer gowns and there were full orchestras or at least string quartets and jazz quintets to provide the music.

She twisted a strand of her hair in her fingers nervously, watching the married couples dance. There was a wistful expression in her eyes. He frowned as he watched her.

"Do you want to dance, Nell?" he asked gently.

She blushed. "No. I, well, I don't dance," she confessed, thrilling to the thought of being in his arms. But that might not be a good thing. He might see how attracted she was to him. She felt helpless when his hand accidentally brushed hers. She wasn't sure she could handle a dose of him at close quarters without giving away her growing infatuation for him.

"I could teach you," he volunteered, faintly amused at her reticence.

"No, I'd better not. I don't want to..." She was going to say that she didn't want to have to explain to the male guests why she wouldn't dance with anyone but Tyler. It was too hard to make him understand that her flesh crawled at the thought of being handled by strange hands. But she coveted *his* touch, and that was new.

"Okay, tidbit. No need to worry the point." He smiled. "But I think I'm about to be abducted, so what will you do while I'm away?" he asked, indicating a heavyset middle-aged woman who was heading toward him with a gleeful smile.

"I'll just help out at the refreshment table," she said, and excused herself. She watched him being led onto the dance floor and she sighed, wishing she was the one dancing with the long, tall Texan. But she was uncertain of herself. It was better if she didn't rush things. Much better.

After that evening, he became her port in a storm. If there were business meetings or problems that she had to discuss with the men or male guests, she always made sure Tyler was included. She began to think of him as a buffer between herself and a world that frightened her. But even as she relied on him, she couldn't help feeling an attraction that was making it impossible for her to go on as she had. She wanted him to notice her, to see her as a woman. It was the first time in years that she'd wanted to show off her femininity, to look the way a woman should.

But as she stared at herself in her mirror one morning, she wanted to cry. There wasn't even good raw material to work with. She'd seen photos of movie stars who looked almost as bad as she did without their makeup, but she didn't have the first idea how to make herself look beautiful. Her hair, while long and lustrous, needed shaping. Her eyebrows almost disappeared because they were so sun bleached. She had a good figure, but she was too shy to wear revealing clothes. Maybe it wasn't a good idea to go overboard, anyway, she told herself. It had taken years to get over her bad experience and the brutal honesty of the first man she'd set her cap at.

Finally, she'd braided her hair into two long pigtails and looped Indian beaded holders around them. That didn't look too bad, considering that her paternal grandmother was a full-blooded Apache. She only wished her face looked as good as her hair did. Well, miracles did happen. Maybe someday one would happen for her. And Tyler did actually seem to like her.

She tried a hint of lipstick and put on her newest jeans—the only ones she had that really fit properly—

with a pullover knit blouse. She smiled at her reflection. She really didn't look too bad, she thought, except for her face. Maybe she could wear a gunnysack over it....

Then Bella called her to lunch before she had time to worry anymore.

She bounced into the dining room with more energy than she'd had for weeks. She felt reborn, full of new, shy confidence. She was blooming.

The rain had come to the desert, making the guests uncomfortable and ranching dangerous. The men were working overtime keeping cattle and horses out of the dry washes that could kill so suddenly and efficiently when they filled with unexpected rainwater. The past three days had brought a deluge, and two of the guests were giving up and going home. The other eight were going to tough it out. Nell had smiled at their stubbornness and was determined to make life as pleasant as possible for them.

The guests were having their meal half an hour later than Nell, Tyler and Bella in the huge oak-decorated dining room with its heavy chairs and table and comfortable lounge furniture.

Tyler hadn't shown up, but Bella was bustling around putting platters of food on the table when she got a glimpse of the mistress of the house and almost dropped the tray she was carrying.

"That you, Nell?" she asked hesitantly, her gray head cocked sideways.

"Who are you expecting?" Nell asked, laughing. "Well, I won't win any beauty contests, but don't I look better?"

"Too much better," Bella said gently. "Oh, honey, don't do it. Don't set yourself up for such a hard fall."

Nell stopped breathing. "What?" she asked.

"You take him things for the cabin," Bella said. "You sew buttons on his shirts. You make sure he's warm and dry when it rains. You're forever making him special things in the kitchen. And now this transformation. Honey, he's a sophisticated man who was, until just recently, very rich and well traveled." She looked worried. "I don't want to smash any dreams, but he's used to a different kind of woman. He's being kind to you, Nell. But that's all it is. Don't mistake kindness for true love. Not again."

Nell's face went bloodred. She hadn't realized that she was doing those things. She'd liked him and she wanted him to be happy. But it didn't look like that—of course it didn't. And her new appearance was going to put him in a very embarrassing situation.

"I like him," Nell faltered. "But I'm not…not chasing him." She turned and ran upstairs. "I'll change."

"Nell!"

She ignored Bella's remorseful wail and kept going. But she wouldn't come back down for dinner, despite the pleading from the other side of the door. She felt raw and hurt, even though Bella had just meant to be kind. Nell was going to have to watch her step. She couldn't afford to let Tyler think she was chasing him. God forbid that she should invite heartache again.

Downstairs, Tyler and Bella had been sharing a quiet meal. He studied the old woman curiously.

"Something bothering you?" he asked politely.

"Nell." She sighed. "She won't come down. She fixed her hair and changed clothes, and I…" She cleared her throat. "I said something."

"Nell could use a little self-confidence," Tyler said

quietly. "That wasn't kind of you to knock her down when she was just getting started."

"I don't want her to get hurt again," Bella moaned. "You just mean to be kind, I know that. But that child has never had any affection, except from me. She doesn't know what it is to be loved and wanted. Her father lived for Ted. Nell was always an afterthought. And the only other time she was interested in a man, she got hurt bad." She sighed again. "So maybe I'm overprotective. But I just didn't want to see her throw herself at you because you pay her a little attention."

"I never thought she was," Tyler said, smiling. "You're wrong. Nell's just being friendly. She's a cute little kid with pretty brown eyes and a nice way about her. I like her and she likes me. But that's all it is. You don't have to worry."

Bella eyed him, wondering if he could be that blind. Maybe he could. "Nell is twenty-four," she said.

His black eyebrows arched. "I beg your pardon?"

"Well, how old did you think she was?" the woman asked.

"Nineteen. Eighteen, maybe." He frowned. "Are you serious?"

"Never more so," Bella told him. "So please don't make the mistake of putting her in patent leather shoes and ruffled pinafores. She's a grown woman who's lived alone and been slighted all her life. She's just ripe to have her heart torn out by the roots. Please don't be the one to do that to her."

Tyler hardly heard her. He'd thought of Nell as a cute kid, but maybe he'd gotten everything wrong. Surely she didn't see him as a potential romantic interest? That was just too far-fetched. Why, she wasn't even his type. He preferred a much more sophisticated, worldly woman.

He picked at his food. "I didn't realize," he began, "that she might be thinking of me in those terms. I'll make sure I don't do anything to encourage her." He smiled at Bella. "I sure as hell don't want a lovesick tomboy grabbing me by the boots every time I walk by. I don't like being chased, even by attractive women. And Nell is a sweet child, but even a blind man couldn't accuse her of being beautiful."

"Have some more beef," Bella said after a minute, grateful that Nell was still up in her room and not likely to hear what he'd said.

Of course, as fate would have it, Nell had started back down the hall and was standing just outside the door. She'd heard every word, and her face was a pasty white. She just barely made it back to her room before the tears that she'd pent-up escaped.

Maybe it had been for the best that she'd found out early what Tyler really thought of her. She'd gone a little crazy because of the attention he'd paid her, but now that she knew what he really felt about her, she'd keep those stupid impulses under better control. Like Bella said, she'd mistaken kindness for interest. And she should have known better. For God's sake, hadn't she learned her lesson already? She had nothing that would attract a man.

So she'd dried her eyes and put back on her comfortable clothes, and later she'd gone down to supper as if nothing at all had happened. Neither Bella nor Tyler realized what she'd overheard, and she hadn't told them.

But after learning how Tyler felt, Nell's attitude toward him changed. She was polite and helpful, but the light that had been in her eyes when she looked at him had gone out. She never looked directly at him and she never sought him out. The little attentions vanished, as did her shy adoration. She treated him like any other ranch hand, and what she really felt, only she knew. She never talked about him again, even to Bella.

But tonight, in the silence of her room, she still ached for what might have been. It seemed very likely that she wasn't cut out for a close relationship with a man, much less with Tyler Jacobs. But that didn't stop her from being hurt by what had happened. It had been the first time in years that she'd made an effort to look like a woman. It would be the last, too, she vowed. She rolled over and closed her eyes. Minutes later, she was asleep.

A COUPLE OF weeks later, the sun was out, thank God, because the recent rains had been catastrophic. Bookings had been canceled and the ranch's finances had suffered. But now they had all eighteen rooms filled, most of them double occupancy. The ranch catered to families with children, and family fun was emphasized, with hayrides and trail rides and barbecues and square dancing. They did a lot of repeat business. Mr. Howes and his wife had been regulars for ten years, and although Mr. Howes spent a great deal of his time falling off his horse, it never seemed to deter him from trying to keep his girth in the saddle. And despite the fact that Mrs. Sims had been infuriating her ulcer with Crowbait's homemade firehouse chili for the past five years, she kept trying to eat it. She was a widow who taught school back East during the year and vacationed for a week at the ranch every summer.

Most of the regulars were like family now, and even

the husbands didn't bother Nell because she knew them. But there was always the exception, like the very greasy-looking Mr. Cova who had a plain, loving wife whose affection he seemed determined to abuse. He was always watching Nell, and she looked forward to the day when they left.

"You could have Tyler speak to Mr. Cova, if things get too rough," Bella mentioned as she was setting the buffet table for lunch.

"No, thanks," Nell said quietly. "I can take care of myself."

She turned, almost colliding with Tyler's tall form as he appeared quietly in the doorway. She mumbled an apology and dashed past him without a word. He watched her irritably for a minute before he swung himself into a straddling position over one of the kitchen chairs and tossed his hat onto the table. His lean, dark hands lit a cigarette while he nursed a warm regret for the friendliness he'd once shared with Nell. He felt as if he'd hurt her somehow. Her quiet sensitivity disturbed him. She touched a chord in him that no other woman had ever reached.

"You're brooding again," Bella murmured dryly.

He smiled faintly. "It's just that Nell's changed," he said quietly, lifting the cigarette to his chiseled lips. "I thought we were going to be the best of friends. But now, when I come into a room, she can't leave quick enough. She sends me messages through Chappy. If I need to see the books, she has somebody bring them to me." He shrugged. "I feel like a damned leper."

"She's just nervous around men," Bella soothed. "She always has been—ask Chappy."

Tyler's green eyes shifted and met hers. "It wasn't

like this at first. I couldn't turn around without bumping into her. Do you know why things changed?"

Bella shrugged. "If I did," she said, choosing her words carefully, "she wouldn't thank me for saying anything. Although she sure is quiet these days."

"Amen. Well, maybe it's just as well," Tyler murmured absently. He took a draw from his cigarette. "What's for lunch?"

"Open-faced roast beef sandwiches, homemade french fries, salad, homemade banana pudding and iced tea and coffee."

"Sounds delicious. By the way, I've added two new men on the payroll to help do some work on the equipment and renovate the stable and the barn. That's going to have to be done before we finish haying, as I'm sure you know."

Bella whistled through her teeth. "Nell isn't going to like that. She hates having to deal with new men."

He scowled at her. "What happened to her?"

"I can't tell you that. She'll have to."

"I've asked, but all I got was the runaround."

"She's a secretive person. Nell doesn't talk about herself, and I won't." She smiled to soften the words. "Trusting someone doesn't come easy to that child."

"Trust is difficult for most of us." He tilted his hat over his eyes. "See you."

THE BARN, LIKE every other building on the place, leaked in heavy rain, but when it was sunny like today, it was cozy and plenty warm enough. Nell was kneeling beside a small Hereford calf in a rickety stall filled with green-gold hay, stroking its head.

Tyler stood in the hay-filled aisle watching her for a

long moment, his eyes narrowed in thought. She looked like Orphan Annie, and maybe she felt that way. He knew what it was like to live without love, to be alone and alienated. He understood her, but she wouldn't let him close enough to tell her so. He'd made a mistake with Nell. He didn't even know what he'd done to make her back off and treat him with such cool indifference. He missed the way things had been at their first meeting. Her shy adoration had touched him, warmed him. Because of Nell, he felt a kind of emptiness that he didn't even understand.

He moved closer, watching the way she reacted to his approach, the way her dark eyes fell, her quick movements as she got to her feet and moved out into the aisle. As if, he thought irritably, she couldn't bear being in an enclosed space with him.

"I thought I'd better tell you that I've hired two men, temporarily, to help with some repairs," he said. "Don't panic," he added when he saw the flash of fear in her eyes. "They're not ax murderers, and they won't try to rape you."

She blushed furiously and tears burned her eyes. She didn't say a word. She turned and stormed out of the barn, hurting in ways she couldn't have told him about, old memories blazing up like bonfires in the back of her mind.

"Damn it—!" he burst out angrily. He was one step behind her. Even as she reached the barn door, he caught her arm firmly to stop her. The reaction he got shocked him.

She cried out, twisting sharply away from him, her eyes wide and dark and fearful.

He realized belatedly that what had frightened her

was the anger in his face, the physical expression of it in his firm hold on her. "I don't hit women," he said quietly, moving back a step. "And I didn't mean to upset you. I shouldn't have made that crack about the new men. Nell…"

She swallowed, stuffing her hands into her jeans while she fought for composure. She hated letting him see the fear his violence had incited. She glanced away from him and her thick black lashes blocked his view of the emotion in her dark eyes.

He moved closer, looming over her. His lean hands slid into the thick coolness of her hair at her ears and tilted her face up to his.

"Stop running," he said curtly. "You've done it for weeks, and I can't take much more. I can't get near you."

"I don't want you near me," she said, choking on the words. "Let go."

Her words stung his pride, but he didn't let her see. "Tell me why, then," he persisted. His gaze was level, unblinking. "Come on."

"I heard what you said to Bella that night," she said, averting her eyes. "You thought I was just a kid, and when she told you how old I really was, you…you said you didn't want a tomboy hanging from your boots," she whispered huskily.

He saw the tears before he felt them sliding onto the backs of his hands. "So that was it." He grimaced. He hadn't realized that Nell might have heard him. His words must have cut her to the quick. "Nell, I never meant for you to hear me," he said gently.

"It was a good thing," she said, lifting her chin proudly as she fought down embarrassment. "I didn't realize how…how silly I was behaving. I won't embar-

rass you anymore, I promise. I liked you, that was all.
I wanted you to be happy here." She laughed huskily.
"I know I'm not the kind of girl who would appeal to
a man like you, and I wasn't throwing myself at you."
Her eyes closed on a wave of pain. "Now, please, will
you let me go?"

"Oh, Nell," he groaned. He pulled her close, wrap-
ping her up in his arms, his dark head bent to her honey-
brown one under the slouch hat. He rocked her, feeling
the pain in her as if it hurt him, too. His eyes closed as
he swung her in his arms, the close contact easing the
tears, easing the pain. She wept silently at the sweetness of it, even while she knew that she couldn't expect
any more than this. A few seconds of pity mingled with
guilt. Cold comfort for a lonely life.

She let herself rest against him for one exquisite
moment, loving the wiry strength of his tall body, the
leather and tobacco smells that clung to his soft cotton
shirt, the sound of his heartbeat under her ear. This
would be something to dream about when he left. But
now, she had to be strong.

She pulled away from him and he let her go. She
knew that there was no hope for her in his life. Margie
was more like him—she was sophisticated and good-
looking and mature. They'd hit it off like a house on
fire, and Nell had to keep that in mind and not let her
heart get addicted to Tyler. Because Margie wanted
him, Nell was sure of it. And Margie always got what
she wanted.

She drew in a shaky breath. "Thanks for the comfort," she said. She even forced a smile. "You don't
have to worry about me. I won't make things hard for
you." She looked up, her brown eyes very soft and dark,

shimmering with a hurt that she was trying so hard to keep from him.

Tyler felt something stir in him that knocked him in the knees. She had the most beautiful, sensual eyes he'd ever seen. They made him hungry, but for things that had no physical expression. She made him feel as if he'd been out in the cold all his life, and there was a warm fire waiting for him.

Nell felt that hunger in him, but she was afraid of it. His eyes had become a glittering green, and they were so intent that she flushed and dropped her gaze to his chest. He made her weak all over. If he looked at her like that very often, she'd have to go off into the desert forever. She felt as if he were taking possession of her without a physical move.

She stepped back, nervous, unsure of herself. "I'd better go inside."

"About those new men—they're only temporary. Just until we get through roundup." His voice sounded oddly strained. He lit a cigarette, surprised to find that his fingers were unsteady. "They'll be here in a few weeks."

She managed a shy smile. "Well, I'll try not to treat them like ax murderers," she promised nervously. "I'm sorry about the square dance. About leaving you to deal with Margie." She lifted her shoulders jerkily.

"I don't mind. But don't make a habit of it, okay?" he asked, smiling to soften the words. He reached out and tugged a lock of her long, unruly hair. "I'm feeling a little raw right now, Nell. I've lost my home, my job...everything that used to matter. I'm still trying to find my feet. There's no place in my life for a woman just yet."

"I'm sorry about what you lost, Tyler," she said with

genuine sincerity, gazing up at his hard, dark face. "But you'll get it all back one day. You're that kind of person. I can't see you giving up and settling for weekly wages."

He smiled slowly, surprised at her perception. "Can't you? You're no quitter yourself, little Nell."

She blushed. "I'm not little."

He moved a step closer with a new kind of slowness, a sensual kind of movement that made Nell's heart stop and then skip wildly. She could barely breathe, the manly cologne he wore drifting into her nostrils, seducing her. "You're not very big, either," he mused. He touched the very visible pulse in her soft neck, tracing it with a long, teasing finger that made it jump. "Nervous, honey?" he breathed.

She could hardly find enough breath to answer him. "I... I have to go inside."

His head bent so that his green eyes were looking straight into her dark ones while that maddening finger traced a hot path down her throat and up to her jaw. "Do you?" he asked in a husky whisper, and his breath touched her parted lips like a kiss.

"Tyler..." Odd, how different her voice sounded. Strained. Almost frantic.

His eyes fell to her mouth, and he wanted it suddenly and fiercely. His chest rose and fell quickly, his eyes glittered down at her. He almost bent that scant inch that would have brought her soft, full mouth under his. But she was trembling, and he couldn't be sure that it wasn't from fear. It was too soon. Much too soon.

He forced himself to draw back, but his hand gripped her shoulder tightly before he let her go. "See you later," he said with a slow smile.

She cleared her throat. For one wild second, she'd

thought he meant to kiss her, but that was absurd. "Sure," she said huskily. "See you."

She turned and went into the house on wobbly legs. She was going to have to get her imagination under control. Tyler was only teasing, just as he had in the beginning. At least he still liked her. If she could control her foolish heart, they might yet become friends. She could hardly hope for anything more, with Margie around.

CHAPTER THREE

A COUPLE OF weekends later, Margie and the boys were back at the ranch. Curt and Jess were up at the crack of dawn Sunday, and Nell noticed with faint humor that they followed Tyler wherever he went. That gave Margie a good excuse to tag along, too, but the woman seemed preoccupied. She'd tried to get a conversation going with Nell earlier, although Nell hadn't been forthcoming. It was hard going, listening to Margie try to order her life for her. Margie apparently hadn't noticed that her sister-in-law was a capable adult. She spent most of her time at the ranch trying to change Nell into the kind of person she wanted her to be. Or so it seemed to Nell.

"I do wish you'd let me fix your face and help you buy some new clothes," Margie grumbled at the breakfast table. She glared at Nell's usual attire. "And you might as well wear a gunnysack as that old outfit. You'd get just as much notice from the men, anyway."

"I don't want the men to notice me," Nell replied tersely.

"Well, you should," she said stubbornly. "That incident was a long time ago, Nell," she added with a fixed stare, "and not really as traumatic as you've made it out to be. And don't argue," she added when Nell bristled. "You were just a child, at a very impressionable age, and you'd had a crush on Darren. I'm not saying that you invited it, because we both know you didn't. But it's time you faced what a relationship really is between a man and a woman. You can't be a little girl forever."

"I'm not a little girl," Nell said through her teeth. She knew her cheeks were scarlet. "And I know what relationships are. I don't happen to want one."

"You should. You're going to wind up an old maid, and it's a pitiful waste." Margie folded her arms over the low bodice of her white peasant dress with its graceful flounces and ruffles. "Look, honey," she began, her voice softening, "I know it was mostly my fault. I'm sorry. But you can't let it ruin your whole life. You've never talked to me or to Bella. I wish you had, because we could have helped you."

"I don't need help," Nell said icily.

"Yes, you do," Margie persisted. "You've got to stop hiding from life—"

"There you are," Tyler said, interrupting Margie's tirade. "Your offspring have cornered a bull snake out in the yard. Curt says you won't mind if he keeps it for a pet."

Margie looked up, horrified.

Tyler chuckled at the expression on her face. "Okay. I'll make him turn it loose." He glanced at Nell, noticing the way she averted her eyes and toyed nervously with her coffee cup. "Some of the guests are going to services. I thought I'd drive them. I'm partial to a good sermon."

"Okay. Thanks," Nell said, ignoring Margie's obvious surprise.

"Did you think I was the walking image of sin?" Tyler asked the prettier woman. "Sorry to put a stick in your spokes, but I'm still just a country boy from Texas, despite the lifestyle I used to boast."

"My, my." Margie shook her head amusedly. "The mind boggles." She darted a glance at Nell, sitting like a rock. "You ought to take Nell along. She and her hair shirt would probably enjoy it."

"I don't wear a hair shirt, and I can drive myself to church later." Nell got up and left the room, her stiff back saying more than words.

She did go to church, to the late morning service, in a plain gray dress that did nothing for her, with no makeup on and her honey-brown hair in a neat bun. She looked as she lived—plainly. Bella had driven her to town and was going to pick her up when the service was over. It would have been the last straw to go earlier with Tyler's group, especially after Margie's infuriating invitation at Tyler's expense.

So the last person she expected to find waiting for her was Tyler, in a neat gray suit, lounging against the ranch station wagon at the front of the church when services were over.

"Where's Bella?" Nell asked bluntly.

Tyler raised a dark eyebrow. "Now, now," he chided gently. "It's Sunday. And I'd hate to let you walk back to the ranch."

"Bella was supposed to pick me up," she said, refusing to move.

"No sense in letting her come all this way when I had to come back to town anyway, was there?" he asked reasonably.

She eyed him warily. "Why did you have to make two trips to town on Sunday?"

"To pick you up, of course. Get in."

It wasn't as if she had a choice. He escorted her to the passenger side and put her in like so much laundry, closing the door gently behind her.

"You're killing my ego," he remarked as he pulled out onto the road.

Her nervous hands twisted her soft gray leather purse. "You don't have an ego," she replied, glancing out at the expanse of open country and jagged mountains.

"Thank you," he replied, smiling faintly. "That's the first nice thing you've said to me in weeks."

She let out a quiet breath and stared at the purse in her hands. "I don't mean to be like this," she confessed. "It's just—" her shoulders lifted and fell "—I don't want you to think that I'm running after you." She grimaced. "After all, I guess I was pretty obnoxious those first days you were here."

He pulled the station wagon onto a pasture trail that led beyond a locked gate, and cut off the engine. His green eyes lanced over her while he lit a cigarette with slow, steady hands.

"Okay, let's put our cards on the table," he said quietly. "I'm flat busted. I work for your uncle because what I have left in the bank wouldn't support me for a week, and I can't save a lot. I've got debts that I'm trying to pay off. That makes me a bad prospect for a woman. I'm not looking for involvement…."

She groaned, torn by embarrassment, and fumbled her way out of the car, scarlet with humiliated pride.

He was one step behind, and before she could get away he was in front of her, the threat of his tall, fit body holding her back against the station wagon.

"Please, you don't have to explain anything to me," she said brokenly. "I'm sorry, I never meant to—"

"Nell."

The sound of her name in that deep, slow drawl brought her hurt eyes up to his. Through a mist of gathering tears she saw his face harden, then his eyes begin to glitter again, as they had once before when he'd come close to her.

"You're all too vulnerable," he said, and there was something solemn and very adult in his look. "I'm trying to tell you that I never thought you were chasing me. You aren't the type."

She could have laughed at that statement. He didn't know that years ago she'd run shamelessly after Darren McAnders and almost begged for his love. But she didn't speak. Her eyes fell to the quick rise and fall of his broad chest under the well-fitting suit, and she wondered why he seemed so breathless. Her own breathing was much too quick, because he was close enough that she could feel his warmth, smell the expensive cologne that clung to him.

"I'm nervous around men," she said without looking up. "You were the first one who ever paid me any real attention. I guess I was so flattered that I went overboard, trying to make you happy here." She smiled faintly, glancing up and then down again. "But I never really thought it was anything except friendship on your part, you know. I'm not at all like Margie."

"What do you mean by that crack?" he asked sharply.

She shivered at his tone. "She's like the people in your world, that's all. She's poised and sophisticated and beautiful…"

"There are many different kinds of beauty, Nell," he said, his voice softer than she'd ever heard it. With surprised pleasure she felt the touch of his lean fingers on her chin as he lifted her face up to his eyes. "It goes a lot deeper than makeup."

Her lips parted and she found that she couldn't quite drag her eyes away from his. He was watching her in a way that made her knees weak.

"We'd better go…hadn't we?" she asked in a husky whisper.

The timbre of her soft voice sent ripples down his spine. He searched her dark eyes slowly, finding secrets there, unvoiced longings. He could almost feel the loneliness in her, the hidden need.

And all at once, he felt a need spark within him to erase that pain from her soft eyes.

He dropped his cigarette absently to the ground and put it out with a sharp movement of his boot. His lean hands slid against her high cheekbones and past her ears.

"Tyler…!" she gasped.

"Shh." He eased her back until she was resting against the station wagon, with his chest touching her taut breasts, and all the time his eyes searched hers, locked with them, binding her to him.

Her nervous hands, purse and all, pressed against him, but not with any real protest, and he knew it. This close, she couldn't hide her hunger from him.

"But…" she began.

"Nell." He whispered her name just as his lips brushed against hers. It wasn't a kiss at all. It was a breath of shivery sensation against her mouth, a tentative touch that made her stand very still, because she was afraid that he might stop if she moved.

His fingers toyed at her nape as they removed the hairpins and loosened her hair, and all the while his mouth was teasing hers, keeping her in thrall to him. He closed one of her hands around her hairpins and ran his fingers slowly through the mass of honey-streaked hair he'd loosened, enjoying its silky coolness.

"Open your mouth a little," he whispered as his teeth closed gently on her lower lip.

She blushed, but she obeyed him without pause.

His own mouth parted, and she watched it fit itself exactly to the contours of her lips. Her eyes glanced off his fiery ones, and then the sensation began to penetrate her shocked nerves, and she gasped as her eyes closed in aching pleasure.

He murmured something deep and rough, and then she felt the length of his hard body easing down against hers while birds called in the meadow and an airplane flew overhead and the sun beat down on her. She moaned in sweet oblivion.

He felt her tremble, heard the first cry from her lips. His mouth lifted just enough for him to see her face, and he was startled by the pleasure he found there. Her eyes opened, black pools of velvet. His hands slid gently down her back to her waist, and he realized that breathing had become an Olympic event.

"My God," he whispered, but with reverence, because not once in his life had he felt this overwhelming tenderness for a woman.

"You…you shouldn't hold me…like this," she whispered back, her voice shattering with mingled fear and need.

"Why not?" He brushed his nose against hers while he spoke and managed a faint smile for her.

She colored. "You know why not."

"No, I don't." His mouth covered hers slowly, and

he felt her yield, felt her submission like a drug as he drowned in the softness of her body and the sweetness of her mouth. He relaxed, giving in to his own need. His hips slowly pressed against hers, letting her feel what she probably already knew...that he was feverishly aroused by her.

She stiffened and gasped, and without warning he felt her ardor turn to fear as she pushed at his chest in flaming embarrassment.

He drew away gently, releasing her from the soft crush of his body. His eyes searched her scarlet face, noting the way she kept her own eyes hidden.

"You haven't done this before," he said with sudden conviction.

"Not...not voluntarily, no," she replied with forced lightness. She gnawed on her lip. "I'm sorry. It's...it's a little scary." And she blushed again, even more.

He laughed softly, delighted. His mouth pressed gently against her forehead. He nuzzled her face with his. "I suppose it would be, to a quiet little virgin who doesn't chase men."

"Please don't make fun of me," she whispered.

"Was that how it sounded?" He lifted his head, touching her mouth with a slow, tender forefinger as he watched her. "I didn't mean it to. I'm not used to innocents, Nell. The world I came from didn't accept them very readily."

"Oh. I see."

"No, you don't, honey. And that's a good thing. It isn't my world any longer. I'm not sure I even miss it." He toyed with a long, silky strand of her hair. "You're trembling," he whispered.

"I'm...this is...it's new."

"It's new for me, too, although I imagine you don't believe it." He brushed the hair back from her face, and his green eyes searched her dark ones. "How long is it since a man kissed you…really kissed you?"

"I don't think anyone ever did, and meant it," she confessed.

"Why?"

"I don't attract men," she faltered.

"Really?" He smiled but without mirth as he caught her by the waist and pulled her to him. She flushed and tried to pull away, but this time he held her firmly.

"Tyler!" she protested, flustered.

"Just stand still," he said quietly, but he let her hips pull away without an argument. "You're twenty-four years old and damned ignorant about men. It's time you had a little instruction. I won't hurt you, but I can't kiss you from a safe distance."

"You shouldn't," she pleaded, looking up. "It isn't fair to…to play with me."

His dark eyes didn't blink. "Is that what I'm doing, Nell?" he asked softly. "Am I playing?"

"What else could you be doing?"

"What else, indeed," he breathed as his head bent. He pulled her up to meet the hard descent of his mouth, and he kissed her with passion and a little anger, because she was arousing him in ways she couldn't have dreamed. He couldn't stop what was happening, and that irritated him even more. Nell was the last woman in the world he should be kissing this way. He had no right to get involved with her when he had nothing to offer. But her mouth was sweet and gentle under his, softly parting; her body, after its first resistance, melting into his. He lifted her against his chest, drowning in the long, sweet, aching pleasure of the most chaste kiss he'd ever shared with a woman. His body fairly throbbed against her, but he kept himself in full control. This was an interlude that couldn't end in a bedroom; he had to remember that.

He groaned finally and listened to reason. He put her back on her feet, his hands gripping her soft arms hard as he held her in front of him and struggled for both breath and sanity.

Nell was dazed. Her eyes searched his glittery ones, and she could feel the fine tremor in his hands as he held her. He was breathing as roughly as she was. He wanted her. She knew it suddenly and without a doubt. With a sense of shock, she realized how much a man he really was.

"I need to sit down," she said shakily.

"I'm just that unsteady myself, if you want the truth," he said on a rough sigh. He opened the door and let her into the station wagon before he slid his long legs inside and got in under the wheel.

He lit a cigarette and sat quietly, not speaking, while Nell fumbled her hairpins into her purse and dug out a small brush to run through her long, disheveled hair. She would have liked to check her appearance in a mirror, but that would look suspicious. She didn't want him to know how desperately sweet that interlude had been for her.

She put the brush back into her purse and closed it and stared down into her lap. Now that it was all over, she wondered how he felt. Would he think she was that starved for affection that she'd have reacted the same way to any man? She glanced at him nervously, but he seemed oblivious to her presence. He was staring out the windshield, apparently deep in thought.

In fact, he was trying to breathe normally. It was unusual for him to feel so shaken by such an innocent kiss. He couldn't remember the last time a woman had thrown him off balance. But Nell seemed to do it effortlessly, and that bothered him. Loss of control was the last thing he could afford with a virgin. He had to put on the brakes, and fast. The question was, how was he going to do that without making Nell think that he was little more than a playboy having fun?

He turned his head and found her watching the landscape without any particular expression on her soft face.

"We'll be late for lunch," Nell remarked without looking at him. She couldn't. She was too embarrassed by her reaction to his kiss.

He searched for the right words to explain what had happened, but Nell was far too unsophisticated for that kind of discussion. She seemed remarkably naive in a number of ways. He imagined her own abandon had been as embarrassing to her as his lack of control had been disturbing to him.

Better to let things lie, he supposed, for the time being. He started the station wagon without another word and headed for the ranch.

MARGIE GOT THE boys ready to go early in the afternoon, and Tyler volunteered to take them back to Tucson. That seemed to thrill Margie, and it was a relief to Nell, who'd dreaded being alone with her sister-in-law. Margie had a way of dragging information out of her, and Nell didn't want to share what had happened with Tyler. It was a secret. A sweet, very private secret, which she was going to live on for a long time.

"You're not brooding again, are you?" Bella asked that evening as they washed supper dishes.

Nell shook her head. "No. I'm just grateful for a little peace. Margie was on her soapbox again about gussying me up." She sighed. "I don't think I'd like being a fashion plate, even if I had the raw material. I like me the way I am."

"Frumpy," Bella agreed.

She glared at the housekeeper. Nell's soapy hands lifted out of the water. "Look who's talking about frumpy!"

Bella glared back. "I ain't frumpy." She shifted her stance and shook back her wild silvery-black hair. "I'm unique."

Nell couldn't argue with that. "Okay, I give up. I'm frumpy."

"You could do with a little improvement. Maybe Margie isn't the terror we think she is. You know, she does care about you, in her way. She's only trying to help."

"She's trying to help herself into a relationship with Tyler," Nell corrected.

"She's lonely," Bella said. Her knowing eyes sought Nell's suddenly vulnerable face. "Aren't you?"

Nell stared at the soapsuds. "I think most people are," she said slowly. "And I guess Tyler could do worse. At least Margie makes him smile."

"You could, if you'd get that chip off your shoulder."

"I got hurt," Nell muttered.

"That's no reason to bury yourself. You're just twenty-four. You've got a lot of years left to be alone if

you don't turn around pretty soon. You don't gain anything if you're afraid to take a chance. That isn't any
way for a young woman to live."

Nell's mind had already gone back to the morning, to
Tyler's warm mouth so hungry against her own, to the
feel of his lean, strong body against hers. She colored
at the sweet memory, and at that moment, she knew
she was going to die if she could never have it again.

But Tyler didn't want her. He'd said that he didn't
have room in his life for a woman—more than once.
She had to keep her head. She couldn't run after him.
Not when she was certain to be rejected.

"Bella, maybe I'm meant to be an old maid," she
murmured thoughtfully. "Some women are, you know.
It just works out that way. It's the beautiful women who
marry—"

"I ain't beautiful and I married," Bella reminded her
with an arrogant sniff. "Besides, looks fade. Character
lasts. And you got plenty of that, child."

Nell smiled. "You're a nice lady."

"I'm glad you like me. I like me, too, just occasionally. Now wash off that spot, Nell, so we don't get food
poisoning. When you have your own house and kitchen,
you'll have to do all this without me to remind you."

Nell had to stifle a giggle. Bella could be imposing,
but she was an angel.

TYLER THREW HIMSELF into his work for the next couple
of days, and Nell hardly saw him. He came to meals,
but he was looking more and more haggard, and he
was coughing. Since the Sunday he'd picked her up at
church, they'd hardly spoken. He'd been polite but remote, and Nell began to think he was avoiding her. She

understood the reason for it—he didn't want to get involved. He was probably afraid she'd read too much into those warm kisses. Well, she told herself, there was no need for him to worry. She wasn't going to throw herself at him. She just wished she could tell him so, again. But it was too embarrassing to contemplate.

All the same, she couldn't stop being concerned about him. He did look bad. Inevitably, there came a day later in the week when he didn't show up for supper.

Bella went down to the foreman's cabin to find out why. She'd asked Nell to go, but Nell had refused instantly. Another confrontation with Tyler was the last thing she needed now.

Bella came back a half hour later looking thoughtful. "He don't look too good," she remarked. "He's pale and he says he's not hungry. I hope he's not coming down with that virus that went through the bunkhouse last week."

"Is he all right?" Nell asked too quickly.

"He says a night's sleep will do him good. We'll see."

Nell watched her amble off to the kitchen and had to force herself not to go rushing down to the cabin to see Tyler. He was the epitome of good health. She knew because he'd told them that he was never sick. But there was always a first time, and he'd worked like a horse since his arrival.

Sometimes it seemed that he was working off more than the loss of his ranch back in Texas. Perhaps there'd been a girl he'd wanted who hadn't wanted him when he lost everything. That put a new perspective on things and Nell started worrying even more. She hadn't thought of him having a girlfriend. But he was a handsome man, and he was experienced. Very experienced, even to her innocent mind. There had to have been women in his past. He might even have been engaged. She groaned. She didn't like to consider the possibility that he might have kissed her because he was missing some woman he'd left behind in Texas. But it might be true. Oh, if only there was some way to find out!

She paced the living room floor until Bella complained that she was wearing out the rug. She went up to bed, where she could pace uninterrupted.

But the more she paced, the more confused things got. In the end, she undressed, put on her soft long gown and climbed into bed. Minutes later she was blessedly asleep, beyond the reach of all her problems.

THE NEXT MORNING, Nell's first thought was of Tyler. She dressed in jeans and a yellow knit top, looped her long hair into a ponytail, and ran downstairs with her boots barely on.

"Have you been to see Tyler?" she asked Bella.

The older woman scowled at her from a pan of biscuits she was just making up. "I will as soon as I get these biscuits in the oven…."

"I'll go."

Bella didn't say a word. But she grinned to herself as Nell went tearing out the back door.

The foreman's cabin was nice. It was big enough for a small family, but nothing fancy. Nell knocked on the door. Nobody answered. She knocked again. Still nothing.

She paused, wondering what to do. But there was really no choice. If he didn't answer, he was either asleep, which was unlikely, or gone, which was equally unlikely, or too sick to get up.

She opened the door, glad to find it unlocked, and peeked in. It was in good order for a bachelor's establishment. The Indian rugs on the floor were straight, and there were no clothes thrown over the old leather couch and chair.

Her heart beat wildly as she eased farther into the living room. "Tyler?" she called.

There was a soft groan from the bedroom. She followed it, half-afraid that she might find him totally unclothed. She looked around the door hesitantly. "Tyler?"

He was under the covers, but his hair-matted chest was bare, like his tanned, muscular arms. He opened his eyes briefly. "Nell. God, I feel rough. Can you get Bella, honey?"

"What for?" she asked gently, moving closer.

"To call a doctor," he said wearily. "I haven't slept and my chest hurts. I think I've got bronchitis." He coughed.

"I can call a doctor," she said gently. She felt his forehead. It was burning hot. "Just lie there and don't move. I'll bring you something cold to drink, and then I'll get the doctor. I'll take care of you."

He caught her eyes, searching them strangely. It felt odd, the sensation her words had sent through his body. He'd never had to be taken care of, but it occurred to him that there was nobody he'd rather have nursing him than Nell.

"Be right back," she said, hiding her concern under a faint smile. She rushed out, all the antagonism gone in the rush of concern she felt for him. He had to be all right, he just had to!

CHAPTER FOUR

NELL GOT TYLER a cold soft drink from his small refrigerator and helped him get a few swallows of it down before she rushed back to the main house to phone the doctor.

Bella stood listening in the doorway while Nell described the symptoms to Dr. Morrison and was told to bring Tyler in to his clinic as soon as she could get him there.

She felt insecure when she hung up. "I'll bet he thinks it could be pneumonia," Nell told the older woman worriedly. "And I guess it could be. He's coughing something terrible and burning up with fever."

"I'll go get Chappy to help you get him into the station wagon," Bella said. "Or I'll go…"

"No, that's all right," Nell replied. "Chappy can come with us. We'll have to postpone the daily shopping trip with the guests, but Chappy can drive Mrs. Sims and the others to the mall as soon as we get back."

"He'll hate that." Bella chuckled.

"I know, but somebody's got to look after Tyler."

Bella almost strangled herself trying to keep quiet. She could have looked after Tyler, but it was pretty obvious that Nell had already assigned that chore to herself. And Bella wasn't about to interfere. "That's right," she said, grinning. "I'll get Chappy."

But as they went out the door together, they noticed immediately that the station wagon was missing. So was the pickup truck.

"Where's he gone?" Bella yelled to Marlowe, who was leading a saddled horse out of the stable.

"Chappy had to run into town to pick up that stomach medicine for the sick calves. He's been gone a half hour, so he should be back anytime."

"Where's the pickup?" Nell called.

Marlowe shrugged. "Sorry, ma'am, I don't know."

"Great," Nell muttered. She glanced at Bella. "Well, send Chappy down to the cabin the minute he comes back. I just hope he's not inclined to linger at the vet's office."

"I'll phone the vet and make sure," Bella replied. "Don't worry. Tyler's tough."

"I guess he is." Nell sighed. She forced a smile and quickly went down the path to the cabin.

Tyler was sprawled against the pillows asleep when Nell got back to him. She sighed, wondering how on earth he was going to dress himself.

"Tyler?" she called gently, touching his bare shoulder lightly. "Tyler, wake up."

His eyes opened instantly, a little glazed from sleep and fever. "Nell?" he murmured, shifting under the covers.

"Dr. Morrison wants me to bring you to his office," she said. "We have to get you dressed."

He laughed weakly. "That's going to be harder than you think. I'm as weak as a kitten." A sudden bout of coughing doubled him up and he grimaced at the pain it caused him. "Damn! It feels like I've got a broken rib."

Nell's heart sank. It was almost surely pneumonia.

Her mother had died of it, and it held hidden terrors for her because of the memory.

"Can you dress yourself?" she asked hesitantly.

He sighed jerkily. "I don't think so, Nell."

"Chappy isn't here," she said thoughtfully. "But there's Marlowe, or Bella—"

"No," he said shortly. He glared up at her with fever-bright eyes. "As strange as it may seem to you, I don't like the thought of having myself dressed by yahoos and grinning old women. No way. If you want me dressed, honey, I'll let you help. But nobody else. Not even Chappy."

That was surprising. She hadn't thought men minded people looking at them. But then, Tyler wasn't like other men.

She hesitated. "Okay. If you can get the—" she cleared her throat "—the first things on, I guess I can help with the rest."

"Haven't you seen a man without clothes?" he asked with faint humor.

"No. And I don't really want to," she said nervously.

"You may not have a choice." He started coughing again and had to catch his breath before he could speak. "Underwear and socks are in the top drawer of the dresser," he said. "Shirts and jeans in the closet."

She paused, but only for a minute. The important thing was to get him to the doctor. She had to remember that and put his health before her outraged modesty. Since he wouldn't let anybody else help, she didn't have a choice.

As quickly as possible, she laid out everything he was going to need. But when he started trying to sit up, he held his chest and lay right back down again.

"God, that hurts, Nell," he said huskily. "It must have been the dust. We got into a cloud of it a few days ago bringing back some straying cattle, and I inhaled about half an acre, I think. I've had a lot of congestion, but I thought it was just an allergy. Until this morning, anyway."

"Oh, Tyler," she moaned.

"Should have worn my bandanna," he murmured. "That's why the old-timers wore them, you know, to pull up over their faces in dust storms and such."

"How are you going to dress?" she wailed.

He gave her a knowing look. "You mean, how are you going to dress me," he replied. "If it helps, it isn't something I'd choose to saddle you with. I don't even like stripping in front of men."

She colored. "I don't think I can," she whispered.

"It won't be that bad, I promise," he said softly. "Pull the sheet up over my hips and slide my briefs up as far as you feel comfortable. I think I can manage it from there."

The blush got worse as she picked them up. "I'm sorry," she muttered, fumbling the briefs over his feet and ankles. "Old maids aren't very good at this sort of thing."

"Neither are old bachelors." He coughed, groaning. "Come on, Nell, you can do it. Just close your eyes and push."

She laughed involuntarily. "That might be the only way." She eased them up, her hands cold against the warm, hard muscles of his thighs. She couldn't help but feel how well made he was, how powerful. She got them just under the sheet and her nerve gave way. "Is that…far enough?" she asked huskily.

"I'll manage." He eased his hands under the sheet and tugged and then lay back with a rough sigh. "Okay. The rest is up to you, honey."

She slid his socks on his feet. He had nice feet, very well proportioned if a little big, and even nice ankles. His legs were as tanned as his face and arms, and it almost had to be natural, because he certainly hadn't been sunbathing the past few weeks.

"This is the first time in my adult life that I've ever been dressed by a woman," he remarked weakly as she eased his undershirt over his head and pulled it down over his broad, hair-matted chest.

"They tell me there's a first time for everything," she returned, but her eyes were on the rippling muscles of his chest. She could feel the warmth of his skin, feel the thick abrasiveness of the hair that covered the broad expanse until it wedged down to his undershorts. When she reached under his arms to pull the undershirt down over his back, her face was almost pressed to his skin, and she had to grit her teeth not to kiss him there. The most unwanted sensations were washing over her body like fire. This wasn't the time or the place, she had to remind herself. He was a sick man, and she had to get him to a doctor. Besides all that, it was suicidal to feel that way about a man who'd already warned her off.

"You look like boiled lobster," he remarked. "It wasn't as bad as you thought, was it?"

"No, not really," she agreed with a thin smile. She helped him into his chambray shirt and snapped the cuffs and then the snaps down the front of it. "It's just new."

"Didn't you ever have to dress your brother?" he grinned weakly.

"No. Ted was much older than I was," she said. "And he went away to school, so we didn't spend a lot of time together. Dad and Mom worshipped him. He was their world. I guess I was more or less an accident. But they tried not to let me feel left out."

"My father never wanted kids at all," Tyler remarked. "He did his damnedest to break my spirit, and he almost did break my sister Shelby's. But we survived. It's ironic that the ranch had to be sold. He'd have sacrificed both of us to hold on to it."

She unfolded his jeans. "You'll have your own ranch one day," she said gently. "And you won't break your children's spirits to keep it, either."

"If I have children," he replied. "Some men never marry. I may be one of them."

"Yes. I guess you might." She eased his jeans onto his long legs and pulled them up as far as she was able. They were tight and the material was thick, and it took most of her strength just to get them to his upper thighs. She knew that he'd never be able to pull them the rest of the way, not with his chest hurting so badly.

"If you can lift up, I think I can get them over your hips," she said through her teeth, and she didn't look at him as she eased the sheet away and tried not to blush at the sight of his undershorts.

"Sorry, little one," he said huskily. "But I do hurt like hell."

"I know," she said gently. "I'm not a child, after all," she said for her own benefit, as well as his. "Here goes."

She closed her eyes and pulled and tugged until she got the jeans over his hips. But she balked at the zipper, going hot all over.

"Fetch my boots, will you, honey?" he asked. He saw her hesitation and understood it. "I can manage this."

She almost wept with relief as she went to the closet to get his dress boots. She'd seen them there when she'd found his shirts and jeans. They were Tony Lama boots, exquisite and expensive, black and gleaming like wet coal.

"These are going to be hard to get on you," she said worriedly.

"You push and I'll push," he said. "They're not all that tight."

"Okay."

Between them, they worked the boots onto his feet. Then Nell got a comb and fixed his disheveled hair. And all the while he lay there against his pillow, his feverish eyes watching her, studying her in a silence that was unnerving.

The roar of a car arriving interrupted the tension. "That must be Chappy," Nell said. She caught her breath. "Tyler, you won't tell him that I…"

"That you helped me dress?" He smiled gently. "I won't tell anyone. It's between you and me, and no one else," he said, and the smile faded into an exchanged look that was slow and intensely disturbing. Nell's heart ran wild until she dragged her eyes away and got up to let Chappy in.

Between them, they got Tyler into the backseat of the station wagon, where he could lie down, and to Dr. Morrison's office.

The nurse helped Tyler to the examination room, while Chappy paced and Nell chewed on a fingernail. It took a long time, and she was expecting Tyler to come out with the nurse, but Dr. Morrison came to the doorway and motioned for Nell to follow him.

He beckoned her into his office, but Tyler was nowhere in sight.

"He'll be fine," he told her, perching himself on the corner of his desk, "but he's got acute bronchitis."

"I was so afraid that it was pneumonia," Nell said, slumping into a chair with relief. "That pain in his chest—"

"That pain in his chest is from a pulled muscle, because he's coughed so much," he said with a tolerant smile. He folded his arms across his chest. "I want him in bed until the fever goes. He can get up then, but he can't work for a full week. And then I want to see him again. I've written him two prescriptions. One's an antibiotic, the other's an expectorant for the cough. Give him aspirin for fever and keep him in bed. If he gets worse, call me."

"Did you tell him all this?" she asked.

"Sure. He said like hell he'd lay around for a week. That's why I wanted to talk to you."

She smiled. "Thanks. He's working wonders out at the ranch. I'd hate to bury him on it."

"He seems pretty capable to me," he agreed. "Mind that he doesn't sneak out and start back to work before you realize it."

"I'll tie him in his bed," she promised.

"Bombard him with fluids while you're at it," the doctor added as he got up and opened the door. "He'll be as docile as a kitten until that antibiotic takes hold, then look out."

"I'll post guards at his door," she said with a grin.

She felt lighter than air. Tyler was going to be all right.
The relief was delicious. "Thank you!"

"My pleasure. He's all yours."

She smiled as she went out. If only that were true.

She called Chappy to help her get Tyler out to the
station wagon, but only after she'd whispered to the
receptionist to send the bill out to the ranch. She had a
feeling that Tyler wouldn't appreciate having her pay his
medical bill, but that was something they could argue
about when he was back on his feet.

All the way home, she wondered how she was going
to manage getting him undressed again. But he solved
that problem himself. When they got into the cabin, he
sighed and murmured, "Don't worry, Nell. I think I can
manage getting out of this rig by myself."

"I'll go up to the house and get Bella to make some
chicken soup for you," Nell said quickly, and darted out
the door. It was easier than she'd imagined.

She sent Chappy back to town to get the prescriptions
filled, because it had seemed more sensible to bring
Tyler home first. She gathered the few things she might
need and told Bella where she was going.

"He's not much of a threat in his present condition, I
guess," Bella said, and nodded, ignoring Nell's outraged
glare. "You can sleep on his sofa. But if you need me,
I'm here. I can sit with him while you sleep if he gets
worse in the night."

"You're a doll," Nell said.

"I have a secret Florence Nightingale streak," she
corrected. "Wanted to be a nurse, once, but I faint at
the sight of blood."

"They say some doctors do the first time they see an

operation," Nell replied. "But I'm glad you wanted to cook, instead. You're kind of special to me."

Bella beamed, unaccustomed to the praise. "I'll have that carved on my tombstone one day. Meanwhile, you fill Tyler full of that juice I gave you and don't let him rope cattle out the window."

"I won't. Thanks, Bella."

The older woman shrugged. "I'll bring the chicken soup when it's made. I'll put some in a thermos for you."

"It'll be welcome by then. And some coffee, too, please. I don't know if Tyler has a coffeepot, but I kind of doubt it."

"He carries his around in a thermos," Bella said surprisingly. "I fill one up for him every morning and every afternoon."

"Okay. I'll get going before he escapes. See you later."

She found Tyler asleep again, apparently back in the altogether under the single sheet that covered him. Nell watched his face for a long moment, seeing the lines erased in sleep, the masculine beauty of his mouth. Just the sight of him was like a banquet to her eyes. She had to tear herself away. While he slept, she might as well make herself useful by tidying up his kitchen.

She put the juice Bella had sent in the small refrigerator, and then she washed the few dishes and cleared the counter. With that done, she checked to make sure he was still asleep before she went to the bookcase in the living room to find something to read.

Apparently he was a mystery fan, because he had plenty of books by Sir Arthur Conan Doyle and Agatha Christie on the shelves. There were some biographies and some history books about the old West, and even a book about ancient Rome. She chose a work on the Apache tribe and sat down to read it, glancing curiously at the photograph atop the bookcase. It was of a young woman with long dark hair and green eyes and a rather sad expression on her beautiful face. Beside it was a smaller photo of the same woman in white, standing beside a tall, fierce-looking man in a suit. That, she decided, had to be Tyler's sister, Shelby. Nell knew Shelby had gotten married recently, because Tyler had gone to Texas for the wedding. That man was probably her new husband. He wasn't much to look at, but perhaps he had saving graces, Nell decided.

She didn't see any other photos. That had to be a good sign. If there had been a special woman in his life, surely he'd have a picture of her. Or maybe not. If he'd lost her to someone else, he might be too bitter to keep a picture of her in a prominent place.

Feeling gloomy, she went back to the book and started reading.

Bella brought chicken soup, and Chappy brought medicine. Tyler was still asleep, but when the visitors left, Nell took his medicine, a glass of juice and a bowl of soup into the bedroom on a tray. The medicine was important, and he needed nourishment. He hadn't eaten anything all day.

She sat down gently on the bed beside him, her eyes going helplessly over his broad, bare chest and his face. "Tyler?" she said softly. He didn't stir. She reached out and hesitatingly laid one slender hand on his chest, thrilling to its hard warmth. It was the first time she'd touched a man this way, and despite the circumstances, it was blatantly pleasurable.

"Tyler, I've got your medicine," she said.

He sighed and opened his eyes slowly. "I hate medicine," he said weakly. "How about a steak?"

"Dream on. Right now, it's going to be chicken soup and encouragement. I brought you a tray."

"What time is it?"

"Almost dark," she replied. "Chappy took the guests to town to shop, and now he's holding court at the supper table. I can hear him telling tall tales through the kitchen window, and everybody's laughing."

"He tells a mean story," Tyler agreed. He breathed heavily and touched his side, encountering Nell's warm hand as his own worked its way up his chest. "You're cool," he murmured.

"Only because you have a fever," she said, thrilling to the touch of his fingers on her soft skin. "Here. Let's get some medicine into you, and then you can have soup and juice. Are you hungry?"

"Half-starved," he said. "But I don't have much appetite."

She gave him the antibiotic with a swallow of juice, and then ladled the cough syrup into his mouth.

"That tastes terrible," he muttered.

"Most medicine does," she agreed. "Can you manage to sit up while you eat?"

"Under protest." He let her prop him up with pillows and dragged himself into a sitting position. The sheet lay loosely over his hips, but she caught a glimpse of underwear, not bare skin, as he moved. "That's for your benefit," he said dryly, smiling at her color. "I drew the line at pajamas, but I wouldn't outrage your modesty too much this way."

"Thank you," she said shyly.

"Thank you," he replied. "You're stuck with me, I gather. Didn't Bella rush to play nurse?"

"She did, but I headed her off. Crowbait would have to do the cooking if she came down here, and the whole outfit would quit on the spot."

"He's not that bad," he said. "The military would love to get their hands on him. Imagine, a cook who can make a lethal weapon of an innocent biscuit."

"Shame on you," she said.

He sighed and grimaced. "I guess my biscuits aren't much better, so I don't have a lot of room to talk. Nell, I'm sorry to cave in on you like this...."

"Anybody can get sick," she said easily, and began to feed him the soup without thinking about how much feeling that simple act betrayed. "It's amazing how many people come out here from the East, thinking that their allergies will go away overnight. What they don't realize is that the dust can be as bad as pollen, and that the soil itself harbors plenty of allergens. Just listen to Mr. Davis sneeze and wheeze on trail rides, if you don't believe me."

"Well, it's the first time in my life I've had bronchitis, but I'll buck it," he said quietly. "And I'll be back at work day after tomorrow."

"No, you won't," she replied. "Dr. Morrison said you couldn't get out of bed until the fever's gone, and you can't work for a week."

He eyed her warily. "Did he tell you that?"

"He sure did," she said with a mischievous grin. "So don't try to get around me. If you do, I'll call my uncle, and then where will you be?"

"Out of work and sick, I guess," he said wearily. "Okay. I'll stay put. Under protest, you understand."

"I understand. You'll get through it. Have some more soup."

He might get through it, she thought, but would she? He slept through the night without waking, although she checked on him every hour or so until she was forced to curl up on the couch and sleep.

The next day was pretty much the same. She fed him and gave him his medicine, and he slept most of the day and all night through. But the following day he felt much better and nothing suited him. The breakfast Bella had sent over was too everything. Too hot, too much, too salty, too filling and too starchy. He didn't want to stay in bed, he had to start planning for winter, and he had to get the cattle operation in hand. That meant more work than ever, in between getting the calves ready for the fall sale. He didn't like the medicine, he hated the confinement and Nell was beginning to wear on him, too, come to think of it.

She glared at him from red-rimmed dark eyes framed by long disheveled honey-brown hair, in the rumpled yellow knit shirt and faded jeans she'd slept in. She hadn't even bothered to put on her boots, having met Chappy at the door for the breakfast tray.

"If I wear on you, that's just too bad, Mr. Jacobs," she said shortly. "Somebody's got to keep you penned up, and everybody else is too busy. It's just the second day. The antibiotic's taking hold, and you want to fight tigers. Great. But fight them while you're asleep, please. I don't like people committing suicide on my ranch."

"It isn't your ranch yet, according to your uncle," he reminded her curtly.

"It will be," she said with cool determination. "Now you just lie down and get well."

"I don't want to lie down. I want to go to work. Hand me my clothes," he said firmly, nodding to where Chappy had draped them over his straight chair.

"Oh, no, I'm not going through that again," she said, reddening. "And you're not able to dress yourself yet—"

"Like hell I'm not able!" He pulled himself painfully into a sitting position, drew in a deep breath and tried to get his feet on the floor. He grimaced and groaned and lay back down, turning the air blue on the way down.

"Damn it, damn this disease and damn you, too!" he swore furiously.

"Thank you. What a kind thing to say to someone who's given up regular meals and sleeping to wait on you for two days," she said icily.

"I didn't ask you to!"

"Somebody had to!" she shot back. She stuck her hands on her slender hips and glared at him. He looked all too good that way, lying back against pillows with crisp white cotton pillowcases. His chest was still bare, and his black hair hung down over his forehead, straight and thick. He looked exquisitely masculine, and the sight of his half-clothed body wasn't doing Nell's nerves any good.

"All right, thank you," he said. "You're an angel in disguise and I'll remember you in my will. Now will you get out of here and let me go back to work?"

"You can't work for a week—Dr. Morrison said so," she replied for the tenth time in as many minutes. "And he wants to see you again to make sure you're on the road to recovery. He told me not to let you on a horse."

"I don't take orders from women," he said shortly. "I work for your uncle, and I answer only to him. You don't and never have told me what to do."

"Will you listen to reason?" she demanded, passing over that bit of insolence.

"Sure. If you'll get me my pants."

"Well, I won't."

"Then I'll get them myself," he said shortly.

She folded her arms across her chest with a smile. She knew he had on his underwear, so he wasn't going to frighten her off. "Okay. Go ahead," she invited.

She didn't realize her mistake until he gave her a hard glare and abruptly threw off the sheet. Her face went from pale pink to scarlet red in seconds as he gingerly slid his long, powerful bare legs over the bed and stood up. Without a stitch of clothing on.

CHAPTER FIVE

Nell was grateful that she didn't faint. What she did do was flush from the neck up and, after one long, shocked glance, turn and run out of the room.

Tyler immediately felt like a heel. He sat back down, his bad temper forgotten, and pulled the sheet over his hips. "Nell," he called gently.

She didn't answer him. She was staring out the living room window, with her arms folded tightly across her yellow shirt, trying to decide whether to stay or go. If he was going to be that difficult, she didn't know how she was going to cope. The sight of him had set her back a bit. Due to her experience with Darren McAnders when she was young, she'd led a pretty sheltered life. But she lived on a ranch, and because of that, she knew all about the technicalities of reproduction. But a nude man was a new experience. And a nude Tyler was…extraordinary. She was still shaking when she heard him calling her, more insistently.

With a deep breath, she turned and gritted her teeth and walked back to the doorway, pale and subdued.

"I'm sorry," he said tersely when he saw her face. "I won't do that again."

She shifted a little. "If you're that determined to kill yourself, I can't stop you. But for your own sake, I wish you'd do what the doctor wants."

His green eyes searched her frozen features. "I'll do damned near anything to get that look off your face. Including," he added wearily as he lay back down, "staying in the bed."

He looked tired. Probably he was, and she wished she'd been older and more sophisticated so that she wouldn't have made such a fool of herself. He made her feel about thirteen.

"Can I get you anything?" she asked.

"I could do with some more juice," he said. "And if you'll dig me out some fresh underwear, I'll put it back on again."

She felt hot all over and tried to hide her reaction to him as she got him a glass of juice and then took a pair of briefs from the dresser. As she put them beside him, he caught her wrist and pulled her down onto the bed, holding her there firmly while he looked at her.

"How can you be twenty-four years old and so damned innocent?" he asked quietly. "Especially with all the people who pass through here in a year's time?"

"I don't mix with people very much," she said. Her eyes slid helplessly over his broad, bare chest. "I socialize only to the extent that I have to, and since most people who come here keep to themselves except for organized activities, I don't have many problems. If I had my own way, this would be just a cattle ranch and I wouldn't take in paying guests. But the dude ranch part is paying for the cattle operation, so I don't have much choice."

"Do you date?"

She kept her eyes down. "No, I don't have time."

"So many secrets between us, Nell," he said, caressing her hand lightly. "Too many."

"You told me you weren't interested in involvement. Well, I'm not, either," she lied.

"Really? Or is it that you don't think you attract men?"

She remembered when she'd said that and what he'd done about it on the way home from church. Her lips parted as she remembered the hungry kiss they'd shared, and she had to fight not to throw herself down against him and beg him to do it again.

"I can't attract men," she replied tersely.

"You're a pretty woman," he said. "You downplay your attractions, but they're there. Why don't you buy a new dress, have your hair done and put on some makeup for the next Saturday square dance?" he murmured, reaching up to tug on a long lock of her hair. "And I'll teach you to dance."

Breathing grew harder by the minute. She felt nervous and insecure, and the slow tracing of his long fingers on her hand and wrist was beginning to stir her blood.

"It's not practical," she said inanely, because she could hardly think at all.

"Why not?"

"Because…because you're…" She bit her lip. "You're just bored, Tyler, and when you're back on your feet again, when you're working for yourself again… Oh, I'm just muddling it."

"You think I'm playing."

She sighed. "Yes."

He took her hand and pulled it to his chest, pressing it hard over the hair-covered expanse where his heart was beating like a bass drum. "Nell, am I callous enough to play with a virgin?" he asked softly.

Of course he wasn't, but she couldn't keep her thoughts clear. The effect he had on her was incredible, and she was hungry for an affection she'd never had from a man.

"It doesn't matter," he said huskily, pulling on her hand. "Come here."

"Tyler, you're sick—"

"I don't have any fever, and I feel like a new man." He eased her across him until she was on her back in the bed with his lean bare torso above her, his green eyes glittering down at her. "I've never seen a woman with less self-confidence than you have, Nell," he said. "There's nothing wrong with the way you look or the way you are."

"Tyler, you're scaring me," she whispered. Her hands went to his chest, and part of her tried to protest. This was bringing back terrible memories of another man she'd loved, or thought she loved, and his harsh, hurtful treatment of her. But Tyler wasn't McAnders, and the look on his face was intoxicating. He wanted her. Not as a substitute for another woman, but for herself.

"No, that won't work," he said gently. His lean hands cupped her chin and held her face tilted up to his. "I'm not going to be rough with you, not ever. And anything we do together will be because you want it."

That was as new as her proximity to him, and she began to relax. There was nothing threatening about him. He seemed fully in control and lazily indulgent.

"Yes, that's it," he said as he felt the tension draining out of her body. "I'm not going to hurt you."

As he spoke, his dark head bent. She felt his mouth whispering over her eyelids, closing them, brushing her nose, her chin, and then settling softly over her mouth. Her breath seemed suspended while he found just the right pressure, the right mingling of tenderness and expertise to make her lips part for him. And while he kissed her, his lean hands slid under her blouse at the back, and she thrilled to the faint roughness of their touch on her bare skin.

He was addictive, she thought dizzily, enraptured by the warmth of his caresses. She didn't think she could have pulled away to save her life. Every touch was more exciting than the one before. His mouth became a necessity. Without its warm crush she was sure to die.

Shyly, she flattened her hands against his chest and let them experience the thickness of hair, the strong padding of muscle beneath it. His breath caught against her mouth, and her eyes opened, questioning.

"I'm sorry, I didn't mean to…" she began quickly.

"It feels good," he said, smiling down into her shocked face. "I can drag that sound out of you the same way."

Her body coiled inside, like a kitten anticipating being stroked. She felt herself tremble and wondered at the mental pictures that were flashing sensually through her mind. His hands on her, touching her…there. Her lips parted. "You…you can?" she whispered, which wasn't what she wanted to say at all, but she was too shy and inexperienced to put it into words.

Tyler, with his greater experience, knew immediately that she was going to welcome whatever he wanted to do. It went to his head, making his thoughts spin with new possibilities. His hands had already told him that Nell had been hiding her light, physically at least, under a barrel. He needed the intimacy with her as he'd needed nothing else in his life, although he still didn't quite understand the way she affected his senses.

"Yes," he breathed, bending again to her mouth. "I can."

As his lips toyed with hers, his hand went to the fastening of her bra. Subtly, almost without her knowing it, he released the catch and slid his fingers slowly, exploringly, under her arm to the soft edge of her breast.

She trembled, but she didn't pull away or protest, and his blood ran hot and fast through his veins. He wanted to look at her. He wanted to see her eyes when he touched her.

He lifted his head. The glitter of his eyes unnerved her at first, until she felt again the light tracing of his fingers against her skin. The sensations piled on each other until she went hot all over with the need to make him put his hand on her, to touch her. Her body was more demanding than her mind, because it tried to twist toward him, to force a contact he was deliberately denying her.

"Ty...ler?" she whispered brokenly.

His free hand was under her nape. It moved caressingly in her thick hair while his gaze searched her huge, hungry eyes. "Shh," he whispered gently. The hand under her arm moved again, tracing, and she arched, shuddering, while her big eyes pleaded with him. "It's all right," he whispered. "It's all right, honey."

And all the while, his fingers were driving her mad. She felt as if every single cell in her body was drawn as tight as a rope, as if the tension was going to break her in half. Her nails contracted on his muscular upper arms and dug in, and when she realized it, she was shocked at her own action.

"I'm...sorry," she whispered jerkily, caressing the

red crescents she'd made in his skin. "I'm sorry, I…
couldn't…help it."

"You haven't hurt me," he said gently. "You know
that I'm doing this deliberately. Do you know why?"

"No," she whimpered, jerking as his fingertips edged
a little farther onto her breast.

"It's very much like a symphony, little one," he whispered softly, and he managed a smile. "It starts slowly,
softly, and builds and builds and builds to a crescendo.
When I finally give you what you're pleading for, Nell,
you're going to feel a kind of pleasure that I can't even
describe to you."

Her teeth ground together, because the tension was
growing unbearable. "But…when…?"

"Now." His mouth covered hers and his hand moved,
at last, at last, at…last! It covered her breast, swallowing up the hard tip, giving her the tiny consummation
her body had begged for.

And it was like fireworks. She cried out into his
mouth, shuddered, arched with the anguished fulfillment. Her hand found his through the cloth of her shirt
and pressed against it, holding it prisoner. She sobbed,
and the hand at her neck contracted as his mouth grew
feverishly hungry. For long, fiery seconds, the sounds
of their breathing were audible in the quiet room.

"It isn't enough," he bit off against her mouth. While
he held her, his hand began to unbutton her shirt. He
lifted his head and looked into her eyes. "I won't go
further than this, I promise you," he said huskily. "But
I…need…to look at you."

Her eyelids felt heavy. She couldn't work up the effort to protest. What he'd just given her was like honey,

and she was helpless with pleasure. She wanted more. She wanted his eyes on her.

It was extraordinary, she thought, watching him divest her of her shirt and bra. Extraordinary, that look in his eyes, on his face, as he eased her down against the pillows and sat gazing at her taut, swollen breasts.

"Ty," she whispered. "There was a movie I watched once, and it was just a little racy. But the man…he did more than touch her. He put his mouth…"

"Here?" he whispered back, brushing her taut breast with the backs of his fingers, his eyes intent on hers.

She jerked involuntarily with pleasure. "Yes."

"Do you want that, with me?"

She colored, but she was beyond pretending. "Oh, yes…!"

His mouth eased down over the soft flesh, smoothing her skin, sensitizing it. The sensation was beyond anything she'd ever imagined. She made little whimpers that sent his mind whirling out of control. He groaned against her breast and gathered her up close, giving in to the need to taste her, to pleasure her.

She didn't hear the knock the first time it came. But the second time it was louder. She lay still, listening, and felt Tyler stiffen above her.

He caught his breath slowly, glancing through the open bedroom door toward the living room with glazed eyes and a mind that was still in limbo.

"Mr. Jacobs, I brought your mail. I'll slide it under the door."

It was Chappy's voice, and thank God he went away quickly. Nell colored furiously as she imagined what would have happened if Chappy had just walked in.

Tyler looked down at her quietly, letting his bold gaze

go from her eyes to her swollen mouth to the alabaster skin of her breast.

"Are you all right?" he whispered softly. "I didn't frighten you?"

"No." She was looking at him as intently as he was studying her, measuring memory and imagination against the sweet reality of what they'd done together. "Not at all."

He touched her breast tenderly and smiled at her. "It was good," he whispered.

"Yes."

He eased down on his elbows and slowly drew his chest over her sensitized breasts, watching her shiver and gasp with the delicious sensation of it. "This is good, too," he breathed, bending again to her mouth. "I want you, Nell."

She tensed as his mouth brushed hers, and he smiled against her trembling lips.

"I'm not going to do anything about it," he reassured her. "Kiss me, and then you'd better get out of here."

She slid her arms up around his neck and gave him her mouth in a kiss as sweet and wild as the ones before. But seconds later he drew away and rolled over, taking her with him. He lay on his back, shuddering a little with a need he couldn't fulfill.

"You might as well get rid of the baggy britches and loose blouses," he murmured, holding her bare breasts against his broad chest. "I'll never fall for the camouflage again, after this."

"Am I too big?" she whispered, because it mattered if she was.

He brushed the hair away from her mouth. "No. You're just right. All of you." He brushed a warm kiss against her lips and loosened his arms. "You'd better get your things back on. I'm weak, but I'm still capable. I don't want this to get out of hand."

She touched his face, her fingers cold and nervous, tracing its hard contours, fascinated with him. "You can't imagine what it was like for me," she whispered. "I...well, it wasn't what I thought it would be."

He smiled. "Not even after you saw that racy movie?" he murmured dryly.

She swallowed, remembering when she'd told him about it and what had followed. "Well, no. Seeing and experiencing are different."

"Indeed they are." He helped her to sit up and spent a long minute looking at her before he gathered up her bra and blouse and proceeded to help her back into them. "No," he said when she tried to stop him. "You dressed me. Now it's my turn."

So she sat still and let him dress her, delighting in his gentle touch, in his obvious pleasure in her.

"You can't stay here tonight," he said. "I hope you realize why."

"Yes. I know why."

He buttoned her up to the throat and smoothed back her long disheveled hair. "I would like very much to take your clothes off and pull you under this sheet with me and love you up to the ceiling," he said seriously. "I could do that, despite your innocence. But I'd hate myself for abusing your trust, and you might hate me for backing you into a corner. I don't want anything to spoil what's building between us. I don't think you want that, either."

She linked her fingers into his as he toyed with her

hair. "No. I don't want anything to spoil it, either," she whispered.

He drew her hand to his mouth and kissed it gently. "I won't sleep. I'll remember how it was while we were loving each other in this bed, and I'll ache to have you here with me."

She trembled at his description of what they'd done. It had felt like loving, even if he only meant that in a physical sense. Her warm eyes searched his, and her face was radiant with shared pleasure, with hope, with new dreams that seemed to be turning into reality.

"I never dreamed it would be this way," she said absently.

"How did you think it would be?"

"Frightening," she confessed without telling him why. McAnders had made it into a terrifying thing, a violent act that would have hurt if he'd succeeded. But what she'd experienced with Tyler wasn't terrifying. It had been beautiful.

"And it wasn't?" he persisted gently.

"Not frightening, no," she said with a demure smile. "A little scary, but in a nice way. So many sensations…"

"For me, too, Nell," he said somberly. His eyes held hers. "That was no casual diversion, and don't you forget it. I'm not a playboy."

"You're not a monk, either," she said. She smiled shakily. "I may be innocent, but I'm not stupid."

He sighed, smoothing her closed fingers with his thumb. "If you want the truth, yes, I've had women. But always women who couldn't or wouldn't consider marriage or anything permanent. And never for money. Lovemaking is too beautiful to reduce to a quick coupling that only satisfies a casual hunger."

She couldn't speak. She hadn't expected him to say anything like that, and it occurred to her that she didn't really know him very well. "I'm glad you think of it that way," she said.

"Don't you, honestly?" he asked.

"With you I do," she said after a minute. McAnders's angry handling was fading away like a bad dream. Now when she thought about physical expressions of affection, she was always going to feel Tyler's hands on her body.

He touched her lips with a long forefinger. "Go away," he said softly. "I want you terribly, Miss Regan."

She smiled tenderly. "I'm very glad of that. But I'll go."

She got up from the bed, her eyes possessive as they ran over his taut body.

"Would you like an anatomy lesson?" he asked with a dry smile. "I could pull this sheet away and teach you volumes about men."

She averted her eyes, her cheeks scarlet. "I'll just bet you could," she muttered, because she remembered how his body had changed when hers came into contact with it. "And stop making fun of me because I'm not clued in."

"I happen to like you that way, believe it or not," he mused. "Come back in the morning. We can have another argument."

"I don't really want to argue with you."

"The alternative could get us into real trouble."

She laughed because he sounded so morose and dryly amused all at once. Her face changed with the sound, brightened, went soft and radiant.

"You are lovely when you laugh," he said huskily.

"And if you don't get out of here right now, I'm going to throw off this damned sheet and come after you."

She let out a low whistle and headed for the door. "The mind boggles," she murmured as she glanced over her shoulder and smiled at him. "Sleep tight."

"Oh, that's funny," he agreed. "A real screamer. I'll have to remember to put it in my memoirs."

"I won't sleep, either," she said softly, and left him reluctantly.

She went out the door smiling, her heart so light that it could have floated before her. She'd never been so happy in all her life. The most unexpected things happened sometimes. They'd argued and she'd been sure that there was no hope, and now he'd kissed her so hungrily, handled her so gently that she was building daydreams again. This had to be the real thing, she told herself doggedly. He'd told her he wasn't playing, so it had to be for real. It had to be!

And all of a sudden, she started thinking about the past, about a man who'd teased her and kissed her lazily once or twice, a man she'd thought she loved. And that man had betrayed her trust and tried to force her into bed, all because he'd wanted her bright, beautiful sister-in-law. It didn't bear thinking about. Surely history wasn't going to repeat itself with Tyler. Nell closed her eyes in faint fear. She couldn't bear the thought of that.

If Bella noticed that Nell's lips were swollen and her hair wildly disheveled and her face full of a new radiance mingled with fear, she kept it to herself. But she was less abrasive than usual as Nell helped with the dishes, and she was smiling when the younger woman went up to bed.

Nell awoke the next morning after a sleepless night to hear a furious commotion going on down in the kitchen.

She hurriedly dressed in jeans and a neat checked shirt, left her hair down around her shoulders and went to the kitchen for breakfast. She caught the tail end of a conversation that sounded curious at best.

Bella was still raging at someone. "...can't imagine what possessed him! Of course he didn't know—he isn't a mean kind of man. But we've got to get him out of here!"

"Can't be done." That was Chappy's voice, slow and measured. "Old Man Regan gave him the power to hire and fire. Even Nell can't override him in something like this. It's just a damned shame that one of you women didn't think to tell him!"

"Well, it ain't the kind of thing you talk about to outsiders," Bella grumbled.

"He was up and moving about last I looked. Should I go talk to him?"

"Hold off a few minutes. Give me time to think."

"Okay. Tell me when."

A door slammed. Nell hesitated before she went on into the room. When Bella saw her, she turned beet red.

"Nell! I wasn't expecting you this early," she said with a toothy grin that was as false as fool's gold.

"I heard you," Nell said. "What's going on? Is it something to do with the new men? They're supposed to show up today." She gnawed her lower lip. "I guess we can send them on over to Tyler. He was much better yesterday. He can't work, but he can still delegate—"

"You'd better sit down," Bella began.

"Why? Has he hired Jack the Ripper?" Nell grinned. She felt great. It was a beautiful day, and she wanted to get this over with so that she could see Tyler. Her whole life had changed overnight. Everything was beautiful.

"Worse." Bella took a deep breath. "Oh, there's just no use in pussyfooting around. He's hired Darren McAnders."

There was a hush like death in the room. Of all the things Nell might have expected to hear, that was the last. She did sit down, heavily, with her heart in her throat. Nightmares were rushing in on her, old wounds were opening.

"How could he?" she asked huskily. "How could he give that man a job here? I thought Darren was working on a ranch in Wyoming."

"Obviously he came home, and it seems he thought nine years had healed old wounds."

"Not mine," Nell said, her dark eyes flashing. "Not ever. He used me. He hurt me, scared me out of my mind… Well, he isn't going to work here. Tell Chappy to fire him."

"You know Chappy can't do that. Neither can you," Bella said. "You'll have to go and tell Tyler what happened."

She went white. After what she and Tyler had shared the day before, the thought of telling him about what McAnders had done to her was sickening. Not only that, she'd have to tell him all of it. That McAnders had flirted with her and teased her, just as Tyler had done. That he'd made a little light love to her, and she'd gone off the deep end and thrown herself at him. It had never been all Darren's fault—even in the beginning. Nell hadn't been able to talk to Bella or Margie, to tell them how much at fault *she'd* been. But she'd loved Darren, or thought she had, and she'd assumed from his affectionate advances that he felt the same way. She'd had the shock of her young life when he'd come into her room, expecting her cooperation to help get Margie out of his blood, and found her unwilling and apparently scared to death. He'd had some harsh things to say, and he'd been drinking. She still didn't know if he'd have gone far enough to force her, because her screams had brought Bella and Margie running. Surely Darren didn't think Nell was still carrying a torch for him and would welcome him back? He had to know how she hated him.

"Tell Tyler what happened," Bella said. "He'll understand."

Nell wasn't at all sure that he would. She thought of approaching Darren, but she couldn't bear to talk to him. Nine years hadn't erased her shame and fear of him, or her embarrassment for her own behavior that had led to such a tragic confrontation.

"I'll try," Nell promised as she went out the back door. She wasn't going to confess, she knew that. But maybe there was another way.

She knocked on Tyler's door, shaking in her boots. He called for her to come in, and she found him in the kitchen frying eggs.

He glanced at her with a strange reserve, as if he'd forgotten the day before or didn't want to remember it. "Good morning," he said quietly. His eyes slid over her and quickly away, back to what he was doing. "Do you want some breakfast?"

His coolness robbed her of courage. He didn't seem like the same man who'd kissed her half to death. Perhaps he was ashamed. Perhaps he regretted every kiss. Or perhaps he was just afraid she might throw herself at him. Shades of the past fell ominously over her head.

"I'm not hungry." She took a deep breath. "One of the new men you hired is Darren McAnders. I want you to let him go. Right now."

His black eyebrows arched. He moved the pan from the burner and shut off the stove before he turned slowly to face her. "I don't think I heard you right."

"I said I want you to fire McAnders right now," she returned stiffly. "I won't have him on this ranch."

"How many available cowboys do you think I can find at roundup time?" he asked shortly. "I'm already a man short, even with McAnders, and he comes highly recommended by the Wyoming outfit he was working for. He's steady, he doesn't drink and he knows what to do with a rope. And you want me to fire him before he's even started? You little fool, he could sue us to hell for that and bring down half the government on our heads!"

"You won't do it?" she asked coldly.

"No." He glowered at her. "Not without cause. If you want him fired, tell me why," he said, and his eyes were oddly intent.

She tried. She started to speak. Her sweet memories were turning black in her mind, and she was already mourning for what might have been. Tyler looked formidable. He also looked fighting mad. She'd gone about it all wrong. She should have tried honey instead of vinegar, but it was too late now. He'd see right through that tactic, anyway.

"We're old enemies," she said finally. "That's the best I can do by way of an explanation."

He smiled mockingly and there was a new coldness in his tone. "Now that's interesting," he said. "Because McAnders told me this morning that you were old friends. Very close friends, in fact."

CHAPTER SIX

NELL JUST STOOD, staring blankly at Tyler while she tried to decide what to say. His tone was enough to convince her that he was well on the way to believing that she'd lied to him. God knew what Darren had said about the past, but it had made a terrible difference in Tyler's attitude toward her. She could feel the distrust in him, and it chilled her.

"You don't have to agonize over an explanation," Tyler said when he saw her hesitation. It was obvious that McAnders had meant something to her. "But don't expect me to fire a man because he's one of your old flames," he added mockingly. "That isn't reason enough."

She didn't say another word. He was looking at her as if he was prepared to disbelieve anything she said. He didn't know her well enough to see that she'd never have asked him to fire a man out of some personal grudge. It went much deeper than that. McAnders was an unpleasant part of her past, a constant reminder of her own lack of self-control, her vulnerability. Tyler had shown her that physical desire wasn't the terrible thing she'd remembered. But that was over before it began, all because she couldn't bring herself to tell him the truth.

"Nothing else to say?" he asked.

She shook her head. "No, thank you. I'm sorry I disturbed you."

Tyler scowled as she left. She was subdued now when she'd been fiery-tempered before. What was McAnders to her? Was she still in love with him and afraid of succumbing? Or was it something more? He wished he'd made her tell him. Now, he had a terrible feeling that he might have left it too late.

Nell was keyed up and frightened of her first confrontation with Darren. It came unexpectedly that same day, at dusk, when he was passing the back porch as she went out the door.

She looked up and there he was. Her first love. Her first crush. Until Tyler had come along, her only crush. Darren McAnders had been in his early twenties nine years ago. Now he was in his early thirties, but he hadn't changed. He had dark auburn hair, threaded with gray at the temples now, and blue eyes. He was a little heavier than he had been. But it was his face that drew Nell's attention the most. He'd aged twenty years. He had lines where he shouldn't have had them, and the easygoing smile she remembered was gone completely.

"Hello, Nell," he said quietly.

She didn't flinch, although she felt like it. He brought back memories of her own stupidity and its near-disastrous consequences. He was walking proof that her self-control was a myth, and she didn't like it.

"Hello, Darren," she replied.

"I suppose you've given the word to have me thrown off the place by now," he said surprisingly. "Once I knew you still lived here, I was sure I'd made a mistake in hiring on without telling your new ramrod the truth."

He frowned slightly, pushing his battered hat back on his head. "You don't mind that I'm here?"

"Of course I mind," she said coldly, and her dark eyes flashed. "I mind that I made a fool of myself over you, and that you used me because of Margie. But if you don't mind the memories, then neither do I. Keep your job. I don't care one way or the other."

He searched her face for a long moment, and then what he could see of her body in her usual clothing, and a kind of sadness claimed his expression. "You might not believe it, but I had a lot of regrets about what happened. It's been heavy on my conscience all these years."

He looked as if it had, too, and that was the most surprising thing of all to Nell. She didn't speak because she couldn't think of anything to say.

He took a slow breath. "How is Marguerite?" he asked finally.

She'd suspected that Marguerite's widowhood had some place in McAnders's decision to take a job at the ranch. Even nine years hadn't dimmed his passion for Margie. Nell wondered how Margie would react.

"She's doing very well," Nell replied. "She and her sons live in Tucson. They come out here for an occasional weekend."

"I heard about your brother," he remarked. "I'm sorry. I always liked Ted. I hated betraying his trust that way."

"He never knew how you felt about her," she said. "Now if you'll excuse me…"

"You've changed," he said suddenly. "I wouldn't have known you in that getup."

She flushed with mingled temper and embarrassment as she remembered the close-fitting outfits she used to wear to try to catch his eye. "I guess not," she said tightly. "We all change with age."

"Not as much as you have." He grimaced. "Oh, Nell," he said softly. "Ted should have shot me for what I did to you. He should have shot me dead."

And he turned on his heels and walked away before she could reply. That wasn't the Darren McAnders she remembered. He was no longer the cocky, arrogant young man who'd alternately teased and toyed with her. He was older and far more mature, and the teasing streak seemed to have been buried. All the same, it was too soon to start trusting him, and Margie was going to have a fit when she heard that he was back on the ranch.

Bella had the same feeling, because after supper was cleared away she mentioned that it might be a good idea for Nell to call and tell Margie about their new hand.

"I won't," Nell said firmly. "She'll find out soon enough. She and the boys are coming this weekend."

Bella sighed. "Going to be fireworks," she said.

"Then she can complain to Tyler. I didn't hire him."

"Nell!"

She jumped. Tyler's deep voice carried even when he didn't raise it, but it was clearly raised now, and irritated as he came down the hall toward the kitchen.

"Is that you, or did somebody stick a pin in a mountain lion?" Nell asked with more courage than she felt.

He didn't smile. He was bareheaded and grim, and there were several bills held in one lean hand. "We've got to talk," he said.

Nell glanced apprehensively at Bella, but the older woman began to whistle as if she hadn't heard a word.

Nell put down the dishcloth and followed Tyler back down the hall to the front room that served as an office.

The desk was cluttered, and it looked as if Tyler had been at the books for at least a couple of hours. He'd been going over the ranch's finances for several weeks now, in his spare time, trying to make sense of Nell's hit-or-miss bookkeeping system. Apparently he'd just figured it out, and he didn't like what he saw.

"These—" he indicated a new set of books "—are the new books. I've boiled everything down to credits and debits. From now on, every purchase comes through me. If you want a needle and thread, you'll have to have a purchase order. This—" he held up a book of purchase orders "—is a book of them. It's going to be locked in the desk, and I have the only key."

"Why?" she asked.

He motioned her into a chair and perched himself on the corner of the desk to light a cigarette. "The way things have been run here, any cowboy could go to the hardware store and charge butane or vaccination supplies or go to the feed store for feed or salt and charge it without any authorization." He handed her the bills he'd been carrying. "Read a couple of those."

She frowned curiously, but she did as she was told. "A pair of spurs," she murmured, reading aloud, "a new saddle…" She looked up. "I never authorized those."

"I know you didn't." He smiled faintly. "That's the problem with giving carte blanche to the cowboys."

"Who had the saddle and spurs on here?" she demanded.

"Marlowe."

"You ought to fire him."

"I already have," he said. "Good thing I hired on two

new men instead of one." He eyed the tip of his cigarette. "I saw you talking to McAnders. Is there still a
problem?"

She didn't feel comfortable discussing it with him.
"There won't be one. Darren and I will work things out."

That sounded ominous to him. As if she had ideas
about recapturing the past. He scowled at her, his green
eyes almost sparking with bad temper. "As long as you
keep your dalliance after working hours, I don't care
what you do."

She felt something inside her dying. He couldn't
know how badly he was hurting her with his indifference. She supposed he wouldn't care if he did. She
lowered her eyes to her jeans. "Have you told the men
about the purchase orders?"

"I told the crew in the bunkhouse at supper. I'll tell
the married hands in the morning. There are going to
have to be other changes, as well." He picked up the led-
ger and went through it. "For one thing, we're going to
have to cut back on the activities that require cowboy
participation. It's getting time for roundup, and I'll need
every man I've got. This open range may be fine for a
big outfit, but it's hell on one this size. We'll spend the
better part of a week just getting the saler calves into
holding pens."

"We can borrow Bob Wyler's helicopter, if you want
to," Nell said. "He always helps out that way, and he
supplies the pilot, too."

"For what kind of payment?" Tyler asked narrowly.

Nell grinned involuntarily. "For a case of Bella's
strawberry-rhubarb preserves," she said.

He chuckled, too, in spite of himself. "Okay. That's

a deal. But can you manage the trail rides without Chappy?"

"I managed well enough before Ted died," she said. "I can do it again. What else?"

"This is the worst of it. We're spending a fortune on having a golf pro on the payroll for visitors who want to tee off on the Western Terrace greens. That's fine for the big dude ranches, but we're operating on a shoe-string here. I can show you on paper that only one out of every ten guests avails himself of this service, but the pro collects his fee just the same."

"That was Ted's idea," she said. "I've just let it drag on. You may have noticed that most of the people who come here aren't really very athletic." She blushed and he laughed.

"Yes, I've noticed." He searched her dark eyes slowly, and little sparks of attraction seemed to leap between them before he drew his gaze down to his cigarette. "Then I'll take care of the pro. As for this daily shopping trip into Tucson, is that mandatory?"

"We could cut back to every other day," she compromised. "I realize that it's pretty hard on the gas budget, what with the van being used for transportation. I guess the city tour is hard on the budget, too."

He nodded his dark head. "That was going to be my next question. Can we subcontract the tours out to an existing agency in town?"

"Sure! I know a terrific lady who'd love the business, and her fees are very reasonable."

"Okay. Give her a call and work something out."

"You've been working," Nell remarked, nodding toward all the ledgers and paperwork.

"It's been a long job. But I didn't want to make specific recommendations until I had a handle on how the ranch was run. You haven't done a bad job, Nell," he said surprisingly. "Except for a few places, you've budgeted to the bone. You've only continued old policies. But we're going to change some of those and get this place operating in the black again."

"You sound encouraging."

"It's a good little operation," he replied. "It shouldn't be hard to make it a paying one. Anyplace you think you may need more help?"

She thought for a minute, trying not to notice the way his jeans clung to his long, powerful legs, or the fact that the top three buttons of his red-checked shirt were unbuttoned over that tanned expanse of hair-covered chest. She remembered all too well how it had felt to touch him in passion.

"I'd like to have someone come with me on the trail ride while that man from back East is here," she confessed with a faint smile. "His wife is rather cold-eyed, and she seems to have some insane idea that I'm chasing him."

Tyler's eyes went narrow. "Yes, I saw how he tried to come on to you at the square dance. They leave Thursday, don't they?" He saw her nod. "I'll go on the next two trail rides with you. Chappy can keep things in order for Bella while we're out."

"Thanks."

"Unless you'd rather I let McAnders go with you?" he added with a mocking smile.

She wanted to protest, but that would be a little too revealing. She swallowed. "Whatever suits you," she said. "It doesn't matter to me."

Which wasn't the answer he wanted. He put out his

cigarette with faint violence. "McAnders can go with you, then," he said. "I've got enough work to do without playing nursemaid."

The words were meant to sting, and they did. She got up, avoiding his eyes as she went to the door. "Thanks for all you're doing," she said over her shoulder.

"My pleasure. Good night."

"Good night."

She didn't see him alone after that. There was always some reason to have other people present or to put off discussions until she could arrange for reinforcements. But that didn't stop Tyler from cutting at her verbally at every opportunity.

What hurt the most was that Darren McAnders didn't mind accompanying her on trail rides, and seemed even to enjoy her taciturn company. He began to smile again, as if being with her brightened his life. She didn't understand why, and she understood even less Tyler's new antagonism.

But the fire hit the fan on the weekend, when Margie and the boys arrived by taxi.

Nell had just come back from the trail ride, with Darren McAnders at her side. Marguerite, immaculate in a white linen suit, stepped out of the cab she'd recklessly hired in Tucson, with her long reddish-gold hair wafting in the breeze, and looked straight up into Darren McAnders's stunned face.

"Darren!" she exclaimed, missing her step.

She went down on her knees in the dust, and Darren vaulted out of the saddle to pick her up, his hands strong and sure on her upper arms, his eyes intent on her flushed face.

"Margie," he said softly. "You haven't aged. You're as beautiful as ever."

"What are you doing here?" Margie gasped. She glanced at Nell, even more shocked to find Nell apparently voluntarily in Darren's company.

"He's our newest hand," Nell told her. "Tyler hired him."

"Doesn't he know?" Margie asked, and then flushed when she saw Darren's rueful smile. "Oh, I'm sorry. It's just that…"

"The past is only a problem if we let it be," Nell said stubbornly. "Darren and I are getting along very well. Aren't we, Darren?" she asked.

He smiled ruefully. "As well as could be expected. Nell's been very generous. It was this job or welfare, and I couldn't have blamed her if she'd thrown me off the place. It's as much as I deserved."

Margie searched his face slowly and then glanced up at Nell, sitting still on her horse. "It took a lot of courage for you to come back here, Darren," she remarked, even though she was looking at Nell, waiting, questioning.

"I found out that running away doesn't solve much," he said enigmatically. He glanced past Margie. "Are these your boys?" He asked the question softly, and his eyes echoed that softness as he looked at them. "Curt and Jess, aren't you? Your aunt Nell's said a lot about you."

They piled out of the car like marauding pirates and stared at him enthusiastically. "Did she, really?" Curt asked. "Did she say nice stuff? Me and Jess are lots of help around the ranch—Tyler says so. We help him find snakes and lizards and stuff and keep them from eating up Aunt Nell's cattle!"

Aunt Nell's eyes widened with amusement. "Did Tyler tell you that?"

"Well, not really," Jess murmured. "But it sounds good, don't it?"

"Doesn't it," Margie corrected absently. She was just beginning to get her self-confidence back after the shock of seeing Darren. "Boys, we'd better get inside." She paid the driver, and Nell got off her horse to help with the luggage, but Darren was one step ahead of her.

"I'll take care of this if you can manage the horses, Nell," he said with a hopeful glance in her direction.

She knew he'd never gotten over Margie. It didn't surprise her that he was anxious to renew that acquaintance. What Margie felt was less easy to perceive. But it certainly wasn't like the older woman to lose her step and pitch headfirst into desert sand.

"Sure," Nell agreed easily. "I'll take them to the barn. Margie, I'll see you and the boys in a few minutes."

"That's fine," Margie said absently, but she was looking at Darren as if she'd been poleaxed.

Nell was faintly relieved. With Darren around, maybe Margie wouldn't bat her eyelashes so luxuriously at Tyler. Not that it mattered anymore. Tyler had certainly made it clear that he wasn't interested in Nell. He avoided her like the very plague.

She led the horses to the barn, where Chappy took the reins with a curious glance at her rigid features.

"You okay?" he asked.

She smiled. "I'm fine." She glanced around. "Where's Caleb?"

Caleb was the big black gelding that Tyler always rode. Asking for the horse's whereabouts was a little less obvious than inquiring about Tyler's.

Chappy saw right through her. "He's out riding the boundary fence we put up around the holding pens."

She blinked. "He hates riding fence."

"He overheard two of the boys talking about the way McAnders hangs around you since he's been here," the wrinkled cowboy said with a twinkle in his pale blue eyes. "He set them to cleaning out the stables, and he went off to ride fence. I don't reckon anybody will mention such things around him again, once word gets through the outfit."

She bit her lower lip. "Why should he care?"

Chappy started to lead the horses toward the stable, where two sweating, swearing cowboys were mucking out the stalls and pitching fresh hay. "You need glasses," he said dryly.

Nell drifted back to the house slowly, her eyes everywhere on the horizon, looking for a glimpse of Tyler. Things had been strained between them. That, and McAnders's presence, were making her life miserable. Not that she minded Darren being around. He'd changed so much from the shallow, careless man she'd known. She felt no remnant of the old crush she'd had on him, nor any sense of bitterness. He was like a friendly stranger whom she began to like, but nothing more.

If only she could go to Tyler and tell him that. But despite his odd behavior this afternoon, he hadn't said anything that would lead Nell to believe he had any lasting affection for her. In fact, he'd said more than once that there wasn't any place for a woman in his life right now. And the thought of throwing herself at another man, after the misery her encounter with Darren had brought her, was unwelcome. Tyler might be kind about it, but she knew he wouldn't appreciate having her "hang on his boots," as he'd mentioned to Bella.

She sighed. She knew so little about men. If only she could talk to Margie, perhaps she could find a way out of the corner she'd painted herself into.

She went into the house to help Bella get supper on the table before the guests were called onto the elegant patio to eat. The wooden tables each had umbrellas and sat beside an Olympic-size swimming pool, which did a lot of business during the day. All meals were taken here, with Bella and Nell setting a buffet table from which guests could choose their portions. All around were palo verde trees, along with every conceivable form of cactus known to the desert Southwest. It was amusing to watch the guests from back East ask about the flower garden mentioned in the brochure and then see it for real. The native plants were surrounded by rock borders, and their arrangement was both mysterious and compelling. In bloom, the cacti were beautiful, like the feathery palo verde with its fragrant yellow blossoms.

"You aren't eating?" Nell asked when Margie sat down a good distance away from the guests while, as a special treat, the boys had their meal in the bunkhouse with the cowboys.

Margie shook her head. She'd changed into designer jeans and a red tank top, and she looked elegant and moody. "I'm not hungry. How long has he been here?"

"A few days," Nell said. "Tyler hired him."

"And you let him stay?"

"Not voluntarily," Nell said after a minute. "I tried to bulldoze Tyler into letting him go, but he wouldn't.

He wanted to know why." She lowered her eyes. "I couldn't tell him."

"Yes. I understand." She sat up suddenly, leaning her forearms on the table. "Nell, it isn't terribly bad, is it? Having him around?"

The intensity of the question was interesting. Nell smiled faintly. "No, it isn't terribly bad," she said gently. She studied the pale, beautiful features. "You still care about him, don't you?"

Margie stiffened. She actually flustered. "I…well, no, of course not. I didn't really care about him!"

"Ted has been dead for a long time," Nell said quietly. "And I'm sure he never meant for you to live without love forever. If you're asking me how I feel about Darren, he's very much like a nice stranger." She smiled gently. "I guess you and Bella were right about what happened. I blew it all out of proportion because I didn't have any experience to measure it against. I didn't exactly invite what happened, but I'd led him to believe that I wanted him without realizing it."

"It was my fault, too," Margie admitted. "But I never meant you to be hurt." She looked at the table instead of at Nell. "I cared about him. Not in the way I loved Ted, but in a different way. But I was married, and despite the way I teased him, I never would have had an affair with him."

"I know that," Nell said.

Margie smiled at her sadly. "I've spent a lot of years trying to make you over in my image, haven't I? Being bossy, taking you for granted. But I meant it in the nicest way. I wanted to help. I just didn't know how."

"I don't need help," Nell told her dryly. "And I'm not

going to try to recapture the past with Darren McAnders."

"And Tyler?" Margie fished. "Where does he fit in?"

That question threw her again. Was Margie infatuated with Tyler? Was her interest in Darren only pretended so that she could find out how Nell felt about Tyler? Nell started drawing into herself again, defensively. "Tyler is my foreman, nothing more. He doesn't give a hang about me in any way," Nell said tautly. She got up from the table. "I'm not hungry, Margie. I think I'll go watch TV."

"Okay. I've got to go get the boys."

"They're already on the way," Nell remarked with a bitter smile, and gestured to where Tyler was coming with both boys by the hand. They were laughing and so was he. Margie was gazing at the group with such naked hunger that Nell turned away. "See you later," she said, but Margie wasn't really listening. Her whole attention was focused on Tyler. Actually, it was focused on Darren, who was right behind Tyler, but Nell didn't see the second man. She was sure now that Margie was using Darren as an excuse to mask her feelings for Tyler.

Nell went inside and threw herself into housecleaning until she was nearly exhausted, getting rooms ready for the boys and Margie. When she came back downstairs, she was surprised to find Tyler in the living room, already watching the news.

He looked tired. Dead tired. He'd showered and changed, but he had an oblivious kind of expression on his face that brightened a little when he saw Nell come into the room.

"Can I get you a lemonade?" he asked, hoisting his.

"Not a brandy?" she mused.

"I don't drink. I never have."

She sat down in the armchair across from him, feeling her way. "Why?"

He shrugged. "I don't know. I don't like either the taste or the effect, I guess." His green eyes went over her like hands, and she flushed, because memories were glittering there. It was shocking to remember exactly how intimate he'd been with her, for all the distance that had been between them since then.

"I don't drink, either," she said absently. "I'm frightfully old-fashioned."

"Yes, I know," he said softly, and the memories were there again, warm and overwhelming. His eyes caught hers and held them relentlessly. "How do you feel about McAnders?"

She sat up straight. She had to hide her real feelings from him, so she said, "I'm not sure."

"Aren't you? You seem to spend enough time with him lately," he accused quietly.

"You spend plenty around Margie," she shot back.

He smiled mockingly. "Yes, I do, don't I? But you don't seem to spend much time considering why."

"It's obviously because she attracts you," she said haughtily. "I'm not blind."

"Oh, but you are," he said quietly. "More blind than you know."

"I can spend time with anyone I please," she continued coldly.

"Have you been intimate with McAnders?" he asked suddenly.

She gasped. Her face went bloodred as she remembered what had happened that night, what Darren had tried to do to her.

Tyler saw the expression, but he took it for guilt, and something inside him exploded. No wonder Nell had eyes for McAnders. He'd been her first love, and now he was back and he wanted her, and she'd let him touch her in all the ways Tyler had. Maybe even more. His eyes glittered at her furiously.

"How could you do that?" he asked bitterly.

She blinked. "Do what?"

He threw up his hands and paced angrily. "And all the time I thought—" He stopped short, turning. "Well, if it's McAnders you want, consider him yours. I'll run the business end of the ranch and take care of the livestock. But don't make the mistake of running after me if McAnders dumps you," he added venomously. "I don't want another man's castoff."

Nell gasped with outrage. "You lily-white purist!" she threw at him. "How many women have you cast off, if we're going to get personal?"

"That's none of your business," he said shortly.

"Well, Darren is none of yours." She clenched her hands, hating his arrogance.

He wanted to throw things. He hadn't realized until then just how deeply Nell was under his skin. He had to face the possibility that a man from her past was about to carry her off, and he didn't know what to do to stop it. She'd got the wrong end of the stick about Margie. He liked Margie, yet he saw right through her antics. But Nell was so insecure that she couldn't see the forest for the trees. Considering that insecurity it was a miracle that she could even contemplate a relationship with Darren McAnders. But she might love him...

He sighed heavily. "Fair enough," he said finally

and with a long, quiet stare. "Do what you please, Nell. I won't interfere. As you say, your life is your own."

He turned to go and she felt sick all over at the way things were working out. She didn't care about Darren. She wanted to call him back and tell him the truth, but something stopped her. She couldn't tell him, she couldn't face his contempt when he knew that she'd invited Darren's advances, that she'd chased him all those years ago and brought it on herself. So she let him go, watching with sad eyes as he left the room only to run into Margie in the hall.

Nell heard him laughing and caught a glimpse of Margie's rapt expression. She couldn't bear it. She was going to lose him to Margie, and she couldn't bear it. She went back into the living room, forcing herself not to cry.

She'd let Tyler think she'd been deliberately intimate with Darren, and that was a lie. She sat down on the sofa, remembering what had happened all those years ago. She'd been mistaken about McAnders's feelings back then, and she'd become obsessed with him after he'd paid her a little attention. She recalled how she'd teased him until one night she went a little too far. Margie had given a party and that evening Nell had flirted with McAnders, who'd been rejected by Margie and had had too much to drink. McAnders had come to Nell's room and found her asleep in her scanty gown, and since she hadn't locked her door, he'd thought she was waiting for him. He'd climbed into bed with her and, despite her protests, he'd been about to seduce her when Bella had come to her rescue.

But that had been years ago, long before she knew Tyler. He hadn't been talking about the past, though.

He'd asked her if she'd been intimate with Darren, and he was talking about the present.

The impact of the realization hit her between the eyes like a hammer. Now she'd done it! She'd inadvertantly let him think that what she'd shared with him she'd also shared with Darren. She'd stung his pride by letting him think that she could go straight from his arms into Darren's and without a twinge of conscience.

She got up, shaking with reaction, and wondered if she could go after him, explain.

But before she got to the door, Curt and Jess came careering down the hall, and she looked past them to where Tyler was holding Margie's arm, escorting her laughingly out the front door.

It was too late now to smooth things over, she knew. She'd left it just a few seconds too long. She'd lost him.

CHAPTER SEVEN

"HI, AUNT NELL," they chorused. "Can we watch that new science fiction movie on the DVD player?"

"Sure. Go ahead," she said with forced tolerance, but her heart was breaking. "Where'd your mother go?"

"Uncle Tyler's taking her into town," Curt volunteered disinterestedly as he searched for the right DVD. "I sure like Uncle Tyler."

"Yeah, me, too," Jess agreed.

So it was "uncle" already, Nell thought, groaning inwardly. She made some brief excuse and left the room before the boys could see the tears forming in her eyes.

After that day Nell started avoiding him again. Not that it was necessary. Tyler cut her dead every time he saw her, his eyes hard and accusing, as if she'd betrayed him somehow. Nell began to wilt emotionally.

Margie and the boys left, but she and Tyler had seemed to spend a lot of time together during that visit, and Margie had been very nervous and standoffish around Darren. So any hope Nell had that her sister-in-law might be interested in her old flame was washed away almost immediately. It was Tyler Margie wanted, and Nell didn't have a chance anymore. Not with Tyler nearly hating her for what he thought she'd done. As if she could have borne the touch of any man's hands but his; it seemed impossible that he didn't know that.

After Margie left, a morose Darren McAnders began to seek Nell out to talk about the way Margie had avoided him. He was hurt, just as she was, and their common pain brought them together as friends. She even found an odd kind of comfort in his presence.

It was an odd turn of events all around, she thought as she walked with Darren to the corral fence to see two new mares Tyler had bought. Darren was turning out to be a friend.

"You're looking moody lately," Darren remarked as they watched Chappy work one of the unbroken mares on a lunging rein. He glanced at her and smiled mischievously. "And the boss is explosive. The men are betting on how long it's going to be before he throws a punch at somebody just to let the pressure off."

She flushed. "It's complicated," she said.

He propped a boot on the lowest rail of the corral fence. "It's pretty funny for me to be offering you a shoulder to cry on, when I was your worst enemy at one time. But times have changed and so have I. And if you need somebody to listen, here I am, honey."

She looked up at him tearfully. He was different, all right. A new man altogether. She managed a smile.

He smiled back and pulled her against him to give her a friendly, totally platonic hug.

But Tyler happened to be looking out the window in the bunkhouse and he saw them. And what was a platonic hug didn't look that way to a man already trying to cope with emotions he was feeling for the first time in his life, and eaten up with unfamiliar jealousy, to boot. Tyler let out a string of range language, turned and stormed off to where he'd tied his horse. He swung

up into the saddle and rode away without the slightest
idea of where in hell he was going.

The square dance was the following Saturday night,
and most of the present guests were leaving on Sunday to make room for a new group of people. A one-
week stay was about standard for most of them. By that
time they were sore enough and rested enough to go
home and cope with their routines. Margie and the boys
showed up Saturday afternoon, and the older woman
thrust a huge box at Nell, with a mischievous smile.

"For you," she said with dancing eyes. "Open it."

Nell eyed her curiously, but she put the box on the
dining room table and opened it, aware of Bella's frank
interest as she did.

It was a square-dancing outfit. A red-checked full
skirt with oceans of petticoats and a pretty white Mexican peasant blouse in cotton, both of which had probably cost the earth. Nell just stared at it without speaking.
It was the prettiest set she'd ever seen.

"For me?" she asked Margie blankly.

"For you," came the smiling reply. "And don't put
your hair up in a ponytail, will you?"

"But, Margie, I can't dance," she began.

"Wear that and someone will be sure to teach you,"
Margie promised.

So Nell wore the new outfit and brushed her long
honey-colored hair until it shone thick and gleaming
around her shoulders. Margie taught her how to put on
a thin coat of makeup, and they were both surprised
at the results. Nell didn't look like Nell anymore. She
wasn't beautiful, but she was certainly attractive enough
to make a man notice her.

Margie was wearing a similar outfit, the difference

being that Margie could do anything from a square dance to a samba. Nell was too aware that she herself had at least two left feet.

Once she tried to ask Margie about Tyler, but she lost her nerve. Margie was so beautiful, and she had a way of making every man she met want her. If Tyler fell victim to her charm, who could blame him?

Nell couldn't help but wonder, though, why Margie had bought her a dress. Did she possibly sense that Nell cared about Tyler, and was trying to help her get over him by attracting Darren? But surely Margie didn't think she was interested that way in Darren, because she'd already denied it.

Downstairs, Bella made a big fuss over Nell's new image, and Nell had a feeling it was to make up for the last time she'd dressed up and Bella had been worried about Tyler getting the wrong idea. But this time praise was certainly forthcoming.

The band could be heard tuning up in the barn, which had been cleared out for the dance. Bella grinned.

"Well, at least Tyler hasn't complained about that forty dollars we have to pay the band twice a month," she said dryly.

"Give him time." Nell sighed. "Lately he complains about most everything. I hear he even made Chappy take back a rope he bought without permission."

"In case you haven't heard," Bella told Margie, "Tyler is in a snit lately. He walks around glowering at people and talking to himself."

Margie lifted an eyebrow at Nell, who flushed angrily.

"I don't have anything to do with it," Nell said shortly. "Maybe he's missing your company."

Margie exchanged glances with Bella and smiled mischievously. "Well, that's possible, of course." She eyed Nell's averted face. "Shall we go find out? Bella, you're sure you can manage the boys? They're in their pajamas, waiting for that story you promised to read them."

"Sure, me and the boys will do fine." Bella picked up a book and started toward the staircase. "Don't you worry about us."

"What are you going to read them?" Margie asked.

Bella turned and grinned wickedly. "All about the pirate raids in the Caribbean, in gory detail."

Nell gasped, but Margie laughed. "Good for you."

"Won't they have nightmares?" Nell asked.

Margie shook her head. "They love that sort of thing. I'm told that most boys do—it's normal. Their young worlds are made up of monsters and battles."

"Isn't everybody's?" Bella chuckled. "Have fun."

Nell didn't have a wrap, and it was a chilly night, but she tried not to notice the goose bumps as she and Margie walked down to the barn. Things were already in full swing, and Nell noticed that Margie's eyes were restless, as if she were looking for someone. She sighed, thinking that Margie was apparently going to single out Tyler for the evening. Nell had once been certain that Darren was the recipient of Margie's affections, but she must have been wrong.

The guests were already dancing, with Chappy calling the square dance with gleeful abandon and clapping his hands as he stood at the microphone in front of the band. Tyler was standing to one side, near the refreshment table, braiding three strands of rawhide carelessly while he glared at the dancing. He had on jeans and a blue-plaid Western shirt, and with his black hair neatly combed and his face freshly shaven, he made Nell's heart race. He was the handsomest man she'd ever seen.

"There you are!" Margie grinned, taking possession of his arm. "How are you?"

"Fine." Tyler looked past her at Nell, glared even more at Nell, then turned his attention back to Margie. "You look like a dream, honey," he said in a tone that would have attracted bees.

"Thank you," Margie purred. She glanced at Nell. "Doesn't Nell look nice?" she added.

Nell colored and Tyler didn't say a word. He caught Margie's hand in his. "Let's get in the circle," he told her, and dragged her off without noticing the surprise in her face.

Nell moved back out of the circle of dancers and sat down in one of the chairs, feeling alone and rejected and uncomfortable. It was there that Darren found her. He was wearing a black shirt and red bandanna with his jeans, and he looked almost as handsome as Tyler but in a totally different way.

"Hi, pal," he said, smiling at Nell. "Hiding out?"

She shrugged. "I don't dance," she said with a rueful grin. "I never learned."

He cocked an eyebrow. "No time like the present," he remarked. The band had just changed to a slow, dreamy tune, and he held out his hand.

But she shook her head. "I'm not really in the mood."

He turned to look at the throng of dancers, and his face hardened when he saw Margie dancing with Tyler. He moved beside Nell to lean against one of the posts with folded arms, glaring at what he saw.

"He doesn't waste much time, does he?" he asked under his breath.

"They come from the same kind of world," Nell said quietly. "They've spent a lot of time together since he came here, and the boys love him."

"The boys don't exactly treat me like a plague victim," Darren said coldly. "Well, faint heart never won fair lady, Nell."

She smiled up at him. "In that case, good luck."

He smiled back. "Don't let him see you looking like that," he advised. "You'll blow your cover."

She sat up straighter. "God forbid."

He winked at her and moved into the dancers to tap Tyler curtly on the shoulder, nod and sweep Margie into his arms.

Tyler moved off the floor. He gave Nell a cursory glance before he picked up the rawhide strands he'd left on the corner of the refreshment table and began to braid them again.

"Lost your escort, I gather," he said coolly without looking down at her.

"What's the matter? Is the competition too much for you?" she shot back with uncharacteristic venom.

He blinked at the unfamiliar heat in her tone. His green eyes glanced over her composed features. "I thought that was your big problem, honey," he said. "Although you're dressed for it tonight."

"This old rag?" she said with a vacant smile. "Until just recently, it was the kitchen tablecloth."

He didn't smile. His eyes went to Margie and Darren, dancing like shadows, oblivious to the world.

"It's a nice crowd," Nell remarked when the silence between them lengthened.

"So it is." He finished the braid and tied it off.

"How are roundup plans coming?"

"Fine."

She took a deep breath. "My goodness, you'll talk my ear off."

"Will I?"

"You might offer to teach me to dance," she said shyly and not without reservations. Inside she was shaking as she tossed off the light remark. "You said once that you'd like it if I wore a dress, and you'd show me how."

His green eyes met hers like bullets. "Most men get poetic when they've been without a woman for a few months," he said with blunt insolence. "But you take things to heart, don't you, Nell?"

She felt the color run up her neck like fire. "I... I didn't mean..."

"Sorry, honey, but my taste doesn't run to tomboys," he said mockingly. "You might as well stick with your current favorite, if you can hold on to him. He seems to have a wandering eye."

She stood up. "That was unfair."

"Was it?" His eyes narrowed. "As for your offer, I don't want to dance with you, now or ever. And you might as well throw that—" he indicated her dress "—in the trash if you bought it to catch my eye. I'm not interested in you."

She felt the world caving in around her. She looked up at him like a small, wounded animal, tears glistening in her eyes.

She couldn't even fight back for the pain his careless words had caused. She'd had such hopes. But then, he'd made no secret of his interest in Margie. She'd been crazy to pit her charms against her sister-in-law's!

"I'm sorry!" she whispered, but her voice broke. Without another word, she turned and ran out of the barn, her skirts flying against her legs as she darted onto the porch, into the house and up the stairs. She didn't stop until she was locked in her room, and the tears came like rain.

Tyler had watched her go with anguish. He hadn't expected that reaction, especially since she'd been sitting with McAnders. Well, maybe it was the sight of Margie dancing with her lost love that had set her off that way, and not what he'd said to her at all. He had to hold on to that thought. If he started believing that what he'd said to Nell had put those tears in her eyes, he wasn't sure he could stand it.

Nell had cried herself to sleep. She woke up dry-eyed and miserable, wondering how she was going to bear it if she had to see Tyler again. Margie had come by her room last night as if she wanted to talk, but Nell had feigned sleep. She didn't know what Margie had to say, but it was probably a lot of sighing memories of Tyler and the dance, and Nell didn't want to have to listen to her.

She was only sorry that she'd shown Tyler how he'd hurt her. She never should have lost control that way. She should have thrown herself into the spirit of the dance, laughed and danced with Darren and given Tyler the cold shoulder. But she wasn't the kind of woman who could carry off that kind of charade. She wore her poor heart on her sleeve, and Tyler had crushed it.

She was surprised to find Tyler in the dining room

when she went downstairs to breakfast, especially after the way they'd parted the night before.

"I want to talk to you," he began slowly.

"I can't imagine about what," she replied. She did look up then, and her dark eyes were almost black with cold rage.

"About last night," he said shortly. "I didn't mean what I said about your outfit. You looked lovely."

"Thank you," she said, but without warmth. "Last night that would have meant a lot."

"I got tired of watching you with McAnders," he admitted shortly.

She wasn't sure she'd heard him right. "Watching me with him?" she probed.

"Watching you throw yourself at him," he said with a mocking smile. "That's what it was, wasn't it? Dressing up in that fancy rig, putting on makeup. I hope he appreciated all your efforts."

She took a deep breath and felt her entire body bristling as she glared at him with her dark eyes flashing. "To be perfectly honest, I hadn't aimed my charms at Darren specifically. But thanks for the idea. Maybe I will 'throw myself' at Darren again! At least he told me I looked nice and offered to teach me to dance!"

"He felt sorry for you!" Tyler burst out without choosing his words.

"Doesn't everybody?" she shouted. "I know I'm not pretty! I'm just a stupid little tomboy who can't tell the right man from a hole in the south forty! And I'm glad he felt sorry for me—at least he didn't make fun of me!"

"Neither did I!"

"What would you call it?"

Bella came ambling into the room, her eyes like saucers, but neither of them noticed her.

"I got the wrong end of the stick!" he tried to explain.

"Well, why don't you get hold of the right end?" she invited. "And I'll tell you exactly where you can put it and how far!"

"Nell!" Bella burst out, shocked.

"If that's how you feel, we'll drop the whole subject," Tyler said through his teeth. One lean hand was almost crushing the brim of his hat, but he seemed to be beyond noticing it.

"Good! Why don't you go out and ride a horse or something?"

"You won't even listen…!"

"I did listen!" Nell raged, red-faced. "You said I might as well throw my clothes in the trash as wear them to impress you, that you weren't interested and that I took things to heart…!"

"Oh, God!" he groaned.

"And that it was just abstinence that was responsible for everything!" she concluded fiercely. "Well, that works both ways, cowboy! And you can get out of my dining room. You're curdling my eggs!"

His face was like rock, and his eyes blazed up like green fires. "Damn your eggs! Will you listen?"

"I will not, and I'm not eating the damned eggs. Here, you can have them, and welcome!" And she flung the plate at him, eggs and all, and stalked out of the room.

Tyler stood there, quite still, with egg literally on his face, his shirt, his jeans. A piece of egg had even landed in his hat.

Bella cocked her head warily as she waited for the

explosion. He glared at her for a minute and deliberately stuck the hat on his head.

"Would you, uh, like some bacon to go with your eggs?" she asked.

"No, thanks," he said calmly. "I don't really have anyplace left to put it."

He turned and walked out, and Bella was hard put not to collapse with hysteria. Imagine, Nell actually shouting at anybody! That young lady was definitely getting herself together, and Tyler was going to be in for some hard times if Bella didn't miss her guess.

The cold war had truly begun. Nell sent messages to Tyler by Chappy during roundup and she never went near the holding pens. The most she did was to call Bob Wyler about the helicopter and make arrangements with the transport people to get the calves to the auction barn. Otherwise, she busied herself with the guests, who were enjoying the warm autumn climate and especially the cookouts and trail drives that Nell led herself.

Her confidence was beginning to grow, except where Tyler Jacobs was concerned. She felt like a new woman. She discarded her old wardrobe and bought a new one. This time, she bought jeans that fit and tops that clung. She had her hair trimmed and shaped. She began to wear makeup. And she learned from Margie how to gracefully get out of potentially disturbing situations with male guests without hard feelings. She was beginning to bloom, like a delayed spring flower blossoming before winter.

Margie began spending more and more time at the ranch, and every time Nell looked out, she saw her sister-in-law with Tyler. Darren grew moody and frankly angry, and began cutting at Margie every time he saw her. She cut back. It got to the point that they were avoiding each other like the plague, but Tyler seemed to benefit from that, because Margie spent most all her time with him. He enjoyed it, too, if the expression on his face and in his eyes was anything to go by. The boys had even started teasing them about their preoccupation with each other. But it was a loving kind of teasing, because the boys were crazy about Tyler. Darren had captured at least some of their attention during the frequent visits, though, because they began to seek him out to show them about horses and cattle and tell them stories he'd heard from his grandfather about the old days in the West. That irritated Margie, but she couldn't make them stop following Darren around. And Tyler wouldn't. That, too, was puzzling to Nell.

Meanwhile, Tyler was becoming more and more unapproachable. He glared daggers through Nell when she was looking, and watched her hungrily when she wasn't. Bella knew, but she kept her mouth shut. It wouldn't do to interfere, she reckoned. Things had a way of working out better without meddling from interested bystanders. She'd learned her lesson.

Roundup ended and the calves brought a better than expected price at auction, which pleased Uncle Ted to no end. He praised Nell for the way things were going at the ranch and then asked with elaborate carelessness what she thought of his foreman.

Nell made an excuse to get off the phone without answering the question. It was too hard thinking up nice ways to tell her uncle that she thought his foreman would be best barbecued.

She'd no sooner hung up than the phone rang again.

She picked it up. The voice on the line was a woman's and unfamiliar.

"Is this Nell Regan?" she was asked hesitantly.

"Yes."

"I'm Shelby Jacobs Ballenger," came the quiet reply. "I was hoping that I might be able to speak to my brother."

Nell sat down. "He's gone into town to pick up some supplies," she said, remembering the fondness Tyler's voice had betrayed when he mentioned his only relative, his sister, Shelby. "But he'll be back within the hour. Can I have him call you?"

"Oh, dear." Shelby sighed. "Justin and I are leaving for Jacobsville in just a few hours. We're just in Tucson on a quick business trip, and I was hoping that we could see him." She laughed self-consciously. "You see, he's been worried about me. Justin and I got off to a rocky start, but things are wonderful now and I wanted him to see us together, so that he'd be sure I was telling him the truth."

"Why don't you come down here," Nell offered impulsively. "We're only about thirty minutes out of Tucson. Have you a car?"

"Yes, Justin rented one for his meeting. It would be all right? You wouldn't mind having two strangers barge in on you?"

"You're not a stranger," Nell said with a smile. "Tyler's talked about you so much that we all feel as if we know you. We'd love for you to come. Bella can make a cake—"

"Oh, please, don't go to any trouble."

"It's no trouble, really. You just come on down." And she proceeded to give Shelby directions. Although God

only knew why she should go to so much effort to give
Tyler a nice surprise when he'd been simply horrible
to her. It must have been a touch too much sun, she decided after she'd hung up.

"Tyler's sister, coming here?" Bella grinned from
ear to ear. "I'll go bake a nice chocolate cake. You tidy
up the living room."

Nell glowered. "It's already tidy."

"Good. Then lay a tray and make sure the silver's
nice and polished."

Nell threw up her hands. "Botheration!"

"It was your idea to have them come down," she
was reminded. Bella smiled with sickening superiority.
"What a sweet surprise for Tyler. And here I thought
you hated him. Slinging scrambled eggs all over him,
yelling at him…"

"I'll just see about that silver," Nell murmured, and
got out of Bella's sight.

A little more than half an hour later, a rented lim-
ousine pulled up at the sidewalk and two people got
out. Nell recognized Shelby Jacobs Ballenger almost
at once, because she looked so much like her brother.
She was lovely, very slender and tall and elegant with
her dark hair in a French twist and wearing a green silk
dress. She was no surprise, but the tall man with her
was. He was very masculine, that was apparent, but he
wasn't handsome at all, and he looked as if he didn't
smile much. Nell felt immediately intimidated and tried
not to show it when she went to the door to greet them.

"You have to be Nell." Shelby smiled. She reached
forward and hugged the younger woman warmly. "It's
so nice to meet you. I'm Shelby, and this is Justin." She
looked up at the tall man, her expression full of love.

He smiled back at her for an instant and then diverted his lancing dark gaze to Nell. "Nice to meet you."

Nell nodded, tongue-tied, she was glad that she'd put on clean jeans and a nice blue-checked blouse and brushed her hair. At least she didn't look scruffy.

She led them into the living room and Bella came in to be introduced, carrying a coffee tray laden with the necessities and a platter of fresh chocolate cake.

"My favorite," Justin murmured, grinning at Bella. "Thank you, but what are they going to eat?" he asked with an innocent glance at the women.

The ice was immediately broken. Nell relaxed visibly and sat down to pour coffee.

"When Tyler comes, waylay him and send him in, but don't tell him why," Nell called to Bella.

"I'll tell him you want to give him some more eggs," Bella said smugly and left the room.

Nell's color intrigued Shelby, who stirred cream into her coffee absently and began to smile. "Eggs?" she probed.

Nell cleared her throat. "We had an, er, slight misunderstanding."

"Eggs?" Justin asked, looking dryly interested.

It was getting more uncomfortable by the second. "I sort of lost my temper and threw my breakfast at him," Nell confessed. She looked at Shelby pleadingly. "Well, he insulted me first."

"Oh, I can believe that." Shelby nodded, smiling. "I'm not going to put all the blame on you."

"How's he fitting in here?" Justin asked as he leaned back against the sofa with his coffee cup in one hand.

"He fits in fine with the men," Nell said restlessly.

Justin's dark eyes were piercing, and they didn't seem to miss much.

Shelby was watching her just as closely, and with a faintly amused smile. "You know," she said, "you don't seem anything like Tyler's description of you at my wedding."

Nell cleared her throat. "Am I better or worse?" she asked.

"If you answer that, I'll disown you," came Tyler's deep voice from the doorway.

"Ty!" Shelby got up and ran into his arms, to be swung high and kissed while he smiled in a way Nell had never seen him smile. It made her see what she'd missed, and it made her sad.

"Good to see you again," Justin said, rising to shake hands with Tyler before he drew Shelby close to his side.

That simple gesture told Tyler how things were between the recently married couple. Justin looked at her with open possessiveness, and Shelby stayed as close to him as she could get. Apparently they'd solved their difficulties, because no couple could pretend the kind of explosive emotion that crackled between them like electricity. Tyler relaxed, sure of Shelby's future. That was one load off his mind. He'd been worried about the marriage's rocky start.

"We thought we'd call you before we left Tucson," Shelby explained while they drank coffee and ate chocolate cake. "But Nell invited us down to see you before we fly home to Texas."

"Nice of her, wasn't it?" Justin asked with that smug, lazy smile that made Tyler's neck hair bristle.

"Nice," Tyler said shortly. He didn't look at Nell, who

was sitting in an armchair while he shared the sofa with Shelby and Justin.

"Don't strain yourself thanking me," Nell said with venomous politeness. "I'd have done the same thing for anyone."

Tyler's green eyes glittered at her across the coffee table. "I'm sure you would, you tenderhearted little thing."

He said it with deep sarcasm and Nell stiffened. "I used to have a tender heart all right," she told him flatly, "but I wore it out on men."

"That's right," he invited, "put all the blame on us. Men can't put a foot right where you're concerned, can they?"

"They can if they have a woman to lead them," Nell said, and smiled icily.

"Let me tell you, I won't live long enough to let a woman lead me anywhere! Furthermore…" He stopped, clearing his throat gruffly when he noticed the attention he was getting from the visitors. He smiled. "How are things back in Jacobsville?" he asked with pleasant interest.

It was to Justin's credit that he didn't fall on the floor laughing when he tried to answer that. Meanwhile, Shelby smiled into her coffee and exchanged a highly amused glance with her husband. They didn't need a program to see what was going on. It looked very much to Shelby as if Tyler had met his match, and not a minute too soon.

CHAPTER EIGHT

SHELBY AND JUSTIN stayed for another half hour, giving Tyler some interesting news from back home. Justin's brother, Calhoun, and sister-in-law, Abby, had flown to Europe for a belated honeymoon, and a neighbor had bought Geronimo, Tyler's prize stud stallion.

"I'm glad Harrison got him," Tyler murmured, his face faintly bitter because the remark reminded him of all he and Shelby had lost. "He was a good horse."

"He'll be well taken care of," Shelby added. "I'll make sure of it." She smiled at her brother. "Don't brood over it, will you? We can't do anything about the past."

Justin saw storm clouds coming and quickly headed them off. "I hate to cut this short," he said with a glance at his thin gold watch, "but we've got to go, honey."

Shelby clung to Justin's hand as they stood up, releasing it for just a minute while she hugged Tyler and then Nell. "Thanks for letting us come, Nell. Ty, try to write once in a while, or at least call and let us know you're alive."

He smiled at his sister. "I'll do my best. Take good care of her, Justin."

"Oh, that's the easy part," Justin said, and his expression as he smiled at his wife was loving and possessive and very sexy. Justin might look formidable, but Nell had a feeling he shared with Shelby a side of himself that no one else would ever see. That was what marriage should be, Nell thought. Not that she was ever going to have a chance at it.

She walked to the door with Tyler to see Justin and Shelby off. It was already dusk and getting darker by the minute. In the distance, the guest houses were all alight and there was the sound of a guitar and a harmonica playing down at the bunkhouse. Nell wrapped her arms around herself, reluctant to leave Tyler, but too nervous of him to stay.

She turned, only to find his hand sliding down to grasp hers.

"Not yet," he said, and there was a familiar deep note in his voice.

She should have had more willpower, but things had been strained between them for too long already, and the touch of his hand on hers made her weak.

"Come for a walk with me, Nell," he said quietly, and drew her along with him down the path that led to his cabin.

Even as she went along, she knew that she shouldn't go. He was leading up to a confrontation. But the night was perfumed with flowers, and the stars were above them, and silence drew around them like a dark blanket. His hand in hers was warm against the chill of the desert night, and she moved closer, feeling the strength of his body like a shield at her side. She sensed his sadness and bitterness, and all the hostility fell away from her. He needed someone to talk to; that was probably all he wanted. She understood that. She'd never had anyone who she could really talk to, until Darren McAnders had come back and become her friend. But she'd much rather have talked to Tyler. She couldn't do anything to change his past, but she could certainly listen.

He stopped at the corral fence and let go of her hand to light a cigarette while they listened to the night sounds and the silences.

"I like your sister," she said softly.

"So do I. She and I have been close all our lives. All we ever really had was each other when we were growing up. After our mother died, our father became greedy and grasping. He was hell to live with most of the time, and he wasn't above blackmail."

"Have she and Justin known each other a long time?" she asked curiously.

"Years." He took a draw of the cigarette, and his smile was reflected by the orange glow from its tip. "Six years ago they got engaged, but Shelby ended it. I never knew why, although I'm sure my father had a hand in it. Justin wasn't wealthy and Dad had just the right rich man picked out for Shelby. She didn't marry anyone as it turned out. Then when we lost everything, Justin went to see her because she had no one—I'd just come out here to work. And the next thing we knew, they were married. I thought he'd done that for revenge, that he was going to make her life miserable. She didn't seem very happy on their wedding day." He glanced down at her. "But I think they've worked things out. Did you notice the way they look at each other?"

Nell leaned against the fence and kept her face down. "Yes. They seem to be very happy."

"And very lucky. Most people don't get a second chance."

She lifted her eyes. "If that's a dig at me because I've avoided you since the square dance…"

"I was jealous, Nell," he said unexpectedly. He smiled faintly at the stunned expression on her face that was barely visible in the dim light from the house. "Jealous as hell. I'd seen you and McAnders in a clinch, and then you dressed up for him, I thought, when you'd never dressed up for me. I just blew up. I didn't really mean the things I said to you, but you wouldn't listen when I tried to explain."

"Jealous of me?" She laughed bitterly. "That'll be the day. I'm a tomboy, I'm plain, I'm shy—"

"And sadly lacking in self-confidence," he finished for her. "Don't you think that a man could want you for yourself? For the things you are instead of how you look?"

"Nobody ever has," she said shortly. "I'm twenty-four and I'll die an old maid."

"Not you, honey," he said softly. "You're too passionate to live and die alone."

Her face went hot. "Don't throw that up to me," she snapped, her eyes flashing. "I was... I was off balance and you're too experienced for me, that's all."

"Experienced, hell," he said shortly. "There haven't even been that many women, and you weren't off balance—you were starved for a little love."

"Thanks a lot!"

"Will you just shut up and listen?" he demanded. "You never would give me a chance to say anything about what happened, you just slung scrambled eggs at me and stomped off in a fury."

"I was entitled to be angry after what you said to me," she reminded him curtly.

"Oh, hell, maybe you were," he conceded tautly. "But you could have let me explain."

"The explanation was obvious," she replied. "Darren was poaching on what you considered your territory."

He smiled in spite of himself. "You might say that."

"Well, you don't have to worry about Margie," she said after a minute. "I mean, it's obvious that she's crazy about you. And the boys like you…"

"What are you talking about?" he asked pleasantly.

"Nobody could blame you for being attracted to her," she went on. "And I'm sorry if I've made things difficult for you—I didn't mean to. You've lost so much. You should have somebody to care about. Somebody who'll care about you."

"Coals of fire," he murmured, watching her as he smoked his cigarette. "Do you want me to be happy, Nell?"

"I want that very much," she said, her voice soft in the darkness. "I haven't meant to be difficult. It's just…"

"You don't have a scrap of self-confidence, that's just what it is," he said for her. "That's a shame, Nell, because you've got a lot going for you. I wish I knew why you had this hang-up about men."

"I got hurt once," she muttered.

"Most people get hurt once."

"Not like I did." She folded her arms across her breasts. "When I was in my middle teens, I had a terrible crush on one of the cowboys. I plagued him and followed him around and chased him mercilessly. To make a long story short, he was in love with a woman he couldn't have, and in a drunken stupor he decided to take me up on my offer." She laughed bitterly. "Until then, I had no idea that romance was anything except smiling at each other and maybe holding hands. It never actually occurred to me that people in love went to bed together. And what made it so bad was that physically I didn't feel anything for him. I guess that's why I panicked and screamed. Bella came and rescued me and the cowboy left in disgrace."

Tyler had listened intently. The cigarette burned away between his fingers without his noticing. "It was McAnders," he guessed with cold certainty.

"Yes. He was in love with Marguerite, but I didn't know it until he tried to make love to me. I realized that night what a terrible mistake I'd made." She smiled halfheartedly. "So then I knew that I couldn't trust my instincts or my judgment anymore. I stopped wearing sexy clothes and I stopped running after anybody."

"One bad egg doesn't make the whole carton spoil," he said.

"That's true, but how do you find the bad egg in time?" She shook her head. "I've never had the inclination to try again."

"Until I came along?"

She flushed. "I told you, I was only trying to make you feel welcome. You paid me a little attention and it flattered me."

"Where does McAnders fit into this now?" he asked. "I gather that you were fairly intimate with him before Bella came to the rescue, but how about today? Did you go from me to him?"

She shifted restlessly. "No," she said under her breath.

He brightened a little. "Why not?"

She had to remember that he was interested in Margie, not her. He might feel a little sorry for her, but he didn't want her for keeps. She straightened. "He still doesn't appeal to me physically."

He wondered if she realized what she was giving away with that remark. If she didn't want McAnders she probably didn't really love him. But he was going to have to make her see that, and it wouldn't be easy.

"I appealed to you physically, once," he said gently, his voice deep and drugging in the still night. He moved closer, his fingers lightly touching her face, her loosened hair. His warmth enveloped her, his breath was like a faint breeze, moving the hair at her temples, making her heart race. "If McAnders hadn't shown up, I might have appealed to you in other ways. We didn't have enough time to get to know each other."

She put her hands slowly, flatly against his shirtfront, hesitating as if she thought he might throw them away. But he caught them gently and pressed them to the soft cotton of his shirt.

"You wouldn't want to, now," she said, and her voice shook. "Margie's here half the time."

"And, of course, you think I'm madly in love with her."

"Aren't you?" she asked stubbornly.

"I'm not going to tell you that," he said. He lifted her chin. "You're going to have to come out of your shell, little one, and start looking around you. You can't learn to swim if you keep balking at the water."

"I don't understand."

"Very simply, Nell, if you want me, you're going to have to believe that I can want you back. You're going to have to believe in yourself a little and start trusting me not to hurt you."

"Trust comes hard," she said, although what he was saying was more tempting than he realized. She did want him, terribly, but she was playing for keeps. Was he?

"It comes hard to most people." He smoothed the hair away from her face. "It depends on whether or not you think it's worth the chance. Love doesn't come with a money-back guarantee. There comes a time when you have to trust your instincts and take a chance."

She shifted restlessly, but he wouldn't let go of her hands. "Why?" she asked abruptly. "You said you wanted me, but at the same time you said you weren't interested in any relationships with women."

"I said a lot, didn't I, honey?" he murmured dryly.

She searched what she could see of his dark face. "I'm not the kind of woman you could care about," she said miserably.

"My whole life has turned upside down, Nell," he told her. "I'm not the same man I used to be. I don't have wealth or position, and about all that's left is my good name and a lot of credit. That makes me pretty vulnerable, in case you've missed it."

"Vulnerable, how?" she asked.

"You might think I was interested in you because you're a woman of property."

"That'll be the day," she murmured dryly. "There's no way I can see you chasing a woman for her money."

His quiet eyes pierced the darkness, looking for her face. "At least you know me that well," he said. "But part of you is afraid of me."

"You want Marguerite," she moaned. "Why bother with me?"

"Margie sends out signals. You could learn to do that, too," he said conversationally. "You could waylay me in the office and kiss me stupid, or buy a new wardrobe to dazzle me with."

She blushed and her heart jumped into her throat.

"Fat chance when you made Chappy take back a rope he bought," she reminded him to lighten the tension that was growing between them.

He grinned. "Buy a new dress. I promise not to fuss."

"Margie bought me a new dress and you made me feel dowdy when I wore it," she said.

"Yes, I know." He sighed. "I keep trying to apologize, but you don't hear me."

Her heart was running wild; while he spoke his hands had gone to her hips and pulled them slowly to his. She tried to step back, but he held her there very gently.

"No," he said softly. "You can't run away this time. I won't let you."

"I have to go inside," she said. Panic was rising in her at the intimacy of his hold. It was bringing back dangerously sweet memories.

"Frightened, Nell?" he asked quietly.

"I won't be just another conquest!" she groaned, struggling.

"Stand still, for God's sake." He gasped suddenly, and his powerful body stiffened. "God, Nell, that hurts!"

She stopped instantly. Her color was rising when she felt what he was talking about and realized that she was only complicating things.

"Then you shouldn't hold me like this," she whispered shakily.

He took a steadying breath and his hands contracted on her waist. "We've been a lot closer, though, haven't we?" he asked at her forehead, brushing his lips against her skin. "We've been together without a scrap of fabric between your breasts and my chest, and you pulled my head down and arched up to meet my mouth."

She buried her embarrassed face in his shirt, shaking with remembered pleasure. "I shouldn't have let you," she whispered.

"Then Chappy came to the door and broke the spell," he murmured at her cheek. "I didn't want to answer it. I wanted to go on loving you. But I guess it was a good thing he came along, because things were getting out of hand, weren't they? We wanted each other so much, Nell. I don't really know that we could have stopped in time."

He was right. That didn't make her guilt any easier to bear. "And that would have been a disaster, wouldn't it?" she asked, waiting stiffly for his answer.

"I'm an old-fashioned man, honey," he said finally. His hands smoothed down her back, holding her against him. "I wouldn't ask you to sleep with me, knowing that you're a virgin. You aren't that kind of woman."

She bit her lower lip hard. "I've got all these hang-ups..."

"Most of which we removed that day in my bed," he reminded her. "But your biggest hang-up, little Nell, is your mental block about your attractiveness. You're the only person around here who doesn't see what a dish you are."

"Me?" she asked breathlessly.

"You." He bent to her mouth and brushed it with his. "You've got a warm heart," he whispered, bending again. The kiss lingered this time, just a second longer. "You're caring." He kissed her again, and this time he parted her lips briefly before he raised his head. "You're intelligent." His mouth teased, brushing hers open breath by breath. "And you're the sexiest woman I've ever made love to..."

He whispered the words into her trembling lips before he took them, and this time he didn't draw back.
His tongue began to penetrate her mouth in slow, exquisite thrusts. This was a kind of kiss Nell hadn't experienced before, not even that day in Tyler's cabin, and
she was afraid of it.

She tried to draw back, but his lean hand at her nape
held her mouth under his.

"Don't fight it," he whispered coaxingly. "I won't
hurt you. Relax, Nell. Let me have your mouth. I'll
treat it just as tenderly as I'd treat your body if you gave
yourself to me, little one," he breathed, and his mouth
whispered down onto hers.

The words in addition to the expert teasing of his
tongue shook away every last bit of her reserve. She
melted into the length of him, trembling with the fierce
hunger he was arousing in her body. She moaned helplessly and felt his mouth smile against hers. Then he
deepened the pressure and the slow thrust of his tongue
into the sweet, soft darkness of her mouth.

But what about Margie? she wanted to ask. How can
you hold me like this when you want her? She couldn't
have asked him that to save her life, because he was
working magic on her body. She wanted him. Tomorrow she could hate herself and him for leading her on,
for toying with her. But tonight she wanted nothing except the sweet pleasure of his mouth and his hands and
a few memories to carry through the long years ahead.

She felt his hands at the back of her thighs, pulling
her shaking legs closer so that her hips were grinding
into his, so that she knew how aroused he was. She
didn't protest. Her hands found their way around him,
to his back and down, returning the pressure shyly even

as the first shudder of desire ripped through her and dragged a cry from her lips.

He lifted his head abruptly. His eyes glittered and he was trembling a little; his heartbeat was rough against her breasts. "Come home with me. I'll sit with you in that big leather armchair by the fireplace, and we'll love each other for a few minutes."

She was crying with reaction. "It's so dangerous," she pleaded, but it was no protest at all, and he had to know it.

"I've got to, Nell," he whispered, bending to lift her so gently into his arms. He turned, carrying her the rest of the way to his porch in the darkness. "I've got to, sweetheart."

Her arms went around his neck, and she buried her face in his warm, pulsating throat. "I can't… I can't sleep with you," she whispered.

"I'd never ask that of you," he breathed ardently. He caught her mouth hungrily with his while he fumbled the door open with one hand and carried her into the dark stillness of his cabin.

He kicked the door shut and moved to the big armchair, dropping into it with his mouth still hard and sure on her lips.

There was no more pretense left. He was hungry and he wasn't trying to hide it. He fought the buttons of her blouse out of his way and deftly removed it and the lacy covering beneath. His mouth found her warm breasts, and he nuzzled them hungrily, nibbling, kissing, tasting while she shuddered and arched her back to help him.

"So sweet, Nell," he groaned as his lips moved on her. "Oh, God, you taste like honey in my mouth."

Her hands touched his cool dark hair, savoring its

clean thickness while she fed on the aching sweetness of his mouth. "Oh, please!" she moaned brokenly when he lifted his head to breathe. "Tyler, please…!"

He held her quietly while he tore open the snaps of his own shirt and dragged her inside it, pressing her breasts against the hair-covered warmth of his chest, moving her sensually from side to side so that her breathing became as rough and torturous as his own.

His mouth ground into hers then, rough with need, his restraint gone, his control broken by the sounds she was making against his lips, by the helpless movement of her body against him, silky and bare and terribly arousing.

His lean hands caressed her soft, bare back, holding her to him so that he could feel the hard tips of her breasts like tiny brands on his skin.

"Nell," he groaned. His mouth slid away from hers and into her throat, pressing hard against the wildly throbbing artery as he drew her up close and held her, rocked her, until the trembling need began to drain out of her.

"I ache all over," she whispered with tears in her voice. She clung closer. "Tyler, this is scary!"

"This is desire," he breathed at her ear, and his arms contracted. "This is the raw need to mate. Don't be afraid of it. I'm not going to take advantage of something you can't help. I want you just as much as you want me."

She shuddered helplessly. "It must be…so much worse for you," she whispered.

"A sweet ache," he confessed huskily, and his mouth brushed her cheek, her throat. "I don't have a single regret. Do you?"

"I shouldn't admit it."

He chuckled, delighted with her headlong response to him, with her helpless hunger. "Neither should I. But wasn't it good, Nell? Wasn't it delicious?"

"Oh, yes." She sighed, nestling closer with a tiny sound deep in her throat. "I want to stay with you all night."

"I want that, too, but we can't."

"I could just sleep with you," she murmured drowsily.

"Sure you could. Platonically. And nothing would happen." He turned up her face and kissed her mouth hard. "You know as well as I do that we'd devour each other if we got into a bed together. We're half-crazy to be together already, and I've barely touched you."

She pulled back a little. "You call that barely touching?" she asked, awed.

"Compared to what I'd do to you in bed, yes."

She hesitated, but he read the thought in her mind and chuckled helplessly.

"Shall I tell you?" he whispered softly.

"You wouldn't dare."

But he would. And he did, sensuously, whispering it into her ear while he touched her, lightly caressed her, brought every nerve in her body to singing, agonizing pleasure.

"I never dreamed…!" she gasped, hiding her face in his chest when he finished.

"You needed to know," he said gently. "You're still very innocent, despite what happened in your teens. I want you to understand that what you and I would share wouldn't be painful or frightening. Physical love is an expression of what two people feel for each other so strongly that words aren't enough to contain it. It isn't anything to dread."

"Certainly not with you it wouldn't be," she said tenderly. She touched his hard face, loving its strength, its masculine beauty. "Tyler… I could love you," she whispered hesitantly.

"Could you, honey?" He bent, brushing his mouth with exquisite softness against her lips. "If you want me, Nell, come after me."

"That isn't fair," she began.

"It's fair," he said. "For your own peace of mind, you need to regain the confidence you lost because of what happened with McAnders. Oh, I could back you into a corner and force you into a decision, but that would rob you of your right to choose. I won't do it for you. You have to do it, alone."

Her worried eyes studied his profile. "You said you didn't want a lasting relationship…." she said again.

He turned his head and looked down at her in the dimness of the unlit room. "Make me want one," he challenged. "Vamp me. Buy some sexy dresses and drive me crazy. Be the woman you can be. The woman you should have been."

"I'm not attractive," she argued faintly.

His hand swept slowly, lovingly, over her breasts. "You're beautiful, Nell," he said huskily. "Firm and soft and silky to touch."

"Tyler…"

"Come here," he groaned. He stood up with her in his arms and let her slide down his body, bent to kiss her hungrily before his hand shot out and fumbled with a light switch.

"No!" she protested, but it was too late. The soft light

flooded the living room, and Tyler caught her hands before she could cover herself. He gazed down at her with an intent masculine appreciation of her attributes, which brought a wave of color up her neck and into her face. His chest rose and fell heavily, and his expression showed that he was having a monumental battle with his conscience to do nothing more than look.

"I'll live on this for a while," he breathed, lifting his eyes to hers.

Her lips parted as she stared back at him, all too aware of the tense swelling of her breasts, of their hard arousal, which he could see as well as feel.

"It embarrasses you, doesn't it?" he asked softly, searching her eyes. "I can see how lovely you are, how aroused I've made you. It's like letting me see you totally nude, isn't it? But you've seen me that way already, Nell. Remember?"

She lowered her eyes to his bare chest. "I couldn't forget if I tried. I thought you were perfect," she whispered shyly.

"I feel just that way about you. I love the way you look without your blouse. I'd give everything I have to carry you into my bedroom and love you in my bed. But as things stand, that's a decision I can't make." He let go of her hands and gazed at her one last time before he forced himself to turn his back and light a cigarette. "You'd better dress, sweetheart. I want you desperately right now, and I'm not quite as controlled as I thought I was."

She stared at his back for an instant, thinking of pressing herself against him. But she knew what would happen, and it would be her fault. She sighed softly and went to find her blouse and bra.

He got into his shirt and buttoned it and smoked half his cigarette before he turned around again. His eyes were dark with frustrated hunger as he looked at her. "We can't do much of that," he said with a tender smile. "It gets worse every time."

"Yes." She smiled back. "Oh, I want you so," she whispered helplessly.

"I want you, too." He held out his hand, and she put hers into it without hesitation. "I'd better walk you home."

"All right."

He went with her up the path in the darkness. He didn't speak and neither did she, but she clung to his hand and felt as if they'd become lovers in every sense of the word. There would never be, could never be, anyone after him. She felt that with a sense of faint despair, because she still didn't know where she stood with him.

He stopped at the front steps and turned her. His face was clearly visible in the light pouring out the window from the front room.

"No more pretense, Nell," he said softly. "If you want me, show me."

"But men don't like being chased," she whispered.

"Try it and see," he challenged with narrowed eyes. "You've got to believe in yourself before other people will."

"You won't mind?" she asked. "You're sure?"

He bent and put his mouth warmly against hers in a brief kiss. "I won't mind."

"But what about Margie?" she groaned.

"You'll find out about that all by yourself when you start putting your life back in order," he said simply. "It's right under your nose, but you just can't see it."

"Tell me," she whispered.

"No. You work it out. Good night, Nell."

Impulsively she moved closer and lifted her mouth. "Would you…kiss me again?" she whispered.

He did, half lifting her against him, and so thoroughly and hungrily that when he let her down again, she gasped.

"I like that," he said roughly. "You might try it again from time to time. Sleep well."

"You, too." She watched him turn and walk back the way they'd come, lighting a cigarette on the way. His stride was moody and thoughtful, but as she turned to go in, she heard him whistling a light, cheerful tune in the darkness. She smiled, because it was a popular love song. She knew that she might be reading too much into what they'd done, but her heart was on fire for him. Maybe he didn't really care that much about Margie. Maybe she could worm her way into his affection if she tried. But it was going to take some hard thinking before she risked her heart again. She needed time.

CHAPTER NINE

NELL WORRIED ALL night about Margie and Tyler and what she was going to do. Her own insecurities haunted her.

She went downstairs, her thoughts murky and still without concrete answers. She half expected Tyler to be there again, waiting for her, but he wasn't.

Bella bustled in with breakfast and sat down beside Nell. "Too early for the new arrivals to be up and hungry, so you and I can have ours in peace," she said, pouring two cups of coffee. "Tyler's having his in the bunkhouse."

"That's nothing unusual, is it?" Nell sighed. "He always seems to be eating down there lately."

"I don't think he's felt very welcome here in recent days," Bella told her bluntly. "Pity, because he sure is a nice fella and you could do worse."

"It isn't me he wants," Nell said curtly, glaring at the older woman as she helped herself to a fresh biscuit and buttered it. "It's Margie."

Bella sipped her coffee. "Did he tell you that?"

"No. But he didn't deny it, either."

The older woman spooned scrambled eggs onto her plate and reached for bacon. "Nell, I steered you wrong when Tyler came here. I should have encouraged you to dress up and act like a young lady. I should have realized what kind of man he was. But I didn't, and I've helped complicate things. I'm sorry."

"You didn't do anything," Nell said. She glowered at her eggs. "I'm not the kind of woman a man like Tyler needs. I'm just a country tomboy. I don't even know how to dance."

"Stop running yourself down," Bella said gruffly. "Listen, child, just because Darren McAnders couldn't see past Margie to you is no reason for you to bury yourself in baggy britches forever. You're young and pretty, and if you tried, you could be everything Tyler needs. Don't forget, he isn't a rich man anymore. He doesn't need a social butterfly, he needs a woman who can help him build a new legacy for his children."

"Margie can work," Nell said halfheartedly.

"Oh, sure, like she does when she's here?" Bella scoffed. "Fat chance. Tyler would be out of his mind after the first week and you know it. She'd never cook supper—she'd be too busy trying on dresses in town or gossiping on the telephone."

"She's pretty and flamboyant."

"A sensible man doesn't want a wall decoration, he wants a flesh-and-blood woman."

"I guess I'm flesh and blood," Nell agreed.

"And a hard worker, a good little cook and a companion who listens more than she talks. You're a jewel," Bella concluded. "You should think positively. At least you've made a start. You're wearing clothes that really fit, and you've put away that horrible slouchy hat and let your hair down. You look like a different Nell."

"I decided that you and Margie were right about what happened with Darren," she conceded. "I overreacted because I didn't know what a man was like when he was hungry for a woman. Well, not then, at least."

Bella's eyes widened. "And now you do?" she asked with a slow, wicked smile.

Nell felt the flush working its way up her neck. She reached blindly for her coffee and turned it over onto the tablecloth and herself.

"Oh, my, what little fumble fingers." Bella chuckled.

"I meant to do that," Nell protested as she got to her feet, brushing at a tiny spot on her blue-checked Western shirt and her new jeans. She glared at Bella. "I just hate coffee. And I don't fumble!" she added.

Then she turned around and tripped over the chair and fell flat on her face.

Bella doubled over laughing while Nell, bruised and furious, disentangled herself from the chair. She was turning the air blue when she saw a pair of boots come into view past her nose.

"She don't fumble," Bella explained to the boots, and walked off into the kitchen.

Nell scrambled to her feet, assisted by a familiar lean, strong hand.

"Having trouble?" Tyler asked pleasantly.

She did fumble then, nervous with him and still uncertain of her ground. She looked up into his dark face, wondering at the secret pleasure it gave her just to stare at him.

"I was looking for a contact lens," Nell said, flustered.

"You don't wear contact lenses," he pointed out.

She cleared her throat. "That doesn't mean that I can't look for one if I want to."

He smiled slowly. "Whatever turns you on," he said dryly.

She brushed back her unruly hair. "What can I do for you?" she asked abruptly.

"You can come on the campout trail ride with me this afternoon," he said. "Chappy's tied up with those new mares, so I told him we'd take the greenhorns out today."

She colored. "You and not Darren?"

He pursed his lips. "That's right. Is that a problem?" he added quietly.

She was still feeling her way, but telling the truth might be a good start, she decided. "No, it's not a problem," she said. "Darren has been a good friend. But I'd rather be with you."

He smiled slowly because her face flamed when she said it, and her shyness made her even more delectable to him. She was a pretty woman when she didn't dress like a baggy orphan.

"I'd rather be with you, too, sunshine," he said softly.

Her heart soared. Heaven must be this sweet, she thought dazedly. She smiled at him, her dark eyes like brown velvet.

Bella came through the door and broke the spell. Nell excused herself as the housekeeper giggled wickedly, and went out into the hall to get her hat. She did her usual chores, feeling as if she were walking on air, and the day was all too long until it was time to pack the bedrolls and the cooking utensils and the food that Bella had provided and head out for an overnight campout. The Double R Ranch was one of the few left that did it for real, complete with bedrolls and rough accommodations and no luxuries. Only a few hardy souls were willing to rough it the way the old-time cowboys had.

There were six people in the party, three couples. Four of that number were good riders already, and they weren't afraid of snakes or coyotes or rolling into the campfire in their sleep. It was a beautiful day, with the ragged mountains ringing around the flat grassy plain, and Nell felt on top of the world as she rode along at the head of the group with Tyler at her side. She kept looking back to make sure she wasn't losing any of their small parade.

"They're doing fine," Tyler told her as he lit a cigarette with steady hands. "Don't worry so much."

"Two of them have never even seen a real horse before," she reminded him.

"The Callaways?" He grinned, referring to a newly married, middle-aged couple who were, to put it politely, well fed. "No, but you've taught them how to stay on, at least, and they're getting the hang of it. Just relax."

She tried, but being a mother hen had become a habit, and she had a bad feeling about doing this campout without Chappy and the chuck wagon that usually came along with a bigger crowd.

And sure enough, things did begin to go wrong suddenly. They rode for an hour and then turned back toward the ranch house and stopped about a mile out to make camp just before dark.

Mrs. Callaway, a pleasant cheerful little blonde lady, came down off her horse too suddenly and caught her blouse on the pommel. There she hung, two inches above the desert floor, while the horse shook his head and pranced restlessly.

Tyler leaped forward to lift Mrs. Callaway while Nell soothed the horse and extricated the blouse.

"Are you all right, Mrs. Callaway?" Nell asked anxiously when the red-faced little woman had stopped shaking in her concerned husband's arms.

"Oh, I'm fine," she said with a grin. "What a story to tell the folks back home!"

Nell relaxed, but Mrs. Callaway's experience was only the beginning. Her husband went to help Tyler and the other men gather brush to make a fire and unearthed a long, fat, very unsocial rattlesnake.

He let out a war whoop, which startled Mrs. Donnegan, who backed into a cactus and let out a war whoop of her own. By the time the rattlesnake was disposed of by Tyler, and Mrs. Donnegan had her cactus spines removed by Nell, everybody was ready to eat. Tyler had a roaring fire going and had passed out wieners and buns and marshmallows and sticks for the guests while he brewed up a pot of black coffee.

"I really hate coffee," Mrs. Harris remarked. She was the only sour note in the bunch, a city woman who'd come to the desert only because her husband had coaxed her into it. She hated the desert, the cactus, the heat, the isolation—she hated everything, in fact. "I'd rather have a soft drink."

"No problem," her husband said. "We'll ride down to the ranch and get one."

"On that horse?" Mrs. Harris wailed, her black eyes going even blacker. "I hurt in places I didn't even know I had!"

"Then you can drink coffee, can't you, sweetheart?" her husband continued.

She pouted, but she shut up. The Callaways sat close

together, sharing condiments for the hot dogs while they munched on potato chips and carried on a casual conversation with the other guests on a variety of newsy subjects.

Nell enjoyed the quiet wonder of night on the desert as she never had, especially when Tyler started telling their guests about the surrounding territory and something of its history. She hadn't realized how much he knew about southeastern Arizona, and some of it she hadn't even known herself.

He talked about places like Cochise Stronghold, where the famous Apache chief was buried. There was a marker there, he added, telling that Indian Agent Tom Jeffords, a friend of Cochise, was the only white man privileged to know the exact spot of the chief's burial. The Apaches had run their horses over the ground and dragged it with brush behind them to conceal forever the place where Cochise rested.

There was also the famous Copper Queen Hotel in Bisbee, a landmark from old copper mining days in the Lavender Pit, where guests drank French champagne and were entertained by famous singers.

Farther south was Douglas, where Agua Prieta lay just over the border in Mexico. Pancho Villa had raided the border town, and a hotel in Douglas bore the marks of his horse on its marble staircase, which could still be seen today.

"You know a lot about this part of the state, Mr. Jacobs," Mr. Callaway remarked. "Do you come from around here?"

"No. I'm from south Texas." He smiled. "Near Victoria. My people founded a little place called Jacobsville, where I was raised."

"I love Texas," Mrs. Callaway said, sighing. "I guess you have cactus and mesquite and sagebrush…"

"Actually, it's more like magnolias, live oaks and dogwood trees," Tyler mused. "West Texas has those plants you're thinking about."

She blushed. "Sorry."

He laughed out loud. "Don't feel bad, a lot of people don't realize just how many different geographic sections there are in Texas. We've got everything from beach to desert to mountain country and plains. Texas had the option of becoming five separate states if it wanted to. But nobody ever did."

"I can see why," Mrs. Callaway said. "I've heard that you can drive from sunup to sunset and never leave Texas."

"That's very nearly true," he agreed.

"I suppose you'll go back there one day?" the small woman asked.

Tyler looked at Nell, his eyes narrow, thoughtful as they caressed hers until she caught her breath. "Maybe. Maybe not," he added softly, and smiled at Nell.

She felt lighter than air all over again, invincible. She laughed delightedly. "Anybody want more marshmallows?"

They roasted marshmallows until nobody could stuff another one into his mouth, and then they laid out the bedrolls and settled down for the night, while the orange flames of the campfire drifted lazily back and forth in the faint wind. It was cold on the desert at night. The guests had been told that and were prepared.

Nell moved her sleeping bag close to Tyler's, to his secret delight, and with a shy glance at him as he rested with his saddle for a pillow, she settled down beside him.

"Comfortable?" he asked, his voice deep and soft in the firelit darkness as he turned on his side to watch her.

"Yes." She gave in to the need to look at him, to memorize the lines and curves of his face, his body. She felt a kind of possessiveness toward him that she didn't really understand. "Do you miss Texas, Tyler?" she asked hesitantly.

"I got pretty homesick at first," he conceded. "But there's something about this desert that gets into your blood. It's full of history, but the cities are forward-looking, as well, and there are plenty of conservationists around who care about the land and water resources. Yes, I miss Texas. But I could live here, Nell," he said, smiling at her.

She wanted so badly to ask him if it was just because he liked the land, but she couldn't get the words to form properly. She blurted out, "With Margie?"

His eyebrows lifted. "Did I say with Margie?"

"No, but…"

He reached out a lean hand and touched her fingers where they lay cold and trembling on her stomach. His covered them, warmed them and made her tingle from head to toe. "I told you, Nell, you're going to have to figure it out for yourself. I won't tell you how I feel about Margie, or how I feel about you, for that matter."

"Why?" she asked more plaintively than she knew.

"Because I want you to understand a little more about trust than you do, honey," he replied. "There's a part of you that draws back and shies away from me. Until you get it worked out, I'm not going to influence you one way or the other."

She sighed. "I guess maybe I'll work it out, then."

"Want to come closer?" he coaxed with a warm

smile. "You're pretty safe, considering how we're surrounded by curious eyes."

She yielded to the temptation to be close. Inching her way, she moved her sleeping bag right up against his and turned on her side to rest beside him, with her head pillowed on one of his hard arms.

"That's better," he said softly. He eased forward a fraction of an inch and brushed her warm lips gently with his, savoring their faint trembling, their helpless response. "You might keep something in mind," he whispered.

"Oh? What?" she breathed against his lips, and her eyes opened straight into his.

"You aren't wearing makeup or a fancy dress," he whispered quietly. "And I'm not drawing back because you don't appeal to me the way you are."

Her fingers touched his face, loving its strength. "I'm not pretty," she said.

"You are to me," he said. "That's all that matters in the long run, if you'd open your eyes and see what's right under your nose."

"I see you," she said, her voice achingly tender as she adored him with her eyes.

"That's what I mean," he replied. He drew her closer. The saddle protected their faces from prying eyes, and he bent slowly to press his mouth hard against hers. "I want you, Nell," he said into her parted lips as he bit at them.

She wanted him, too. Her body was already on fire, and all he was doing was kissing her. She nibbled helplessly at his teasing mouth, and her hand smoothed into his thick hair, trying to draw him down.

"No," he breathed. "You can't have my mouth that

way, not tonight. I can't lose my head with you, honey. There are too many witnesses."

"What if we were alone?" she moaned under her breath. She slid her arms around his neck to press her breasts against his hard chest.

"Nell...damn it." He shuddered. He lifted his tormented eyes to the campfire. It was dying down and he needed to get up and put some fresh wood on it. The other campers were in their sleeping bags and turned toward the fire in a semicircle, which he and Nell were behind. No one could see them. He realized that now, and his powerful body trembled with the need to ease Nell onto her back and slide his leg between both of hers and show her how much he wanted her. He could feel her skin against his, the silken warmth of her breasts hard-tipped under his broad chest, the cries that he could tease out of her throat while he seduced her body slowly and tenderly and penetrated its virginal purity....

He groaned. His fingers on her arms hurt, but she didn't mind. Something powerful and mysterious was working in him, and she was too hungry to be afraid of it. This was Tyler, and she loved him with all her heart. She wanted memories, all that she could get, to press to her mind in the years that would follow.

"What is it?" she asked.

He looked down at her. In the dim light he could see her soft eyes, he could feel her quickened breathing. His hand moved with quiet possession over her blouse and smoothed around her breast until he found the hard tip. He watched her bite her lip and jerk toward him, trying not to cry out lest someone heard her.

"This is not sane," he whispered as the arm under her

nape contracted with desire. "Of all the stupid places to make love...."

"Touch me," she whispered brokenly.

His breath was audible as the words shattered his control and made him vulnerable. "Oh, Nell, you can't imagine what I'm thinking." He laughed huskily as his hand slid to the buttons of her blouse and began to lazily unfasten them. "You can't imagine what I want to do to you."

"Yes, I can," she whispered back, "because you told me, remember?" Her eyes met his searchingly. "You told me every single detail."

His powerful body trembled as he reached the last button. "Yes. And I dreamed it that night. Dreamed that I took you under me and felt your body like a field of flowers absorbing me so tenderly." He was whispering, but the tone of his voice drugged her. His fingers slid under the fabric and stopped with delighted surprise when he found nothing except soft warm skin.

Her lips parted. "I've never done this before," she whispered unsteadily. "Gone without...without what I usually wear, I mean."

He could have jumped over the moon. His fingers delved farther under the soft fabric and found a hard tip that brought a pleasured gasp from her lips when he touched it. "Lie still, honey," he whispered, his voice as unsteady as her own as he peeled away the cotton. "And for God's sake, don't cry out when I put my mouth on you...."

She had to bite her lower lip almost until it bled to manage that, because his lips were hungry and demanding. When he took her inside the warm darkness of his mouth, she felt tears well up from her closed eyes because it was like a tiny fulfillment in itself. She writhed helplessly, her nails biting him, her mouth as hungry as his, while the stars boiled down around them in white-hot flame.

He drew back first, and suddenly fastened her blouse with trembling hands before he rolled away from her and got to his feet.

She lay there, on fire for him, her eyes watching him as he moved near the campfire. Her body trembled with a need she'd never felt before. She wanted him, she wanted him!

His back was arrow straight as he began to build up the fire. He stood there for a while, and by the time he came back to his bedroll, her heart was beating normally again and she could feel the tension easing out of her body. But when he climbed into his sleeping bag, the tension came back all over again.

"Tyler," she whispered achingly.

"It passes," he whispered back. "I'm sorry, little one. I didn't mean to take you that far. It's impossible, in more ways than one."

She felt for his lean hand and curled her fingers into it trustingly. "I know. But it was sweet, all the same. I love it when you touch me like that. I'm not even embarrassed to tell you so."

His fingers contracted. "Then I don't mind telling you that I almost couldn't pull back." His head turned and his eyes searched hers in the blazing orange reflection of the fire beyond them. "One day I won't be able to stop. What then?"

Her lips parted. "I don't know."

"You'd better start thinking about it," he said bluntly.

"Because things are getting totally out of hand. Either we part company or risk the consequences."

She lowered her worried eyes to the steady rise and fall of his chest. "I...don't want to lose you," she said, burying her pride.

He brought her hand to his mouth. "That would be harder than you realize. Do you still want me, or is it easing off?"

She flushed. "It's easing off," she whispered back.

"At least now you understand why I get short-tempered from time to time, don't you?" he mused.

"Yes." She nuzzled her face against his arm. "What are we going to do?"

"What are *you* going to do?" he said, rephrasing the question. "The ball's in your court, honey. Make your move."

"But what do you want?"

"You."

"Just my body?" she asked softly.

"All of you."

She took a slow breath. "For how long?" she asked bravely.

"I told you, Nell. Love doesn't come with a money-back guarantee—if you do love me. What you feel might be infatuation, or just your first sensual experience making you vulnerable to me."

She searched his face, trying to see if he really believed that. "Is that what you think?"

"Not really. Why don't you tell me what you feel?"

She hesitated, and despite what she did feel, she couldn't lower her pride enough to tell him. She moved her fingers closer into his, feeling his own part and accept them in a warm, strong clasp.

"That reserve is the biggest part of our problem," he murmured. "You won't give in because you don't think I want you."

"I know you want me," she corrected.

"But not how badly, or in what way," he returned. "You're still locked up in the past, afraid of being hurt again."

"I know you wouldn't hurt me," she said unexpectedly, and her eyes were eloquent. "I never knew that a man could be so gentle."

He brought her fingers to his mouth. "That seems to come naturally with you," he said softly. "I've never felt as tender with a woman until now."

She moved her head on his arm. "Tyler, is it just physical with you?"

"If it was," he replied with a dry smile, "would I give a damn about your old-fashioned ideas on chastity? Would I even try to pull back?"

She felt her cheeks burn, and then she laughed self-consciously. "No. Of course not."

"Take it from there and think about it. Now we'd better get some sleep. We've already talked and…other things…for more than an hour."

"It didn't seem that long," she said shyly.

"For me, either, Nell." He let their clasped hands relax between them and closed his eyes. "After tonight," he murmured drowsily, "you'll never be able to deny that we've slept together."

"No, I won't." She curled a little closer and closed her own eyes. Her last thought before she fell asleep was that she'd never felt more secure or happy in all of her life.

SHE WOKE AT dawn to the delicious smell of percolating coffee and bacon and eggs being fried. Tyler was already hard at work on breakfast, with a little good-intentioned help from a couple of the guests. Everyone ate quietly, enjoying the silence of the desert at dawn and the incredible colors of the sky on the horizon.

"I've never seen anything so beautiful," Mrs. Callaway said with a sigh, nestling close to her husband.

"A living art gallery," Tyler agreed, smiling at Nell. "With a new canvas every minute of the day. It certainly is beautiful." *Like you*, his eyes were telling Nell, wooing her.

She sighed, her heart in her eyes, in her smile, in her rapt attention. His gaze locked with hers while he smoked his cigarette, and the exchange lasted long enough to make her blood run wildly through her veins and her knees get weak.

They rode back to the ranch a few minutes later, and Nell helped Tyler get the horses unsaddled, unbridled and put back in their stalls.

"I've never enjoyed anything more," Nell told him honestly, and laughed uninhibitedly. "It was wonderful."

"I thought so myself," he murmured. He leaned against a closed stall, and his green eyes glittered over her. "Come here," he challenged from deep in his throat.

Her heart raced. She didn't hesitate. She went straight to him and deliberately let her hips melt into his, her legs rest against the powerful strength of his own.

She raised her face for his kiss, blatantly inviting, without fear or inhibitions or reservations.

"Now I want an answer," he said solemnly. "I want to know what you feel for me. I want to know where I stand. You're going to have to trust me enough to tell me."

"That isn't quite fair," she argued. "I have to lower my pride, and you won't lower yours."

"I'm not the one with all the hang-ups," he reminded her. "Any good relationship has to be built on absolute trust to be successful."

"Yes, I know. But…" She avoided his gaze.

He tilted her face up to his. "Take a chance, Nell."

She took a deep breath, gathered her courage and started to speak. And just as she opened her mouth, a familiar voice called, "Tyler, darling, there you are! The boys and I arrived yesterday evening, and we're going to spend the week—isn't that nice?"

Nell moved away from Tyler as Margie came laughing into the stable and threw her arms around him. "Oh, you darling man, how have I managed to live all these years without you? Nell, isn't he wonderful? I'm so happy! Tyler, have you told her our news?" she prompted, her face radiant.

"No, he hasn't," Nell said, turning away. "But he doesn't need to, now. I can guess. See you later. I need a bath and a change of clothing."

"Nell," Tyler called after her, but she wasn't listening. She kept going into the house, with her dreams around her ears. Only a blind fool wouldn't know what Margie had hinted at. She and Tyler had something going, it was just plain obvious. And how could he have touched Nell so hungrily only last night, knowing that Margie was going to be here, waiting for him? Nell could have thrown things. Once again she'd been taken in by her own stupid, trusting nature. Well, this was the last straw. She was going to call Uncle Ted and tell him he could keep the ranch forever—she was going to leave and find something else to do. And as far away from Arizona and Tyler Jacobs as she could get!

CHAPTER TEN

"WHAT DO YOU look so unhappy for?" Bella asked Nell. "Didn't you enjoy the campout?"

"It was all right," Nell said with deliberate carelessness. She didn't want to remember what she and Tyler had done together. Margie had spoiled everything. Whatever Tyler had been going to say would never be said, and it looked as though Margie had pulled out all the stops and was going after him headlong.

"Hand me that mixer." Bella nodded toward the appliance she was going to use on a cake mix. "That Mrs. Norman was back in here again complaining about the menu. She's another Mrs. Harris, but at least Mr. Harris is here. Mrs. Norman doesn't like the way I cook. And besides all that, she thinks the entertainment stinks and there's nothing to do but ride horses."

Nell's eyes bulged. "Did you tell her that this is a dude ranch? People come here to ride horses."

"I told her that and plenty more." Bella looked at the younger woman sheepishly. "She's packing to leave. She says she's going to tell the whole world what a miserable operation we've got here. Oh, and we don't even have a tennis pro," she added.

"Tyler fired him, along with the golf pro," Nell reminded her. "He said they weren't paying their way."

"You mad at me?" Bella asked.

Nell put her arms around the older woman. "I love you. If people say cruel things about your cooking, they deserve to be sent packing. I think you're terrific."

Bella smiled and hugged her back. "That goes double for me. But I'll apologize all the same, if you want me to."

"No. Mrs. Norman may leave, with my blessing. In fact," she said, moving toward the door, "I'll even refund her money."

"Tyler won't like that," Bella called after her.

"Tyler can eat worms and die," Nell muttered.

"So that's it," Bella said to herself, and giggled once Nell was out of earshot.

Mrs. Norman had finished packing. She had her full-length mink coat wrapped around her thin body and her black eyes were flashing. "I am leaving," she told Nell, who was waiting outside the apartment when the older woman came out with her nose haughtily in the air. "You may have someone bring my luggage and call me a cab."

"With pleasure," Nell said, and even smiled. "If you'll stop by the office, I'll gladly refund your money."

Mrs. Norman eyed her suspiciously. "Why?"

"You don't like it here," Nell said. "There's no reason you should pay to be made miserable. The cooking is terrible, there's nothing to do…"

Mrs. Norman actually squirmed and pulled the mink coat closer, despite the fact that it was ninety degrees outside and she was already sweating. "That won't be necessary," she said. "Money is the least of my problems." She averted her eyes, then suddenly blurted out, "I'm allergic to horses and the dust is choking me. All my husband's friends go to dude ranches, and he sent me here because he didn't want to take me to Europe with him." She lifted her chin proudly, even though it trembled. "It's just that…that this room…is so empty," she finished, choking the words out. "I'm so alone."

She broke down into tears and Nell did what came naturally. She took the weeping woman in her arms and just stood holding her and rocking her and murmuring soft words of reassurance.

"There's nothing wrong with the food," Mrs. Norman said with a hiccup. Mascara ran like black tears from her huge, hurting eyes. "It's delicious. And the people are nice, too, but they're all couples. My husband only married me as a business proposition—he doesn't even like me. He never tried to make our marriage anything else."

"You might consider that men don't read minds," Nell told her gently, and even as she said it she smiled inwardly at the irony of telling this sophisticated woman anything about men, when her own love life was so confusing and unfamiliar. "Your husband might think you didn't want to go with him."

Mrs. Norman pulled away self-consciously and dried her eyes with a pure white linen handkerchief. Then she smiled a little shakily. "I'm sorry, I never go to pieces like this." She blew her nose. "Actually, he asked me if I wanted to go, and I laughed at him. He's not a handsome man, but I… I do love him." She glanced at Nell. "Can I make a long-distance call to Europe and have it charged to my account?"

"Of course you can!" Nell smiled. "He might even decide to come back home."

Mrs. Norman smiled back, suddenly looking ten years younger. "I'll do it right now." She took off the

mink coat. "That's my security blanket," she added ruefully, draping it over one arm. "I hate the damned thing,
it makes me sneeze, and it's too hot to wear it anywhere
except during blizzards in Alaska. I'll just make that
phone call." She went inside the apartment, and before
she closed the door she turned to look at Nell. "Thank
you," she said sincerely.

Nell couldn't get over what had just happened. She
felt on top of the world; she'd just learned a valuable
lesson about human nature, and she might have helped
save a marriage.

It wasn't a good time for Tyler to come around the
corner of the apartment block, glaring into space.

He stopped, looking at her. "Are you lost?" he asked.

"Not lately." She put her hands in her back pockets
and studied him quietly. "You look peaked."

"Do I? Why did you go rushing out of the stable?"
he demanded.

She lifted her eyebrows. "Three is still a crowd, isn't
it?"

"You thought I might have been waiting breathlessly
for you to leave so that I could seduce Margie in one of
the stalls?" he said with a cold tone to his deep voice.

Put that way, it sounded ridiculous. "Well, I guess
not. But she was waiting for you."

"She had some good news. You won't get to hear it,
of course," he continued. He lit a cigarette and threw
her a mocking smile. "Margie and I don't think you deserve to hear it. You jump to conclusions on the shab-
biest evidence, and you won't listen to explanations.
You're still running away from involvement."

"I've had some hard knocks in the past," she defended herself.

"I know all about that," he said. "I wormed the rest of it out of Margie, and I'm sorry about what happened to you. But I thought you and I were on the way to something more important than a few stolen kisses—yet I still can't get close to you."

She flushed, remembering the trail ride. "I wouldn't exactly say that," she faltered.

"I'm not talking about physical closeness," he said curtly. "I can't get close to you emotionally. You back away from me."

"I have good reason to!" she shot back.

"Not with me, you don't," he said, his voice deep and quiet as he watched her. "I'm not asking you to move in with me, or even to spend the night with me in a non-platonic way. I want you to trust me, Nell."

"But I do trust you," she began.

"Not in the way that counts." He drew in a slow breath. "Well, I've had all I can take. I won't run after you, honey. If you want anything more to happen between us, you'll have to make the first move. I'm not going to touch you again. You're going to have to decide."

He moved away without another word, leaving Nell to stand there and watch him leave with her heart down around her ankles.

Mrs. Norman left in a delighted flurry that afternoon. Her husband had been thrilled to hear from her, and he'd decided to come home and meet her in Vermont for a second honeymoon. Nell had driven the older woman to the airport and had been fervently hugged before Mrs. Norman ran like a teenage girl to catch her plane.

At least someone was happy, Nell thought miserably.

But it sure wasn't her. She still didn't understand why Tyler was trying to make her chase him. It didn't really make sense. He was the man, and the man was supposed to make all the moves, not the woman; at least, not in Nell's old-fashioned world.

Of course, Tyler was old-fashioned, too. That was the hard thing to reconcile. And with his attitude, it didn't really make sense that he'd be hanging around Nell when he wanted Margie. And he had to want Margie. Every man did. Margie was beautiful and cultured and sophisticated, just the right kind of woman for a man like Tyler.

During the next few days, Margie kept very much to herself. She smiled at Nell as if nothing were wrong, but she spent a lot of time where the men—especially Tyler—were, and she kept the boys with her. She seemed to understand that her presence irritated Nell, and she did everything she could to make it bearable for the younger woman, right down to sleeping late and going to bed early.

Nell was actually looking for an excuse for a confrontation, because there was a lot she wanted to say to her sister-in-law. But Margie made that impossible, and even Tyler interfered if it looked as though Nell might find an opportunity. So the days went by with Nell getting more frustrated by the minute. What she didn't know was that Darren McAnders had been furious that Margie was spending time with Tyler, and had begun to make his presence felt and heard while Tyler and Nell were away on the campout. He and Margie had it out that very evening while the campout was in full swing. The argument shortly began to have results. When no one was looking, McAnders picked Margie up and carried her off to a quiet spot under the big palo verde tree near the apartments. And there he kissed her until she couldn't stand up or protest. Then he began to tell her how he felt and what he wanted. When he finished, she was smiling. And the next kiss was instigated by her. But they kept their secret, because Margie didn't want to spring anything on Nell until Tyler had a chance to patch things up with his lady. Margie was getting impatient, though. Tyler and Nell seemed to have reached an impasse.

Nell went on teaching the daily riding lessons and avoided going to the dinner table until she was sure it was too late for Tyler to be there, if he'd decided to eat at the big house, that was. He spent more and more time in the bunkhouse or his own cabin.

Nights got longer and Nell's temper got shorter. Until Tyler had come along, she'd never known that she even had a temper, but he seemed to bring out the beast in her.

It was like being half a person. She strained for glimpses of him; she spun beautiful daydreams about him. Her eyes followed him everywhere. But she kept to herself, and spoke to him only when he asked her something directly. Which was all she could do, because he was still spending time with Margie. Actually he was chaperoning her with McAnders so that Bella wouldn't figure out their secret and spill the beans too soon, but Nell didn't know that and she didn't trust him.

Tyler was brooding, too. He almost gave up. Nell seemed more unapproachable now than she ever had, and she was retreating by the day. He wondered if he was ever going to be able to reach her again.

Texas seemed so far away. He remembered how he'd

taken Abby Clark out on a date and how sweet it had been to dance with her. But it was nothing compared to the feel of Nell's body in his arms, her soft, shy mouth under the crush of his, welcoming him. She had a big heart and he wanted it, but Nell didn't seem to want him back.

She thought he was stuck on Margie, and that was a real laugh. Margie reminded him too much of the world he'd had to give up, of all he'd lost. He was going to need a woman who wasn't interested in frills and fancies, a woman who'd be willing to work at his side and help him start over. Nell was just right, in every way, and he cared about her deeply. The problem was getting her to believe he loved her when she had such poor self-image. She couldn't or wouldn't believe that she was infinitely desirable to him. And until he could break her out of that self-ordained mold, he was never going to reach her.

His green eyes glittered as he saw her riding back in from the trail ride with Darren McAnders at her side. Damn McAnders. Why couldn't he stop interfering?

He watched them dismount. McAnders took Nell's mount by the bridle and led both horses into the stable, with a grin and a cheerful greeting to Tyler.

Tyler didn't acknowledge it. He stood glaring at Nell for a long moment, and then he strode toward her.

She watched the way he walked, so tall and easy, which was deceptive. He was all muscle, and she knew the power in that exquisitely male body, the sweetness of being held by him while he brought her every nerve alive. He had on a beige shirt that emphasized his dark coloring, made his green eyes even greener. He came close and she felt the tension grow between them almost instantly.

"Having fun?" he asked.

She didn't like his tone. It was insulting. "No, I'm not," she replied tersely. "I hate running a dude ranch. I'm scared to death that a rattlesnake is going to bite somebody or a horse is going to run away with a greenhorn rider or that we're going to lose somebody out on that desert and find them several days later. I hate budgeting, I don't like the need to cut out half of our recreational facilities, and if I have to hear one more remark about how desolate and disgusting my desert is, I'm going to scream!"

"I just asked if you were having fun," he pointed out. "I didn't ask for a rundown on the world economy."

"Don't mind me," she said mockingly. "Pat yourself on the back."

He did, and her face flamed with bad temper.

"Why don't you go back to Texas?" she muttered.

"Oh, I like it here," he told her. "Dust and rattlesnakes grow on a man."

Her eyes narrowed. "Don't you start," she dared.

His eyebrows lifted. "What a nasty temper you're in, little Nell. Why don't you go and eat something bland and see if it'll take the pepper off your tongue?"

"I'm going to tell my uncle how you're ruining the place," she threatened.

"He won't listen," he said with a lazy grin. "He's too busy depositing the money we've been making lately."

She took a sharp breath. "That's it, go ahead, put all the blame on me!"

"Mind you don't split a blood vessel with all that temper, honey," he said.

"Don't call me honey!"

"How about vinegar?"

She aimed a kick at his shin, but he was faster. He caught her up in his arms and carried her toward the corral, where the horses' watering trough was sitting innocently.

Through her kicking and cursing, she noticed where he was headed and clung to his neck.

"You wouldn't dare," she snapped.

He chuckled. "Of course I would."

Her arms tightened. "I'll take you with me."

"Promises, promises," he breathed huskily, and his mouth lowered so that it almost touched hers. "Will you, indeed?"

The threat of his lips made her heart race. She felt her breasts pressed against his chest; she smelled the leather and tobacco scent of his body mingling with the cologne he wore. She felt the strength of the arms under her and a kind of feminine delight in his maleness grew within her.

"Will I what?" she breathed. Her nails scraped gently against his nape as unfamiliar sensations trembled through her.

"Don't tease," he whispered. "If I start kissing you now, we're going to have the biggest audience this side of Denver."

Her lips parted. "I'm not teasing," she said softly.

His face hardened. "No? Then tell me how I feel about Margie."

She felt the spell shatter. "I don't know," she muttered. "Anyway, it's none of my business."

"The hell it isn't. You blind little bat!"

And with a suddenness that put her between shock

and fear, his mouth went down on hers savagely for one long instant before he took advantage of her helpless reaction and threw her, bottom first, right into the horses' trough.

CHAPTER ELEVEN

TYLER HAD STRODE off in a black temper by the time Nell dragged herself, dripping and swearing, out of the horses' trough. A couple of the men were watching, and she gave them her best glare as she sloshed off toward the house. It didn't help her dignity that they were laughing behind her.

She stormed into the house and upstairs to shower and change her clothes before anybody got a good look at her and guffawed some more. Then she returned downstairs, cooler but still fuming, and dialed her uncle Ted's number with fingers that trembled in her haste. And all the while she wanted to fling Tyler and Margie down a mine shaft.

"Hello?" A deep, masculine voice came over the other end.

"Hello, yourself. I don't want to run this ranch anymore," she said without preamble. "I don't care if it means I lose everything, I won't stay at the same place with that foreman of yours!"

Uncle Ted was getting a new lease on life. His man-hating niece was suddenly losing her temper, something she never did, and over a real live man! He could have jumped for joy. He knew it had been a good idea to send Tyler Jacobs out to the Double R.

"Now, now," Uncle Ted soothed, "I can't let you

throw away your inheritance, Nell. No, you'll just have to stay there and work things out, I'm afraid."

"I can't!" she wailed. "Look, I'll sign everything over to you—"

"No." He hung up.

She stared at the dead receiver as if it had sprouted flowers. Talk about finality! He hadn't even said goodbye.

She slammed the receiver down with a bang and glared at it. "I hate you!" she raged. "I think you're an overbearing male chauvinist, and just because you're rich doesn't give you the right to try and run people's lives for them!"

She was screaming by now, and Curt and Jess, standing unnoticed in the doorway, were watching her with saucer-size eyes. They motioned to their mother, who joined the rapt audience.

"I don't want him here," she fumed at the telephone. "I never did! I don't understand why you wouldn't give me a chance to straighten things out by myself before you stuck your big nose into my business. It's my ranch, my father left it to me and Teddy, and he never meant for you to dangle it over my head like a guillotine!"

"What's a guillotine?" Jess whispered to his mother.

"It's stuff you put on your joints when you have rheumatism," Curt whispered.

"Hush!" said their mother.

"Well, you can just tell him to go back to Texas, or I'll go there and live myself and he can have the ranch! I hate him, and I hate you, and I hate Margie, too!"

"It must be the insecticides in the groundwater table affecting your brain," Margie said, shaking her head.

Nell whirled, aghast to find three pairs of eyes staring at her. She stared back, speechless.

"Aunty Nell, why are you talking to the telephone?" Curt wanted to know.

"I was talking to your great-uncle Ted," she said with mangled dignity.

"Wouldn't you communicate better by talking into the receiver?" Margie mused.

Nell glared at her. "I haven't congratulated you yet. I'll make sure I send you a suitable gift when the time comes."

"How sweet of you, Nell." Margie sighed. "He's soo handsome, and I can't believe he really loves me."

"We love him, too," the boys chorused, grinning. "And we can come and live here now—"

Nell screamed. She actually screamed. She did it and then stood stock-still, astonished that the sound had really come from her throat.

"I love you, too." Margie added fuel to the fire, making a kissing motion with her lips. "We'll be one big happy family."

"Like hell we will!" Nell burst out, and tears fell from her eyes. "I'm leaving, right now!"

"Leaving for where?" Margie asked.

"I don't know and I don't...care." She hiccuped from stuffy tears. "Oh, Margie, how could you!"

"Boys, go and find a new lizard to scare me with," Margie told her sons. She shooed them out and closed the door.

"I want to leave," Nell wailed.

"After you listen to me," Margie said. "Now dry up for a minute. How do you feel about Tyler?"

Nell tried to avoid the question, but Margie wouldn't

budge. She drew in a shaky breath. "I…love him," she bit off.

Margie smiled. "Do you? A lot?"

"Yes."

"But you think that he's the kind of man who plays with one woman at the same time he's courting somebody else?"

Nell blinked. She turned her head slightly, and her great, dark eyes fixed on Margie's face. "Well, no, actually, he isn't," she admitted. "He's kind of old-fashioned about things."

Margie nodded. "That's right. You're doing very well, darling. Keep going."

"If he'd been going to marry you, he'd have told me himself," Nell ventured. "He wouldn't have let me find out by accident from someone else."

"Yes. And?"

Nell drew in a slow, exquisite breath. "He'd never play around with an innocent woman unless he was serious about her. Unless he was playing for keeps."

Margie smiled gently. "And you were going to cuss out Uncle Ted and run away."

Nell dried her tears. "I've been such a fool. I was scared, you know, Margie."

"We're all scared. Commitment isn't easy, even when people love each other." She went close to Nell, smiling. "I'm going to marry Darren. Will you be my maid of honor?"

Nell burst out laughing. "Oh, Margie, of course I will!" She hugged the older woman fervently, laughing and crying all at once. "I'm so sorry for the things I said. I was so jealous, and my heart was broken! But now I think I'm going to be all right, after all."

"I know you are. Wouldn't you like to take a nice, refreshing walk?" she added. "You might walk down by the holding pens. The scenery there is really something."

"Nice, is it?" Nell probed.

"Dark and handsome, to coin a phrase." Margie grinned. "But it may not last long, so you'd better hurry."

"I'll do that. But first, can you lend me a dress? Something very feminine and lighter than air and suitable for a woman to chase a man in?"

Margie was delighted. "You bet I can. Come on!"

It was a dream of a dress in creamy spring green with a full, flowing skirt and a pretty rounded neckline and puffy sleeves. Nell felt like a young girl again, all heart and nerves as she brushed her long, clean hair and put on makeup and a little perfume.

Nell smiled, thinking how sweet it was going to be to make her first move toward Tyler, to flirt openly with him, sure of herself at last.

She slipped on a pair of soft shoes and tore down the staircase and out the door toward the holding pens. It seemed to take forever to get there, and she was breathless from her haste when she finally reached them.

The pens were empty now, with roundup over, but Tyler was leaning back lazily against the fence with a cigarette in his fingers, his long legs crossed and one arm propped on the second fence rail. His hat was pulled low over his eyes so that Nell couldn't quite see them through the shadows, but he looked approachable enough.

"Hello," she said nervously.

He nodded. His green eyes glittered over her possessively before he turned back to the horizon and took a draw from his cigarette. "Lose your way?"

"Not this time." She went closer and stood beside him to look over the pasture. "Do you make a habit of throwing women into water troughs? Because if you do, we're going to have a rocky life together."

He couldn't believe he'd heard that. He turned, his eyes hungry on her face, his pulse racing. She'd dressed up and fixed her face and hair, and she looked radiant. "No, I don't make a habit of it," he replied. "But at the time I'd had about all I could stand. Nell, I'm thinking of going back to Texas."

"Running out on me?" she asked with pure bravado. "I'll come after you."

He touched his forehead unobtrusively to see if he was dying of fever or having hallucinations. "I beg your pardon?"

She gathered up her shaken nerve. "I said, I'll follow you back to Texas."

He finished the cigarette and ground it out under his boot, taking so long to speak that Nell felt her knees getting ready to buckle in case she'd gotten it wrong and he didn't care.

"No doubts?" he asked suddenly, and his eyes met hers with a fiercely sensual impact.

It was hard to get enough breath to answer him, because he was even closer now, and she had to fight not to put her body right against his and hold on for dear life. "No doubts, Ty," she whispered. She looked up at him and went for broke. "I love you."

His eyes closed for an instant and then opened on a heavy exhaled breath. "My God." He drew her into his arms and held her there, rocking her hungrily from side to side, with his lips on her cheek, her ear, her neck, and finally, crushing into the warmth of her soft mouth.

She held on to him with all her strength, loving the furious beating of her heart, the weakness he engendered in her body, the warm wonder of knowing that he cared about her, too. She sighed under his devouring mouth and it lifted, fractionally, while he searched her eyes with all the barriers gone.

"Did Margie tell you that it isn't me she's going to marry?" he asked quietly.

"Not really," she hedged, because it was a dangerous time to go into all the details.

He frowned. "She didn't talk to you?"

"It was more a case of her making *me* talk. And I worked it out by myself." She smiled tenderly at him. "If you were going to marry Margie," she began quietly, "you'd never have touched me, not even out of pity."

He didn't move for a minute. Then he began to stroke her bare arms very gently with his warm, work-roughened hands. "It took you a long time to realize that," he said deeply, and his heart sang because of the look in her eyes.

"Yes," she said with a faint grin. "Of course, I didn't work it out at first. After I got out of the horses' trough and dried off," she said with a glare that didn't faze him, "I called Uncle Ted and yelled at him and told him what he could do with the ranch and that I was leaving forever. He just hung up on me. I guess I'll have to call him back and apologize."

"I wouldn't just yet," Tyler advised. "He's probably laughing too hard. I get the idea that before I came along, you never yelled at anybody."

She nodded. "There was never any reason to." She

sighed, looking hungrily at his dark face. "Oh, I want you," she whispered, letting down her pride. "I want to live with you and have children with you and grow old with you."

"And what do I want, do you think?" he asked, leading her on.

It didn't work. She just smiled. "You want me, of course."

He burst out laughing, the sound full with joy and delight. He lifted her up against his chest to kiss her with exquisite tenderness. "I'm sorry about the horses' trough. I'd waited and hoped, and we were almost there, and then Margie came along after the campout and set us back several weeks. She didn't mean to. Her news, of course, was that she and McAnders were engaged. But when you took off, she decided to keep the secret awhile longer."

"I'm sorry about that," she murmured. "I didn't think I could compete with her. I never dreamed that you could feel for me what I felt for you. It was like wishing for the moon."

"Not anymore, is it?" he mused, and brushed his mouth sensually across hers.

"Not anymore," she agreed huskily.

"When were you sure that I didn't want Margie?"

"When I remembered that you'd made the sweetest kind of love to me, without asking me to go all the way with you," she whispered, and for the first time, she kissed him, with shy hunger. "And a man like you wouldn't do that unless he had something permanent in mind. Because I'm still a virgin," she breathed into his mouth. "And you're an old-fashioned man. You even said so."

"It took you long enough to remember it," he murmured dryly. He nuzzled her cheek with his, floating, warm from the touch of her body against his, the clasp of her soft arms. "I love you, Nell," he whispered huskily. "And I do want you for keeps. You and a houseful of children and the best future we can make together."

"I love you, too," she whispered fervently.

"You grew on me," he mused, lifting his head to search her soft eyes. "But long before that time I was sick and you nursed me, I knew I'd lost my heart. I wasn't able to think about another woman after that."

"I'm very glad. I loved you from the beginning, although I was afraid to. You see, I thought you were just being nice to me because you felt sorry for me."

"I liked you," he said simply. "And when you started avoiding me, it was like a knife in my heart."

"I didn't think you could care about someone like me," she said quietly. "Then after you began to talk about my low self-image and my lack of confidence, I started thinking about things. I guess none of us is perfect, but that doesn't mean we can't be loved. It doesn't have much to do with beauty and sophistication and money, does it? Love is more than that."

"Much more." He framed her face and bent slowly to her mouth. "I'll cherish you all my life. I don't have a lot to give you, but you can have my heart."

She smiled against his mouth. "I'd rather have that than anything else in the whole world. I'll give you mine for it."

He smiled back. "That," he whispered before he kissed her, "is a deal."

A long time later, they walked back to the house

hand in hand, and Margie and the boys and Bella stood on the porch, anxious to find out what had happened.

"Well?" Bella demanded, out of patience. "Is it going to be a wedding or a farewell party?"

"A wedding." Nell laughed and ran forward to hug Bella and Margie and the boys. "And we're going to be so happy together."

"As if anybody could believe otherwise," Bella said, sniffing. "Well, I'll go cook supper. Something special." Her eyes narrowed in thought. "And a cake…"

"You snake in the grass, leading me on like that!" Nell accused Margie. "Making me so jealous that I couldn't stand it!"

"I knew it would either open your eyes or close them for good." Margie smiled. "You could have gone on forever the way you were, untrusting and alone. I thought you needed a chance."

"Well, thank you," Nell said. She glanced at Tyler's radiant expression and then back at Margie as the other woman started to speak.

"I love Darren so much, Nell. Are you going to mind having us both on the place? Because he insists that he's going to support me."

"I don't have any problem at all with that," Nell said at once.

"I called Uncle Ted back after you went out to meet Tyler," Margie said with a secretive smile. "He said if you and Tyler got married, he'd turn over control of the ranch early—as a wedding present."

Tyler didn't say anything, and Nell went close to him. "Look," she said, "it isn't much of a ranch right now. It's lost a lot of money and times are still pretty bad. You are getting nothing but a headache, so don't look on it as a handout."

That took the bitter look off his face. "Then I guess you and I are going to have the challenge of building it up again," he said finally, and his hard features relaxed. He had to start back somewhere, and he loved Nell. The two of them together, working to build a future and a family. Yes, that sounded good. He smiled down at her. "Okay, honey. We'll give it a try."

"And Darren and I can live in the cabin with the boys," Margie suggested. "Or we can build a house close by. I think I'd rather do that. I still have a nest egg, and so does Darren--he's been saving for years. We'll do that. Your foreman will have to have someplace to live."

Tyler glanced amusedly at Nell. "I thought we might offer it to Chappy. He's been here a long time, and he bosses everybody around anyway. What do you think?"

Nell laughed. "I think it's a great idea!"

"So do I," Margie agreed. "Well, shall we go inside and call Uncle Ted one more time?"

Nell slid her hand into Tyler's, and they followed the others back inside. Tyler looked down at her just before they went through the open door. The look on his face made Nell catch her breath. The awe and wonder of love blazed from it as surely as the Arizona sun warmed the desert. Nell's own face reflected a love for her long, tall Texan that would last forever.

* * * * *

CALHOUN

To Mary Wheeler at Micro Pro—
Thanks a million!

CHAPTER ONE

ABBY COULDN'T HELP looking over her shoulder from time to time as she stood in line at the theater ticket counter. She'd escaped by telling Justin that she was going to see an art exhibit. Calhoun, thank God, was off somewhere buying more cattle, although he was certain to be home later this evening. When he found out where his ward had been, he'd be furious. She almost grinned at her own craftiness.

Well, it took craftiness to deal with Calhoun Ballenger. He and Justin, his older brother, had taken Abby in when she'd been just fifteen. They would have been her stepbrothers, except that an untimely car accident had killed their father and Abby's mother just two days before the couple were to have gotten married. There hadn't been any other family, so Calhoun had proposed that he and Justin assume responsibility for the heartbroken teenager, Abigail Clark. And they did. It was legal, of course; technically Abby was Calhoun's ward. The problem was that she couldn't make Calhoun realize that she was a woman.

Abby sighed. That was a problem, all right. And to make it even worse, he'd gone crazy on the subject of protecting her from the world. For the past four months it had been a major ordeal just to go out on a date. The way he stood watch over her was getting almost comical. Justin rarely smiled, but Calhoun's antics brought him close to it.

Calhoun's attitude didn't amuse Abby, though. She was desperately in love with Calhoun, but the big blond man still looked upon her as a child. And despite her frequent attempts to show Calhoun that she was a woman, she couldn't seem to get through his armor.

She shifted restlessly. She had no idea of how to attract a man like Calhoun in the first place. He wasn't as much of a rounder now as he had been in his youth, but she knew that he was frequently seen in nightclubs in San Antonio with one sophisticated beauty or another. And here was Abby, dying of love for him. She wasn't sophisticated or beautiful. She was a rather plain country girl, not the sort to immediately draw men's eyes, even though her figure was better than average.

After brooding over the problem, she had come up with a solution. If she could manage to get sophisticated, he might notice her. Going to a strip show wasn't exactly the best first step, but in Jacobsville it was a good start. Just being seen here would show Calhoun that she wasn't the little prude he thought she was. *When* he found out about it—and eventually he would hear she'd attended the show.

Abby smoothed the waistline of her pretty gray plaid skirt. She was wearing a pale yellow blouse with it, and her long, wavy brown hair was in a neat chignon. Her hair, when it was loose, was one of her best assets. It was thick and silky. And her eyes weren't bad. They were big, quiet grayish-blue eyes, and she was blessed with a peaches-and-cream complexion and a perfect bow of a mouth. But without careful makeup she was hopelessly plain. Her breasts were bigger than she wanted them to be, her legs longer than she would have liked. She had friends who were small and dainty, and they made her feel like a beanpole. She glanced down at herself miserably. If only she were petite and exquisitely beautiful.

At least she did look older and more sophisticated than usual in her burgundy velour jacket, and her blue-gray eyes sparkled as she thought about what she was doing. Well, it wasn't so bad for a woman to go to a male dance revue, was it? She had to get educated somehow, and God knew Calhoun wasn't about to let her date any men who knew the score. He saw to it that her only escorts were boys her own age, and he screened every one and made casual remarks about how often he cleaned his guns and what he thought about "fooling around before marriage." It wasn't really surprising to Abby that few of her dates came back.

She shivered a little in the cold night air. It was February, and cold even in south Texas. As she huddled in her jacket, she smiled at another young woman shivering in the long line outside the Grand Theater. It was the only theater in Jacobsville, and there had been some opposition to having this kind of entertainment come to town. But in the end there had been surprisingly few complaints, and there was a long line of women waiting to see if these men lived up to the publicity.

Wouldn't Calhoun just die when he found out what she'd done? She grinned. His blond-streaked brown hair would stand on end, and his dark eyes would glare at her furiously. Justin would do what he always did—he'd go out and dig postholes while Calhoun wound down. The two brothers looked a lot alike, except that Justin's hair was almost black. They both had dark eyes, and they were both tall, muscular men. Calhoun was by far the handsomer of the two. Justin had a craggy face and a reticent personality, and although he was courteous to women, he never dated anybody. Almost everybody knew why—Shelby Jacobs had thrown him over years ago, refusing to marry him.

That had been when the Ballengers had still been poor, before Justin's business sense and Calhoun's feel for marketing had skyrocketed them to success with a mammoth feedlot operation here in south Texas. Shelby's family was rich, and rumor had it that she thought Justin was beneath her. It had certainly made him bitter. Funny, she mused, Shelby seemed like such a wonderful woman. And her brother, Tyler, was nice, too.

Two more ladies got their tickets, and Abby dug out a ten-dollar bill. Just as she got to the ticket counter, though, her wrist was suddenly seized and she was pulled unceremoniously to one side.

"I thought I recognized that jacket," Calhoun murmured, glaring down at her with eyes that were dark and faintly glittering. "What a good thing I decided to come home through town. Where's my brother?" he added for good measure. "Does he know where you are?"

"I told him I was going to an art exhibit," Abby replied with a touch of her irrepressible humor. Her blue-gray eyes twinkled up at him, and she felt the warm glow she always felt when Calhoun came close. Even when he was angry, it was so good to be near him. "Well, it is an art exhibit, sort of," she argued when he looked skeptical. "Except that the male statues are alive…"

"My God." He stared at the line of amused women

and abruptly turned toward his white Jaguar, tugging at her wrist. "Let's go."

"I'm not going home," she said firmly, struggling. It was exciting to challenge him. "I'm going to buy my ticket and go in there—Calhoun!" she wailed as he ended the argument by simply lifting her in his hard arms and carrying her to the car.

"I can't even leave the state for one day without you doing something insane," Calhoun muttered in his deep, gravelly voice. "The last time I went off on business, I came home to find you about to leave for Lake Tahoe with that Misty Davies."

"Congratulations. You saved me from a weekend of skiing," Abby murmured dryly. Not for the world would she have admitted how exciting it was to have him carry her, to feel his strength at such close quarters. He was as strong as he looked, and the subtle scents of his body and the warmth of his breath on her face made her body tingle in new and exciting ways.

"There were two college boys all set to go along, as I remember," he reminded her.

"What am I supposed to do with my car?" she demanded. "Leave it here?"

"Why not? God knows nobody would be stupid enough to steal it," he replied easily, and kept walking, her slight weight soft and disturbing in his hard arms.

"It's a very nice little car," she protested, talking more than usual because the feel of his chest was unnerving her. His clean-shaven chin was just above her, and she was getting drunk on the feel of him.

"Which you wouldn't have if I'd gone with you instead of Justin," he returned. "Honest to God, he spoils you rotten. He should have married Shelby and had kids of his own to ruin. I hate having him practice on you. That damned little sports car isn't safe."

"It's mine, I like it, I'm making the payments and I'm keeping it," she said shortly.

He looked down at her, his dark eyes much too close to hers. "Aren't we brave, though?" he taunted softly, deliberately letting his gaze fall on her mouth.

She could barely breathe, but he wasn't going to make her back down. Not that way. She didn't dare let him see the effect he had on her. "I'm almost twenty-one," she reminded him. He looked into her eyes, and she felt the impact of his glance like a body blow. It made her feel like a lead weight. And there was a sudden tautness about his body that puzzled her. For seconds that strung out like hours, he searched her eyes. Then abruptly he moved again.

"So you keep telling me," he replied curtly. "And then you go and do something stupid like this."

"There's nothing wrong with being sophisticated," she mumbled. "God knows how I'll ever get an education. You seem to want me to spend the rest of my life a virgin."

"Hang out in this kind of atmosphere and you won't stay in that sainted condition for much longer," he returned angrily. She disturbed him when she made such statements. She had been talking like that for months, and he was no nearer a solution to the problem than he had been at the beginning. He quickened his pace toward the car, his booted feet making loud, angry thuds on the pavement.

Calhoun was still wearing a dark suit, Abby noticed. His thick dark-blond hair was covered by his cream dress Stetson. He smelled of Oriental cologne, and his dark face was clean-shaven. He was a handsome brute, Abby thought. Sexy and overpoweringly masculine, and she loved every line of him, every scowl, every rugged inch. She forced her screaming nerves not to give her away and attempted to hide her attraction to him, as usual, with humor.

"Aren't we in a temper, though?" she taunted softly, and his dark expression hardened. It was exciting to make him mad. She'd only realized that in the past few weeks, but more and more she liked to prod him, to see his explosive reactions. She loved the touch of his hands, and provoking him had become addictive. "I'm a big girl. I graduated from the trade school last year. I have a diploma. I'm a secretary. I'm working for Mr. Bundy at the feedlot sales office—"

"I remember. I paid for the trade school courses and got you the damned job," he said tersely.

"You sure did, Calhoun," she agreed, her mischievous gaze darting up at him as he opened the passenger door of the vehicle and put her on the smooth leather seat, slamming the door once she was settled. He went around the gleaming hood and got in under the steering wheel. There was muted violence in the way he started the powerful white car, shot away from the curb and drove down the town's main street.

"Abby, I can't believe you really wanted to pay money to watch a bunch of boys take their clothes off," he muttered.

"It beats having boys try to take mine off," she returned humorously. "You must think so, too, because you go nuts if I try to date anybody with any experience."

He frowned. That was true. It upset him to think

of any man taking advantage of Abby. He didn't want other men touching her.

"I'd beat a man to his knees for trying to undress you, and that's a fact," he said.

"My poor future husband," she sighed. "I can see him now, calling the police on our wedding night…"

"You're years too young to talk about getting married," he said.

"I'll be twenty-one in three months. My mother was twenty-one when she had me," she reminded him.

"I'm thirty-two, and I've never been married," he replied. "There's plenty of time. You don't need to rush into marriage before you've had time to see something of the world," he said firmly.

"How can I?" she asked reasonably. "You won't let me."

He glared at her. "It's the part of life that you're trying to see that bothers me. Male strip shows. My God."

"They weren't going to take all their clothes off," she assured him. "Just most of them."

"Why did you decide to go tonight?"

"I didn't have anything else to do," she sighed. "And Misty had been to see this show."

"Misty Davies," he muttered. "I've told you I don't approve of your friendship with that flighty heiress. She's years older than you and much more sophisticated."

"No wonder," she replied. "She doesn't have an overbearing guardian who's determined to save her from herself."

"She could have used one. A woman who treats her body cheaply doesn't invite a wedding ring."

"So you keep saying. At least Misty won't faint of

shock on her wedding night when her husband takes his clothes off. I've never seen a man without a stitch on. Except in this magazine that Misty had—" she began, warming to her subject.

"For God's sake, you shouldn't be reading that kind of magazine!" He looked outraged.

Her eyebrows went up suddenly, and her eyes were as round as saucers. "Why not?"

He searched for words. "Well…because!"

"Men ogle women in those kind of magazines," she said reasonably. "If we can be exploited, why can't men?"

He finally gave in to ill temper. "Why can't you just shut up, Abby?"

"Okay, Calhoun, I'll do that very thing," she agreed. She studied his hard, angry profile, and almost smiled at the way she'd gotten him ruffled. He might not be in love with her, but she certainly did have a knack for getting his attention.

"All this sudden fascination with male nudity," he grumbled, glaring at her. "I don't know what's gotten into you."

"Frustration," she replied. "It comes from too many nights sitting home alone."

"I've never tried to stop you from dating," he said defensively.

"Oh, no, of course you haven't. You just sit with my prospective dates and make a big deal of cleaning your gun collection while you air your archaic views on pre-marital sex!"

"They're not archaic," he said curtly. "A lot of men feel the way I do about it."

"Do tell?" She lifted her eyebrow. "And I suppose that means that you're a virgin, too, Calhoun?"

His dark eyes cut sideways at her. "Do you think so, Abby?" he asked, in a tone she'd never heard him use.

She suddenly felt very young. The huskiness in his deep voice, added to the faint arrogance in his dark eyes, made her feel foolish for even having asked. Of course he wasn't a virgin.

She averted her eyes. "Foolish question," she murmured softly.

"Wasn't it, though?" He pressed on the accelerator. For some reason, it bothered him to have Abby know what his private life was like. She probably knew more than he'd given her credit for, especially if she was hanging around with Misty Davies. Misty frequented the same kind of city hot spots that Calhoun did, and she'd seen him with one or two of his occasional companions. He hoped Misty hadn't talked to Abby about what she'd seen, but he couldn't count on it.

His sudden withdrawal puzzled Abby. She didn't like the cold silence that was growing between them any more than she liked thinking about his women. "How did you know where I was?" she asked to break the rigid silence.

"I didn't, honey," he confessed. The endearment sounded so natural coming from him that she'd never minded him using it, though she disliked its artificiality when other men did. "I happened to come home through Jacobsville. And who should I see in line—in front of all the lurid posters—but you?"

She sighed. "Fate. Fate is out to get me."

"Fate may not be the only one," he returned, but his voice was so low that she couldn't hear.

He turned onto the road that led past the feedlot to the big Spanish house where the Ballengers lived. On the way they passed the Jacobses' colonial-style house, far off the road at the end of a paved driveway, with purebred Arabian horses grazing in sprawling pastures dotted with oak trees. There wasn't much grass—the weather was still cold, and a few snow flurries had caused excitement the day before. Big bales of hay were placed around the property to give the horses adequate feed, supplemented with blocks of vitamins and minerals.

"I hear the Jacobses are having financial problems," Abby remarked absently.

He glanced at her. "Since the old man died last summer, they're close to bankrupt, in fact Tyler's borrowed all he can borrow. If he can't pull it together now, he never will. The old man made deals Ty didn't even know about. If he loses that place, it's going to be damned hard on his pride."

"Hard on Shelby's, too," she remarked.

He grimaced. "For God's sake, don't mention Shelby around Justin."

"I wouldn't dare. He gets funny, doesn't he?"

"I wouldn't call throwing punches at people funny."

"I've seen you throw punches a time or two," she reminded him, recalling one particular day not too long before when one of the new cowhands had beaten a horse. Calhoun had knocked the man to his knees and fired him on the spot, his voice so cold and quiet that it had cut to the bone. Calhoun didn't have to raise his voice. Like Justin, when Calhoun lost his temper he had a look that made words unnecessary.

He was an odd mixture, she thought, studying him.

So tenderhearted that he'd go off for half a day by himself if he had to put down a calf or if something happened to one of his men. And so hotheaded at times that the men would actually hide from his anger. In temperament, he was like Justin. They were both strong, fiery men, but underneath there was a tenderness, a vulnerability, that very few people ever saw. Abby, because she'd lived with them for so many years, knew them better than any outsider ever could.

"How did you get back so fast?" she asked to break the silence.

He shrugged. "I guess I've got radar," he murmured, smiling faintly. "I had a feeling you wouldn't be sitting at home with Justin watching old war movies on the VCR."

"I didn't think you'd be back before morning."

"So you decided you'd go watch a lot of muscle men strip off and wiggle on the stage."

"Heaven knows I tried." She sighed theatrically. "Now I'll die ignorant, thanks to you."

"Damn it all," he laughed, taken aback by her reactions. She made him laugh more than any woman he'd ever known. And lately he'd found himself thinking about her more than he should. Maybe it was just his age, he thought. He'd been alone a long time, and a woman here and there didn't really satisfy him. But Abby wasn't fair game. She was a marrying girl, and he'd better remember that. No way could he seduce her for pleasure, so he had to keep the fires banked down. If he could.

Justin was in his study when they got back, frowning darkly over some figures in his books. When he looked up, his craggy face was devoid of expression, but his dark eyes twinkled when he glanced from Calhoun's irritated expression to Abby's furious one.

"How was the art show?" he asked her.

"It wasn't an art show," Calhoun said flatly, tossing his Stetson onto the coffee table. "It was a male strip show."

Justin's pencil stopped in midair as he stared at Abby. His shock was a little embarrassing, because Justin was even more old-fashioned and reactionary than Calhoun about such things. He wouldn't even talk about anything intimate in mixed company.

"A what?" Justin asked.

"A male revue," Abby countered, glaring at Calhoun. "It's a kind of…variety show."

"Hell," Calhoun retorted, his dark eyes flashing. "It's a strip show!"

"Abby!" Justin scolded.

"I'm almost twenty-one," she told him. "I have a responsible job. I drive a car. I'm old enough to marry and have children. If I want to go and see a male variety show—" she ignored Calhoun's instantly inserted "strip show" "—I have every right."

Justin laid his pencil down and lit a cigarette. Calhoun glared at him, and so did Abby, but he ignored them. The only concession he made to their disapproval was to turn on one of the eight smokeless ashtrays they'd bought him for Christmas.

"That sounds like a declaration of war," Justin remarked.

Abby lifted her chin. "That's what it is." She turned to Calhoun. "If you don't stop embarrassing me in front of the whole world, I'll move in with Misty Davies."

Calhoun's good intentions went up in smoke. "Like hell you will," he countered. "You're not living with that woman!"

"I'll live with her if I want to!"

"If you two would…" Justin began calmly.

"Over my dead body!" Calhoun raged, moving closer. "She has parties that last for days!"

"…just try to communicate…" Justin continued.

"She likes people! She's a socialite!" Abby's eyes were almost black now as she clenched her fists by her sides and glared up at Calhoun.

"…you just might…" Justin went on.

"She's a featherbrained, overstimulated eccentric!" Calhoun retorted.

"…COME TO AN UNDERSTANDING!" Justin thundered, rising out of his chair with blazing eyes.

They both froze at the unfamiliar sound of his raised voice. He never shouted, not even when he was at his angriest.

"Damn, I hurt my ears," Justin sighed, putting his palm to one while he glared at his brother and Abby. "Now, listen, this isn't getting you anywhere. Besides that, any minute Maria and Lopez are going to come running in here thinking someone's been murdered." Just as he finished speaking, two robed, worried elderly people appeared, wide-eyed and apprehensive, in the doorway. "Now see what you've done," Justin grumbled.

"What is all this noise about?" Maria asked, pushing back her long salt-and-pepper hair and glancing worriedly around the room. "We thought something terrible had happened."

"¡Ay de mí! Another rumble." Lopez shook his head

and grinned at Abby. "What have you done now, *ni-ñita*?"

She glared at him. "Nothing," she said tersely. "Not one thing—"

"She went to a male strip show," Calhoun volunteered.

"I did not!" she protested, red faced.

"What is the world coming to?" Maria shook her head, put her hands to it and went out mumbling in Spanish, followed by a chuckling Lopez. The couple, married more than thirty years, had been with the family for two generations. They were family, not just cook and former horse wrangler.

"But, I didn't!" Abby called after them. She darted a speaking glance at Calhoun, who was perched on a corner of Justin's desk looking elegant and imperturbable. "Now see what you've done!"

"Me?" Calhoun asked coolly. "Hell, you're the one with the lurid curiosity."

"Lurid?" She gaped at him. "Go ahead, tell me you've never been to a female strip show."

Calhoun got up, looking uncomfortable. "That's different."

"Oh, sure it is. Women are sex objects but men aren't, right?"

"She's got you there," Justin said.

Calhoun glared at both of them, turned on his heel and left the room. Abby gazed after him smugly, feeling as if she'd won at least a minor victory. There was little consolation in her triumph, though. Calhoun had been harder to get along with than a bone-dry snake at a poison water hole lately. She didn't know how or what, but she was going to have to do something about the situation, and soon.

CHAPTER TWO

ABBY ARRANGED TO miss breakfast the next morning. Calhoun's attitude irritated her. He didn't want her himself, but he was so possessive that she couldn't get near another man. His attitude was frustrating at best. He had no idea how she felt, of course. She was careful to hide her feelings for him. A man like Calhoun, who was rich and moderately handsome, could have any woman he wanted. He wouldn't want a plain, unsophisticated woman like Abby. She knew that, and it hurt. It made her rebellious, too. She didn't want to spend the rest of her life grieving for a man she could never have. It was far better to look in other directions. But how could she, when Calhoun refused to let go?

She drove several miles from the ranch to the office at the mammoth feedlot in the small red British sports car she'd talked Justin into cosigning for when she'd graduated from the local vocational school. Because of the attention Calhoun and Justin paid to hygiene, there wasn't as much odor as most feedlots generated, which surprised a lot of visiting cattlemen. Abby had once gone with Calhoun to tour some other feedlots and had come out with a new respect for the one back home. The Ballenger brothers' operation was a little more expensive to run, but there were hardly any cattle deaths here because of disease. And that was a prime consideration. A rancher who contracted with the feed-lot to fatten his cattle for slaughter didn't want to lose the animals to disease.

Since Abby was early, the office was deserted. There were three other women who worked here, all married, and they helped keep records on the various herds of feeder cattle being fattened for ranches all over the country. There were contracts to sort and file, records on each lot of cattle to keep, and ongoing vaccination and management reports. There was the constant hum of the heavy equipment used to feed the cattle and to remove waste to underground storage to be used later to fertilize pastures where grain was grown. The phones rang constantly and the computers had to be programmed. There was a payroll department, as well as a salesman, a staff veterinarian and a number of cowboys who moved cattle in and out and saw to feeding them and maintaining the machinery that kept it all going. Abby hadn't realized until she'd come to work here how big the operation was.

The sheer size of it was staggering, even for Texas. Fenced areas filled with steers stretched to the horizon, and the dust was formidable, as was the smell, which was inevitable even when sanitary management practices were employed.

The Ballengers didn't own a packing plant—that wasn't legal, just as it wasn't legal for packers to own custom feedlots. But the brothers did own a third of their feeder cattle, and the other two-thirds were custom fed. Abby had grown up hearing terms like profit margin, break-even prices and ration formulation. Now she understood what the words meant.

She put her purse under her desk and turned on her

computer. There were several new contracts waiting to be filled in for new lots of four-footed customers.

The feedlot took in feeder cattle weighing six hundred to seven hundred pounds and fed them up to their slaughter weight of one thousand to eleven hundred pounds. The Ballengers had a resident nutritionist and an experienced stockman who handled the twice-daily feeding routine with its highly automated machinery. They had the feeding down to such a fine art that the Ballenger operation was included in the top five percent of feedlots nationally. And that was a real honor, considering all the things that could go wrong, from falling cattle prices to unexpected epidemics to drought.

Abby was fascinated by the workings of it all. There were thousands of bawling steers and heifers out there. There were always big cattle trucks coming and going and men yelling and herding and vaccinating and dehorning, and the noise could get deafening despite the soundproofed office walls. Visiting cattlemen came to see their investments. Those who didn't come were sent monthly progress reports. Daily records were kept on everything.

Abby fed the first contract into her electronic typewriter, trying to decipher the spidery scrawl of Caudell Ayker, the feedlot office manager. He was second only to Calhoun in the chain of command, because Calhoun's name went in as manager. He and Justin owned the feedlot jointly, but Justin held the lion's share of the stock. Justin preferred money management to meeting with clients, so Calhoun did most of the day-to-day management on the feedlot. That was one reason Abby loved the job. It meant she got to see a lot of Calhoun.

When Calhoun walked in the door in a dashing pale

tan suit, Abby hit the wrong key, covering the contract with a flock of *X*s. She grimaced, backspacing to correct her mistake, and then discovered that she couldn't do it. The correction was too little, too late. Irritated, she ripped the paper out of the machine, put a clean sheet in and started all over again.

"Having problems this morning, honey?" Calhoun asked with his usual cheerful smile, despite the way they'd parted in anger the night before. He never carried grudges. It was one of his virtues.

"Just the usual frustrations, boss," she answered with a blithe smile.

He searched her eyes. They had such a peculiar light in them lately. He found her more and more disturbing, especially when she wore close-fitting suits like the blue one she had on today. It clung lovingly to every line of her tall, slender body, outlining the thrust of her high breasts, the smooth curve of her hips. He took a slow breath, trying to hide his growing attraction to her. It was odd how she'd managed to get under his skin so easily.

"You look nice," he said unexpectedly.

She felt color blush her cheeks, and she smiled. "Thank you."

He hesitated without knowing why, his dark eyes caressing her face, her mouth. "I don't like your hair like that," he added quietly. "I like it long and loose."

She was having a hard time breathing. Her eyes worked up his broad chest to his face and were trapped by his steady gaze. Like electricity, something burst between them, linking them, until she had to drag her eyes down again. Her legs actually trembled.

"I'd better get back to work," she said unsteadily, fiddling with the paper.

"We both had," he replied. He turned and walked into his office without knowing how he got there. Once inside, he sat down behind his big oak desk and stared through the open door at Abby until the buzz of the intercom reminded him of the day's business.

Things went smoothly for a little while, but it was too much to expect that the serenity would last. Just before lunch, one of the cattlemen who had feeder steers in the lot came by to check on them and got an eyeful of Abby.

"You sure are a pretty little thing," the man said, grinning down at the picture she made in her neat blue knit suit and white blouse with her hair in a French twist and a minimum of makeup on her pretty face. He was about Calhoun's age.

She flushed. The man wasn't as handsome as Calhoun, but he was pleasant-looking and he seemed harmless. "Thank you," she said demurely, and smiled at him, just as she smiled at other customers. But he took it as an invitation.

He sat down on the corner of her desk, giving her a purely masculine scrutiny with his pale blue eyes. "I'm Greg Myers," he introduced himself. "I just stopped in on my way to Oklahoma City, and I thought I'd take Calhoun to lunch if he's in. But I think I'd rather take you instead." He lowered his voice, then reached out unexpectedly and touched Abby's cheek, ignoring her indrawn breath. "You pretty little thing. You look like a tea rose, ripe for the picking."

Abby just gaped at him. All her reading and imagining hadn't prepared her for this kind of flirtation with an experienced man. She was out of her depth and frankly stunned.

"Come on, now," Myers drawled, caressing her cheek. "Say you will. We'll have a nice long lunch and get to know each other."

While Abby was searching for the right words to extricate herself from the unwelcome situation, Calhoun came out of his office and stood directly behind Mr. Myers, looking suddenly murderous.

"I'm afraid you'll have to settle for me," Calhoun said tersely. "Abby's my ward, and she doesn't date older men."

"Oops." Myers stood up, grinning sheepishly. "Sorry, old son, I didn't know."

"No harm done," Calhoun said carelessly, but his eyes were dark and cold and dangerous-looking. "Let's go. Abby, I'll want the latest progress report on his cattle when we get back."

Only a few months before, Abby might have had some snappy reply to that, or she might have jumped back at Calhoun for acting so possessive. But now she just looked at him, feeling helpless and hungry and awash on a wave of longing because he was acting jealous.

He seemed to stop breathing, too. His dark eyes searched hers, aware of her embarrassment, her confusion. He let his gaze fall to her mouth and watched her lips part suddenly, and his body reacted in a way that shocked him.

"Lunch. Now." Calhoun ushered the other cattleman to the door. "If you'll get in the car, I'll just get my hat and be right with you," he told the man with a glued-on smile and a pat on the shoulder. "That's right, you go ahead…." He turned to Abby, his expression un-readable. "I want to talk to you." Calhoun took her arm and pulled her up, leading her into his office without a word. He closed the door, and the way he looked at her made her feel threatened and wildly excited all at the same time.

"Mr. Myers is waiting…." she faltered, disturbed by the darkness of his eyes as they met hers.

He moved toward her, and she backed up until his desk stopped her, her eyes riveted to his. Maybe he was going to make a declaration!

His chin lifted then, and it was anger that glinted in his dark eyes, not possessiveness. "Listen," he said curtly, "Greg Myers has had three wives. He currently has at least one mistress. He's forgotten more than you've had time to learn. I don't want you to learn that kind of lesson with a professional Romeo."

"I'm going to learn it with someone eventually," she said, swallowing hard. Her body felt odd, taut and tingling all at once, because his was close enough that she could feel its warm strength.

"I know that," he said impatiently, and his face hardened. "But I'd just as soon you didn't join a queue. Myers is no serious suitor. He's a playboy with a smooth manner, and he'd have you screaming for help five minutes after you were alone with him."

So that was it. More big-brother responsibility. He wasn't jealous, he was upset because his protective instincts had been aroused. She stared at the steady rise and fall of his chest in dull acceptance. *Stupid me*, she thought miserably, *wishing for a star again*.

"I wasn't trying to lead him on," she said finally. "I just smiled at him, like I smile at everyone—even you.

I guess he thought I was sending out smoke signals, but I wasn't, honestly."

His face relaxed. "No harm done." And then he moved. One long, powerful arm slid behind her, bringing his lips within an inch of hers. She almost moaned at the minty warmth of his breath on her mouth. Her gaze dropped to his mouth, curiously tracing every hard line of the thin upper lip and the more chiseled lower one. Her heart throbbed. Her breath seemed to stop altogether, and for one long instant she felt the full weight of his chest against her soft breasts in a contact that was shocking. She looked up at him with wide, stunned eyes.

Then he moved back, the hat he'd been reaching for in one hand, his eyes frankly amused at the look on her face. So she'd never thought of him that way, had she? It irritated him to think that she didn't feel the new and very unwelcome attraction he was discovering for her. It was just as well that he had a business function tonight; it would keep his overimaginative brain away from Abby.

"Were you expecting something?" he asked coldly. "I just wanted my hat." He watched a shadow pass across her eyes before she mumbled something and lowered her gaze. He put his Stetson on his thick blond-streaked hair and tilted it over one eye. "I hired you to work here, not to send out signals, intentional or otherwise, to clients."

"I hate you," she said suddenly, sick of his accusations and his hateful remarks.

"Sure you do. What else is new?" He tapped her chin with a long finger. "Get busy."

While she was still struggling with her composure

he opened the door and went out without a backward glance.

Abby hardly got anything done for the next hour. She couldn't remember a time when she'd felt so turned around, so confused. She was sure she hated Calhoun, but in an hour he'd be back, smiling, and then she'd forgive him. That was what made her so miserable, the knowledge that he could commit murder and she'd still love him. Damn this hateful attraction!

She took a half-hour break and went to the canteen and had a sandwich that she didn't taste. She was barely back at her desk when Mr. Myers returned—with Justin instead of Calhoun.

She handed the progress reports to Justin, who herded Mr. Myers into his brother's office, kept him there a scant ten minutes and then herded him out again. Abby kept her head down and didn't even say hello. That was just as well, because Mr. Myers didn't look in her direction.

Justin gave Abby a curious look afterward. "That's unusual," he remarked. "Calhoun called me out of a board meeting to have lunch and talk over that contract with Myers. Then he waltzed off and left me there. What's going on?"

Abby cleared her throat. "Why, Justin, I have no idea," she said, even managing a smile. Justin lifted an eyebrow, shrugged and went back into Calhoun's office without another word. Abby stared after him, curious herself about Calhoun's behavior. Then it occurred to her that maybe he just didn't like Greg Myers, which led to the unpalatable thought that perhaps they'd fallen out over a woman. Maybe one of Myers's mistresses... She turned back to her typewriter. She hated even thinking about that side of Calhoun's life.

Justin was quiet for the rest of the afternoon, but he had plenty to say when Calhoun came in just before quitting time. The door was half-open, and Abby, who was the last of the office group to leave, got an earful as she was straightening up her desk.

"This has got to stop," Justin was telling his brother. "One of the office girls told me that Myers got friendly with Abby just before you cleared out. It's gotten to the point that Abby can't even smile at a man without having you come down on her head like Judgment. She's almost twenty-one. It isn't fair to expect her to live like a recluse."

"I wasn't," Calhoun said curtly. "I just warned her off him. My God, you know his reputation!"

"Abby's no fool," came the reply. "She's a level-headed person."

"Sure, she's proved that," Calhoun said with biting sarcasm. "Going to a strip show—"

"It was not!" Abby called through the open door. "It was a male variety show."

"My God, she's standing out there listening!" Calhoun jerked the door all the way open, glaring at her. "Stop eavesdropping! It isn't polite!"

"Stop talking about me behind my back, then," she returned, picking up her purse. "I wouldn't have gone out with a man like Greg Myers even to spite you, Calhoun. I know a line when I hear one."

Calhoun glared at her. "I'm not sure it's a good idea, your working here."

Her eyebrows went up. "Really? Why?"

"The place is full of men," Calhoun muttered, and Justin had to smother a grin.

Abby lifted her eyebrows and smiled. "Why, so it is," she gushed. "Lovely, unshaven men who smell of cattle and cow chips. Sooo romantic," she sighed.

Justin had turned away. Calhoun's dark eyes were glittering.

"Myers didn't smell of cow chips," he reminded her.

She arched her eyebrows at him. "How interesting that you noticed," she said in a theatrical whisper.

He looked as if he wanted to throw something at her. "Will you cut that out?" he muttered.

She sighed. "Suit yourself. I was just trying to help. God forbid that I should be seduced by some strange, sweet-smelling man."

"Go home!" Calhoun roared.

"My, my, what a nasty temper we're in," she said demurely. She reached for her purse, glancing back at him. "I'll have Maria make you a nice bowl of razor-blade soup, just to keep your tongue sharp."

"I won't be home for supper, thank God," Calhoun said coldly. "I've got a date," he added, for no other reason than to irritate her. He didn't like the idea of her knowing how much Myers's flirting had upset him. He didn't want her to know that he'd been so violently jealous that he couldn't even trust himself to have lunch with the man and had had to call Justin to intervene.

But Abby didn't know that, and she was sure that it was just Calhoun being overprotective as usual. It hurt her to hear about where he was going. Abby felt as if she were being choked to death. If only she were beautiful and blonde, if only she could cope! But she managed to hide her emptiness. "That's great, Calhoun, you just enjoy yourself while I sit home alone. I'll never get a date as long as you're two steps behind me."

"Dream on," Calhoun told her. "Hell will freeze over before you'd go out with a man like that."

"There's a little town called Hell, you know," Abby told him. "It does snow there...."

"If I were you I'd go home, Abby," Justin said, eyeing his brother. "It's Friday night. You might find a nice movie to watch. Come to think of it, I just bought a new war movie. You can watch it with me if you want to."

She smiled. Justin really was nice. "Thanks. I might do that, since my watchdog doesn't want me out after dark," she added with a glare at Calhoun. "I'll bet Elizabeth the First had a guardian just like you!"

Justin caught Calhoun in the nick of time, and Abby took off running, her heart in her throat. It was odd how Calhoun, usually so easygoing, had turned explosive lately. She did goad him, of course, but she couldn't help it. Fighting him was the only way she could stay sane and hide her feelings for him. If she ever started batting her eyelashes and sighing over him, he'd probably shoot her off the place like a bullet.

She started her car and drove home, all the fury dying into misery as she left the feedlot behind. What good was pretending? Her heart was broken, because Calhoun was going out with one of his women and she didn't qualify for that title. She never would. She'd grow old with Calhoun patting her on the head. Once or twice she'd almost thought he felt something for her, that he'd begun to notice her. But if he had, he certainly wouldn't be running all over the place with other women. And he wouldn't ignore Abby unless she started a fight or got into trouble. She was his responsibility, of course.

His headache. To him she was anything but a warm, attractive woman whom he might love eventually. That she'd never be.

By the time she got to the house, she felt sick all over, but a plan was beginning to form in her mind. If Calhoun thought she was giving in that easily, he was in for a shock. She could have a good time, too, even if she didn't have a date. By golly, she'd get out and find herself one!

CHAPTER THREE

ABBY ATE A solitary meal. Justin was called to the phone shortly after they got home, and he told Maria to put his dinner on a tray so he could eat it while he watched the movie he'd bought. Calhoun had come home to change for his date, and Abby had made a beeline for her room and stayed there until after he'd left. She didn't even care how it looked; she was sick at the thought of Calhoun with some faceless blonde. That was when she knew she had to break out, even if just for the evening.

She hadn't started out to rebel. But she couldn't sit home and watch the movie with Justin. She'd never hear a word of it; she'd just brood about Calhoun.

So she got dressed in slacks and a blouse and brushed her hair. Then she called Misty.

"How do you feel about helping me rebel?" she asked the older girl.

Misty laughed huskily. "You're lucky my date canceled out. Okay. I'm game. What are we rebelling against?"

"Calhoun caught me at the revue last night and dragged me home," Abby told her. "And today he... Well, never mind, but he set me off again. So tonight I thought I'd like to sample that new dance bar in Jacobsville."

"Now that is an idea worthy of you, Abby. I'll pick you up in fifteen minutes."

"I'll be ready."

Abby ran downstairs, giving no thought at all to how Calhoun was going to react to this latest rebellion. Well, he had his woman, damn him. Horrible pictures of his bronzed body in bed with the faceless blonde danced in front of Abby's eyes. No, she told herself, she wasn't going to let Calhoun's actions hurt her like that. She was going to get out and live!

She poked her head into the living room. Cigarette smoke drifted in front of a screen on which men in uniforms were blowing each other up.

"I'm going out with Misty," she told Justin.

He glanced up from where he was sitting. His long legs were crossed over the coffee table, and he had a snifter of brandy in one hand and a cigarette in the other. "Okay, honey," he said agreeably. "Stay out of trouble, will you? You and Calhoun are hell on the digestion lately, and he doesn't seem to need much excuse to go for your throat."

"I'll behave. Misty and I are just going to that new dance place. I'll be good, honest I will. Good night."

"Good night."

He went back to the bullets and bombs, and she closed the door with a sigh. Justin was so nice. He never tried to hog-tie her. Now why couldn't Calhoun be like that? She felt murderous when she considered Calhoun's possessiveness. She was entitled to a life that didn't revolve around him. There was just no sense in wearing her heart out on his taciturn indifference. None at all!

Misty came ten minutes later. Thank God, Calhoun didn't reappear. With a sigh of relief, Abby ran out to Misty's little sports car, all smiles, her breaking heart carefully concealed from her all-too-perceptive girl-friend.

It was Friday night, and the Jacobsville Dance Palace was booming. It had a live Western band on the week-ends, and while it did serve hard liquor, it wasn't the kind of dive Calhoun had forbidden her to frequent. Not that she cared one whit about his strictures, of course.

Abby glanced apprehensively toward the doorway, across the crowded room where cigar and cigarette smoke made a gray haze under bright lights. The band's rhythm shook the rafters. Couples danced on the bare wood floor, the men in Western gear, the women in jeans and boots.

"Calhoun won't know you're here, I tell you." Misty laughed softly. "Honestly, it's ridiculous the way he dogs your footsteps lately."

"That's what I keep telling him, but it does no good at all," Abby replied miserably. "I just want to get out on my own."

"I'm doing my best," Misty assured her. "Any day now I'll have some new apartment prospects for us to look at. I've got a real estate agent helping."

"Good." Abby sipped her drink, trying not to notice the blatant stare she was getting from the man at the next table. He'd been eyeing her ever since she and Misty had walked in, and he was giving her the willies. He looked about Calhoun's age, but he lacked Calhoun's attractive masculinity. This man was dark headed and had a beer belly. He wasn't much taller than Abby, but what he lacked in height he made up in girth. He had a cowboy hat pulled low over his small eyes, and he was obviously intoxicated.

"He's staring at me again," Abby muttered. She lifted

her gin and tonic to her lips, wondering at how much better it tasted every time she took a sip. She hated gin, but Misty had convinced her that she couldn't sit at the table drinking ginger ale.

"Don't worry." Misty patted her arm. "He'll give up and go away. There's Tyler! Hi, Ty!"

Tyler Jacobs was tall and rangy-looking. He had green eyes and an arrogant smile, and Abby was a little afraid of him. But he didn't carry his wealth around on his shoulders as some rich men did, and he wasn't a snob, even though the town of Jacobsville took its name from his grandfather.

"Hello, Misty. Abby." Tyler pulled out a chair and straddled it. "What are you doing here? Does Calhoun know?" he asked quietly.

Abby shifted restlessly in the chair and raised her glass to her lips again. "I am perfectly capable of drinking a drink if I want to," she said, enunciating carefully because her tongue suddenly felt thick. "And Calhoun doesn't own me."

"Oh, my God," Tyler sighed. He gave Misty a rueful glance. "Your doing, I gather?"

Misty blinked her long false lashes at Tyler, and her blue eyes twinkled. "I provided transportation, that's all. Abby is my friend. I'm helping her to rebel."

"You'll help get her killed if you aren't careful. Where's Calhoun?" he asked Abby.

"Out with one of his harem," she said with a mocking smile. "Not that I mind, as long as he's out of my hair for the evening," she added carelessly.

"He dragged her out of line at the male revue last night at the Jacobsville theater," Misty explained. "We're getting even."

Tyler's eyes widened. "You tried to see a male strip show? Abby!"

Abby glared at him. "Where else do you expect me to get educated? Calhoun wants me to wear diapers for the rest of my life. He doesn't think I'm old enough to go on dates or walk across the street alone."

"You're like a kid sister to him," Tyler said, defending his friend. "He doesn't want you to get hurt."

"I can get hurt if I like," Abby grumbled. Her eyes closed. She was feeling worse by the second, but she couldn't let on. Tyler was as bad as the Ballenger brothers. He'd have her out of here like a shot if he thought she was sick.

"What are you drinking?" Tyler asked, staring at her glass.

"Gin and tonic," she replied, opening her eyes. "Want some?"

"I don't drink, honey," Tyler reminded her with a slow smile. "Well, I've got to pick up Shelby at the office. She had to work late tonight. Watch out for Abby, Misty."

"Of course I will. Sure you won't stay and dance with me?" Misty asked.

Tyler got up, his eyes worried as they trailed over Abby's wan face. "Sorry. I don't usually have to get Shelby, but her car was in the shop today and they didn't finish with it."

"Lucky Shelby, to have a brother like you," Abby mumbled. "I'll bet you don't have a kamikaze pilot fly behind her when she goes to work, or a gang of prize-fighters to walk her home after dark, or a whole crew of off-duty policemen to fend off her suitors...."

"Oh, boy," Tyler sighed.

"Don't worry," Misty told him. "She's fine. She's just miffed at Calhoun, that's all. Although how anybody could get upset at a dishy man like that being so protective—"

"Dishy isn't a word I'd use to describe Calhoun if he finds Abby like that and thinks you're responsible for it," Tyler cautioned. "Have you ever seen him get angry?"

Misty pushed back her curly hair uncomfortably. "Justin's temper is worse," she reminded him.

Tyler lifted an eyebrow. "Don't be so sure. They're cut from the same cloth." He touched Abby's shoulder. "Don't drink any more of that." He gestured toward her drink.

"Whatever you say, Ty," Abby said, smiling. "Good night."

"Good night."

He waved and left them there.

"I wonder what he was doing here," Misty said, puzzled. "Since he doesn't drink."

"He may have been looking for somebody," Abby murmured. "I guess a lot of cattlemen congregate around here on the weekends. This stuff is pretty good, Misty," she added, taking another sip.

"You promised you wouldn't," she was reminded.

"I hate men," Abby said. "I hate all men. But especially I hate Calhoun."

Misty chewed her lower lip worriedly. Abby was starting to tie one on, and that wasn't at all what Misty had had in mind. "I'll be back in a minute, honey," she promised, and got up to go after Ty. She had a feeling she was going to need his help to get Abby to the car, and now was the time to do it.

The minute she left, the burly, intoxicated man who'd been watching Abby for the past hour seized his opportunity. He sat down next to her, his small, pale eyes running hungrily over her.

"Alone at last," he drawled. "My gosh, you're a pretty thing. I'm Tom. I live alone and I'm looking for a woman who can cook and clean and make love. How about coming home with me?"

Abby gaped at him. "I don't think I heard you?"

"If you're here with a girlfriend, you've got to be out looking for it, honey." He laughed drunkenly. "And I can sure give it to you. So how about it?" He put his pudgy-fingered hand on her arm and began to caress it. "Nice. Come here and give old Tom a kiss…."

He pulled her toward him. She protested violently, and in the process managed to knock her drink over onto him. He cursed a blue streak and stood up, holding her by the wrist, homicide in his drunken eyes.

"You did that on purpose," he shot at her. "You soaked me deliberately! Well, let me tell you, lady, no broad pours liquor on me and gets away with it!"

Abby felt even sicker. He was hurting her wrist, and there was a deathly hush around them. She knew that most people didn't involve themselves in this kind of conflict. She couldn't fight this man and win, but what else was she going to do? She wanted to cry.

"Let her go."

The voice was deep, slow, dangerous and best of all, familiar. Abby caught her breath as a tall, heavily built blond man came toward her, his dark, deep-set eyes on the man who had Abby's wrist. He was in a gray vested suit and a dressy cream-colored Stetson and boots, but Abby knew the trappings of civilized company wouldn't save this ruddy cretin if he didn't turn her loose. Abby had seen Calhoun lose his temper, and she knew how hard he could hit when he did.

"What's she to you?" the drunken cowboy demanded.

"My ward."

Calhoun caught the smaller man's wrist in a hard grasp and twisted. The man groaned and went down, holding his hand and cursing.

"Hey, you can't do that to Tom!" one of the man's cronies protested, standing up. He was almost Calhoun's size, and a lot rougher-looking.

"Want to make something out of it, sonny?" Calhoun asked in a soft drawl that was belied by the dark glitter in his eyes.

"You bet I do!"

The younger man threw a punch, but he was too slow. Calhoun's big fists put him over a table. He reached down and picked up the Stetson that the man's blow had connected with and looked around the room as he ran his fingers through his thick, silky blond hair.

"Anybody else?" he invited pleasantly.

Eyes turned the other way, and the band started playing again. Then Calhoun looked down at Abby.

She swallowed. "Hi," she said, and tried to smile. "I thought you were out on a date."

He didn't say a word, but his glittering eyes told her every single thing he was feeling. He wouldn't admit for a minute that his dinner date was strictly business, or that he'd expected something like this after the argument he and Abby had had. She was giving him fits, but he didn't let his expression show how concerned he really was.

"Did you see Misty?" she asked hopefully.

"Luckily for her, no," he said in a tone that could have boiled ice water. "Get your purse."

She fumbled on the chair beside hers for it, weak and shaky. He had a gift for intimidating people, she thought, watching him slam his Stetson over his eyes at a slant. The men who were picking themselves up off the floor didn't seem anxious to tangle with him twice. It was amazing, she thought, how unruffled he looked for a man who'd just been in a fight.

He caught her arm and propelled her out of the bar and into the night air. Misty and Ty were standing just outside, both looking faintly apprehensive.

"It wasn't all my fault, Cal," Misty began in a subdued tone.

Calhoun eyed her coldly. "You know what I think of this so-called friendship. And I know the reason behind it, even if she doesn't."

Abby was puzzled by that remark. The cold, level look in Calhoun's dark eyes and the uncomfortable flush in Misty's pretty face didn't add up.

"I'd better go get Shelby," Ty said quietly. "I was going to offer to take Abby home, but under the circumstances I'm a bit relieved that you came along," he told Calhoun.

"If Justin finds out you were in the same room with her, there'll be hell to pay," Calhoun agreed. "But thanks all the same." He turned Abby toward his Jaguar. "I assume you rode into town with your girlfriend?" he added.

"We came in Misty's car," Abby murmured. She felt weary and a little sick. Now she really looked like a child, with all the concerned adults making a fuss over her. Tears burned in her eyes, which she was careful to keep hidden from the angry man beside her.

"Honest to God," he muttered as he put her into the passenger seat and went around to get into the driver's seat. "I don't know what the hell's wrong with you lately. Last night I find you in line at a male strip show, and tonight you're getting drunk and eyeing strange men in bars!"

"I was not eyeing that lewd creature," she said unsteadily. "And you can't say I was dressed to invite his kind of comment. I'm not wearing anything that's the least bit immodest!"

He glanced at her. "You were in a bar unescorted. That's all the invitation that kind of man needs!"

She felt his gaze on her, but she wouldn't look at him. She knew she'd cry if she did. She clasped her hands firmly in her lap and stared out the window instead as he started the car and headed for home.

It was a long ride, over deserted paved roads and dirt ones that led past the huge feedlot and then uphill to the house, which sat on a level plain about three miles away.

"Do you want me to carry you?" he asked stiffly as he helped her out of the car and she stumbled.

She pushed away from him as if she'd touched hot coals. "No, thank you." He was making her more nervous than ever tonight. The scent of him filled her nostrils, all leathery and spicy and clean. She averted her eyes and walked as straight as she could toward the kitchen door. "Are you going to sneak me in the back way so that Justin doesn't see me?" she challenged.

"Justin told me where to find you," Calhoun said as he put the key in the lock and opened the back door. "He's still watching his war movie."

"Oh." She walked through the door he was holding open for her. "I thought you were out on a date."

"Never mind where I was," he said curtly. "My God, I really must have radar."

She flushed. Thank God he couldn't see her face. She felt odd tonight. Frightened and nervous and a little unsure of herself. The gin had taken away some of her inhibitions, and she had to be careful not to let Calhoun see how vulnerable she felt when he came close to her.

She went in ahead of him, barely noticing the huge, spotless kitchen with its modern conveniences, or the hall, or the mahogany staircase she began to climb. Behind the closed living room door, bombs were going off in a softly muted way, indicating that Justin's war movie was still running.

"Abby."

She stopped, her back to him, trying not to show how nervous she felt. He was behind her, much too close, and she could smell the fresh, clean scent of his body and the spicy cologne he wore.

"What's wrong, honey?" he asked.

His tone broke her heart. He used it with little things—a newborn kitten, or a filly he was working for the first time. He used it with children. He'd used it with Abby the day her mother had died in the wreck. It had been Calhoun who'd found her and broken the news to her and then held her while she cried. It was the tone he used when something was hurt.

She straightened, trying hard to keep her back straight and her legs under control. "That man…" she began, unable to tell him he was breaking her heart because he couldn't love her.

"Damn that drunken—" He turned her, his strong

hands gentle on her upper arms, his dark eyes blazing down into hers. He was so big, and none of it was fat. He was all muscle, lean and powerful, all man. "You're all right," he said softly. "Nothing happened."

"Of course not," she whispered miserably. "You rescued me. You always rescue me." Her eyes closed, and a tear started down her cheek. "But hasn't it occurred to you that I'm always going to land in trouble if you don't let me solve my own problems?" She looked up at him through a mist. "You have to let go of me," she whispered huskily, and her eyes reflected her heartbreak. "You have to, Calhoun."

There was a lot of truth in what she said, and he didn't really know how to respond. He worried about her. This strange restlessness of hers, this urge to run from him, wasn't like Abby. She was melancholy, when for the past five years or more she'd been a vibrant, happy little imp, always laughing and playing with him, teasing him, making him laugh. She couldn't know how somber the house had been when she'd first come to live with him and Justin. Justin never laughed anyway, and Calhoun had come to be like him. But Abby had brought the sunshine. She'd colored the world. He scowled down at her, wondering how she did it. She wasn't pretty. She was plain, and she was serious a good bit of the time. But when she laughed... When she laughed, she was beautiful.

His hands contracted. "I wouldn't mind if you'd go to conventional places," he muttered. "First I catch you in line to watch a bunch of nude men parade around a stage, and the very next night you're drinking gin and tonic in a bar. Why?" he asked, his deep voice soft with curiosity and concern.

She shifted. "I'm just curious about those things," she said finally.

He searched her eyes quietly. "That isn't it," he replied, his own gaze narrowing. His hands shifted, gentle on her arms, Abby could feel their warmth through the fabric. "Something's eating you alive. Can't you tell me what it is?"

She drew in her breath. She'd almost forgotten how perceptive he was. He seemed to see right through to the bone and blood sometimes. She let her gaze drop to his chest, and she watched its lazy rise and fall under his gray vest. He was hairy under his shirt. She'd seen him once in a while on his way to or from the shower, and it had been all she could do not to reach out and run her hands over him. He had thick brown hair across his tanned chest, and it had golden tips where it curled. There was a little wave in his thick blond hair, not much, but enough that it was unruly around his ears. She let her gaze go up, feeding on him, lingering just above his dimpled chin at the thin but sensuous curve of his upper lip and the faintly square, chiseled fullness of his lower lip. He had a sexy mouth. His nose was sexy, too. Very straight and imposing. He had high cheekbones, and thick eyebrows on a jutting brow that shadowed his deep-set eyes. He had black eyes. Both the Ballengers did. But Calhoun was something to look at, and poor old Justin was as rangy-looking as a longhorn bull by comparison.

"Abby, are you listening to me?" Calhoun murmured, shaking her gently because her faintly intoxicated stare was setting his blood on fire.

Her eyes levered up to his, finding darkness in them, secrets, shadows. Her lips parted on a hopeless sigh. When Misty had told her last week about seeing him with some ravishing blonde up in Houston, it had knocked her for a loop, bringing home the true hopelessness of her situation. Calhoun liked sophisticated women. He'd never look twice at drab little Abby. Once Abby had faced that unpalatable fact, she'd been on a one-way road to misery. She'd been looking for an escape, last night and tonight, but she couldn't find one. Wherever she turned, Calhoun was there, hounding her, not realizing how badly he was hurting her.

"What did you say?" she asked miserably.

His chest rose and fell roughly. "It's hopeless trying to talk to you in this condition. Go to bed."

"That's just where I was headed," she said.

She turned and started up the staircase ahead of him, her eyes burning with tears that she was too proud to let him see. Oh, Calhoun, she moaned inwardly, you're killing me!

She went into her room and closed the door behind her. She almost locked it, but realized that would be a joke and a half. Locking a door against Calhoun was a hilarious idea. He'd as soon come looking for a lady vampire as to look at Abby with amorous intent. She started laughing as she went into the bathroom to bathe her face, and she almost couldn't stop.

CHAPTER FOUR

ABBY MANAGED TO get into the silver satin nightgown, but she couldn't seem to fasten it in the front. The gown hung open over her full, firm breasts. She looked at herself in the mirror as she passed it, fascinated by the sophistication the unbuttoned state lent her. She looked oddly mature with the pink swell of her breasts blatantly revealed and her long hair tangled around her face. Then she laughed at her own fancy and stretched out on top of the pale pink coverlet on her canopied bed.

The whole room was decorated in shades of pink and white with blue accents. She loved it. The Ballengers had let her choose her own colors, and these were what she favored. Very feminine colors, even if she wasn't a sophisticated blonde. She shifted restlessly on the cover, and the bodice of her gown came completely away from one breast. Her eyes closed. What did it matter, she thought as she drifted off to sleep. There was no one to see her.

No one except Calhoun, who eased the door open with an expression of concern in his dark eyes. He saw something that knocked the breath out of him.

Abby was barely conscious. She didn't even open her eyes when he came into the room. It was just as well, because he knew he wouldn't be lucid if he had to speak. He'd never thought of Abby as a woman, but the sight of her in that silky drift of silver fabric, with one exquisite breast completely bare and her slender body outlined to its best advantage, shot through him like fire.

He stood frozen in the doorway, facing for the first time the fact that Abby was an adult. No sane man who saw her lying there like that could ever think of her as a child again. And even as the thought formed he realized why he hadn't been himself lately, why he'd deliberately antagonized her, why he'd been so overprotective. He...wanted her.

He closed the door absently behind him and moved closer to her. God, she was lovely! His face hardened as he stared down at her, helplessly feeding on the sensuous nudity she wasn't even aware of.

He wondered if she'd ever let any of her dates see her like this, and a murderous rage stiffened his tall form. He hated the thought of that. Of another man looking at her, touching her, putting his mouth on that soft swell and searching for a tip that he could make hard with the warm pressure of his open mouth....

He shook himself. This wouldn't do. "Abby," he said tersely.

She stirred, but only to shift on the bed so that the whole damned bodice fell open. He actually trembled at the sweetness of her pretty pink breasts with their delicate mauve tips relaxed in sleep.

He muttered something explosive and forced himself to bend over her, to pull the fabric together and fasten it. His hands shook. Thank God she wasn't awake to witness his vulnerability.

She moaned when his hard knuckles came into contact with her skin, and she arched slightly in her sleep.

His lips parted on a rough breath. Her skin was like

silk, warm and sensuous. He gritted his teeth and caught the last button. Then he scooped her up in his arms and stood holding her propped on one knee while he tore the covers loose and stripped back the colorful pink patterned top sheet over the soft blue fitted one.

Her eyes blinked and opened lazily. She searched his hard face, smiling faintly. "I'm asleep," she whispered, nuzzling close. Her sweet scent and the feel of her soft body in his arms overwhelmed him.

"Are you?" he asked, his voice deeper, huskier than he wanted it to be. He laid her down on the sheet, cupping the back of her head in his hand while he drew a pillow under it, his mouth just above hers.

Her hands were around his neck. He drew them down and pulled the covers up over her with a feeling of relief.

"I never had anybody tuck me in before," she mumbled drowsily.

"Don't expect a bedtime story," he murmured, his deep voice lazy with forced humor. "You're too young for the only ones I know."

"I guess I am. Too young for everything. Much too young." She sighed heavily, as her eyes closed. "Oh, Calhoun, I wish I was blonde...."

"Now what brought that on?" he asked, but she was asleep again. He looked down at her softly flushed sleeping face, his eyes narrow and dark and thoughtful. After a minute he turned and went out, flicking off the light behind him.

Justin was coming out of the living room when Calhoun got back downstairs.

"Did you bring Abby home?" Justin asked his brother.

"Yes. She's in bed. Dead drunk," Calhoun added

with a faintly amused smile. He'd already taken off his Stetson, along with his jacket and vest.

Justin's dark eyes narrowed. "What's wrong with you? Your lip is cut."

"A slight altercation in the local bar and dance hall," Calhoun said sardonically. He went to the brandy bottle and poured himself half a snifterful. He swirled it, staring into the glass. "Want one?"

Justin shook his head and lit a cigarette instead, ignoring Calhoun's pointed glare of disapproval.

"What were you fighting about?"

Calhoun sipped his brandy. "Abby."

Justin turned, his dark eyebrows arching. "Abby?"

"Misty Davies took her to a bar."

"Last night a nude revue, tonight a bar." Justin stared at his cigarette. "Something's eating our girl."

"I know. I just don't know what. I don't like what Misty's doing, either, but I can't tell Abby."

Justin cocked his head as he drew on the cigarette. "She's trying to get back at you through Abby, I gather."

"Got it in one." Calhoun raised the brandy snifter mockingly before he drained it. "She came on to me hard, and I turned her down. My God, as if I'd be crazy enough to seduce Abby's best friend."

"Misty should have known that. Is Abby all right?"

"I guess," Calhoun said, not adding that he'd put her to bed himself or that she was the reason he was drinking, something he rarely did. "Some red-faced jackass was manhandling her."

Justin whirled. "And?"

"I think I knocked one of his teeth out."

"Good for you. All the same, she needs watching."

"I'll say amen to that. Shall we flip a coin?" Calhoun asked with pursed lips.

"Why should I interfere when you're doing such a good job of looking out for her interests?" Justin asked, smiling faintly. His smile faded as he searched the younger man's troubled eyes. "You do remember that Abby turns twenty-one in three months? And I think she's already been apartment-hunting with Misty."

Calhoun's face hardened. "Misty will corrupt her. I don't want Abby passed around like an hors d'oeuvre by some of Misty's sophisticated boyfriends."

Justin's eyebrows arched. That didn't sound like Calhoun. Come to think of it, Calhoun didn't *look* like Calhoun. "Abby's our ward," he reminded his brother. "We don't own her. We don't have the right to make her decisions for her, either."

Calhoun glared at him. "What do you want me to do, let her be picked up and assaulted by any drunken cowboy who comes along? Like bloody hell I will!"

He turned on his heel and walked out of the room. Justin pursed his thin lips and smiled softly to himself.

ABBY WOKE THE next morning with a headache and a feeling of impending doom. She sat up, clutching her head. It was seven o'clock, and she had to be to work by 8:30. Even now, breakfast would be underway downstairs. Breakfast. She swallowed her nausea.

She got out of bed unsteadily and went into the bathroom to wash her face and brush her teeth. She managed that and felt much better. As she started to get out of her gown, she noticed that the buttons were fastened. Odd. She was sure she'd left the thing unbuttoned. Oh, well, she must have gotten it buttoned and climbed in under the covers sometime before dawn.

It was Saturday, but ordinarily the feedlot stayed open. The cattle still had to be looked after, and the paperwork had to be done no matter what day it was. Abby had gotten used to the long work week, and it was just routine not to have her Saturdays free. She could get off at noon sometimes if she needed to go somewhere. But that hadn't been her habit in recent months. She was hungry for the sight of Calhoun, and he was there most weekends.

She got into a pale gray suit with a blue silk print blouse and put her hair into a French twist. She used a little makeup—not much—and slid her nylon-encased feet into tiny stacked high heels. Well, she was no ravishing beauty, that was for sure, but she wouldn't disgrace herself. She was going down with all flags flying. Calhoun would be mad as fury, and she couldn't let him see how pale she was.

The Ballenger brothers were both at the table when she got downstairs. Calhoun glanced at her, his gaze odd and brooding, as she sat between him and Justin.

"It's about time," he said curtly. "You look like hell, and it serves you right. I'll be damned if I'll have you passing out in bars with that Davies woman!"

"Please, Calhoun, not before I eat," Abby murmured. "My head hurts."

"No wonder," he shot back.

"Stop cussing at my breakfast table," Justin told him firmly.

"I'll stop when you do," Calhoun told his brother, just as firmly.

"Oh, hell," Justin muttered, and bit into one of Maria's fluffy biscuits.

Ordinarily that byplay would have made Abby smile, but she felt too dragged-out to care. She sipped black coffee and nibbled at buttered toast, refusing anything more nourishing.

"You need to take some aspirins before you go to work, Abby," Justin said gently.

She managed to smile at him. "I will. I guess gin isn't really my drink."

"Liquor isn't healthy," Calhoun said shortly.

Justin's eyebrows lifted. "Then why were you emptying my brandy bottle last night?"

Calhoun threw down his napkin. "I'm going to work."

"You might offer Abby a lift," Justin suggested with a strangely calculating expression.

"I'm not going directly to the feedlot," Calhoun said. He didn't want to be alone with Abby, not after the way he'd seen her the night before. He could hardly look at her without remembering her lying across that bed....

"I'm not through with breakfast," Abby replied, hurt that Calhoun didn't seem to want her company. "Besides," she told Justin with a faint smile, "I can drive. I didn't really have all that much to drink."

"Sure," Calhoun replied harshly, dark eyes blazing. "That's why you passed out on your bed."

Abby knew she'd stopped breathing. Justin was pouring cream into his second cup of coffee, his keen eyes on the pitcher, not on the other occupants of the room. And that was a good thing, because Abby looked up at Calhoun with sudden stark knowledge of what he'd seen the night before and had her fears confirmed by the harsh stiffening of his features.

She blushed and started, almost knocking over her cup. So she had gone to sleep on the covers. Calhoun found her with her bodice undone, he'd seen her—

"Never mind breakfast. Let's go," Calhoun said suddenly, his lean hand on the back of her chair. "I'll take you to the feedlot before I do what I have to. You're not fit to drive."

Justin was watching now, his gaze narrow and frankly curious as it went from Abby's red face to Calhoun's taut expression.

That look was what told Abby that Calhoun was the lesser of the two evils. She couldn't tell Justin what had happened, but he'd have it out of her in two seconds if she didn't make a run for it. Calhoun must have realized that, too.

He took her arm and almost pulled her out of the chair, propelling her out of the room with a curt good-bye to his brother.

"Will you slow down?" she moaned as he took the steps two at a time. "My legs aren't long enough to keep up with you, and my head is splitting."

"You need a good headache," he muttered without a glance in her direction. "Maybe it will take some of the adventure out of your soul."

She glared at his broad back in silence as she followed him to the Jaguar and got into the passenger seat.

He started the car and reversed it, but he didn't go toward the feedlot. He went down the driveway, turned off onto a ranch road that wasn't much more than a rut in the fenced pastures and cut off the engine on a small rise.

He didn't say anything at first. He rested his lean hands on the steering wheel, studying them in silence, while Abby tried to catch her breath and summon enough nerve to talk to him.

"How dare you come into my room without knocking," she whispered after a long minute, her voice sounding husky and choked.

"I did knock. You didn't hear me."

She bit her lower lip, turning her gaze to the yellowish-brown pastures around them.

"Abby, for God's sake, don't make such an issue out of it," he said quietly. "Would you rather I'd left you like that? What if Justin had come to wake you, or Lopez?"

She swallowed. "Well, I guess they'd have gotten an eyeful," she said, her voice unsteady. After a minute, her face flushed, she turned toward him and asked plaintively, "Calhoun... I wasn't uncovered all the way, was I?"

He looked into her eyes and couldn't quite manage to look away. She was lovely. He reached out involuntarily and touched the side of her neck, his fingers tender and exquisitely arousing.

"No," he managed, watching the relief shadow her eyes as he told the lie with a straight face. "I buttoned you back up and tucked you in."

She let out a hard breath. "Thank you."

His fingers moved up to her cheek. "Abby, have you ever let a man see your breasts?" he asked unexpectedly.

She couldn't handle a remark that intimate. She dropped her eyes and tried to catch her breath.

"Never mind, tenderfoot," he chided softly. "I can guess."

"You mustn't talk like that," she whispered.

"Why?" he mused, tilting her chin up so that her shocked eyes met his. "You're the one trying to grow up, aren't you? If you want me to treat you like an adult, Abby, then this is part of it."

She shifted nervously. He made her feel so gauche it was ridiculous. She twisted her purse out of shape, afraid to meet the dark eyes that were relentlessly probing her face.

"Don't," she pleaded breathlessly, and her eyes closed.

"Are you really afraid of me?" he asked, his voice deeper, silkier.

He touched her mouth with a lean forefinger and she actually jumped, her eyes flashing open, all her hidden hungers and fears lying vulnerable there. And that was when his self-control fell away. She was hungry for him. Just as hungry as he was for her. Was that why she'd been so restless, because she'd become attracted to him and was trying to hide it? He had to know.

She couldn't answer him. She felt as if he were trying to see inside her mind. "I'm not afraid of you. Can't we go?"

"What are you trying to do?" he whispered, leaning closer, threatening her lips with his. "Block it out? Pretend that you aren't hungry for my mouth?"

Her heart went wild at the soft question. If he didn't stop, she was going to go in headfirst. He could be playing, and to have him tease her without meaning it would kill her. Her fingers touched his shoulder, pushed experimentally against the hard muscle under the soft fabric of his suit. They trembled there as her eyes suddenly tangled with his and her mouth echoed the faint tremor of her body.

He stared at her. It was a kind of exchange that Abby had never experienced before. A level, unblinking, intense look that curled her toes and made her heart race. Very adult, very revealing. His dark eyes held hers, and his lean fingers traced up and down her soft throat, arousing, teasing. His hard mouth moved closer to hers, hovering above it so that she could feel his warm, minty breath on her parted lips, so that she was breathing him.

"Cal...houn," she whispered, her voice breaking on a hungry sob.

She heard his intake of air and felt his hand curl under her long hair, powerful and warm, cradling her nape to tilt her head up.

"This has been coming for a hell of a long time, baby," he whispered as his head bent and he started to give in to the hunger that had become a fever in his blood. "I want it as much as you do...."

He leaned even closer, but just as his hard mouth started down over hers, before his lips touched her pleading ones, the sound of an approaching vehicle broke them apart like an explosion.

Calhoun felt disoriented. He looked in the rearview mirror and saw one of the ranch trucks coming up behind, but it took a moment to register. He was having trouble breathing. His body felt rigid, like drawn cord.

He glanced at Abby. She'd moved away and the realization that she was trembling brought home the total shock of what he'd been about to do. Damn it, she'd knocked him for a loop without even trying. That made him mad, and so, ironically, did the fact that she'd given in so easily. It infuriated him even more that he'd been about to kiss her. He didn't want complications, damn it, and Abby was the biggest he'd ever faced. Was she vulnerable because she wanted him or just because she'd suddenly discovered that she was a woman and wanted to experiment?

"We'd better get to work," he said tersely, starting the Jaguar. He drove down the path, waving to the men in the vehicle behind them. He cut off at the next dirt road, and minutes later they were at the feedlot. "Go on in. I've got to drive over to Jacobsville and talk to our attorney for a few minutes," he said as coolly as he could. That was a bald-faced lie, but he needed time to get hold of himself. He was as tense as a boy with his first woman, and he was losing his sense of humor. He didn't want Justin to see him like this and start asking embarrassing questions.

"All right," Abby said, her voice faltering.

He glanced at her with narrowed eyes. She'd give the show away all by herself if she went inside looking like that. "Nothing happened," he said shortly. "And nothing will," he added, his voice cold, "if you can manage to stop looking at me like a lovesick calf!"

A sob tore from her throat. Her wide, hurt eyes sought his and quickly fell away. She opened the door and got out, closing it quietly behind her. She straightened and walked toward the office without looking back.

Calhoun almost went after her. He hadn't wanted to say that to Abby, of all people, but he was off balance and terrified of what he might do to her if she kept looking at him that way. He couldn't make love to her, for God's sake. She was a child. She was his ward. Even as he told himself that, a picture formed in his mind of Abby lying on the bed with her breasts bare.

He groaned and jerked the car into gear, sending it flying down the road.

Abby didn't know how she got through the day. It was impossible to act as if nothing had happened, but since Justin knew she had a hangover he didn't question her pale complexion or her unusually quiet demeanor. And Calhoun didn't come back to the office. That was a godsend. Abby didn't think she could have borne seeing him after what he'd said to her.

"You need a diversion," Justin remarked later in the day, just about quitting time. "How about a steak in Houston? I've got to meet a man and his wife to talk about a new lot of stocker calves, and I'd hate to go alone."

He was smiling, and Abby warmed to his gentle affection. Justin wasn't the cold creature most people thought him. He was just a sad, lonely man who should have married and had several children to spoil.

"I'd like that very much," Abby said honestly. It would be nice to go out to dinner, especially if it meant she could avoid Calhoun. Of course, it was Saturday night. He wasn't usually home on Saturday nights anyway, but it would be so much better if she didn't have to dread seeing him.

"Good," Justin said, rising. "We'll get away about six."

Abby wore a soft burgundy velour dress. It had a slightly flared knee-length skirt and bishop sleeves, and a neckline that was V-shaped and not at all suggestive. She wore black accessories with it and, because it had turned cold, her heather-colored wool cape.

"Very nice," Justin said, smiling. He had on dark

evening clothes and looked elegant and sophisticated, as he always did on the rare occasions when he dressed up.

"I could return the compliment," Abby said. She clutched her purse, sending a restless look down the hall.

"He won't be home," Justin told her, intercepting her worried glance. "I gather the two of you had another falling-out?"

She sighed. "The worst yet," she confessed, unwilling to tell him any of the details. She looked up at him. "Calhoun acts as if he hates me lately."

Justin searched her eyes quietly. "And you don't know why," he mused. "Well, give it time, Abby. Rome wasn't built in a day."

She blinked. "I don't understand."

He laughed softly and took her arm. "Never mind. Let's get going."

Houston was big and sprawling and flat as a pancake, but it had a very special personality and Abby loved it. At night it was as colorful as Christmas, all jewel lights and excitement.

Justin took her to a small, intimate dinner club where they met the Joneses, Clara and Henry. They owned a small ranch in Montana where they raised stocker calves to supply to feedlots. They were an older couple but full of fun, and Abby liked them instantly. She and Clara talked fashion while Justin and Henry talked business. Abby was really having a good time until she glanced across the room and saw a familiar face on the cozily intimate dance floor.

Calhoun! Her eyes widened as she followed his blond head through the crowd until there was a clear space. Then she saw the ravishing blonde with him. He was holding the woman, who was at least his own age, with both hands at her waist, and she was curled up against him as if they'd been dancing together for years. They were smiling at each other like lovers.

Abby felt sick. She could almost feel herself turning green. If Calhoun had worked at it for years, he couldn't have hurt her any worse. Coming on the heels of the insulting remark he'd made just a few hours earlier, it was a death blow. This was his kind of woman, Abby realized. Sleek, beautiful, sophisticated. This was one of his shadowy lovers. One of the women he never brought home.

"What's wrong, Abby?" Justin asked suddenly. But before she could answer he followed her gaze to the dance floor, and something in his dark eyes became frightening, dangerous.

"Isn't that Calhoun?" Henry Jones grinned. "Well, well, let's get him over here, Justin, and see what he thinks of our proposition." Before anyone could stop him, he got up and headed for the dance floor.

"Mrs. Jones, shall we go to the powder room?" Abby asked with a pale but convincing smile.

"Certainly, dear. Excuse us, won't you, Justin?" the white-haired woman asked politely, and started out of the restaurant ahead of Abby.

Justin unexpectedly caught Abby's upper arm and drew her back. "Don't panic," he said quietly. "I'll get you out of here as soon as I can. Do you want a drink?"

She looked up, almost in tears at his unexpected understanding. "Could I have a piña colada with just a little rum?" she asked.

"I'll order it. Keep your chin up."

She smiled at him softly. "Thanks, big brother," she said gently.

He grinned. "Any time. Get going."

She glanced away in time to catch Calhoun's dark eyes. She nodded her head at him and turned away with no apparent haste.

Ten minutes later, she and Mrs. Jones returned to find Calhoun about to leave the table, the blonde still clinging to his arm. He looked up at Abby. His face was unreadable, but there was something in his expression that disturbed her. She wasn't about to let it show, though. Lovesick calf, indeed. She'd show him, by gosh.

She smiled. "Hi, Calhoun!" she said easily, sliding into the chair next to Justin's. "Isn't this a nice place? Justin decided I needed a night on the town. Wasn't that sweet of him?" She picked up her piña colada and took a big sip, relieved to find that it had barely enough rum to taste and even more relieved that her hand didn't shake and betray her shattered nerves.

"She's a big girl now," Justin told his brother, leaning back in his chair arrogantly and daring Calhoun to say a word. His cool smile and level, cold stare had a real impact, even on his brother.

But Calhoun didn't look any too pleased at the implication of the remark, especially when Justin slid an arm around Abby's shoulders. In fact, Calhoun seemed almost ready to leap forward and shake his brother loose from Abby.

"I'm tired," the blonde sighed, nuzzling her face against Calhoun's arm. "I need some sleep. Eventually," she teased gently, with a meaningful look at Calhoun's rigid expression.

Abby lifted her chin, looking straight at him. "Enjoy

yourself, big brother," she said with forced gaiety. She
even managed a smile. Thank God for Justin. She lifted
her glass, took a sip of her drink and winked at the
blonde, who smiled at her, obviously thinking Abby
was a relative and no threat even if she wasn't.

Calhoun was trying to find his voice. The sight of
Abby with his brother was killing him. He hadn't even
considered that possibility. And while Justin might not
be a playboy, he was a mature, very masculine man, and
he had, after all, attracted a beauty like Shelby Jacobs.

Calhoun hadn't meant to ask the blonde out. She
was a last-ditch stand against what he was feeling for
Abby, and a very platonic one at that. He didn't even
want her physically; she was just someone to talk to
and be with who didn't threaten his emotions. But he'd
never thought Abby might see him with her. It cut him
to the bone, embarrassed him. Did Abby care? Try as
he might, he couldn't find the slightest hint of jealousy
in her face. She was wearing more makeup than usual,
and that dress suited her. She looked lovely. Had Justin noticed?

"I said, I'd really like to go home, Cal," the blonde
drawled, laughing. "Can we, please? I've had a long
day. I'm a model," she added. "And we had a showing
this afternoon. My feet are killing me, however unro-
mantic that sounds."

"Of course," Calhoun said quietly. He took her arm.
"I'll see you later," he told Justin.

"Sure you will," Justin mused, his tone amused and
unbelieving, and he smiled at the blonde, who actually blushed.

Calhoun noticed then how Abby reacted to the remark. She lowered her eyes, but her slender hand was

shaking as it held the piña colada. He felt murderous. He wanted to pick her up and carry her out of here, out of Justin's reach.

But Justin had his arm around Abby, and he tightened it. "We may be late," Justin told his brother. "So don't wait up if you beat us home. I thought I might take Abby dancing," he added with narrowed eyes and the arrogant smile Calhoun hated.

"Yes, I'd like that," Abby told him, smiling.

Calhoun felt his throat contracting. He managed a smile, too, but not a normal one. "Good night, then," he said tautly. He hardly heard what the others said as he escorted the blonde out of the restaurant.

"It's all right," Justin told Abby, his voice quiet. "They've gone."

She looked up, her eyes full of tears. "You know, don't you?"

"How you feel, you mean?" he asked gently. He nodded. "Just don't let him see it, honey. He's still got a wild streak, and he'll fight it like hell even if he feels what you do. Give him time. Don't hem him in."

"You know a lot about men," she said, sniffing into the tissue she took from her purse.

"Well, I am one," he replied. "Dry your eyes, now, and we'll take the long way home. That ought to give him hell. He hated the very idea of your being out with me."

"Really?"

He smiled at her expression. "Really. Chin up, girl. You're young. You've got time."

"What do I do in the meantime? He's driving me crazy."

"You might consider looking for that apartment," he

said. "I hate to see you move out, but it may be the only answer eventually."

"I'd already decided that." She wiped her eyes. "But he hates the idea of my rooming with Misty."

"So do I," he remarked honestly. "Did you know that she made a pass at Calhoun and he turned her down?"

"Can't I trust anybody?" she moaned. "Aren't there any women who don't like him?"

"A few, here and there," he mused, his dark eyes twinkling. "I think you might do better to find a room in somebody's house. But that's your decision," he added quietly. "I'm not going to tell you what to do. You're old enough to decide alone."

"Thanks, Justin," she said gently. She smiled. "You'll make some lucky girl a nice husband one day."

His expression hardened, and the humor went out of his dark eyes. "That's a mistake I won't make," he said. "I've had my fill of involvement."

"You never asked about Shelby's side of it," Abby reminded him. "You wouldn't even listen, Calhoun said."

"She said it all when she gave me back the ring. And I don't want to discuss it, Abby," he cautioned, his eyes flashing warning signals as he rose. "I talk to no one about Shelby. Not even you."

She backed down. "Okay," she said gently. "I won't pry."

"Let's go," he said, reaching for the check. "We'll take two hours getting home, and I hope Calhoun has kittens when we get there."

"I doubt he'll notice," Abby said miserably. "She was very pretty."

"Looks don't count in the long run," he replied. He

looked at Abby. "Odd, isn't it, how embarrassed he was when you saw him with her?"

She turned away. "I'm tired. But it was a lovely dinner. Thank you."

He lifted an eyebrow. "Don't thank me. I had a good time. It beats watching movies at home, anyway." He chuckled gently.

Abby wanted to ask him why he never dated anyone and whether he was still carrying a torch for Shelby Jacobs after six years. Calhoun had said he was, but Justin was a clam when it came to his private life. And Abby wasn't about to pry any further. She wasn't that brave, not even with a piña colada inside her.

CHAPTER FIVE

ABBY WAS MISERABLE by the time they got home. She'd done nothing but think of Calhoun and the model. Justin had been kind, talking as if she were really listening to him. But she was reliving those few tempestuous minutes in Calhoun's Jaguar, when he'd come so close to kissing her and then had insulted her so terribly. She didn't understand his hot-and-cold attitude or his irritability. She didn't understand anything anymore.

Justin parked his elegant black Thunderbird in the garage, and Abby was surprised to find Calhoun's Jaguar already there.

"Well, well, look who's home," Justin murmured, glancing at Abby. "I guess he felt like an early night."

"Maybe he was exhausted," Abby said coldly.

Justin didn't comment, but he seemed highly amused and smug about something.

Calhoun was in the living room with the brandy bottle when they got home. He was down to his white shirtsleeves, which he'd rolled up to his elbows. His shirt was almost completely open in front, and Abby had to bite her lip to keep from staring helplessly at the broad expanse of his muscular chest. He was the most sensuous man she'd ever known, so powerful and tall and huge. Just the sight of him made her body tingle.

"So you finally brought her home," Calhoun shot at his brother. "Do you know what time it is?"

"Sure," Justin said imperturbably. "It's two o'clock in the morning."

"What were you doing?"

Justin cocked an eyebrow. "Oh, riding around. And things. Night, Abby," he said, and winked at her before he turned and went up the staircase.

Abby felt as if she'd been poleaxed. Now why had Justin said that? It had made Calhoun look frankly murderous. She cleared her throat.

"I think I'll go up, too." She started to turn, only to have her arm caught by huge warm fingers and be pulled into the living room.

Calhoun slammed the door behind her, his chest heaving with rough breaths. His dark eyes were really black now, glittering, dangerous, and his sensuous mouth was a thin, grim line.

"Where were you?" he demanded. "And doing what? Justin's thirty-seven, and he's no boy."

She stared at him blankly. The sudden attack had knocked the wind out of her for a minute, but then her temper came to the rescue.

"That blonde you were out with was no schoolgirl, either," she replied as calmly as she could, even though her knees were shaking under her. She leaned back against the door for support.

His heavy brows drew together. "My private life is none of your business," he said defensively.

"Of course not," she agreed. "You've already said that you didn't want me hanging around you like a love-sick calf, and I'm doing my best not to," she added, although it hurt terribly to try to make light of that hurtful remark.

His heavy shoulders made a jerky movement as he looked at her and away again, as if her answer made him uncomfortable. "Justin's too old for you."

"Bullfeathers," she replied, lifting her chin. "You've objected to every other man I've ever gone out with, but you can't object to your own brother. Justin would never hurt me, and you know it."

He did know it, but that didn't help. He was dying at the thought of Abby and Justin together.

"Oh, for God's sake!" he burst out, lost for words.

She took a steadying breath, though her heart was still doing a tango in her chest. "Why should it matter to you what I do?" she challenged him. "And you're a fine one to sit in judgment on other people! My gosh, Calhoun, everybody in the world knows what a playboy you are!"

He glared at her, trying to keep his temper. "I'm not a playboy," he said tersely. "I may date women occasionally—"

"Every night," she returned. Even though she knew her assertion wasn't completely true, she was too angry to split hairs. "Not that I mind," she added with a cold smile. "I don't care who you go out with, as long as you stop poking your nose into my business. I'll date whom I please, Calhoun, and if you don't like it, you know what you can do!"

He started to tell her what she could do, but before he could get the words out she'd jerked the door open and gone out and up the staircase.

"If you stay out until two o'clock in the morning

again, with or without Justin, you'll regret it!" Calhoun yelled up the stairs.

Abby made a sound that almost drove him crazy. He muttered something obscene and went back into the living room, slamming the door so hard it shook the room.

Damn women! He could have screamed at the effect she was having on him lately. She was ruining his love life, ruining his business life. All he did was think about her damned pretty breasts....

Abby cried herself to sleep. It had been a rotten evening altogether, and every time she thought of Calhoun kissing that model she got sicker. She hated him. She hated every bone in his body, and she most especially hated his possessiveness. She had to find an apartment. She had to get away. After tonight it was going to be just plain horrible trying to stay in the same house with Calhoun until her birthday.

The next morning she slept late. She usually got up and went to church, but this time she played hooky. She didn't want to risk running into Calhoun.

But as it was, there was nothing to worry about. When she finally went downstairs at lunchtime, wearing jeans and a beige knit top, her hair in a ponytail, Calhoun was nowhere in sight.

"Good morning," Justin said from the head of the table, smiling faintly. "How did it go last night?"

"Don't ask," she groaned. She sat down and glanced nervously at the door. "Is he here?"

He shook his head and filled his cup with coffee then passed the carafe to Abby. "He's still asleep," he said. That was surprising, because Calhoun was usually up early. Justin actually grinned then. "What happened?"

"He thinks I should be in before two o'clock in the

morning, even if he isn't," she said calmly. "And you're too old for me," she added with a faint grin, eyeing him.

He chuckled. "What else?"

"He's going crazy, Justin," she said. "I don't know what's gotten into him lately. It can't be his love life—his model seemed to be more than willing," she added cattily.

Justin looked at her, but he didn't reply. He poured cream into his coffee. "Oh, I almost forgot. Misty phoned. Something about having an apartment she wanted you to look at today if you want to go with her."

"Yes, I think I do," she murmured with a cold glance at the staircase.

"You know I don't approve of Misty as your prospective roommate," Justin told her honestly. "But it's your decision."

"You're a nice man."

"I'm glad you think so. Obviously my brother thinks I'm as big a rake as he is." He chuckled.

"Thank God you aren't," she sighed. "One in the family is enough!"

"If you're going out, you'd better wear a jacket," Justin warned. "I stepped out to get the paper and almost froze in place."

Abby sighed again. "And they keep saying spring is just around the corner."

She finished her breakfast and called Misty to tell her she'd be right over. Then she returned to her room to get her burgundy velour jacket. She was looping the last button when she turned to the open door and found Calhoun standing there, looking at her broodingly.

He'd just showered. He was bare chested, and his blond hair was damp. But Abby's eyes stopped at his brawny chest in helpless appreciation of the sheer masculinity of him. He leaned idly against the doorjamb, and muscles rippled under the wedge of thick brown hair that ran down into the wide belt around his slender hips. He didn't smile, and his dark eyes had heavy circles underneath them. He looked as tired as Abby felt.

"Where are you going now?" he asked coldly.

"Out to look at apartments," she said carelessly. "In a little over two and a half months I'll be needing one."

"How does Justin feel about that?" he asked, his eyes narrowing angrily.

"Justin isn't the one who's trying to keep me in a cage," she replied. She was tired of the whole thing, of his unreasonable anger and even of Justin playing cupid. "Look, Justin just took me out for a meal. He didn't park the car and try to make love to me. He isn't that kind of man, and you should be ashamed of yourself for thinking he is. Justin's like a brother to me. Just…as you are," she finished, averting her eyes. "I don't have romantic thoughts about either one of you."

"And that's a damned lie," he said in a cold tone. He jerked away from the door, slamming it behind him, bringing her shocked eyes to him as he advanced toward her. "I'm no more your brother than I'm your great-uncle."

She backed up into a chair, swerved and made it to the wall. He looked dangerous, and she didn't know how to handle this lightning mood switch.

"That's what you want me to be," she said accusingly, pressing against the cold wall. "You want me to be a kid sister and not get in your way or make eyes at you—"

"My God, I don't know what I want anymore," he ground out as he placed his big hands on either side of her head, his body too close, too sensuous, too deliciously masculine. The scent of him filled her nostrils, excited her senses. She could see the tiny golden tips of the hair on his chest now, glittering in the light. Glittering…like the dark, intent eyes that caught hers and held them.

"Calhoun, I have to go," she said, her voice faltering.

"Why?" he asked.

She could see him breathing. His chest rose and fell roughly, as if he were having a hard time getting air in and out. She felt that way herself. He was too close, and her vulnerability was going to start showing any minute. She couldn't bear to have him see her weakness and make fun of it.

"Stop it," she whispered huskily, closing her eyes. "Damn you, stop…oh!"

He had her mouth under his so smoothly and easily that her heart seemed to stop beating. He wasn't gentle, either. It was as if the feel of her soft body under his made him wild, made him hungry.

In fact, he was starving for her. He leaned down so that his hips and thighs were fully against her, so that his bare chest was against the velour of her jacket. He didn't like not being able to feel her breasts, so he snapped open the buttons of the jacket and pushed the material aside. He felt her gasp as her breasts pressed against him, and he groaned, marveling at the warm softness of her. Nudging her lips apart, he nipped sensuously at the lower one. That was arousing, too, and he wanted her. He wanted her mouth as he wanted her soft, sweet young body. His tongue pushed into her mouth, past her lips, tangling with her own, and he groaned and gave her his full weight, pressing her against the wall.

Abby was frightened. She hadn't expected anything quite so adult, and she'd never been kissed by anyone who had any expertise. Calhoun was experienced, and he was kissing her as if she knew all the answers, too. But she didn't. The feel of his body in such unfamiliar intimacy was embarrassing, and his mouth was doing shocking things to her own. She pushed at his chest, afraid of his lack of control.

"No!" she whimpered.

He barely heard her. His mind was spinning, his body in torment. He managed to lift his head, breathing roughly, and look down at her. But the passion and delight he had expected to see in her pale eyes was missing. They were wide, but not with desire. With…fear!

He scowled. Her hands were on his chest, but they were pushing, not caressing, and she was crying.

"Abby," he whispered gently. "Honey…"

"Let me…go," she sobbed brokenly. "Oh, let me go!" She pushed again, harder.

This time he flexed his hands against the wall and pushed away from her, leaving her cold, empty. She moved past him, putting half the length of the room between them. So that—that!—was what passion felt like. She shivered a little at the memory. Her mouth hurt where his had ground against it, and her breasts were sore from the hard pressure of his chest. He hadn't even tried to be gentle. She stared at him accusingly, her eyes bright with tears as she drew her jacket closer and shivered.

Calhoun felt as if he'd been hit in the head with a hammer. Her reaction hadn't been anything like what he'd expected. He'd almost kissed her once before, and she'd been yielding then, willing. But now she looked as if she hated him.

"You hurt me," she whispered shakily.

He was lost for words. Concerned, he stared at her, his dark eyes quiet on her wan face. She looked as if she had never experienced a man's passion. Was that possible? Could any woman be that unawakened in this day and age?

"Haven't you ever been kissed?" he asked softly.

"Of course I have," she replied stiffly. "But not... not like that!"

His eyebrows went up. At last he was catching on. "My God," he said huskily. "Abby, adults kiss that way!"

"Then I don't want to be an adult," she returned, coloring. "Not if I have to be mauled like that!"

He watched her turn and leave the room, and he was powerless to stop her. Her reaction had floored him completely. He'd expected her to know a little about lovemaking, at least, but she seemed totally innocent. She'd never known a deep kiss or the intimacy of a man's body.

It should have pleased him, but he found it irritating that she thought he'd mauled her. By God, he should have let her go out with Myers. Then she'd know what it was to be mauled!

He left the room and closed the door, his expression thunderous as he heard her footsteps going down the staircase and then her muffled goodbye to Justin.

Calhoun went back to his own room. He was breathing roughly, and his heart wouldn't beat properly. He felt hot all over. Frustrated. Furious. Damn Abby and her soft body. It was driving him out of his mind!

He went into the bathroom and turned on the shower.

Well, it was a good thing she didn't like his kisses, because hell would freeze over before she ever got another one.

Abby was blissfully unaware of Calhoun's thoughts. She climbed into her car and started it with hands that were still trembling. How could Calhoun have hurt her like that if he'd cared anything about her? He'd just proved how little she meant to him. He'd only been interested in his own pleasure, not hers. Well, he could go back to his blondes for all she cared. She was sure she hated him now.

Misty was already dressed and waiting when Abby got to the colonial mansion the older girl shared with her parents. Misty took them to town in her little sports car, and for once Abby didn't mind the wind. It might blow away her misery. Just thinking about Calhoun's rough treatment made her miserable. She loved him and it hurt terribly that he could treat her that way. But she had to pretend that nothing was wrong, so that Misty wouldn't start asking questions that Abby didn't want to answer.

They parked in town and went to the first address on Misty's list. It was an apartment above a sweet shop, on the corner across from the bank. Misty didn't like the place, because there was only one bedroom and she wanted her privacy. Abby deliberately put the implications of that remark in the back of her mind and added that she didn't like the view. It was too close to the center of town, and there was a good deal of traffic on Saturday night.

The second place they went was just right. The room being rented was upstairs in a private house owned by a Mrs. Simpson, who was friendly and bright and welcoming. That turned Misty off completely. She didn't want an old busybody watching out for her. But Abby was rapidly coming to the conclusion that Misty was going to do some entertaining once they were on their own, and her association with the Ballengers made her balk at the thought of Misty's plans.

"I'll take it," she told Mrs. Simpson, "if you don't mind having just me instead of both of us, and if you aren't in a hurry for me to move in. It will be a few weeks…."

"That will work out fine. I'm going off to my sister's for a week or so, anyway." Mrs. Simpson smiled broadly, her blue eyes lighting up. "My dear, I'd be delighted." She leaned forward while Misty was still upstairs grumbling about the lack of privacy. "Your friend seems very nice, mind you, but I'm rather old-fashioned…."

"So am I," Abby whispered, putting her finger to her lips when Misty came downstairs again.

"No, I'm sorry, it won't do," she sighed.

"I have the perfect solution," Abby told her. "I'll take this one, and you take the other one. It'll be great. We can visit each other, and we'll both have our privacy."

Misty raised an eyebrow. "Well…it might be nice at that. But you said you wanted to room with me."

Mrs. Simpson excused herself, asking Abby to phone her later about a date for moving in.

Abby moved with Misty to the door. "Let's face it," she told her friend, "you want to entertain men, and I'll have Calhoun and Justin all over me if they find out about it. I'm sure you don't want them on your case."

Misty shuddered delicately. "Are you kidding? Calhoun, maybe, but not Justin! That man doesn't have a humorous bone in his whole body."

Abby remembered how amused Justin had been about Calhoun's behavior, but she just nodded her head.

"Let's have coffee," Misty suggested. She drove them back into town in her little sports car and parked beside the bank. The two women had just gotten out of the car when Tyler Jacobs and his sister Shelby came around the corner looking somber and disturbed.

Abby greeted them. "Tyler. Shelby. How are you?"

"This isn't a good time to ask," Shelby sighed, but she smiled. She was a dish. Short dark hair framed her elfin face, and she had eyes that were an odd shade of green, almost glassy in color. Her mouth was perfect, and she was tall. She would have made a fortune as a model, but her parents wouldn't have heard of such a profession for their only daughter.

Tyler was like his sister in coloring. He had thick dark hair, almost black, and an olive complexion and the same odd-colored green eyes. He was as big as Calhoun, but slender. Whipcord-lean and dangerous-looking. He wasn't handsome at all, but he had character, and women usually found him irresistible.

Misty turned to see where Abby had gotten to and smiled delightedly at Tyler.

"Well, hello," she drawled. "Fancy seeing you here."

"Hello, Misty," he said, smiling lazily. "You look devastating, as usual. What are you two doing in town on a Sunday?"

"Looking for an apartment to share, originally." Abby sighed. "But we wound up with one each, across town from the other. I'm renting from Mrs. Simpson, and Misty has a neat place overlooking the bank."

"Right up there, in fact." Misty pointed across the street. "It needs decorating, but I can take care of that."

Abby grinned. "I'll bet you can."

"Come and have coffee with us," Shelby invited. "Tyler needs cheering up. We had a bad blow yesterday, and an even worse one today."

Abby looked up at him. He did seem reticent. And moody, which was totally unlike him. "I'm sorry. Can I help?"

"You little doll," he murmured, and touched her hair gently. "No. But thanks for the offer. How's Calhoun?"

Abby averted her eyes. "He's fine, I guess. He and Justin are both at home."

"No problems the other night after Calhoun got you home?" Tyler persisted with a teasing smile.

"Only the usual lecture," Abby said. She managed a shaky smile as all four of them went down the street and entered a small cafeteria.

They were quickly seated, and the waitress brought four cups of coffee and a pitcher of cream.

Shelby cast a glance at Abby and laughed softly. "You devil," she teased.

"I just wanted to see how the other half lived," Abby sighed.

"I did my best to help you," Misty sighed. "On the other hand, weren't you lucky that it was Calhoun and not Justin who came after you? Calhoun is a little more easygoing."

"Not lately, he isn't," Abby said tautly.

At the mention of Justin, Shelby became quiet and shy. Abby felt sorry for her. Justin had never gotten over Shelby's defection. He probably never would, and Shelby had to know that.

"How is Justin?" Tyler asked casually. Too casually.

"He goes to work and comes home and goes to work

and comes home," Abby said as they added cream and sugar to their coffee.

Misty yawned. "What an exciting life."

"He's lonely, I suppose," Abby said deliberately. "He never goes anywhere."

"I know somebody else like that," Tyler murmured with a hard glance at Shelby, who shifted restlessly in her seat.

"How's the horse business going?" Abby interrupted, posing the question to Tyler as she sipped her coffee.

"Going bust, I'm afraid," he said heavily. "Dad made some bad investments before he died. So far, I've managed to meet the payments. This month I defaulted." His face hardened. "I'm going to have to sell Geronimo."

"Oh, Tyler, I'm sorry." Abby grimaced. "He was your favorite."

"Mine, too," Shelby said with a sigh. "But we can't keep him and pay off Dad's debts. I don't suppose you'd want him, Abby?"

"I don't ride that well," Misty confessed.

"If I can talk Justin into it I'd like to have him," Abby said gently.

"Thank you, Abby, but that wouldn't be a good idea," Shelby replied. "Justin would go right through the roof if you asked him."

"Like a rocket," Tyler said, smiling at Abby. "No, we'll do it through an agent. We won't have any problems selling him. I'd rather know who he was going to, that's all. Some people want a horse strictly for breeding purposes. They look at dollars and cents, not at the horse itself."

"I've got a cousin in Texas," Misty piped up. "She's

trying to hold on to the ranch all by herself. It's a horse ranch," she added. "Does that tell you anything?"

He smiled. "Enough. I'd appreciate it if you'd put her in touch with me."

"I'll give her your number, if you don't mind."

"Fine."

Lights gleamed in Shelby's black hair as she lifted the cup and finished her coffee. Abby wondered at her elfin beauty, and thought it strange that a man like Justin could attract such a lovely woman when he wasn't handsome or even very personable. Then Abby remembered how kind he'd been to her in Houston, and the way he'd supported her with Calhoun. On the other hand, maybe it wasn't so surprising that he could attract her. What was surprising was that he'd ever let her go. It made Abby uncomfortable, thinking about how two people could be so much in love one day and bitter enemies the next. Love didn't last, after all.

"Tyler, we'd better go. I've got to call Barry Holman about those bonds and securities we're selling," Shelby said gently. "I'm sorry. I'd love to stay and talk. We hardly ever see each other these days, and I guess Justin would burn the house to the ground before he'd let me through the front door to visit you."

Tyler sighed. "He holds a grudge longer than any man I've ever known, that's for sure. And without reason."

"No," Shelby pleaded, her green eyes seeking his. "Please don't. Abby owes him her loyalty. Don't put her in the position of having to defend him."

"Sorry," he said, his green eyes glittering with controlled rage. Then he smiled at Abby. "There's a square dance at the dance hall next Friday night. How about going with me?"

Abby hesitated. Justin would be furious, and she didn't like to think about what Calhoun might say or do. He was so unpredictable lately. On the other hand, going out with Tyler would show Calhoun that she wasn't going to make eyes at him anymore....

"Don't do it," Shelby pleaded. "Can't you see, it will only make things worse."

"For whom?" Tyler shot back. "Could the situation possibly be any worse for you? My God, you're living like a nun!"

Shelby put her napkin down with calm, steady fingers. "The way I live is no one's concern except my own." She stood up. "Abby, Justin would come down on your head like Judgment. He isn't the man he was. I'd hate to see you caught in the cross fire."

"I'm not afraid of him, Shelby," Abby said gently. "Not much, anyway. I'm trying to get out from under Calhoun's thumb. Tyler and I would kind of be helping each other."

"You see," Tyler told his sister. "And here you were thinking I was just doing it to irritate your ex-fiancé."

"Well, aren't you?" Shelby said challengingly.

He lifted his chin arrogantly. "Maybe."

"Sometimes I wonder if Mom and Dad didn't find you under a cabbage leaf," Shelby muttered.

"Not a chance," Misty mused, looking him up and down. "He's much too big."

"Tease," he said, flirting lazily with Misty as he did with most women. But Tyler was deep, like Shelby, and if there was a special woman, nobody knew except himself. He was discreet about his love life.

"Justin used to laugh, you know," Shelby told Abby as they walked out together, with Misty and Tyler talking together ahead of them. "He wasn't always cold and hard and unyielding. Not until I gave him back his ring and made him bitter." She clutched her purse against her breasts. "Abby, don't hurt him," she pleaded, her eyes soft and gentle. "Don't let Tyler hurt him. He hides it, but he's so vulnerable...."

"I know that," Abby said gently. She touched the taller woman's arm, stung by the look in Shelby's eyes. Yes, she was vulnerable, too, and Abby sensed that Shelby was still in love with Justin, even now.... "I'm sorry that things have gone so badly for both of you. Justin doesn't have women, you know. If you live like a nun, he lives like a monk. There isn't anyone."

Shelby's lower lip trembled. She looked away, her head tilting to stop a tear from escaping. "Thank you," she managed huskily.

Abby wanted to say more, but the others were waiting impatiently. "Ready to go?" she called brightly to Misty. "Okay. Can you keep it under ninety going home? Honest to goodness, I don't think that car knows any legal speeds!"

"I'm a good driver," Misty informed her haughtily. "You just come with me and I'll prove it. So long, Tyler. Shelby."

"I'll pick you up at six on Friday," Tyler told Abby. "Wear something sexy."

She curtsied. "You'd better bring a baseball bat when you come to the door. And pray that Justin doesn't have a long cord for his chain saw."

"Dangerous games, my friend," Misty told Abby as

they drove away. "Justin won't like it, and he's pretty frightening when he loses his temper."

"So is Tyler. But they won't come to blows. I'll make sure of it."

"And what will Calhoun say?" Misty added with a quick glance at Abby.

Abby felt herself going pale. She could feel all over again the terrible crush of his mouth, the shattering intimacy of his body. She swallowed. "He won't care," she said coldly.

"Why do it? You're moving out. Isn't that enough of a show of independence for you?"

"No." Abby leaned back against the leather seat and closed her eyes. "But going out with Tyler will be."

Misty sighed and shook her head. "Well, I'll remember you in my prayers. Hang on." She pressed her foot down on the accelerator, and Abby wondered what the Guinness book of world records listed as the top land speed by a wild blonde in a little sports car. Whatever the record was, she thought as she held on for dear life, she'd bet that Misty could break it.

CHAPTER SIX

CALHOUN WAS GONE when Abby got home, and she spent a quiet afternoon watching television. Justin was around long enough to ask about the apartment and to approve Abby's choice of lodgings. But then he left to deal with some problem at the feedlot.

Abby dreaded the moment when Calhoun would return, because of what had happened that morning. She couldn't reconcile the man she knew with the stranger who'd been so rough with her. Boys had kissed her before, but lightly and carefully. Calhoun hadn't been careful, and he'd frightened her with his experience. She'd never experienced adult passion before, and she didn't know what it was. But surely a man like Calhoun, with his love life, couldn't have been thrown off balance so completely by a twenty-year-old virgin.

He'd already said he didn't want her making eyes at him, so maybe he was showing her what she'd be inviting if she let him see her interest. She shivered. What a deft and accurate way he'd picked, if that were the case.

Supper was on the table and she and Justin were about to start serving themselves when Calhoun came in. He sat down, looking worn and rumpled, and poured himself a cup of coffee. He didn't speak to Abby, and she kept her head down so that he wouldn't notice her scarlet flush. It wasn't necessary, anyway, because he didn't even look at her. He started talking to Justin about a prospective new feedlot customer he'd found, and he kept the conversation going until they were having a second cup of coffee. Abby felt shut out and ignored. When Calhoun finally got up to leave and looked at her, she felt worse than she had in her life.

There was barely controlled anger in his eyes, mingled with something darker, something she didn't understand. She dropped her eyes and felt her heart race under his cold scrutiny. He acted as if she were the guilty one. Didn't he realize how he'd hurt her? That his treatment of her had been frightening?

"Hey," Justin said softly as the outside door opened and closed.

She looked up, her eyes faintly misty. "He didn't even speak to me," she whispered.

Justin leaned back in his chair and lit a cigarette, exhaling smoke as he watched her. "He's been like that all day," he said. "While you were gone he stared out the window whenever I tried to talk to him. He didn't even hear me. Finally he lit a cigarette and went outside and just walked."

She stared at him. "Calhoun stopped smoking years ago."

He shrugged. "He's gone through a pack already. You keep telling me that there's nothing wrong, but my brother goes from bad to worse. Now either you tell me or I'll beat it out of him. I love him, but I've had enough silence."

Abby swallowed hard. Justin's tone was unnerving. But she couldn't tell him what Calhoun had done. Justin was unpredictable, and she didn't want him to rake

Calhoun over the coals for something that in all honesty she'd helped to provoke.

Then she remembered what she'd said to Calhoun, and suddenly all the pieces of the puzzle fit together. She must have hurt Calhoun's pride with what she'd said and done after he'd kissed her so intimately. The more she thought about it, the worse she felt. For months she'd dreamed of having him kiss her. Then he had, and she'd been too frightened by his experienced bulldozer technique to even respond. She'd behaved like a child.

Justin lifted an eyebrow and waited expectantly. When she didn't say anything, he prodded, "Well?"

"I said some terrible things to him," she confessed finally. "I was jealous."

"And hurt," he said perceptively.

"And hurt," she sighed. Her blue-gray eyes met his dark ones. "Oh, Justin, he hates me. And I can't even blame him. I hurt his pride so badly that I don't imagine he'll ever talk to me again."

"Incredible, isn't it, that you could hurt him," he mused. "When women have been trying for years to get through that thick hide and never have."

"He's been responsible for me for a long time," she said quietly. "I guess it's hard for him to let go."

"Maybe," he said. He took another draw on the cigarette. "Maybe not. He's acting strangely lately."

"Maybe he's got the gout or something," she suggested with a slight smile.

"Or something."

She sipped her coffee so that she'd have something to do with her hands. She had to talk to Justin about Friday night, and it was only just dawning on her how difficult it was going to be.

"Justin, I have to tell you something."

His dark eyebrows lifted. "This sounds serious," he said with a faint smile.

"It is. And I hope you won't get mad at me."

His chin lifted. "Is it about the Jacobses?"

"I'm afraid so," she sighed. She looked at her coffee, because his eyes were getting darker by the second. "Tyler asked me to a square dance Friday night, and I said I'd go." She clenched her teeth, waiting for the outburst. When it didn't come, she looked up. He was watching her, but without any particular anger. She continued quickly, "I don't have to let him pick me up here. I can meet him at the dance. In fact, Shelby did her best to stop him from asking me, because she didn't want to upset you."

Something passed across his face, too fleeting to identify. But for one wild second his eyes were soft and quiet and full of wonder. Then it was gone, and he stared down at his glowing cigarette. "Did she?"

"She didn't want Tyler to make any trouble," Abby said gently.

"It's been six years," he said after a minute, his face quiet and oddly gentle. "Six long, empty years. I've hated her, and I've hated the family. I guess I could go on hating them until we're all dead. But it wouldn't change anything. It's all over and done with, a long time ago."

"She's so lovely," Abby said.

Justin winced, and there were memories in his dark eyes, in his taut face. He crushed out his cigarette roughly. "Tyler can pick you up here," he said abruptly, and got to his feet. "I won't give him a hard time."

She looked up as he passed by her chair and then

down at her cup, thoughtfully. "She lives like a nun, you know. Tyler says she hasn't dated anyone for years."

Abby thought he stopped then, just for a second, but it might have been her imagination, because he kept walking and he didn't say a word.

What a pity, Abby thought with quiet melancholy, that love could die so violent a death. And the saddest part of it was that in spite of what Justin said, she'd have bet Justin and Shelby were still madly in love, even though it had been six years since they'd broken up. What had Shelby done to make Justin turn against her so vehemently? Surely just being given back his engagement ring wouldn't make a man so vindictive!

Abby got up from the table and went to her room. It was much too early to go to bed, but she didn't relish the idea of staying downstairs and having Calhoun stare holes through her. Avoiding him had suddenly become imperative.

That wasn't too hard. But avoiding the memories that lingered in her room was. The wall where he'd pinned her with his big body and kissed the breath out of her was all too empty. In the end she pushed a bookcase against it, just to keep her mind from replaying the scene.

She went to work as usual for the rest of the week, and so did Calhoun. But there was a difference. There was no soft greeting, no smile, no teasing grin. This Calhoun was more and more like his older brother. The fun had gone out of him, leaving behind a hard, formidable businessman who alternately ignored Abby or chewed her out for any nervous mistakes she made. It was impossible to get near him, even to talk.

By quitting time on Friday, she was a nervous wreck.

She looked forward to the square dance like a doomed prisoner coveting an appeal. At least the dance would get her out of the house and take her mind off Calhoun. Not that she expected him to be home on a weekend. He'd probably be up in Houston with his model. Abby gritted her teeth as she thought about that.

Hindsight was a sad thing, Abby reflected, and she'd only begun to realize why Calhoun had been out of control with her in the bedroom. It hadn't been because he was angry or because he was punishing her. He'd been out of control because he'd wanted her. She was almost sure of it now, having asked Misty some subtle but intimate questions about men. Calhoun had wanted her, and she'd stabbed his pride bloody. She could have cried, because she'd had his attention and hadn't even known it. He was well and truly cured now. He didn't speak to her unless he had to, and he avoided her like the plague. She was glad she'd had that room reserved at the boarding house, because she had a feeling she was going to need it any time now.

She dressed in a red-checked full skirt with several crinolines and a perky white blouse with puffy short sleeves and a button front. It was almost March, but it was still cold, and she got out her long tan coat to wear with it. Tyler was due at six, and it was almost that when she went downstairs, her long hair silky and clean around her shoulders, wearing just enough makeup to give her a rosy-cheeked glow. She'd never wished more that she was blonde or that she could have a second chance with Calhoun. Just her luck, she thought miserably as she made her way down the staircase, to foul everything up on the first try. Why hadn't she realized that Calhoun felt passion, not anger? Why hadn't she waited to give him a chance to be tender? He probably would have been if she hadn't struggled with him.

She reached the bottom of the staircase just in time to watch Calhoun open the front door for Tyler, because Maria and Lopez had the night off. Abby's heart jumped helplessly at the sight of those broad shoulders and that long back. Calhoun was so big he even towered over Tyler.

Abby's body tensed as she wondered if Justin had told Calhoun she'd be going out with Tyler. But he finally opened the door all the way and let the other man inside.

Tyler, in jeans and a red checked Western shirt and bandanna and denim jacket, looked as Western as a man could get, from his black boots to his black hat. Calhoun was dressed in a similar fashion, except that his shirt was blue. They stared at each other for a long moment before Calhoun broke the silence.

"Justin said you were taking Abby out," he said tersely. "You can wait in the living room if you like."

"Thanks," Tyler said, equally tersely, as he met Calhoun's eyes and glanced away.

"I'm already dressed," Abby said with forced cheerfulness, smiling at Tyler and getting a smile back. She didn't look at Calhoun. She couldn't. It would have been like putting a knife in her heart.

"Then let's go," Tyler replied. "I hear the Jones boys are going to play tonight. You remember Ted Jones, Calhoun; he was in our senior class back in high school."

"I remember him," Calhoun said quietly. There was a smoking cigarette in his hand, and he looked like a stranger.

A minute later, Justin came out of his study, stopping short when he saw the three of them. He and Calhoun were wearing almost identical clothing, and it was odd for Justin to dress up on a Friday night. Unless…

"Where are you off to?" Abby asked the oldest of the three men with a smile.

"The square dance, of course," Justin said, glancing at Tyler. "Not to keep tabs on her, in case you were wondering," he added with a cold smile. "We're meeting a business contact there."

Abby's heart jumped. Calhoun was going to the dance, too. She hated her own helpless pleasure at the thought that she might have at least a few minutes in his arms.

Tyler studied Justin warily. "You aren't meeting Fred Harriman, by any chance?"

Justin's eyebrows arched. "Yes. Why?"

Tyler grimaced. "He just bought our place."

Calhoun caught his breath. "For God's sake, you weren't forced out?"

"I'm afraid so," Tyler replied with a sigh. "Funny, you never think you'll go under. I was sure that I could undo the damage Dad had done, but I was too late. At least it's not a complete loss. We've still got a couple of stallions, and we can hold on to at least the house and an acre or two of land."

"If you need a job, we've got one open at the feedlot," Justin said unexpectedly. "It's not charity, damn it," he added when he saw Tyler's incredulous look and glinting green eyes. "I don't have to like you to know how good you are with livestock."

"That's a fact," Calhoun agreed, raising a cigarette to his chiseled mouth. "The door's open."

Abby, watching them, was struck by the sheer force

of so much masculinity at close range. The three of them were like patterns cut from the same rough cloth. Long, tall Texans. She was suddenly proud to be a friend to two of them, even if the third hated her.

"Thanks for the offer, then," Tyler said. He stared at Justin. "I didn't think you went to dances, business or not."

"I don't. Calhoun gets drunk if I don't baby-sit him," he said, grinning at his brother's outraged expression.

"Like hell I do," Calhoun replied. "I remember a night when you tied one on royally and I put you to bed."

Justin pursed his lips. "We all lose our heads occasionally," he said. "Don't we, Abby?" he added with a glance in her direction and then in Calhoun's. Abby flushed, and Calhoun turned his back and headed for the front door, holding it open for the rest of them without another word. Justin only smiled.

"Shelby's going, too," Tyler remarked to Abby as they walked out. "I had to twist her arm, but she needs some diversion. She's working a six-day week for the first time in her life, and it's rough."

Justin didn't say a word, but if that quiet unblinking gaze meant what Abby thought it did, he was listening intently. She wondered just how many fireworks a dance hall could stand. Behind her, Calhoun was glaring at her and at Tyler with a scowl so hot that she would have grown warm if she'd seen it.

The dance hall was jumping. The Jones boys' band was playing a toe-tapping Western medley, and the dance floor was full. Old Ben Joiner, his fiddle in his hand, was calling the dance, his voice rising deep and clear above the music as he told the dancers what to do and when.

"Nice crowd," Tyler remarked. He and Abby had arrived after Justin and Calhoun. The two of them were at a table with a third man who looked pitifully out of place.

"Yes, it is nice. What do the brothers want with Fred Harriman, I wonder?" she asked, thinking out loud as she and Tyler headed toward the table where Shelby was sitting all alone.

"You're in a position to know better than I am," Tyler returned, "but I expect he wants the brothers to feed out his new cattle for him." Tyler glanced at his sister and saw where her big, soulful green eyes were staring. "God, she's got it bad," he said under his breath.

Abby noticed, too, and touched his sleeve. "Justin doesn't date, either. Do you suppose there's any chance for them?"

"Not after what he thinks she did," Tyler replied tersely. "And talking about it won't butter any biscuits. Hi, sis," he said more loudly, smiling at his sister as he pulled out a chair for Abby and then sat down himself.

"Hi," Shelby said with a grin. "Abby, you look gorgeous."

"So do you." Abby sighed. "You don't know what I'd give to be as pretty as you are."

"Oh, go on," Shelby murmured, embarrassed. But she did look pretty, her dark hair coiled on her head with a bow holding it, her green Western-style dress exactly matching her eyes and showing off her beautiful figure.

"I wish things had worked out for you. Your job must be rough," Abby commiserated.

Shelby smiled back. "Oh, I like it," she said. "And at least we've got the house. We'll finish the last details of the sale next week, and then all the gossip will die down and we'll have our privacy back." She picked up her glass of ginger ale and sipped it. "I hope you don't mind my being a third wheel…."

"You go on," Abby replied. "You know Ty and I are just friends. I'm glad to have your company, and I'm sure your brother is, too."

Tyler smiled, but the look he sent her over Shelby's oblivious head wasn't quite platonic.

"Let's get in that next set," Tyler said, pulling Abby up by the hand. "Shelby, order Abby and me a ginger ale, would you?" he asked his sister.

She grinned. "Of course."

Abby stared at Tyler as he led her into the throng of dancers. "I can have a gin and tonic if I want to."

"Not while you're out with me," he said firmly, leading her into place in front of him. "I don't drink. That means you don't drink."

"Spoilsport," she sighed.

He chuckled. "Shame on you. You don't need booze to have a good time."

"I know. But I had looked forward to being treated like an adult," she told him.

"Well, don't give up hope," he said, his voice deep and soft as his lean hand curled around her waist. "The night's still young yet."

Abby smiled, because of course he was just flirting. She let him jostle her around the dance floor, graceful on his feet, expertly leading her through the twists and turns and shuffles and exchanges. Abby was having a great time until she glanced at the table where Justin and Calhoun were sitting. Justin's dark eyes kept darting over to Shelby. Abby was too far away to read his expression. Calhoun, on the other hand, was glaring at Abby and Tyler with enough venom for ten rattlesnakes.

Her heart leaped at the jealousy she saw on his face. Maybe there was still a little hope. The thought perked her up, and she began to smile, and then to laugh. Tyler mistook her response for pleasure in his company, and so did Calhoun. By the time the dance was over, Abby was caught in the middle of a building storm.

It threatened to explode when Calhoun, sick of watching Abby with Tyler, went and asked Shelby to dance.

Shelby was hesitant because Justin had just straightened at his table and looked capable of starting a world war all by himself.

"He won't mind," Calhoun said. "You look lonely sitting here by yourself."

"Oh, Calhoun, don't start anything," she pleaded.

"I won't," he promised. "Now come and dance with me."

Shelby gave in, but her lovely face was troubled.

Abby watched them go onto the dance floor, and her spirits fell. Shelby and Calhoun looked good together, her brunette beauty a perfect foil for his blond good looks. Abby felt plain and unattractive by comparison. She stared at Ty's chest, hopelessly depressed. What if Calhoun had come because of Shelby? What if he was courting her now? She felt sick.

"I feel like I'm sitting on a time bomb," Tyler mused as he watched Calhoun and Shelby and then got a look at Justin's face. "I don't know what Calhoun's up to, but Justin looks dangerous. Even if he hates my sister, he still seems to consider her his personal property. Would you look at that scowl?"

Abby saw Justin's expression and was ashamed of herself for wishing he would get out of his chair and beat the hell out of Calhoun. She flushed with embarrassment. "If Justin was dancing with another woman, how do you think Shelby would feel?" she asked, looking up at him.

He pursed his lips, his green eyes dancing as they searched her face. "I hadn't considered that."

"Calhoun probably thought Shelby was uncomfortable sitting by herself with nobody to dance with," Abby added.

Tyler sighed, his eyes wandering quietly over Abby's distracted expression as she looked toward the other couple on the floor. And all at once a lot of things became clear for him. Foremost was that Abby was jealous. Her eyes weren't any softer than Justin's. If she wasn't already in love with Calhoun, she was well on the way to it. Tyler felt all his chances slipping away, and there wasn't a thing he could do about it.

The evening wore on, and the tension rose. Calhoun seemed to enjoy dancing with Shelby. Abby stuck with Tyler. Justin sat and drank quietly by himself after he finished his business with the other gentleman, who left. The tall man began to look more coldly violent by the minute.

Toward the end of the dance, Calhoun left Shelby long enough to saunter over to Abby, who was sipping ginger ale while Tyler spoke to someone he knew at a nearby table. Abby hadn't been watching Calhoun, because he was making her miserable. He didn't smile at her anymore. He hated her, she was sure of it. So when Calhoun appeared in front of her, Abby grew flustered and nervous and almost spilled her drink.

Calhoun saw the nervous motion, and it gave him hope. "How about dancing one with me?" he asked quietly.

She looked up, her eyes searching his face almost hungrily. "No, I'd better not," she said softly.

He caught his breath at the wounded sound in her voice. "Abby, why not?" he asked.

"It might hurt Shelby's feelings," she said, and turned away, searching the room desperately for Tyler. "I can't imagine where Tyler got to," she added huskily.

Calhoun looked like a radio with the transistors removed. He blinked, doubting that he'd really heard what she'd just said. Shelby might be hurt? Surely she didn't think— it suddenly dawned on him that if Abby was crazy enough to imagine he was getting involved with Shelby, Justin might, too.

He turned toward the table where Justin was sitting like a statue, and whistled under his breath. "Oh, my God," he breathed. "I've done it now."

Abby didn't say another word. She watched Calhoun move through the crowd toward Justin and wondered absently if his life insurance was paid up. Justin looked murderous.

There were two full ashtrays in front of Justin, and one half-empty whisky glass. The older man drank on occasion, but usually not when he was angry. If he did, he limited himself to one drink. The glass was what told Calhoun how angry his older brother was.

Calhoun sat down across from him, leaning back to study the older man. "She was lonely," he told Justin.

Justin drained his glass and rose, his eyes blacker than Calhoun had seen them in a long time. "Then I'll see what I can do about it."

While Calhoun was catching his breath, Justin walked to Shelby's table. He didn't say a word. He looked at the woman until her face colored, then simply held out his hand. She put hers into it. He pulled her onto the dance floor, and they melted into each other to a slow, dreamy tune.

Abby sighed as she watched them. They were stiff, as if there were more than just space between them, but the look on Shelby's face was hauntingly beautiful. His expression was less easily read, hard and rigid. But Abby would have bet that he was as close to heaven as he'd been in six years.

"How about that for a surprise?" Tyler murmured over her head, watching. "My God, look at them. They're like two halves of a whole."

"Why did they ever split up?" she asked him.

"I don't know," he said with a sigh. "I think my father was mixed up in it somehow, and one of his friends. But Shelby never talks about it. All I know is that she gave him back his ring and he's been bitter ever since."

As the music ended, the couple stopped dancing. Justin released Shelby very slowly and abruptly turned and walked out of the dance hall. After a minute, Shelby went back and sat down. Calhoun returned to the table.

Abby, turning to watch Calhoun bend toward Shelby, felt even sicker when she saw Shelby get up and leave the building, holding Calhoun's arm.

She toughed it out for several more dances, but when Calhoun didn't come back, she finally realized that he'd more than likely taken Shelby home. And was still there...

"Can we go home, Ty?" she asked huskily.

"Are you sure that's what you want?" Ty asked, his voice full of sympathy.

"I'm tired," Abby replied, and it was no lie. She really was. She was tired of watching Calhoun in action. First the blonde, now Shelby, and all in one week. But plain little Abby didn't figure in his world. She didn't even matter. She looked up at Ty, her eyes misty with unshed tears. "Do you mind?"

"Of course I mind," he said gently. "But if that's what you want, we'll go."

Abby didn't speak all the way home. It was unlike Calhoun to deliberately start trouble. It was almost as if he were getting back at Justin for something, but for what? Justin hadn't done anything to him.

Tyler walked her up the steps onto the long front porch with its graceful arches and porch furniture.

"Sorry the evening ended so abruptly," Tyler said. "But I hope you had fun."

"I did, honestly," she said, smiling up at him.

He took a deep breath and bent toward her hesitantly. When she didn't resist, he brushed his mouth gently against hers. There was no response, and after a minute he lifted his dark head.

His green eyes searched hers, and he wasn't smiling. "You don't have a clue, do you, honey?" he asked gently. "And I think it's lack of interest more than just lack of experience."

"You think I'm green as grass, too, I guess," she sighed miserably.

He cocked an eyebrow and tweaked her chin with his lean fingers. "So that's how it is." He pursed his lips. "Well, little Abby, with some cooperation from you I could take care of the green part in about five minutes. But I think that's a lesson the man you're mooning over should teach you." He touched his lips to her forehead. "I hope he appreciates his good luck. You're a special girl."

"He doesn't think so, but I'm glad you do." She looked up at him with a faint smile. "I wish it could be you."

His expression hardened for just an instant before the old mocking humor came back. "So do I. Want to go to dinner one night? Just a friendly dinner. I know when a door's being closed, so you won't have any worries on that score."

Her smile grew brighter. "You're a nice man."

"Not always." He touched her cheek gently. "Good night."

"Good night, Tyler. I had a good time."

"So did I."

He took the steps two at a time, and Abby stood quietly, watching him drive off. It was a long time before she turned and went into the house.

She closed the front door and started toward the staircase, only to be stopped in her tracks by an off-key rendition of a Mexican drinking song. Somewhere in the back of her mind she recognized it as one Justin sang on the very rare occasions when he had had too many glasses of whiskey.

CHAPTER SEVEN

ABBY WENT ALL the way inside the house and closed the door. Then she slipped down the hall to the study and peeked in.

Justin was holding a square whiskey glass. It was empty. He was sprawled on the leather sofa with his dark hair in his eyes and his shirt rumpled, one big boot propped on the spotless leather seat, singing for all he was worth. On the coffee table beside him were a smokeless ashtray, a crumpled cigarette pack, a fresh cigarette pack, and half a bottle of whiskey.

"No puedo hacer..." He stopped at the sound of her footsteps and looked up at her with bloodshot eyes.

"Oh, Justin," she moaned.

"Hello, Abby. Want a snort?"

She grimaced at the glass he held up. "It's empty," she told him.

He stared at it. "Damn. I guess it is. Well, I'll fill it up, then."

He threw his leg off the sofa, almost ending up on the floor in the process.

Abby put down her purse and coat and helped him onto the sofa. "Justin, this won't help," she said. "You know it won't."

"She cried," Justin murmured. "Damn it, she cried. And he took her home. I want to kill him, Abby," he said, his eyes blazing, his voice harsh. "My own brother, and I want to kill him because he went off with her!"

She bit her lower lip. She didn't know what to say, what to do. Justin never drank, and he never complained. But he looked as if he were dying, and Abby could sympathize. She'd felt that way, too, when Calhoun had left with Shelby.

"I saw them go," he ground out. He put his face in his lean hands and sighed heavily. "She's part of me. Still part of me after all the years, all the pain. Calhoun knew it, Abby, he did it deliberately...."

"Calhoun loves you," she defended him. "He wouldn't hurt you on purpose."

"Any man could fall in love with her," he kept on. "Shelby's beautiful. A dream walking."

Abby knew how attractive Shelby was. The knowledge didn't help her own sense of failure, her own lack of confidence or her breaking heart.

"Drinking isn't the answer," she said softly. She touched his arm. "Justin, get some sleep."

"How can I sleep when he's with her?"

"He won't be for long. Tyler just went home," she said tautly.

He took a deep breath, letting it out in jerks. His hands came away from his eyes. "I don't know much about women, Abby," he said absently. "I don't have Calhoun's charm, or his experience, or his looks."

She felt a sense of kinship with him then, because she had the same problem. Justin had always seemed so self-assured that she'd never thought of him having the same doubts and fears that she did.

"And I don't have Shelby's assets," Abby confessed.

She sat down beside him. "I guess we'd both lose a beauty contest. I wish I was blonde, Justin."

"I wish I had a black book." Justin sighed.

She grinned at him, and he grinned back. He poured whiskey into the glass, getting half again as much on the heavy coffee table. "Here," he offered it to her. "To hell with both of them. Have a shot of ego salve."

"Thanks, masked man," she sighed, taking it. "Don't mind if I do."

It tasted horrible. "Can you really drink this stuff and live?" she wondered. "It smells like what you put in the gas tank."

"It's Scotch whiskey," he returned. "Cutty Sark."

"It would cutty a shark all right," she mused, sipping it.

"Not cutty a shark. Cutty Shark. Sark. Hell." He took the glass and finished what little whiskey she'd left. "Now, if you're going to drink Cutty Sark, Abby, you have to learn to sing properly. I'll teach you this song I learned down in Mexico, okay?"

And he proceeded to do just that. When Calhoun walked in the front door about thirty minutes later, there was a very loud off-key chorus coming from the study.

He stared in the door incredulously. Justin was lying back on the sofa, his hair in his eyes, one knee lifted, a whiskey bottle in his hand. Abby was lying against his uplifted knee, her legs thrown over the coffee table, sipping from a whiskey glass. She looked as disreputable as his brother did, and both of them looked soaked to the back teeth.

"What in hell is going on?" Calhoun asked as he leaned against the doorjamb.

"We hate you," Abby informed him, lifting her glass in a toast.

"Amen." Justin grinned.

"And just as soon as we get through drinking and singing, we're going to go down to the feedlot and open all the gates, and you can spend the rest of the night chasing cows." She smiled drunkenly. "Justin and I figure that's what you do best, anyway. Chasing females, that is. So it doesn't matter what species, does it, old buddy?" she asked Justin, twisting her head back against his knee.

"Nope," Justin agreed. He lifted the whiskey bottle to his lips, rolling backward a little as he sipped it.

"We were going to lock you out," Abby added, blinking, "but we couldn't get up to put on the chain latches."

"My God." Calhoun shook his head at the spectacle they made. "I wish I had a camera."

"What for?" Justin asked pleasantly.

"Never mind." Calhoun unbuttoned his cuffs and rolled up his sleeves. "I'll make some black coffee."

"Don't want any," Abby murmured drowsily. "It would mess up our systems."

"That's right," Justin agreed.

"You'll see messed-up systems by morning, all right." Calhoun grimaced and moved off toward the kitchen.

"We should check his collar for lipstick!" Abby told Justin in a stage whisper.

"Good idea." Justin frowned. He started to sit up, then fell back against the arm of the sofa, cradling the bottle. "In a minute. I have to rest first."

"That's okay," she said. "I'll do it." She yawned. "When he gets back." Her eyes closed.

By the time Calhoun got back, they were both snoring. The whiskey bottle was lying on the floor, with the neck in Justin's lean hand. Calhoun righted it and put it on the table along with Abby's empty glass. The sight of them was as puzzling as it was amusing. Both Justin and Abby were usually the teetotalers at any gathering, and here they were soused. He wondered if his leaving with Shelby had set them off and realized that it probably had. In Justin's case it was understandable. But Abby's state was less easily understood, after the way she'd treated him since he'd kissed her. Unless…

He frowned, his dark eyes quiet and curious as he watched her flushed, sleeping face. Unless she'd finally realized why he'd been rough with her and was regretting her hot words. Was that possible? She'd seemed jealous of the time he'd spent with Shelby at the dance, and here she was three sheets to the wind. Well, well. Miracles did happen, it seemed.

He still wasn't sure about Tyler Jacobs's feelings toward Abby, but at least now he didn't have to worry about Justin's. If just seeing his brother with Shelby had this effect on Justin, he was still crazy about Shelby.

Calhoun lifted Abby and sat her crookedly in a chair while he laid Justin down on the sofa, pulled the older man's big boots off and covered him with one of the colorful serapes that were draped on chairs all over the room. Then he swung Abby up in his arms, balanced her on his knee while he turned off the overhead light, and closed the study door. Justin was going to hate himself in the morning.

Abby stirred as he carried her up the staircase. Her eyes flickered open, and she stared up drunkenly at the hard, quiet face above hers.

"You're with Shelby," she muttered drowsily. "We know you are. We know what you're doing, too." She laughed bitterly, then sighed and broke into the Mexican song Justin had taught her.

"Stop that." Calhoun scowled at her. "My God, you shouldn't use language like that."

"What language?"

"That song Justin taught you," he muttered, topping the staircase and heading down the hall toward her room. "It's vulgar as all hell."

"He didn't say it was."

"Of course he didn't. He wouldn't have taught it to you if he'd been sober. He'll have a heart attack if he hears you singing it when he's back on his feet."

"Want me to teach it to you?" she asked.

"I already know it."

"That isn't surprising," she sighed. She closed her eyes as he walked through the open door into her room and kicked it shut behind him. There were memories in this room, he thought angrily as he headed toward the bed. Abby, half-naked on that pink coverlet. Abby's soft body under his against that far wall—where she'd put a bookcase. He frowned at it. The new furniture arrangement was fairly revealing. Why would she shift the bookcase there unless it bothered her to remember?

He laid her down on the bed and watched her curl up. "No, you don't," he murmured. "You can't go to sleep like that."

She yawned. "Yes, I can."

He pulled off her shoes, and after a moment's hesitation his hard fingers went to her skirt. He removed it and about a hundred layers of full underskirts, and then her panty hose and blouse. Under it all, she was wearing dainty pink lace briefs and a matching bra that was no cover at all over her full, firm breasts.

This, he thought as he looked at her, was a hell of a mistake. But she was the most delicious little morsel. Her body was perfect, the most beautiful he'd seen in his life. And when he realized just how innocent she was, how untouched, his body rippled with pleasure mingled with need.

She sighed then, and her eyes opened. She searched his face, watching where his gaze had fallen. "You undressed me," she said.

"You couldn't sleep in that rig," he replied tautly.

"I guess not." She knew it should bother her that he was seeing her like this, in those wispy pink things she'd been crazy enough to buy at Misty's insistence. But if the way he was staring at her was any indication, he seemed to like what he saw.

"Do you have pajamas or a gown?" he asked after a minute.

"A gown. Under my pillow."

He managed to make his legs move and took out a bit of material that would cover no more of her than her underwear. "You'll freeze to death in this thing," he muttered.

"Misty said it was a sexy outfit," she said drowsily. She moved, her long hair framing her oval face with its delicate flush, her pale blue-gray eyes enormous as they searched the faintly blurred outline of his body. "I thought I'd seduce Ty," she added. "He likes me."

His face hardened. "Like hell you will," he said shortly.

"You did that to Shelby," she accused. "Shame on you, when Justin loves her."

"I didn't touch Shelby," he returned. "I left her at her front door and went back to the dance hall looking for you."

"I wasn't there," she murmured.

"Obviously." He didn't mention that he'd had to fight the urge to go looking for Tyler's car in case he and Abby were parked somewhere. The thought of her with Ty made him want to do something violent.

"Justin is going to beat you up when he can stand up again," she told him gaily.

"I guess he's entitled." Calhoun sighed. "I sure as hell made a mess of things." He sat down beside her, his eyes reluctantly leaving the long, sweet line of her legs and hips and the open seductiveness of her almost-bare breasts. "Do you know how perfect you are?" he said absently.

She was suddenly cold sober. Her eyes opened wide, searching his. "Me?"

"You," he said harshly. "From your legs to your hips to those sweet, pretty brea—" He stopped, hating his own vulnerability. "Come here." He put the gown in her lap and drew her into a sitting position, watching the tips of her firm breasts suddenly harden. He caught his breath.

She looked up at him curiously. "What's wrong?"

"This." He touched her delicately, only the back of his knuckles rubbing softly against her nipples. She pulled away, her breath audible, and he lifted his head to search her shocked eyes.

She looked back at him, relaxed from the alcohol, all her deeply buried longings surfacing without the restraint of a usually protective mind. She touched the back of his hand and intertwined her fingers with his.

And then she pulled gently, watching as she drew his hand across her breasts.

"Abby…" he ground out.

"I'm sorry," she whispered. "About what I said that morning. About how I…reacted." She swallowed, searching for courage. She opened his fingers and pressed them hesitantly just underneath her breast, lifting them so that he could feel the swell against his skin.

"Don't, for God's sake," he groaned.

She moved his hand against her, drowning in the sweetness of his touch, arching toward it. Both her hands went there, pushing his fingers completely over her. "Calhoun," she moaned. She felt so weak that she thought she'd have to lie down again, but she couldn't let go of his hand.

"You aren't sober enough," he whispered roughly, although the feel of her was doing terrible things to his self-control. He was already going rigid with need as he followed her down.

"I'm not sober enough to be afraid," she whispered. Her eyes searched his glittering eyes. "Teach me."

He actually shuddered. "I can't."

"Why?" she asked. "Because I'm plain and unsophisticated, because I'm not blonde—" Her voice broke.

So did his control. He leaned down, his smoky breath mingling with hers as his hand cupped her. "Because you're a virgin," he breathed into her mouth as he took it.

She moaned. It was sweet, so sweet. Nothing like that other time, when he'd been rough and hadn't given her enough room to respond. He'd been impatient and demanding, but now he was gentle. His fingers stroked her body from her breasts to her waist to her flat stomach. His mouth teased at hers, probed it, traced it in a silence that was thick with sensual pleasure. Abby felt warm all over, safe and cared-about. She let her lips admit the probing of his tongue, admit him into the sweet darkness of her mouth. She didn't even protest when the kiss grew much deeper, much slower, or when she felt his hand slide under her to find the catch at her back.

The air was cool on her body. He removed the lacy covering that was no covering at all, and his hands were heaven on her hot skin. She moaned, helping him, pressing his fingers against her, drawing them over her hungry body.

"Abby," he groaned against her mouth, half-crazy with the hunger to make love to her completely, to salve the ache that was throbbing through his body.

She opened her eyes, letting her gaze fall lazily to his chest. Her hands went to his shirt, and she worked at the buttons, feeling him tense. But he didn't protest, even though his heartbeat was shaking his big body as it lay beside hers.

"There," she whispered when she could see and touch the thick wedge of hair that ran down to his belt. "I'll bet women love to touch you there," she murmured as she pressed her fingers hungrily against him.

"I've never let a woman touch me like this before," he said huskily. "I didn't like it until now."

Her eyes searched his, and she shifted restlessly on the coverlet, hungry, aching for something without a name, without an image.

"What do you want?" he asked gruffly, searching her eyes. "Tell me. I'll do anything you want me to."

She swallowed, and her lips parted unsteadily. She

took his head in her hands and tugged at it, lifting her body. And he understood without her having to put it into words.

"Here?" he whispered tenderly, and put his open mouth completely over the swollen tip of her breast.

She moaned helplessly. It was beyond her wildest imaginings of what passion would feel like. Her body was in control. Her mind could only watch, it couldn't slow down what was happening. She twisted the cool, thick strands of his blond hair while he smoothed his warm mouth over her breasts and stomach, her faint cries encouraging him, her body welcoming him.

His mouth slid back up to meet hers. And as she opened her own lips to welcome him, she felt his body slowly cover her.

Her eyes opened then as his mouth lifted fractionally, and she watched his face, hard with passion, as his body fit itself perfectly to her slenderness.

She barely breathed, her eyes wide and full of new knowledge as she felt him intimately and knew without words how badly he wanted her.

"Are you afraid this time?" he whispered quietly.

"I should be," she replied. She reached up and touched his face as he drew his chest slowly, teasingly over her breasts. Her breath caught, but she traced his eyebrows, his cheeks, his mouth with fingers that trembled and adored him.

His big, callused hands slid under her back, lifting her up into the curve of his body. "I want you, Abby," he whispered, bending to her mouth as his body shuddered over hers. "I want you so much...."

She curled her arms around his head and held his

mouth against her eager one. "I want you, too, Calhoun," she whispered into his mouth.

He almost lost control completely then. He kissed her until he had to stop for breath, his body shuddering rhythmically, his knee between her long, soft legs, his hand low on her hips. He felt her trembling and heard her whimper. Oddly, it brought him to his senses.

Slowly, so slowly, he rolled onto his side, bringing her with him, cradling her against his damp body. He slid his hands to her head, holding her forehead to his throbbing chest.

"Lie still, honey," he whispered raggedly when she began to move again. He caught her hips and stilled them. "Just lie against me and breathe. It will be all right in a minute. Lie still, baby."

Her hands were flat against his chest, trembling there in the thick mat of hair, and she felt his unsteady breathing against her hair. He was as shaken as she was, but why had he stopped? She didn't understand. If he wanted her, then why had he stopped?

"Sweet thing," he breathed when the tremor was almost out of his big arms. "Sweet, precious thing, another few seconds and nothing on earth would have stopped me, did you know?"

She nuzzled her head against him. "Why did you stop?" she asked dazedly.

He tilted her head back on the pillow and smiled into her drowsy eyes. "Don't you know?"

"Because I'm not blonde, I guess," she sighed, almost weeping with frustration and disappointment.

"Because you're not lucid," he corrected. He brushed

the long, soft hair away from her face. "Abby, you're half lit."

"I want you," she moaned.

"I know. I can see it. Feel it." He hugged her close for a minute, because he was almost in control now. Then he let go and quickly and efficiently slid her into her gown. "Sit up, honey."

She did, and he eased back the covers and helped her get under them. She lay quietly beneath two layers of fabric and blinked at him sleepily. "Calhoun, stay with me," she whispered.

He smiled gently, his dark eyes possessive on her flushed face. "Justin would love finding us in your bed together. He'd probably make me marry you."

"And I guess that would be the end of your world," she replied.

His expression hardened. He drew in a slow breath and touched her cheek gently, thoughtfully. "I've been alone a long time. I like being my own boss, answering to no one. I've been a rounder, and in some ways I still am. I'm a bad marriage risk."

"One woman wouldn't satisfy you, I guess," she murmured, hiding her eyes from him. All her dreams were dead now. Every last one. He wanted her, but not enough for marriage. He was telling her so.

He shrugged, confused and feeling faintly hunted. "One woman never has," he said curtly. "I don't want to be tied."

"God forbid that I should try," Abby said, forcing a smile. "Don't worry, Calhoun, I was just…experimenting. I wondered why you were so rough with me the other morning, and I wanted to see if passion made peo-

ple rough. I guess it does, because that's how I felt tonight. Thanks for the...the lesson."

He frowned slightly, searching her eyes. "Is that all
it felt like? An experiment? A lesson in making love?"

"Tyler said I needed teaching," she said with a yawn,
missing the flash of fury in his face. "But I don't anymore." She closed her eyes and turned her face against
the pillow. "I'm sleepy."

Calhoun sat watching her, his eyes stormy. She'd
used him. That was all she'd wanted. She'd been exper-
imenting, seeing how it felt to be touched. Damn her!

He got up, glaring at the lacy bra he'd removed from
her soft breasts just before she'd let him touch them.
Let him! God, she'd helped him! His blood ran hot at
the memory of how uninhibited she'd been with him
tonight. Had she been competing with Shelby, or had
it been curiosity alone? Could she care about him and
be hiding it? And how did he feel? Did he just want her
physically, or was it more than that? Could he bear the
loss of his freedom? Because it would come to that if
he took her. Marriage. Trap.

He tossed the bra onto the chair beside her bed and
took a long last look at her sleeping face. She didn't
need to be blonde. She was exquisite. Her long hair was
spread out around her, her lashes were feathering her
flushed cheek, and her parted lips were pink and faintly
swollen because he'd been hungry. She was delicious.
Virginal and sweet-tasting and exquisitely beautiful
without her clothes. He wondered if he'd ever get over
the taste of her—if he'd be able to forget. Hell, would
he ever be able to have another woman, or would the
memory of Abby always stand in the way?

He opened the door and went out, closing it quietly behind him. He should never have touched her in the first place, he thought furiously.

He had to get away for a while. Far away, so that he could think things through. Now that he'd touched Abby, it was going to be the purest kind of hell keeping his hands off her. And Justin wouldn't like having that sort of loveplay going on, not if it threatened Abby. Calhoun knew that if he took Abby into his arms again, it wasn't going to end with a few kisses. He wanted her too badly, and she was too responsive. He aroused her as no man ever had. That meant she'd give herself to him with hardly any coaxing. Calhoun was terrified that he might lose his head and take her.

He didn't want marriage. He didn't want ties. Abby wouldn't understand that. In her world, lovemaking meant marriage. Maybe in his, too, when the woman was a virgin. He didn't like the noose she was tying around his neck, but he hated the thought of never touching her again almost as much.

She was heaven to love. Her mouth was young and sweet and so eager to learn. Her body was nectar. Just the sight of it made him drunk, not to mention the exquisite feel of it between his hands, under his skin.

Abby, he groaned inwardly as he made his way to his own room. He couldn't have her and he couldn't give her up. He didn't know what in hell he was going to do. Maybe when he got back from wherever he wound up he would have reached a decision.

He sat down at the small desk in a corner of his room and wrote Justin a note telling him he was going away for a few days to check on some stockers in Montana.

Justin might think it strange, but Abby wouldn't. He wondered how she was going to feel when she woke up and found him gone. He hoped she wouldn't even remember what they'd done in her bed together. But even if she did, that was going to be one private memory. Abby wouldn't share it any more than he would.

CHAPTER EIGHT

ABBY GROANED THE minute the light got to her eyes. She had the world's biggest headache, and nausea sat in the pit of her stomach like acid.

She managed to get on her feet and into the bathroom, where she bathed her face with cold water and pressed a cold cloth against her eyes. She remembered drinking whiskey in the study with Justin. Then Calhoun had taken her to bed, and—

Her head jerked up. In the mirror her eyes looked wild, and her paleness had been eclipsed by a scarlet blush. She'd let Calhoun see her. Worse, she'd let him touch her. She swallowed. Well, at least she remembered that he'd stopped before she'd gone to sleep, so nothing unspeakable had happened, thank God. As more of the details of her eagerness came back, she groaned in embarrassment. She'd never be able to look at him again, although what had happened would make the sweetest of memories to tuck in a corner of her mind for solace in her old age. Calhoun would never settle down or fall in love with her. He'd be forever out chasing his blondes. But this was something of him that Abby would always have. A tiny crumb of loving to live on.

Now she understood what had happened that morning in her room. He hadn't been rough on purpose. He'd wanted her. It gave her the oddest feeling of pride that she could have thrown him that far off balance. She was almost sure that no other woman ever had. Looking back, she thought she must have seemed terribly naive to him for reacting that way to an intimate kiss. But at the time his actions had seemed shocking and frightening. For all her dreams about Calhoun, she hadn't realized what the reality of his lovemaking would be like. Now that she knew, it was like an addiction. She wanted more. But could she afford the risk of letting him that close again?

A sob racked her slender body. Well, she had to get herself together. She had to remember her pride. She held her aching head. She had to remember, most of all, to never accept a drink of whiskey from Justin again! Or from anyone, for that matter. Drowning one's sorrows was vastly overrated. She'd tried it, and now she knew that it only brought hangovers, not oblivion.

She put on a gray slacks suit with a blue blouse, left her hair around her shoulders because she was hurting too much to worry with putting it up, and pulled on a pair of sunglasses. Then she felt her way down the staircase and into the dining room.

Justin was sitting at the table with his head in his hands. He was dressed in jeans and a blue checked shirt, and when he looked up, his eyes looked even worse than Abby's.

"Nice touch," he remarked, noticing the dark glasses. "I wish I had mine, but they're out in the car."

"You look like I feel," Abby said as she sat down, very gently, in the chair beside him, grimacing because even that slight jarring made her head feel like bursting. "How are we going to work today?"

"Beats me," Justin replied. "Calhoun's gone."

Her heart skipped a beat, and she was glad she was wearing dark glasses. "Is he?"

"Skipped town. Gone to Montana to look at stockers, or so he said." He fumbled for a cigarette and lit it. "I'm rather disappointed. I had consoled myself all morning with the thought of beating the hell out of him for last night."

"How selfish," Abby muttered as she tried to pour herself a cup of hot coffee from the carafe. "I ought to get in a lick or two of my own."

"I'll sit on him, you can hit him," Justin offered. He sipped black coffee and smoked quietly.

Abby took one swallow of her coffee and sat back, feeling miserable. "Weren't we singing something?" she thought, frowning. "Oh, yes, I remember...." She launched into a few measures of the song. Justin went white, and Maria came running out of the kitchen, beet red, waving her apron.

A tidal wave of Spanish hit Abby between the eyes, delivered in a scolding, furious tone. "For shame, for shame!" Maria wound up breathlessly, crossing herself. "Where you learn such terrible language?"

Abby stared at her blankly. "Justin taught me," she said.

Justin had his face in his hands. Maria launched into him, and he replied in the same tongue, a little sheepishly. Maria shook her head and stormed out of the room.

"What did I say?" Abby asked him, wide-eyed.

He took a slow breath. "You don't want to know," he said finally. "I think you'd better forget the song, Abby, or we're going to be eating burned meals for a month."

"You taught it to me," she pointed out.

He groaned. "I was sauced. That was a drinking song I learned when I was barely out of school from one of the Mexican boys I used to pal around with. I didn't even remember it until last night, and I never should have taught it to you."

"It's all Calhoun's fault," she said.

"I wonder why he started it?" Justin asked, watching her. "He didn't show any signs of wanting to dance until he saw you and Tyler."

Abby shifted restlessly in her chair. "Well, he doesn't want me," she said miserably. "Not on any permanent basis, anyway. He told me last night that he was a bad marriage risk. He likes variety, you see."

"Most men do, until they find themselves so hopelessly enthralled with one woman that they can't even look at anyone else," Justin said tersely, staring at his coffee.

"Is that why you spend all your time alone?" she asked gently, searching his hard, drawn face. "Because your world begins and ends with Shelby?"

He glared at her. "Abby..."

"Sorry." She sipped the coffee. "It's just that I know how it feels now." She traced the pattern of her lipstick on the edge of the cup. "I feel that way about your stupid, blind brother."

The brief anger left his face, and he smiled gently. "I could pretend to be surprised, but I'm not. You're pretty obvious. On the other hand," he added, tilting his head back, "so is he. In all the years Calhoun's been dating, this is the first time I've ever seen him behave as if he were jealous."

Abby bit her lower lip. "He...wants me," she said. She couldn't look at him as she said it.

"Of course," he replied carelessly, smiling at her shocked expression. "Abby, for a man that's a big part of caring about a woman."

"I guess I don't know very much about men," she said with a sigh. "In fact, I don't know anything. Except that I want to live with him all my life, and have children with him, and look after him when he's sick, and keep him company when he's lonely." She bit her lower lip. "So, that being the case, Justin, I think I'd better get out while I still can. Before something happens and Calhoun winds up trapped." She looked up at Justin, her fear plain in her eyes. "You understand, don't you?"

He nodded. "I think you're very wise, Abby. If he cares enough, he'll come after you. If he doesn't…you might save both of you a lot of heartache by heading off trouble." He shrugged. "But I'll miss having you around."

"I'll come back and visit." She sipped more coffee, and as she began to feel a little better she took off her dark glasses. "Can I still have my twenty-first birthday party here?"

"Sure," he said readily.

"You may not approve of my guest list," she added gently.

He took a deep breath. "Tyler Jacobs will be on it, I gather."

"And Shelby." He glared at her, and she smiled hesitantly. "Justin, I can't very well invite him and not her. How would it look?"

"Calhoun might—" He stopped short.

Abby lifted her chin. "I have to stop caring what Calhoun does, and so do you. And if you don't like Calhoun paying attention to Shelby, why not do something about it?" she added impishly. "You might get her drunk and teach her that terrible song."

He almost smiled. "I did once," he said, his dark eyes softening at the memory. "The night we got engaged." Then he flinched and got up from the table. "I've got to try and go to work. How about you? Can you make it?"

"Of course I can." She stood up, feeling as wobbly as he looked. She glanced at him ruefully. "Shall we flip a coin and see who drives?"

He chuckled. "I think I'd better. I've got more practice at it than you have. Come on."

They muddled through the day, and at the end of it Abby called Mrs. Simpson and asked if she could go ahead and move in later that week. The older woman was delighted and promised to have the room ready. Then, with a heavy heart, Abby began to pack up her things, getting ready to say goodbye to the only home she'd known for the past five and a half years. Worst of all was the realization that once she left it she'd probably never see Calhoun again. Although she hadn't mentioned it to Justin yet, she'd decided to quit her job at the feedlot, too. The prospect of seeing Calhoun every day, knowing that he wanted her but had no love for her, would tear her heart out.

Justin and two of the cowhands helped her get her possessions over to Mrs. Simpson's house. Since the room was furnished, she hadn't tried to take furniture with her, but she had plenty of clothes and records and books to carry. Her stereo and her color television went with her, along with her memorabilia. It was easier to think about living elsewhere with her belongings around. But after having a home of her own, even if she had shared it with the brothers, it was hard to adjust to a small apartment in someone else's house.

She gave notice at the feedlot the very next day. It was hard, but Justin seemed to understand. He didn't say a word. He just smiled.

But Calhoun didn't understand. He came back unexpectedly in the middle of the following week, and when Abby came back from lunch it was to find him sitting on the corner of her desk, looking worn and smoking like a furnace.

She stared at him with eyes that adored him. It had only been a few days. A little over a week. But she'd ached for him. To be without him was like having part of her body cut away, and she didn't know how she was going to manage to hide her feelings from him.

He was wearing a beige suit with a striped shirt, and his blond hair gleamed clean and thick in the light from the office window. He scowled over his cigarette.

She straightened the skirt of her pale blue dress nervously, waiting for him to look up. Then he did, and she saw the darkness of his eyes, the faint shadows under them.

He looked at her for a long time, oblivious to the noise around them, the ringing telephones, the buzz of printers. He looked at her until she felt uncomfortably warm and she blushed.

"You've moved out," he said without preamble.

"Yes," she replied huskily.

"And you've put in your notice here."

She took a deep breath, moving a little closer. He smelled of spice and soap, and she stared unconsciously at his mouth, remembering its exquisite sweetness on her lips. "I… I'm going to work for George Brady and his father," she said. "At the insurance office. I'm used to working with forms, so it won't be so unfamiliar."

"Why?" he ground out.

She smoothed her lower lip with her tongue, looking up at him with soft, wounded eyes.

"Here," he muttered, catching her arm. He pulled her into his office and closed the door behind them, frowning down at her. He didn't let go even then. His fingers were warm and firm through her soft sleeve, and their touch made her tingle.

"You know I can't stay in the house anymore," she whispered. "You know why."

"Are you that afraid of me?" he asked quietly.

She shifted restlessly, letting her eyes slide down to his firm jaw. "I'm afraid of what could happen."

"I see."

It was embarrassing to talk to him about it, but he had to know how vulnerable she was. It wasn't anything he hadn't guessed. She studied his patterned red tie carelessly.

"I suppose I sound conceited," she added. "But... but if you—" Her eyes closed. "I'm vulnerable," she whispered. Her lower lip trembled, and she bit it. "Oh, Calhoun, I'm so vulnerable—"

"Don't you think I know?" he said under his breath, and the eyes that met hers were dark with emotion. "Why do you think I left?"

She couldn't look at him anymore. She felt naked. "Well, I'm saving you from any more complications," she said tightly. "I won't be around."

He couldn't seem to breathe. His cigarette had burned out, and it hung in his hand, as dead as he felt. "Is that what you want?"

She straightened. "Tyler's taking me to dinner tonight," she said out of the blue, just to let him see that she wasn't going to try to hang on to him or act lovesick. "He's got a job, too, by the way. He's going to manage old man Regan's ranch for him. In no time at all he'll be settled and able to take on more responsibilities."

Calhoun's heart felt like lead in his chest. Was she saying what he thought she was? Was she implying that she might marry Tyler?

"You don't love him," he said harshly.

She looked up. "I don't need to," she replied quietly. "Love isn't anything. It's just an emotion that blinds people to reality."

"Abby!" he burst out. "You can't believe that?"

"Look who's talking." She glared at him. "You're the one who said it was for the birds, aren't you? You've never let your emotions get in the way of a good time!"

He took a slow, steadying breath, and his dark eyes searched hers in the static silence that followed. "Maybe that was true a few years ago," he admitted, his voice deep and slow and measured. "I've never had any trouble attracting women, and I had a sizable appetite back then. But I learned that sex by itself has very little flavor, and it didn't take long to realize that most of those women were trading their bodies for what I could give them." He laughed bitterly. "How would that appeal to you, tidbit? Being traded a few kisses and a night in bed for a car or a coat or some expensive jewelry, so that you never could be sure that it was you or your wallet they really wanted?"

She'd never heard him talk like this. He never had, at least not to her. She searched his face, finding cynicism and faint mockery in his smile, in his hard eyes.

"You're very attractive," she replied. "Surely you know that."

His big shoulders rose and fell. "Plenty of men are," he said without conceit. "But I'm rich with it. My money has appeal."

"Only to a certain type of woman," she reminded him. "One who doesn't want ties or emotional liabilities. One with mercenary tendencies who could walk away from you if you lost everything, or if you were sick or old." She smiled gently. "I suppose you liked that, too. You could be independent and still enjoy yourself."

He frowned a little, watching her. "I haven't had a woman since the night you went to the strip show," he said quietly.

She didn't want to hear about his love life. She turned her head. "You had dates…."

"Well, my God, I can date women without seducing them!"

"It's none of my business." She started to reach for the doorknob, but his big, warm hand engulfed hers, sensuously caressing her fingers as he moved closer, drowning her in the clean cologne-rich scent of him.

"Make it your business," he said tautly.

She looked up at him slowly, searchingly. But there was nothing readable in his face or his eyes or even the set of his head. It was like trying to learn from stone. "I don't understand," she said, her voice faltering.

"I don't like bridles," he said shortly. "I don't like the thought of ropes around me, or a ring through my nose. I hate the thought of marriage." He grimaced, but his eyes held hers. "But you're in my blood," he breathed. "And I don't know what to do about it."

"I won't sleep with you," she said with quiet pride.

"And yes, I want to." She laughed bitterly. "More than I want to breathe."

"Yes. I knew that when I left." He touched her hair, smoothing it, tracing its length down to her shoulder with a possessive touch that made her tremble. "I know all too well how you feel about me. I suspected it the night you went to that bar with Misty and you whispered that you wished you were blonde...." His dark eyes lanced up to her shocked ones. "And the night of the square dance cinched it. I did a lot of thinking while I was away. I managed to put two and two together at last."

She felt as if he'd cut the ground from under her feet. Stark naked. She'd thought her secret was safe, and now it wasn't.

"You don't need to deny it," he added when he saw her expression. "There's no reason to. I'm not going to make fun of you or try to embarrass you. But I told you the night I left how I felt. I'm twelve years older than you. I'm a rounder, and I haven't ever tried abstinence. You're even my ward. If I had any sense I'd let you go and wave you off, laughing. You're a complication I don't want or need."

"Thanks," she said shortly. Her face was flaming. It was embarrassing to have him see right through her, when she hadn't realized how transparent she must be to an experienced man.

"That's what my mind is telling me," he added, laughing with faint mockery as he moved closer. "Now let me show you what my body says—"

She opened her mouth to protest, but his lips covered hers before she could speak. His kiss was warm and slow, and when his hands went to her hips and pulled them against his and he let her feel the blatant hunger of his body, she gave in.

"So soft," he whispered as he brushed his lips over her mouth. "So sweet. I dream about kissing you. I dream about your body and the way you are with me when I make love to you. I want you more than I've ever wanted a woman in my life."

"That's…physical," she protested.

"That's all I can offer you," he replied. His lips moved to her eyelids, closing them with kisses. "Now do you see, Abby? I've never loved anyone. I've never wanted that. All you can have of me is this."

She swallowed. What a bitter, hopeless relationship that would be. She loved him with all her heart, and all he had to offer her was his body.

He tasted the tears before he saw them. His blond head lifted, and he winced at the sight of her drenched blue-gray eyes. "Oh, God, don't," he breathed, wiping the wetness away with his thumbs.

"Let me go, please," she pleaded, pushing at his broad, hard chest.

"You want something I can't give you."

"I know that now," she whispered. She bit on her lower lip to stop it from trembling, and stared at his tie. "I guess I was never cut out to be a mercenary blonde," she said with an attempt at humor, feeling his body stiffen as she made the remark. She looked up then, with drenched eyes that couldn't hide her hunger for his heart. "But I would have loved you so—"

"Abby," he groaned. His mouth silenced her, ardently, roughly. He wrapped her up in his hard arms, kissing her with such force that her head bent back against his arms, and still he didn't stop, couldn't stop. He began to tremble faintly, the hunger a living thing in him, torturously sweet.

But Abby couldn't bear the bitter mockery of a kiss that screamed of pity and desire. She twisted her mouth from under his and buried her face in his jacket, her hands gripping the fabric as she shook with frustrated need.

"I'm young," she whispered after a minute. "I'll get over you."

"Will you?" His voice sounded odd. His big hands were in her hair, holding her head to him. They were just a little unsteady, and the chest under her forehead was shuddering with the force of his heartbeat.

"I'll have to," she said. She took a slow, soft breath. "It was enough that you and Justin have taken care of me all these years," she murmured. "I can't expect anything more from you. I shouldn't have. It was…just proximity, and a huge crush, and…and curiosity, that's all. I didn't mean—"

"Stop it," he said harshly. He pulled her closer, enfolding her in his big arms, holding her, rocking her. "My God, stop it. Am I laughing at you? Am I making fun of how you feel, or trying to shame you for it? I never should have said that to you at the feedlot that day about hating the way you looked at me. I didn't mean it. I wanted you so badly all I could think about was getting you out of the car before I lost my head." He laughed coldly. "And a hell of a lot of good it did. I lost it anyway, that morning in your room, and scared the hell out of you."

"I didn't understand what intimacy was until then," she confessed quietly.

"And the way I was holding you made you all too aware of what I wanted," he added with a faint laugh.

She flushed. "Yes."

He smoothed her hair, noticing the way her body was resting against his, so trustingly, even though he was just as aroused now as he had been the morning he'd mentioned. "And now it doesn't frighten you, does it?" he whispered, tilting her eyes up to his.

She searched his face softly. "No. Nothing about you frightens me or embarrasses me."

He touched her cheek, her mouth, and his powerful legs trembled at the contact with hers. "Not even knowing how badly I want you?"

She shook her head. "Not even that. I—" She dropped her gaze.

"You—" He made her look at him. "Say it," he whispered. "Say the words. I want it all."

She should have denied how she felt. Or run. Something. "I love you," she whispered with faint anguish in her tone.

His eyes caressed her face. "Such big eyes," he breathed. "So soft. So full of secrets." He bent and drew his mouth tenderly against hers. "You're very special to me, Abby. Part of my life. I wish I could give you what you want. I wish I could give you back those words and offer you a future. But that would cheat us both ultimately. Marriage should be a joint commitment, with a foundation of shared love." He sighed bitterly. "I... don't know how to love. Justin and I were raised by our father, Abby. Our mother died when I was born. We never had a woman's touch, and until your mother came along, Dad went from one woman to another like a bee to pollen." He toyed with a strand of her hair. "I don't understand commitment, because I never got a good look at it. The only thing I know about love is that it doesn't last. Look at Justin. See what happened to him because it all went wrong."

"At least he took the chance," she said gently. "And it does last. Or didn't you see how Justin and Shelby looked at each other while they were dancing?"

"Is that your idea of a perfect relationship?" he asked with a cold laugh. "A little love, followed by years of hating each other?"

"What's your idea of perfection, Calhoun?" she replied. "A succession of one-night stands and a lonely old age at the end of the road, with no family, no one to love you, nothing to leave behind?"

He scowled down at her. "At least I won't die of a broken heart," he said.

"No," she replied. "You won't." She pushed at his chest, but he wouldn't move. "Let me go, please."

"Why?"

"Because I've got a lot of work to get through."

"And a date with Tyler," he added mockingly.

She glanced up. "Tyler is solid, capable, very masculine and a good marriage risk. He isn't afraid of commitment. He'll make a good husband."

"You aren't marrying Tyler," he said shortly.

"Not unless he asks me," she agreed.

"You aren't marrying him even if he does."

"How do you plan to stop me?" she asked curiously.

"Guess."

She cocked her head, staring up at his stubborn face. "Why bother? You don't want me, except in bed. I want someone who can love me."

He shifted restlessly. "Maybe love can be taught,"

he said uncomfortably. He stared down at her hands on his chest. "Maybe you could teach me how."

She didn't feel as if her feet were touching the floor anymore. Could she possibly have heard him say that?

"I'm only twenty," she reminded him, "and your ward, and you don't want commitment—"

His mouth covered hers in midsentence, tenderly probing, pushing at it, savoring it. "Kiss me, Abby," he whispered into her mouth.

"I don't want—" she tried to protest.

"Love me, baby," he breathed.

Her arms slid under his jacket and around him. She pressed close, holding him, giving him her mouth with all the wonder and generosity of her love for him. She felt his lips smile against hers, heard his soft breathing, and then he increased the pressure of his mouth and his arms and she went under in a maze of stars.

A long time later, he groaned and his mouth slid to her throat, his arms contracting as he tried to breathe. "That," he whispered roughly, "was a mistake."

She could hardly get her own breath, and she knew it was much harder for him. She smoothed his cool, thick hair, gently soothing him, comforting him as he fought for control.

Her lips pressed light, undemanding kisses to his cheek, his temple, his closed eyelids. He stood very still, giving her that freedom with a sense of wonder at how it felt to be caressed so tenderly.

His eyes opened when she stopped. "That was a nice touch," he whispered, cupping her face in his warm hands. "Have you been talking to Misty again, or did you just think it might calm me down?"

"I read it in a book," she confessed, lowering her flushed face.

"Reading about it and doing it are pretty different, aren't they?" he asked gently.

"Yes." She was still trying to breathe properly. Her fingers toyed with a button on his patterned shirt. He was warm, and she loved the feel and smell and closeness of his body towering over her.

"I've never made love to a virgin," he whispered. His mouth touched her forehead with breathless tenderness. "I'd have to hurt you a little, maybe, at first."

She felt waves of embarrassment wash over her at the vivid pictures in her mind. His big, nude body over hers in bed, covering her, his hands holding her...

"Does it always hurt?" she asked shyly.

"Not for a man," he whispered, lifting his eyes to hers. "Not for you, either, if I could keep my head long enough to arouse you properly."

Her heart was going like a trip hammer. "H...how... would you?"

He kissed the very tip of her nose. "Go out with me and I'll show you."

"On a date?" she whispered.

"Mmm-hmm." He nuzzled his cheek against hers. "Tomorrow night. I'll take you to Houston. We'll wipe out the bad memory of that last time there. We'll dance and walk." He brushed his mouth over her ear. "Remember, I have an apartment there," he said slowly.

She closed her eyes. "No. I won't go to your apartment."

"It isn't the last century," he whispered. "We could be alone. We could make love."

Her face flamed. "No," she repeated.

"Abby…"

She pulled away from him, hating her own inhibitions and his attitude, as well. If he'd loved her, it might have been different. But he didn't. He wanted her. And after that first time, she'd be just like every other woman he'd slept with. She'd be just another one of Calhoun Ballenger's conquests, an ache that he'd satisfied and forgotten. A used toy.

"I have work to do," she said, and tried to smile. "And… I don't think I'll go to Houston with you, thanks all the same."

He realized only then what she thought. He'd made it sound as if he was going to round off the evening with a night in bed. He'd made it sound cheap, and that hadn't been his intention at all. He'd meant that he'd make love to her, very light love, and then he'd take her home. He hadn't meant—!

"Abby, no!" he burst out. "I didn't mean what you think!"

She opened the door. "I have to go." She went out, and he followed her, intent on having things out. But as he reached for her, Justin came in with two businessmen. Abby escaped into the bathroom, shaking, broken inside by hopelessness and rejection. Calhoun not only didn't love her. Now he didn't even respect her.

CHAPTER NINE

ABBY WAS GRATEFUL that business kept Calhoun occupied for the next two days. She could hardly bear the thought of seeing him when he knew so well how she felt about him. And now that he'd reduced their relationship to a strictly physical one, some of the joy had gone out of life for her. She hadn't expected that he'd actually proposition her. But if inviting her to his apartment wasn't a proposition, what was it?

She managed to avoid him when he was in the office that Thursday and Friday, since things stayed hectic. Abby was training a new secretary, and Calhoun seemed reluctant to discuss their private lives around the other woman. She was a year older than Abby, bright and quick-witted. And, unfortunately, already stuck on Calhoun. She had a habit of sighing and batting her long eyelashes every time he passed her desk. Abby was glad Friday was her last day. Having to watch Calhoun with a potential new conquest—the girl was blonde and very pretty—was just unbearable.

There was a small farewell party for Abby late Friday afternoon. Justin and Mr. Ayker and the women who worked in the office had taken up a collection to buy her a beautiful cardigan in a pale yellow shade. There was a cake, too, and Justin made a brief speech about how valuable she'd been to them and how they hated losing her. Calhoun wasn't there. Abby left with mingled relief and disappointment. Apparently she wasn't even going to get to say goodbye to him. Well, that suited her. She didn't care if he was glad to be rid of her. Not one bit.

She cried all the way to Mrs. Simpson's house because she didn't care.

Tyler was right on time to take her to dinner. He looked good dressed up. He was wearing a navy blazer with tan slacks, a white shirt and a natty blue striped tie. He looked elegant and very masculine. His green eyes danced as Abby came downstairs in a gray crepe dress with a full skirt and a low, crosscut bodice with fabric buttons. Her hair was neatly styled, and she looked elegant and sexy.

"You look pretty," he commented with a slow smile.

She curtsied. "So do you. Good night, Mrs. Simpson," she called out. "I'll be in by midnight!"

Mrs. Simpson came to the doorway, grinning. "Mind that no good-looking woman tries to take Ty away from you," she teased.

"No chance of that," he replied carelessly, smiling down at Abby. "This dishy lady is enough for me. Good night, Mrs. Simpson."

"Good night," the older woman replied. "Have fun."

Tyler walked her out to his white Ford, opening the door for her. "I like your landlady. Her husband used to work for Dad. Did you know that?"

"She mentioned something about it," Abby told him. "She's a nice landlady."

He got in, started the car and pulled out onto the road. "Do you miss the big house?"

"I miss the brothers," she said quietly, fingering her

small purse. "It's hard getting used to my own company. There was always something going on at home."

"Can I ask why you moved out?" he persisted, glancing in her direction.

She smiled at him. "No."

His eyebrows arched wickedly. "Don't tell me. Calhoun wrestled you down on the desk and tried to ravish you."

Her face turned scarlet. She cleared her throat. "Don't be absurd."

He chuckled. "It isn't absurd, considering the way he was watching you dance with me that night at the bar."

"He was too busy dancing with Shelby to notice," she murmured. "Justin went home and got drunk afterward," she added, neglecting to mention her own participation.

"Shelby cried all night." He sighed. "Hell of a thing, isn't it, Abby, the way they still care about each other. Six years, and they're as far apart now as they were then."

"And both of them dying inside," she added. She thought about herself and Calhoun and hoped that she wasn't going to end up like Shelby, grieving for a man she could never have. She forced a bright smile. "Where are we going?"

"To that new Greek restaurant," he told her. "They say the food is really good. Have you ever had Greek food?"

"No. I'm looking forward to trying it," she said, and the conversation was back on safe territory again and away from the disturbing subject of Calhoun.

Meanwhile, Calhoun was pacing in Justin's study at

the house, his dark eyes black, his hands linked behind his back, scowling.

"Will you stop?" Justin muttered as he tried to add figures and ignore the distraction of his restless brother. "Abby's not our responsibility anymore. She's a grown woman."

"I can't help it. Tyler's been around. He's no boy."

"So long as Abby isn't interested in him, none of that will matter."

Calhoun stopped pacing and glared at him. "And what if she is? What if she's throwing herself at him on the rebound?"

Justin laid down his pencil. "Rebound from whom?" he asked, lighting a cigarette.

Calhoun rammed his hands into his pockets and stared out the dark window. "From me. She loves me," he said quietly.

"Yes," Justin replied, and for once his tone was sympathetic.

Calhoun hadn't realized how much Justin knew. He turned, his dark eyes curious, wary. "Did she tell you?"

Justin nodded. He took a draw from the cigarette, watching it instead of his brother. "She's young, but that could be an advantage. She isn't cynical or world-weary or promiscuous like most of your women. And she hasn't got a mercenary bone in her body."

"She'd want marriage," Calhoun replied tautly. "Happily ever after. I don't know if I could adjust to being married."

Justin looked up. "How are you going to take to a life without Abby in it?"

For an instant, Calhoun looked hunted. He stared

at the carpet. "And what if it doesn't last?" he replied harshly. "What if it all falls apart?"

Justin blew out a cloud of smoke. "Love lasts. And if you're worried about being faithful to her," he added with a pointed stare, "you may find that fidelity isn't all that difficult."

Calhoun's dark eyes snapped. "Oh, sure. Look at you. Happily ever after. Your perfect relationship fell apart," he said, hurting and striking out because of it. "And how many women have you consoled yourself with in the past six years?"

Justin stared at him for a long moment, his eyes narrow and glittering. He smiled then, faintly. "None."

Calhoun didn't move. He hadn't expected that answer, despite Justin's clamlike attitude toward his private life.

"I had an old-fashioned idea that sex came after marriage with a woman like Shelby," Justin said quietly. "So I held back. After she broke it off, I found that I wasn't capable of wanting anyone else." He turned away, oblivious to Calhoun's shocked expression. "These days I find my consolation in work, Calhoun. I've never wanted anyone but Shelby since the day I met her. God help me, I still don't."

The younger man felt as if he'd been hit by a two-ton weight. His heart ran wild. Justin's words echoed in his mind. He couldn't even feel desire for the ravishing blonde Abby had seen him with in Houston. He hadn't felt it with anyone since that night he'd brought Abby home from the bar and seen her naked to the waist. Was that what he had to look forward to? Would he end up like Justin, imprisoned in desire for the one woman he couldn't have, alone for the rest of his life because he was incapable of wanting another woman?

"I didn't realize," Calhoun said quietly. "I'm sorry."

Justin shrugged. "One of those things," he said philosophically. He sat down behind his desk. "You may not believe in marriage, but you may find that a relationship can tie you up properly without a ring or a legal paper. And I'll throw your own question right back at you," he added, cocking his head at his brother. "How many women have you had since you noticed Abby?"

Calhoun's face grew hard and remote. He glared at Justin, then turned and left the room.

Justin lifted an eyebrow and chuckled softly to himself as he bent over his figures again.

ABBY HAD A nice supper with Tyler, and the moussaka she sampled was delicious, like the elegant baklava they had for dessert and the faintly resinous wine they drank with their meal. But while she was listening to Ty talk about his new job, she was thinking about the empty future, about living without Calhoun. She'd gotten used to listening for his step in the hall late at night as he went to his room, to seeing him across the table, to watching television with him, to being near him at work. Life was so empty now, so cold. She felt as if she'd never know warmth again.

"The only bad part of it is that I'm going to get loaned out," Tyler was telling her resignedly as he drank a demitasse of Greek coffee after dessert. "Old man Regan has a daughter in Arizona who's coping with a dude ranch and two of her nephews for the summer. I'm going to be sent out there to get the place in shape, I gather, while my assistant looks after things here."

He grimaced. "I hate dude ranches. And I don't much care for the woman trying to run this one. Apparently she thought she could and talked Regan into it, but she seems to be losing her shirt."

Abby glanced at him. "What's she like, do you know?"

"I don't have a clue. She's probably one of those feminists who think men should have the children and women should earn the living. I'll be damned if she'll tell me how to do my job."

Abby could see the fireworks already, and she smiled behind her cup at the mental image. Tyler was so much like Justin and Calhoun, a reactionary, a holdover from the old West. It would be fascinating to see how he coped with a modern woman.

He took her home minutes later, bending to kiss her cheek at the door of Mrs. Simpson's house. "Thanks for keeping me company." He grinned. "I enjoyed it."

"So did I." She smiled up at him. "You're a nice man. Someday you'll make some lucky girl a nice husband."

"Marriage is for—"

"The birds," she finished for him, sighing. "You and Calhoun ought to do an act together. You've got the chorus down pat."

"No man wants to get married," he told her. "Men get corralled."

"Oh, sure they do," she agreed. "By greedy, grasping, mercenary women."

"I'd marry you in a minute, Abby," he said. He was smiling, but he didn't sound as if he were joking. "So if Calhoun slips the noose, you just throw it my way. I won't even duck."

"You doll." She reached up and kissed his firm jaw. "I'll remember that. Good night, Ty."

"Good night. I'll give you a call next week, okay?"

"Okay."

She waved at him and then used her key and went inside. She climbed the stairs lazily, relaxed from the resinated wine and worn out from her long week of avoiding Calhoun. So it was a surprise to find the telephone ringing in her room, where she had her own private extension.

She put down her purse and sat on the bed to answer it. "Hello?"

A deep, familiar voice that made her pulse leap said, "Hello."

"Calhoun?" she asked softly.

"I can't sit up and wait for you anymore," he said. "So I thought I'd make sure you got home all right."

"I did."

"Where did you go?"

She lay back on the bed, her head on the pillow. "To the new Greek place."

"Ummm," he murmured, sounding as if he were stretched out on his own bed. "I've been there for business dinners a time or two. Did you try the moussaka? It's delicious."

"Yes, that's what I had, and some of that resinated wine. It's very strong."

He paused. "Did you come straight home?"

She almost smiled at his concern. "Yes, I came straight home. He didn't even try to seduce me."

"I don't remember accusing him of it."

She touched the receiver gently. "Is everything all right at the house?"

"I guess so." There was a pause. "It's lonely."

"It's lonely here, too," she said.

Another pause. "I didn't mean what you thought I did," he said quietly. "I wouldn't take you to bed on a bet. You aren't the kind of woman to be used and thrown aside. I'm ashamed of you for thinking I could treat you like that after all these years."

Her heart ran away. She clutched the receiver closer to her ear. "But you said—"

"I said we could go to the apartment and be alone," he interrupted. "And that we could make love. I meant we could make a few memories and then I'd take you home." He sighed. "I'd probably do it bent double, but I never had any intention of taking advantage of the situation."

"Oh."

"So now that we've cleared that up, how about dinner tomorrow night?" he asked.

She hesitated. "Calhoun, wouldn't it be better if we just didn't see each other again?" she asked quietly, even though it broke her heart to say the words.

"I've looked out for you, watched over you and ordered your life for years," he replied. "Now you're grown, and things have happened between us that I never expected. We can't go back to the relationship we had, and we can't be intimate. But there has to be a way that we can keep each other," he said heavily. "Because I can't quite put you out of my life, Abby. I hate like hell going past your room at night and knowing you aren't in it. I hate watching television alone and sitting at a table alone when Justin has business dinners. I hate the feedlot because there's going to be another woman at your desk."

"She's blonde," she reminded him.

"She isn't you," he said shortly. "Are you going to come with me or not?"

"I shouldn't...."

"But you will," he returned.

She sighed, smiling. "Yes."

"I'll pick you up at five."

"Five?"

"We're going to Houston, remember?" he laughed softly.

"Dining and dancing."

"Just that, if it's what you want," he said gently. "I won't even touch you unless you want it."

"That apartment," she asked hesitantly. "Have you... have you taken a lot of women there?"

He didn't answer her immediately. "While I was away those few days, I moved. I changed apartments," he said. "This one is across town from the one I had. And I've never taken a woman there."

She wondered at the switch, wondered why he'd bothered. Surely it couldn't be to protect her from the memory of his old life, in case one day she did go there with him?

"I see," she murmured.

"No, I don't think you do," he replied, his voice deep and soft. "Not yet, anyway. I'd better let you get to sleep. It's late."

She didn't want him to hang up. She searched for something to say, something to keep him on the line, but her mind was blank.

"You and Justin never came to blows over Shelby, I guess," she asked then, because it had just occurred to her that Justin had threatened to punch Calhoun the morning after the square dance.

"Justin and I had a long talk," he replied. "Not that I expect it to do any good. He's too set in his ways to bend, and he won't let Shelby get near him."

"Maybe someday he'll listen."

"Maybe." He sighed. "Five tomorrow. Don't forget."

As if she could! She touched the receiver as if she were touching him. "Good night."

"Good night, sweetheart," he said softly, and the line went dead.

She floated into her nightgown and into bed, hearing nothing but the endearment, that unexpected, beautiful word, until sleep finally claimed her.

It was the longest Saturday of Abby's life. She tried to sleep late, but she couldn't. She went downstairs and had breakfast with Mrs. Simpson and then she went back to her room and forced herself to watch television. Having Saturdays free was still new. At the feed-lot, she'd always worked them. Now she had the whole weekend off, and she didn't know what to do with herself.

Time dragged all day long. She went for a ride just to give herself something to do and wound up in town shopping for a new dress to wear on her date with Calhoun.

She came out with a pretty red patterned silk skirt and matching sweater. It brought out her tan and made her look sophisticated. She thought about having her hair cut, but she'd gotten used to its length. She experimented with different hairstyles for an hour, only to brush it out and leave it around her shoulders afterward.

She was dressed and ready at 4:30. She tried to get

interested in a book while she waited. Those thirty minutes were going to be agony.

Apparently Calhoun felt the same way, because he showed up twenty minutes early.

She forced herself not to run to let him in, but she was breathless all the same as she looked up into his dark, quiet eyes.

"Hi," she said.

He smiled slowly, gazing approvingly not only at her outfit but at her hairdo, as well. "Hi," he replied lazily.

He was wearing a charcoal-gray suit with pale gray handtooled leather boots and a pearl Stetson. He looked so handsome that Abby could hardly believe he was really taking her out on a date. It was so new, so unreal.

"Are you sure you want to take me out?" she asked unexpectedly, her eyes troubled as they met his. "You don't feel sorry for me—?"

He put his thumb gently against her lips, silencing her. "I wouldn't take you to the post office out of pity," he replied. "Are you getting cold feet?" he added softly.

She grimaced and stared at his jacket. "Yes."

"I won't hurt you," he said, his voice quiet and deep. "I won't rush you or embarrass you."

She bit her lower lip. "It's just that it's...new."

"You'll get used to it." He moved restlessly. "Are you ready to go? I'm early, but I was afraid I'd get held up if I didn't leave while I could."

"Yes. I'll just get my purse."

She got her purse and her black velvet blazer, as well, and let him escort her out to the Jaguar. She got more nervous by the minute, which was absurd considering how long she'd dreamed of going anywhere with him. She could hardly talk, and her hands shook.

"How do you like living with Mrs. Simpson?" Calhoun asked on the way to Houston.

She smiled. "I like it very much." Her fingers toyed with the handle of her purse. "I miss the house sometimes. It's different, living alone."

He glanced at her, his eyes narrow. "Yes." He turned his eyes back to the road, frowning as he pulled a cigarette from the pack in his pocket and stuck it in his mouth. He reached for the car lighter, noticing her curious stare. "I'm nervous," he said without thinking, and then he laughed at his own confession. "That's one for the books, isn't it, Abby, with my reputation?"

She felt warm all over. She smiled, her eyes carefully lowered. "I'm nervous, too," she said.

"I'm not a virgin," he reminded her as he put the lighter against the cigarette.

"Rub it in," she sighed miserably.

"Don't make it sound like leprosy," he teased as he replaced the lighter in its hole beside the ashtray in the dash. "Frankly, I've had my fill of experienced women telling me what to do in bed."

She stared at him, torn between curiosity and jealousy. "Do women really do that?"

His eyebrows arched. He hadn't realized how innocent she really was. "Don't you go to movies?"

"I tried," she recalled. "You never would let me in to see the really good ones."

He whistled softly. "Well, well." His eyes brushed her slender body, then returned to the road. "You'll take a lot of teaching, won't you, tidbit?" he murmured.

She shifted against the seatbelt. "Which would probably bore you to death."

"I don't think so," he mused. "After all—" he lifted the cigarette to his firm lips "—I could customize you."

She gaped at him. "Now I've heard everything!"

"Tell me you'd hate being my lover, Abby," he challenged softly, glancing her way.

She couldn't. But she couldn't quite admit the truth, either. She averted her face, burning with subdued irritation at his soft, predatory laughter.

They went to the same club where she'd seen him with the blonde, but this time was different. There seemed to be no barriers after the first few awkward minutes.

"I've never had rice made like this," Abby remarked as she enjoyed the small portion that came with her roast beef au jus.

"With scallions, you mean? It's unique. Like you," he added, and she looked up to find his eyes steady on her face. Intent. Unblinking.

She gazed back at him. He made her feel giddy when he looked at her that way. Her whole body tingled.

And she wasn't the only one affected. His heart was doing a tango in his chest at the way she was watching him, at her pleasure in his company. He even liked the way he felt himself, nervous and a little uncertain.

They finished their meal, and the dessert that followed it, in silence. As they lingered over a second cup of coffee, he finally spoke. "Want to dance?" he asked softly.

She swallowed. Her eyes traveled slowly over his big body, and just the thought of being pressed against him on the dance floor frightened her. She'd drown in pleasure, and he'd know it. He'd see how helpless she was, how vulnerable.

"I—don't know," she stammered finally, and swallowed the last spoonful of her apple pie.

"Are you really afraid to let me hold you in front of a roomful of people, Abby?" he asked with narrowed eyes.

She lifted her own gaze. "Yes."

"Why?" he persisted.

Well, why not be honest, she thought fatalistically. "Because I want you," she whispered softly, watching his expression become taut. "And because you'll be able to see how much."

Her lack of guile floored him. He couldn't remember a single woman in his past being quite so straightforward about such things. He took a slow breath and reached across the table for her hand, turning it over to trace the palm tenderly with a long forefinger.

"I want you just as badly," he said, watching her hand instead of her eyes. "And you'll be able to feel how much, as well as see it. And I still want to dance with you."

She was so hungry for him that her body was pulsing softly. Even having him know every thought in her mind, being vulnerable, didn't seem to matter anymore. She worshiped him with her eyes, and he looked up and caught her in the act.

"Let's stop pretending," he said quietly. "Come here."

He got up, drawing her with him. He led her to the small dance floor, where a band was playing a lazy tune, and when he pulled her close, she went without a murmur.

"Have you ever noticed how perfectly we fit together?" he asked against her hair as they moved to the music. His hand at her back contracted, bringing her even closer, and the sound of his voice at her ear was deliciously exciting. "I like the way you feel against me."

She could tell that, because his body was beginning to react in a totally masculine way to her softness. She stiffened a little, but the caressing motion of his fingers on hers relaxed her.

"It's all right," he whispered. "I won't hurt you."

"I know that." She closed her eyes, drowning in his nearness, in the music, in the magic.

He shuddered, a barely perceptible stiffening of his big body, and his hand pressed her against him for one wild second. "This is stupid," he said tautly.

"I tried to tell you that," she whispered shakily as her fingers contracted helplessly in his and she looked up into his eyes.

His jaw clenched. Everything she felt was in those worshipful eyes, in her face, in her body so soft against his. His mind whirled; he was floating. She wanted him.

"For God's sake," he groaned. "Let's get out of here."

Her gaze searched his hard, dark face, the eyes that blazed down into hers. He looked impossibly mature and experienced, and she knew she was out of her league. But she wanted to lie in his arms and let him love her. She wanted nothing in life more than to be alone with him now.

"I…" She swallowed. "I don't know how… I've never had to…about precautions, I mean…"

He bent, brushing his hard mouth against her soft one briefly, silencing her. "Are you scared?"

"Yes."

His nose nuzzled hers. "But you'd give yourself to me anyway."

She clenched her teeth. "Yes."

"And hate me afterward."

Her slender shoulders lifted and fell. "No."

Her expression touched him. "Do you love me that much?"

She lowered her eyes, but he tilted her chin up again and there was something new in his look, in his scrutiny of her face.

"Do you love me that much?" he whispered again.

Her eyes closed. "Yes!" she breathed.

His hand slid up her back into her long, thick hair and pulled her forehead against him, pressed it there as they moved to the rhythm of the music. "Precious," he said in a tone that could have burned water. She hardly heard him over the wild beating of her heart. His lips smoothed her forehead, brushing it tenderly.

"I won't make you pregnant," he whispered. "Come with me."

As if she had a choice, she thought shakily as she let him lead her off the dance floor. She'd never been so helpless in her life. All she could do was look at him with helpless need, love radiating from her oval face like fire from an open hearth.

He paid the bill and drew her out into the cold night air, tucked her in the car and drove across town without saying a single word.

CHAPTER TEN

CALHOUN HAD A penthouse apartment with a private elevator and a view of Houston that was breathtaking. It was furnished in tans and browns, with African carvings and weavings mingled with Western paintings and Indian rugs. It was an apartment that was welcoming despite its purely masculine ambience.

"Do you like it?" Calhoun asked, watching her from the closed door.

"Very much," she said, smiling. "It suits you."

He came into the room, his eyes never leaving her face. "How about something to drink? I can make coffee."

She shifted her eyebrows. "Coffee?"

His dark eyes narrowed. "Just because you got drunk with Justin doesn't mean you can expect the same courtesy here."

She shifted restlessly, her purse clutched against her waist. "Well, I didn't mean to get drunk with Justin."

"I'll bet the pair of you could hardly walk the next morning."

"We sort of leaned on each other," she confessed. She searched his hard face. "He was afraid you were going to use your experience to take Shelby away from him. He didn't come right out and say so, but it was implied."

"As if I could hurt him like that," he said curtly. His

dark eyes wandered quietly over her face, tracing every soft line. "Did you care that I danced with her?"

She turned toward the window. "I like the scenery," she said, trying to change the subject, trying to breathe normally.

"Yes, I like it, too," he said finally. "I wanted something with a view of the city. And I have to spend a lot of time here on business, so that makes it a good investment."

She heard his steps coming closer, and she could feel his warmth at her back, smell the clean, spicy scent of him.

Her pulse jumped as his lean hands caught her waist and pulled her against his big body. She heard his breath and felt it in her hair as he wrapped her up in his arms from behind, rocking her lazily as they watched the city lights spread out below them.

He inhaled the floral scent of her body and the clean, shampooed softness of her hair all at the same time. He bent his head and brushed his mouth against her neck through her silky hair.

"I miss you," he said softly. "You haunt me."

"You'll get used to not having me around," she said sadly. "After all, up until five and a half years ago, you and Justin had the house all to yourselves."

"And then you moved in," he mused, linking his lean hands in front of her. "We got used to running feet and laughter, to music in the living room and movies on television and teenage girls in and out and hot-rodding young men speeding up the driveway."

"You were both very tolerant for old bachelors," she said. "Looking back, I guess I really cramped your style."

He stiffened a little, because it was true. She had at first. But now it hurt to look back, to remember his furtive affairs, his hidden amours. It hurt to think that there'd ever been a woman in his arms except Abby.

"A woman in the dark is just a body," he said softly. "And I never gave my heart, Abby."

"Do you have one?" she asked.

He turned her gently, putting her hand on his chest, over his white silk shirt, against hard, warm muscle and thick hair. "Feel it beat," he whispered.

"That isn't what I meant."

"I know." He looked down at her hand, feeling his body tauten at the light touch. He moved her fingers across his chest to a hard male nipple and held her palm there, letting her feel.

She glanced up at him, her blue-gray eyes wide and searching as he stroked her hand against the hardness.

"That happens to women," she whispered.

"And to men." He gently pulled her closer, his hands moving into her hair as he bent his head. "Unbutton my shirt. I'm going to show you how to touch me."

Her heartbeat sounded and felt unnaturally loud in the stillness of the room. But she didn't protest. Her fingers fumbled with the buttons, and eventually she had the shirt out of his slacks and away from his broad, bronzed chest with its thick covering of hair.

He smiled at her faint embarrassment. "Here. Like this." He pulled her hands against him in long, sensual strokes and watched their slender gracefulness as he drew them down to the wide belt around his slender hips. But when he tried to move them past it, she froze.

He searched her soft eyes quietly, sensing the turmoil in her heart. "You're very innocent," he said, his voice unusually deep and slow. "You've never touched a man intimately, have you?"

She traced a tiny pattern on his chest. "I've never done anything intimate with a man in my life, except with you."

He was incredibly pleased to hear that. His chin lifted. "I need more than a few chaste kisses," he said softly.

She flushed, staring at the heavy rise and fall of his chest. "I'm sorry."

He bent abruptly and lifted her, cradling her against him as he turned and walked down the hall with her.

He went through an open door, and she turned her head to find a huge king-size bed with a cream-and-chocolate quilted cover over it in a darkened room.

"Calhoun, no," she whispered, raising her eyes to his in the dimness of the heavily curtained room.

"I won't even undress you," he breathed, brushing her lips with his. "We're going to make a little love, and then I'll take you home. There won't be a risk. I give you my word on it."

"But you want me," she whispered in protest when he slid her onto the coverlet and stretched out beside her, his body so close that she could feel how aroused he was.

"Of course I want you," he said gently, smiling as he lay poised above her, his lean hands smoothing back her long, soft hair. "But there's no risk involved, as long as you don't do anything to knock me off balance."

She searched his dark face, loving every inch of it. "How could I do that?" she whispered.

"By doing anything I don't invite," he murmured deeply. "Don't touch me, or move against me, or kiss me unless I tell you how." He moved down then, drawing his open mouth lazily over her lips until he managed to get between them. "That's it," he whispered. "Just relax."

He was doing the most sensuous things to her mouth. It amazed her, the sensations he aroused so effortlessly. Her breath was already coming in gasps, and she felt her body tautening as what he did to her mouth began to affect the entire length of her.

"God, you're sweet to kiss," he whispered into her parted lips. "Come here, Abby."

He abruptly rolled over onto his back and turned her with him so that she was above him, looking down into his dark, dancing eyes.

"That's better," he murmured. "Do you feel less threatened on top?"

She colored faintly, and he laughed. Then he drew her mouth down over his and opened it, and the laughter stopped.

She felt his hands moving her, lifting her. She was beside him, then over him, and he had her hips, bringing them down completely over his.

"Don't do that," he whispered when he felt her tautness. "Just lie still and let me feel your body over mine."

She felt shaky. She trembled as his tongue began to probe gently around her lips and past them, teasing its way into the sweet darkness of her mouth.

She caught her breath, and he heard it. His dark eyes opened, looking up at her.

"They call it a soul kiss," he said softly. "It's intimate and wildly arousing and very, very suggestive. Let me kiss you that way."

She felt her legs tremble where they touched his.

"You… You're already wildly aroused," she whispered unsteadily.

"I'm going to make you that way, too," he murmured. He turned her slowly so that she was on her back. His long, powerful leg insinuated itself between hers.

She stiffened as she felt his big, muscular body spread over hers, pushing her down into the mattress. His masculinity was blatant now. The intimacy was shocking, and the sensations it caused were a little frightening.

He saw her fear, and his hands slid into her hair, caressing as he let his weight down on her slender body, his elbows catching a little of it as he moved.

"I won't hurt you," he said softly. "Lie very still for me, Abby. I want to show you what passion is."

"I already know…oh!" She clenched her teeth. Her nails bit into the fine fabric of his jacket, and her eyes widened in shock when he moved against her. She felt him in a way that turned her face blood red with embarrassed knowledge, and a tiny cry forced its way out of her throat.

His mouth covered hers. His tongue teased, probed, withdrew, probed again and began a taunting invasion that was every bit as intimate as his huge, softly moving body on hers. She moaned. She grasped him. She bit at his firm, chiseled lower lip. Her tongue shyly encountered his and began to fence with it. She began to shudder, and so did he, and just when she was going under for the third time he slid away from her and gathered her against his side, holding her cheek to his shoulder while the trembling grew.

"Calhoun." Her voice broke.

"It's all right," he whispered. "I'll make it bearable."

His big hands found her jacket and eased it off. He unfastened the sweater where it buttoned over one shoulder, and levered it up lazily, unfastening the hooks of her lacy bra and tugging the whole of her upper covering over her head and moved it aside.

She started to cover herself, but his mouth was suddenly on her breasts, and what he did to them was too sweet, too addictive to protest.

She gave in, arching toward his mouth, drowning in his ardor. He knew exactly what to do, how to arouse her to a fever pitch. She let him, welcomed him, her body fluid in his hands, her voice softly inciting him.

He sat up for just a minute, long enough to strip off his jacket and shirt. Then he was poised over her, vibrantly male with his hair-roughened chest bare and muscular, his eyes glittering with desire as they caressed her own bareness.

"I can't stop you," she whispered shakily, tears stinging her eyes as she watched him come to her. "I don't want to stop you."

"I want to hold you like this," he whispered, levering his chest over her bare, aroused breasts, rubbing softly against her body. "Isn't it sweet, Abby? Skin against skin. Breast to breast in the darkness, mouth to aching mouth… Kiss me, sweetheart. Open your mouth and kiss me until you can't bear the wanting any longer."

She did. Her arms held him, trembling, her body welcomed the crush of his. The mattress moved under them and the air washed over her body while his mouth fed on hers, seduced hers, intimate and ardent and tender.

His mouth lifted seconds later, and he looked into her eyes in the faint light from the hall. "I don't think I can stop," he whispered, his voice oddly husky.

"I don't want you to stop," she moaned. "Oh, Calhoun, please, please…please!"

His mouth slid down to her breast, taking it inside. His hand went to the fastening of her skirt and loosened it. His lean fingers slid onto the soft skin of her belly, pressing there, savoring the soft skin.

"The…risk," she whispered shakily.

"Of a child?" he murmured against her breasts. He nuzzled her soft skin with his cheek, his eyes closed, the scent of her all around him, in his blood. His hand slid under her hips, lifting them hungrily into the hard contours of his own, holding her there with undisguised passion. "For the first time in my life, I'm not afraid of the consequences, Abby."

His mouth was over hers again, and she wasn't quite sure she'd heard him. Her mind was on fire, her body was burning. Her legs moved helplessly against his. She wanted him. She wanted all of him. She moaned as she tried to get closer, to absorb him, possess him. She felt savage and wild. She wanted to join with him, to be a part of the massive, muscular body that was slowly driving her mad.

Her arms reached up, her fingers tangled in his thick blond hair as she moved her hips sensually under his in movements that made him cry out.

"Abby—!" he bit off, shuddering.

"I love you," she sobbed.

His mouth was over hers, and he began to remove her skirt with unsteady hands. It was going to happen. Here, now, she was going to know him in every way there was.

But in the middle of her feverish pleas, there was the sudden, unexpected pealing of the doorbell.

He paused, his body racked by shudders. "Oh, my God," he said, choking.

"Don't answer it," she whispered tearfully.

He lifted his head, pushing back sweaty hair. He was gasping for breath, his body vibrating with frustrated need, driving urgency. He shuddered. "I can't get up," he whispered with a hollow laugh. He pushed away from her and lay on his stomach, groaning, his lean hands speared into the pillow, crushing it.

Abby didn't know what to do. She knew better than to touch him. She lay there, not moving, sanity coming back slowly. She concentrated on trying to breathe while her heartbeat shook her.

The doorbell kept ringing. After a moment, Calhoun managed to sit up. He looked a little foggy as he got to his feet, but he was breathing almost normally.

"Are you all right?" she whispered shyly.

"I'm all right," he said softly. "Are you?"

At least he wasn't angry. "Yes," she replied, her tone equally soft.

He took a steadying breath and got to the door. Unexpectedly he switched on the light and turned to look at her, his eyes narrow, full of possession and something violent, dark, hungry.

Her breasts were mauve and peach, exquisitely formed, taut with arousal. Where he'd pulled her skirt down, he could see the graceful curve of her hips below her small waist.

"God, I could die looking at you," he said huskily. "I've never seen a woman so perfect."

She flushed, but the intensity of his delight in her was overwhelming. She sat up slowly, watching his gaze move to the firm thrust of her breasts, and she felt herself go hot with pride and pleasure.

He looked up then, catching the light in her eyes. "You belong to me now," he said. "As surely as if I hadn't stopped. We'll work out the details later, but there won't be anyone else for me from this night on. I'll never touch another woman until I die." And with that quiet, terse statement, he turned and left the room.

Abby wasn't sure she hadn't dreamed the whole thing. She got into her clothes in a daze, shaking with pent-up emotion. She wanted to cry and scream and laugh and dance.

He was talking to someone. His voice was curt and almost angry. Frowning, Abby stepped out into the hall, her mouth swollen, her hair in tangles, her silk skirt hopelessly wrinkled. As she went into the living room, she recognized Calhoun's guest. It was the blonde from the restaurant, the one he'd taken out the night Abby had gone to dinner with Justin.

"So that's why you didn't have time for me," the older woman said when she saw Abby. "My God, she's barely out of school!"

"Abby, go back into the bedroom," Calhoun said.

"Yes, Abby, go and hide," the blonde added viciously, although tears were visible in her big eyes.

But Abby didn't. She went quietly to Calhoun and slid her hand trustingly into his.

"I love him with all my heart," Abby told the other woman. "I guess you probably do, too, and I'm sorry. But I'd rather die than lose him."

The blonde looked at her for a long moment, and then at Calhoun. "It would have served you right if she hated you, as many hearts as you've broken," she cried, her lower lip trembling. "But that won't ever happen, any more than you'll ever love any one of us. Not even she can reach that stone you call a heart!" She turned to Abby. "You'll never have all of him." She laughed bitterly. "All he can give you is his body, and he'll soon get tired of yours and go off to conquer new worlds. Men like him don't settle down, honey, so if you're looking for happy endings, you'd better run like hell."

She gave Calhoun a final, bitter glance and was gone as quickly as she'd arrived.

Calhoun closed the door, his face hard, unyielding.

"I'm sorry you had to hear that," he said quietly.

"So am I." Abby searched his eyes sadly, wondering if the other woman was right about his lack of feeling. Perhaps she should run. But how could she, when she loved him?

His eyes narrowed as he saw the indecision and fear in hers. "You don't trust me, do you?" he asked. "You think she might be right, that you can't have a future with me."

"You said yourself that you didn't want to be tied," she replied. "I understand." She dropped her eyes. "Maybe I'm too young for marriage anyway. I've never been out on my own at all. I've hardly even dated. Maybe what I feel for you is just a crush and my first taste of desire."

She didn't really mean what she'd just told him, but it gave him an out if he wanted one. He'd wanted her in the bedroom, and perhaps he'd said things he didn't really mean. She didn't want him to feel obligated just because they'd almost gone too far.

But Calhoun didn't realize that she was trying to save him from himself. He took her words at face value and felt their impact as if they were bullets. She was telling him that she wasn't sure she loved him, and at the worst possible moment. When she'd put her slender hand so trustingly in his, he'd known for the first time what he felt for her. His feelings went deeper than lust, and they wouldn't fade. But now he was afraid to tell her, to put the emotion into words. She was admitting that she might have mistaken infatuation and desire for something lasting. She was young, all right, and inexperienced. He might be taking advantage of a natural step in her progression to womanhood. What if he risked his heart and she kicked it aside when she got through this phase? She was young, and she'd bounce back. But Calhoun had never loved before, and the thought of being rejected terrified him.

He stared down at her with bitter realization darkening his eyes to black. He'd fallen into the trap that he'd sworn he'd never be taken by. Now here they were, almost lovers, and she was telling him that it was all a mistake. He felt as if she'd hit him in the chest with an ax.

"Would you take me home, please?" she asked without looking at him.

He straightened. "Of course."

He turned toward the bedroom, and she sat on the sofa, reaching for the purse she'd tossed there when they'd first arrived. She sat twisting and turning it, listening to his quick, sharp movements in the bedroom while he dressed. Her eyes closed in mingled shame and embarrassment. It had only just occurred to her how many liberties she'd allowed him, how close they'd come to making love completely. She hadn't had the

presence of mind to think of stopping, and neither had
he. If that woman hadn't interrupted them—

Her face went hot. He'd been undressing her. He
wouldn't have stopped at all, he hadn't had any intention
of denying himself. And afterward, how would it have
been? She'd have been eaten up by guilt and sorrow,
and he'd have felt obligated to marry her because she'd
been a virgin. He'd have been well and truly trapped.

She didn't take seriously anything Calhoun had said
in the semidarkness of his bedroom, because men didn't
think when they were engulfed by passion. Even though
she was innocent, she knew that much. He'd wanted her
for a long time, and tonight had been his one chance to
get her into bed. He'd almost taken her. He knew she
loved him, and it didn't even seem to bother him that he
was taking advantage of something she couldn't help.

Calhoun came into the living room minutes later,
pale and strained but neatly dressed. He'd even combed
his thick blond hair. After one quick glance, she didn't
look at him again. She stood up.

He opened the door for her, noticing her unnatural
stiffness. "I don't know what to say, Abby," he said quietly. "I don't know how she traced me here."

"It doesn't matter," she replied, looking only as high
as his chin. "It would be unrealistic to expect that we'd
never run across any of your discarded lovers."

His dark eyes flashed fire. He reached beside her and
slammed the door before she could get out, forcing her
shocked eyes up to his angry ones.

"And that's what you think you would have been if
she hadn't interrupted us?" he asked coldly.

She ground her teeth together to keep from breaking
down. "You weren't going to stop," she said.

"I *couldn't* stop," he corrected. "Any more than you could. If you want to know, it was a first. I've always been able to pull back before."

"Should I be flattered?" she asked on a trembling laugh. "Because I'm not. Bodies are cheap."

"Yours isn't," he returned. "Yours is young and sweet and exquisitely formed. Innocent, when I've never had innocence in my life. I might have been half out of my head, but I'd have managed to make you want me back and I wouldn't have hurt you."

"And after you were through?" she probed, lifting her pained eyes.

He touched her swollen lips with a cool forefinger. "That would have taken all night," he said softly. "And by then you wouldn't have had any doubts left about where we stood with each other. I'd have made sure of it."

She flushed. "I'd have been another conquest...."

He drew her against him, sighing heavily as he smoothed her long, dark hair and felt her body shake with soft sobs.

"It's just frustration, sweetheart," he whispered at the top of her head. "You wanted me and I wanted you, and neither of us had fulfillment, that's all. It passes."

Her curled fingers pressed against him while tears ran down her pale cheeks. "I hate you," she cried.

He only smiled, because he understood. He kissed her hair gently. She was so very young. Too young, probably. He drew in a slow, sad breath and wondered how he was going to live without her.

"You've got to see Maria about your birthday party," he said after a few minutes. "She's going to hire a caterer. And you'll have to provide a guest list for us. I can have one of the women at the office send out the invitations."

She drew back, sniffing, and he pulled out a handkerchief and mopped her face. "You don't have to do that," she mumbled.

"We want to." He touched the handkerchief to her red eyes. "I won't come near you until then, Abby," he added to her surprise. His dark gaze was quiet and unblinking, and it did wild things to her pulse. "I won't call you, or take you out, or see you until then."

"Because of tonight?" she asked with what dignity she still possessed.

"In a way." He put the handkerchief away and searched her face. "You're afraid of giving in to me, aren't you?"

She moved restlessly.

"Aren't you?" he persisted.

She bit her lower lip. "Yes."

"Why?"

"I won't have you forced into a marriage you don't want," she said warily. "Calhoun, you aren't a marrying man. You even told me so."

He brushed his mouth against hers, and he nuzzled her nose with his, teasing her lips, playing with her mouth.

"Abby, I told you not so long ago that my playboy days were over, and I meant it," he said softly. "I haven't lived like a recluse, but in the past few years, I've settled down. And if you want the truth," he added, resting his forehead on hers, "I haven't thought of any other woman since the night I found you bare-breasted on your bed, little one. You've been in my bed every night since then, a vision that haunts me from dawn to dusk."

Her heart jumped straight up. He'd never lied to her. He wasn't doing it now, she knew.

"Me?" she whispered.

He smiled gently. "You." He brushed her mouth lazily with his. "And if you'd given yourself to me in my bedroom a few minutes ago," he whispered, "we'd have been on our way to get a marriage license by morning."

"Because of your conscience?" she asked.

He chuckled softly. "Because of my body," he breathed. "Lovemaking is addictive. The way I want you, little Abby, I'd have you pregnant by the end of the first week."

She flushed wildly and hid her face from him, feeling his chest shake with laughter.

"Did you hear what I said," he whispered, "when you warned me about the risk?"

Her heart ran wild. "Yes."

His mouth bit at hers. "Didn't it seem an odd response for a philandering playboy to make?"

"You wanted me—"

"God, I still do!" he breathed. "But a man interested in nothing but a good time is sure as hell not interested in making babies, Abby."

"Stop that!" she whispered.

He smiled against her mouth, delighting in her innocence, in her reaction. He wasn't worried anymore. Now, at last, he knew why she'd said what she had in front of his visitor. She'd been offering him a way out. But he didn't want one. He wanted Abby. He wanted a future.

"I'll take you home now," he said gently. "And you can have until your birthday to think about me and miss me and want me. And then, if you can't stand it anymore, I'll give you a birthday present you'll never forget."

"What?" she asked breathlessly.

He covered her open mouth with his own. "Me," he breathed into it.

CHAPTER ELEVEN

ABBY PONDERED THAT odd remark for the next few lonely weeks. What had Calhoun meant, that they were going to become lovers? Or had he meant something quite different?

He'd taken her home after that last, passionate kiss, and he hadn't made another single personal remark to her. He'd talked about the feedlot, about things at the house, even about the weather. And he'd left her at Mrs. Simpson's with a warm, secretive smile, contenting himself with a chaste but breathlessly tender kiss on her forehead.

As he'd promised, he hadn't called or come visiting. She hadn't seen him or heard from him since that night. It had been hard going, too. She'd stopped by Misty's a time or two, pretending to be happy so that her friend wouldn't ask too many questions. Tyler had asked Abby out again, but she'd refused without really understanding why. She wanted only the memory of Calhoun. If it was all she could ever have of him, it would be more than a lot of lonely women had.

She enjoyed her work at the insurance office, and her bosses were good to her. She settled in without any problem, but she went home to a lonely room, and as the days went by she was almost frantic with the need to see Calhoun.

She'd gone to the Ballenger house to talk to Maria about the party, and she'd left a list of guests for Justin, but to her disappointment both the brothers had been away at the time. She'd managed to get nothing out of Maria, either, except for a careless remark that everything was fine at home and the brothers seemed to be very happy. Which did nothing for Abby's self-esteem, especially since she missed Maria's wicked, conspiratorial smile.

The night of the party, Abby drove herself to the Ballenger house. She felt starved for the sight of Calhoun. All her memories and all her fantasies only made it worse.

She was wearing a long electric-blue gown that enhanced her blue-gray eyes and emphasized her exquisite figure. It had soft fabric straps and a crisscross bodice, a fitted waist and a long, narrow skirt. She wore her hair up in a braided coiffure with wispy little curls hanging beside her ears and curling on her forehead. She looked mature and sophisticated. She might not be beautiful, but she felt it tonight, and her face radiated with a glow that only the anticipation of seeing Calhoun could give her.

Maria opened the door and hugged her impulsively. "So lovely," the older woman sighed. "Everything has worked out so nicely, even the band was on time. Your guests have started arriving. The Jacobses are in the living room with Justin."

Abby winced, but Maria shook her head.

"No, it is all right," she said quickly. "Señor Justin and Señor Tyler have been talking cattle, and Señorita Shelby—" Maria smiled sadly. "Her soft eyes feed on

Señor Justin like dry flowers welcoming rainfall. It breaks my heart."

"And mine," Abby said gently. "I'll go and keep her company."

She walked into the living room and smiled at Shelby, who was wearing a long green velvet skirt with a simple chemise top in white silk. She looked exquisitely lovely. Justin and Tyler, in dark suits, rose as she entered the room, both pairs of masculine eyes gazing appreciatively at her dress.

"Happy birthday, honey," Justin said gently, and went forward to brush his hard mouth against her cheek. "And at least a hundred more."

"I'll second that." Tyler grinned, his green eyes dancing as he bent and kissed her softly on the mouth. "You look delicious."

"Thank you both," she replied.

"I remember my own twenty-first birthday," Shelby sighed after she'd hugged Abby and congratulated her. "It was very special." Her eyes went helplessly to Justin, who stood very still and looked at her, his dark eyes full of emotion.

Abby could have cried. She hadn't understood before, but now she knew how devastating it could be to want someone that much. She looked around the room. There were several other people there, friends from school, who waved and lifted their glasses in her direction. She smiled back, but her heart was getting heavier by the second.

"Justin, where's Calhoun?" she asked finally.

Justin took a draw from his cigarette and dragged his gaze away from Shelby. Abby had asked the question he'd dreaded ever since she'd walked in the door. "I don't know if he's going to make it, honey," he hedged, because he didn't know where in hell Calhoun was either. She looked devastated, so he improvised. "He said to tell you happy birthday and—Abby!"

She couldn't help it. She burst into tears, shaking with the disappointment. "I'm sorry..." she sobbed.

"Shelby, take her into the study, please," Justin said.

"Of course." Shelby put a gentle arm around her. "Abby, please don't cry. I know Calhoun would have been here if he could have."

"I'll be all right in a minute," Abby told Justin as they passed him and a quietly curious Tyler. "I'm sorry. It's been a long week," she added with a faint smile.

"I'll knock him through a wall for this," Justin said coldly. "I swear to God I will."

"No, you won't," Abby sniffed. "As Shelby said, I'm sure he had a good reason." She laughed coldly. "Probably a blond one..." Tears fell hotly again, and Shelby quickly got her out of the room, across the hall and into the study.

"Now sit down." Shelby helped her to the burgundy leather sofa. "I'll get you a brandy. Is that all right?"

"I hate him," Abby said, burying her face in her hands. "I hate him so much!"

"Yes, I know." Shelby smiled wryly and poured brandy into a snifter. She gave the glass to Abby, and watched her take a sip and grimace at the harsh taste.

Her blue-gray eyes lifted to Shelby's green ones. "I haven't even seen him in weeks," she said brokenly. "He hasn't called or come to see me. I didn't know why then, but now I do. He was letting me down easy. He knows how I feel, and he doesn't want to hurt me...."

"If it means anything, I know how you feel, too," Shelby said gently, her eyes soft and sad.

"Yes, I'm sure you do." Abby touched the older woman's hand. "Justin never looks at anyone else. Calhoun said once that he supposed Justin would die loving you."

"And hating me, all at once," Shelby sighed. "Justin thinks I slept with someone else. He believed my father and a crony of his, and I've never been able to make him listen. As if I could have let any other man touch me, ever!"

Abby stared at her, momentarily distracted. "Oh, Shelby," she whispered.

Shelby grimaced. "Stubborn, proud, hardheaded man." Her eyes lifted. "I'd die for him."

"I hope it works out someday."

The older woman sighed. "Miracles still happen occasionally." She searched Abby's eyes. "Will you be all right now?"

Abby finished the brandy. "Of course I will. I don't care if Calhoun misses my party. I can have a perfectly good time without him. After all, I was only his ward and now I'm not anymore. He's just another man." She got up, smoothing her hair. "I'd better fix my makeup."

She went to the mirror and repaired her lipstick and powder, but there was very little she could do about her red eyes. Then she followed Shelby out the door.

The band was good. They played a succession of dreamy waltzes and country-and-western songs, which their lead singer belted out in a smooth baritone. Abby danced every dance, some with Justin, some with

Tyler, and a lot with old school friends. But still Calhoun didn't make an appearance. Abby grew more vivacious by the minute to cover up her misery.

She was dancing much too close to Tyler in a lazy two-step, when she felt eyes on her back. Without looking, she knew Calhoun had arrived. He'd spoiled her party by not showing up until it was almost over, and she hated him. Having settled that in her mind, she kept her eyes closed and kept dancing.

"Calhoun's here," Tyler murmured into her hair.

"So what?" she said icily.

His eyebrows arched. He glanced at Calhoun, who was thunderously angry, and then at Justin, who was heading toward his younger brother with an expression that would have made a lesser man than Calhoun back off.

"Abby, Justin's going toward Calhoun with blood in his eye."

"Good," she muttered. "I hope he kills him."

"Abby!"

She bit her lower lip. "I don't care."

"You don't care like hell," Tyler replied curtly. He stopped dancing and held her by the arms. "Stop it. If you want him, for God's sake, show him that you do. Don't pout and hem and haw until you lose him."

"You don't understand," she began.

"Abby, look at Shelby and Justin," he said quietly. "Is that how you want to end up?"

She searched Tyler's face and then looked over to the doorway, where Justin and Calhoun were talking in terse monosyllables. "All right," she said wearily.

He smiled. "Good girl. Go on."

She hesitated, but then she walked away. Tyler watched her go, a faint sadness in his own eyes. That was quickly erased when Misty Davies wandered over in a frothy gold party dress and asked him to dance.

Justin stopped talking when Abby came near. He glared at Calhoun. "Tell it to Abby," he said shortly. "She's been having a hell of a good time, though, all by herself."

Justin smiled faintly at them and wandered off to talk to another of the guests, leaving a cold-eyed Calhoun and a fuming Abby staring at one another.

"Thank you for coming," she said with faint hauteur. "I'm having a lovely time."

"How could you think I'd willingly treat you like that?" he asked quietly. "Turn my back on you, deliberately arrive late, embarrass you with your guests... Oh, God, don't you know me better than that?"

He disconcerted her. She looked up at him helplessly. "What happened?"

"I ran the Jaguar into a ditch and damned near wrecked it," he said with a mocking smile. "I was going too fast, and I took a curve where there'd been an oil spill that I didn't know about."

Her face went white. She saw a graphic mental picture of him lying in a ditch, dead. It erased all her stupid suspicions and left her shaking.

Without a word, she pressed hard against him. She held him, trembling, oblivious to her surroundings, to everything but Calhoun.

"You're trembling," he said, faintly surprised. His big hands went to her back, where it was bare over the deep plunge of her dress. "I'm all right, honey."

She held him tighter, fighting tears. The trembling grew worse, and she couldn't seem to stop.

"For God's sake…!"

He drew her out of the room, one big arm supporting her, and into the study. He locked the door behind them, shutting out the music and muffled conversation and other party sounds. His dark eyes looked down into her wild, pale ones.

"I wouldn't have missed your party on purpose, little one," he said gently.

That was the old Calhoun, she thought wildly. Her guardian. Her protector. The kind, caring older man who looked after her and kept her safe. But he didn't look or sound like a lover, and she supposed that he'd used those weeks to good advantage, getting her out of his system. She felt sick and shaken, and she wanted nothing more than to go home and cry herself to sleep.

"No, I'm… I'm sure you wouldn't have," she said, her voice husky. She forced a smile. "It was kind of you and Justin to let me have the party here."

His dark eyes narrowed. He leaned back against the door, elegant in his evening clothes, the white silk of his shirt emphasizing his high cheekbones, his blond hair and dark skin, his powerful build. "You sound strange," he said. "You look strange."

"I've had a long week, that's all." She was beginning to sound like a broken record. "I'm enjoying my new job. I like it very much. We stay busy. And—"

"Stop it," he said softly.

Her eyes closed, tears burning them. Her hands at her sides tautened into fists and she fought for control. "I'm sorry."

"Come here, Abby," he said in a tone that she remembered, deep with tenderness, soft with sensuality.

She opened her eyes. "I don't want pity," she whispered.

His chin lifted. "What do you want?"

She lowered her gaze to his highly polished shoes. "The moon," she said wearily.

He moved forward abruptly. One big, lean hand caught hers and pried it open. He placed something in it and curled her fingers around it. She frowned. Something small and thin and metallic...

She opened her hand. It was a ring, a very simple circle of gold without any flourishes or frills. It was a wedding ring.

He bent, lifting her. He carried her to the burgundy sofa and put her down on it. Then he knelt on the carpet beside her, his lean hands on her waist, his blond hair gleaming like the golden ring in the soft light from the ceiling.

"I love you," he said softly, holding her gaze as he said it.

Her eyes searched his, getting lost in their dark, unblinking intensity. "W-what?"

"I love you," he repeated. "I didn't know it until the night I almost made love to you, and even then I wasn't sure that I could settle down." He laughed faintly, watching her with eyes that adored her. "But I'm sure now. These past few weeks have been the purest hell I've ever known. A dozen times I've almost stormed over to your apartment at three in the morning to get into bed with you. I've thought about kidnapping you from work and carrying you off into the mountains. But

I promised to give you time, and I have. Now I've run out of it. If you don't marry me, so help me, I'll ravish you where you sit."

"I'll marry you," she whispered. "But—"

"But what?" he whispered back.

Her lips parted as she let her shoulders droop, so that the silky fabric of her dress fell and revealed all of her breasts except the hard tips. "But wouldn't you ravish me anyway?"

His breath caught. "As if I needed asking…"

His hands finished the job, stripping the fabric to her waist. He sat looking at the soft, pretty swell of her breasts, watching her breathe for a long moment before he drew her toward him and bent his head.

She began to tremble when she felt his mouth on her soft, heated skin. Her hands cradled his head and she wept softly, kissing his hair, whispering to him. "I love you," she murmured. "I'm sorry I…made a fuss. I thought you were out with some woman, that you didn't want me…. Oh, Calhoun!"

His mouth had opened, taking almost all of one perfect breast inside to taste, to caress with his tongue. His lean hand was at her back, searching for a zipper, and in the next instant she was on the carpet under him, her body bare from the neck down except for her briefs and her stockings.

"I was in Houston buying a ring. Buying two rings. Your engagement ring had to be sized. It's a yellow diamond." He kissed her hungrily. "I got caught in traffic, and since I knew I was going to be late, I rushed back… too fast. But it's all right now, isn't it, sweetheart?" He eased his hands down her body, feeling her tremble. "Abby, suppose we make love right here?" he murmured, stroking her gently with his warm, hard fingers.

"Someone might come in," she whispered breathlessly.

He smiled as he bent. "I locked the door," he breathed into her open mouth. "I'm hungry."

"I'm hungry, too."

His nose nuzzled hers. "Or we could go up to my bedroom," he murmured huskily. "And lock the door. Even Justin wouldn't disturb us there."

"The guests..."

"They'll never miss us. They're too busy enjoying themselves. I want you, Abby. I want you for the rest of my life, until I die. And if I get you pregnant..." He lifted his head, searching her warm, soft eyes. "Would you mind having my child?"

She touched his mouth with aching tenderness. "I love you," she said. "I want to have lots of babies with you."

He actually shuddered. "You're very young."

She smiled. "All the better." She traced his heavy eyebrows with her finger. "I can play with them."

He smoothed back her hair, his eyes full of wonder. "Abby... I never dreamed how sweet it would be to belong to someone. To have someone of my own. And a family." He touched her breasts tenderly. "Ever since the first time I touched you, I've felt as if there'd never been a woman for me. You make it all new and exciting. You make me feel whole."

"You make me feel the same way." She reached up to find his mouth with hers, kissing him slowly, tenderly. "Justin won't like it if we go upstairs together."

"He won't see us," he whispered and smiled wickedly. "Where's your sense of adventure?"

"I'm nervous—"

"We'll be married by tomorrow afternoon. I've already got the license. All we need is a blood test, and we can have that in the morning."

"You rake," she said accusingly.

"Reformed rake."

"All right," she breathed.

He searched her eyes quietly. "I need you badly. But I can wait if you want me to."

"You don't want to," she said.

He smiled. "I've felt married to you since that night in my apartment, Abby. A piece of paper and a few solemn words aren't going to tie me to you any more firmly than I am right now. I love you, honey," he said softly. "That's the beginning and the end of my life, wrapped up in those words."

She pressed against him. "I love you so."

He helped her into her dress and led her out the back door, around through the guest bedroom and to the rear staircase. Then he picked her up, laughing softly, and carried her upstairs. He'd just made it to the landing and was turning the corner toward his own room when they ran headfirst into Justin and almost went down on the floor with the impact.

Abby gasped. Calhoun actually turned blood red. Justin's eyebrows went up expressively. Then they just stared at each other.

"Tired of dancing?" Justin asked after a minute, his lips pursed mischievously.

Calhoun cleared his throat. "We were going to…"

"…talk," Abby improvised.

Justin's dark eyes went over Abby's face, reading all the telltale signs there. Then he glanced toward Calhoun and stared him down.

"Oh, what the hell," Calhoun muttered darkly. "You know damned good and well where we were going and why. But there's something you don't know. I love Abby. We're getting married tomorrow. The license is in my pocket."

"And the ring," Abby added, faintly embarrassed at being caught in such a compromising situation.

"Congratulations," Justin said pleasantly. "I couldn't be happier for both of you. And if I might just add, it's about time."

Calhoun shifted Abby. "Thank you."

"You'll be a lovely brother-in-law," Abby agreed.

"The very best," Calhoun added.

Justin smiled. "It won't work. I'm not going anywhere, and neither are you."

"Damn it, Justin!" Calhoun ground out.

"Twenty-four hours is just overnight," Justin continued. "Then you can both go to Houston and have a honeymoon in that penthouse apartment you bought."

"Listen here…" Calhoun began.

"Abby, you tell him how you really feel about this," Justin said, staring at her.

She grimaced, her hands linked around Calhoun's neck. She sighed. "Well, I love him," she said finally.

"I thought you wanted to," Calhoun said softly, searching her embarrassed face. "I'd never have forced you."

"Oh, I know that," she said, her eyes worshipful. "But I couldn't refuse you."

He smiled ruefully. "You're one of a kind," he said gently. "And I love you."

"I love you, too," she whispered, smiling.

He kissed her softly. "I guess we'd better wait, since Justin is going to stand there until he takes root."

"I guess we had," Abby murmured.

Calhoun put Abby on her feet. "Well, let's go downstairs and dance, Abby," he said. "Then we can sing that terrific drinking song that Justin taught you."

Justin glared at him, looking uncomfortable. "You started that."

Calhoun's eyebrows lanced upward. "All I did was dance with Shelby."

Justin stared at him coldly. "And if you hadn't been my brother, I'd have broken your jaw for it."

There was a faint sound behind them, and Justin turned to find Shelby standing two steps behind him.

"Go ahead, Shelby, get an earful," Justin said icily. "Does it please you that after six years I still feel murderous when another man touches you?"

"That works both ways, Justin," Shelby said quietly. "Or didn't you know that it would kill me to see you with another woman?"

She turned and stormed off downstairs. Justin stared after her, shocked.

"Why don't you carry her upstairs?" Calhoun asked his brother with pursed lips. "Then Abby and I could stand on the landing and block your way."

Justin said something in Spanish that Abby was glad she didn't understand and stomped off downstairs.

Calhoun glanced at Abby's questioning face and grinned. "I'll tell you after we're married," he whispered in her ear.

AND HE DID tell her two days later as they lay together in the big soft bed at his penthouse, sated and close in each other's arms as the sun drifted lazily through the blinds.

"What did Justin say to you the night you started to carry me upstairs?" she asked drowsily.

"He said that if he ever took Shelby to bed it would be on a desert island with mines on the beach." He chuckled. "Poor Justin," he added quietly. "To love like that and not even have a memory to live on."

She lifted her eyes to his, her hand lazily stroking his thick, hair-matted chest. "What do you mean?"

"Justin never slept with Shelby," Calhoun said softly. "And since the engagement broke off, he's never slept with anyone else."

She caught her breath.

"It isn't so incredible, Abby," he mused, rolling over to look down into her soft eyes. The covers had long since been thrown off, and his dark gaze slid over her nudity with possession and exquisite memories of the night before. "I couldn't touch anyone else after I kissed you."

"That's very profound," she whispered, trembling as his lean hand stroked gently over her taut breasts and down over her belly to the silken softness of her thighs.

"It's that," he agreed, bending to brush his lips across her mouth. "Have I hurt you too badly, or is it all right if we make love again?"

She flushed, remembering their first time, the softness of his voice whispering to her to lie still after he'd realized how difficult it was going to be. And then he'd bridled his own needs so that he could rouse her all over again. The pain had been minimal, because the savage hunger he'd kindled in her had surpassed pain or fear or even thought. She'd given everything he'd asked in the end, her body so completely his that he could have done anything to her.

"I'm all right now," she whispered, adoring his hard face with her eyes. "You made it all right."

"You were very much a virgin, Mrs. Ballenger," he said with faint traces of satisfied delight. "And it wasn't the easiest initiation."

She traced his chin. "I love you. And any way you loved me would have been all right."

He kissed her softly. "You make me feel humble."

"You make me feel wild," she gasped, arching as his hand moved. Her eyes widened as it moved again. "Yes…do…that…"

He smiled through his own excitement as she responded to him. He enjoyed her innocence as he'd never imagined he could. He held back this time, drawing out his possession until she was crying with her arousal, until she was almost in torment from the need. And then he eased down, tenderly, coaxing her to bank down her own fires and settle into a new and achingly sweet rhythm that brought with it a fulfillment beyond her wildest dreams, beyond even his experience.

Afterward, he cradled her against his hard, damp body, trembling as he held her, stroked her. She'd gone with him every step of the way, and she was exhausted. So was he. She made an adventure of lovemaking, an exquisite expression of shared love. It was something he'd never known in a woman's arms. Whispering softly, he told her that.

She smiled as she lay nestled against him. "I don't have anyone to compare you with," she whispered. "But on a scale of ten, I'd give you a twenty."

Calhoun laughed softly, closing his eyes and sighing contentedly as he felt her snuggle close to him, her body fitting perfectly against his.

"Abby, how would you feel about living in the old Dempsey place?" he asked unexpectedly.

She opened her eyes. "That big Victorian house that you and Justin bought last year? It's been remodeled and furnished, hasn't it? I thought you were going to use it for offices."

"I'd thought about it," he told her. "But I want to live there with you."

"There, and not with Justin?" she asked softly.

He touched her hair. "It will make life hell for him if we're under the same roof."

"Yes, I know. To see how happy we are will only point out what he's lost." She smiled. "I'll live with you wherever you say."

He searched her eyes gently. Then he folded her up against him and drew the sheet over their damp bodies. "I love you, Abby," he said drowsily.

"I love you, too." She slid her arm across his broad chest and sighed contentedly. It was spring, and soon the pastures would be dotted with wildflowers and seed would begin sprouting everywhere. She closed her eyes, thinking about the long horizons and lazy summers and the promise of children playing around her skirts while she sat in the circle of Calhoun's arm and watched the cattle graze. It sounded like the most exciting kind of future to share—with a long, tall Texan at her side.

* * * * *

HARLEQUIN
PLUS

Announcing a **BRAND-NEW** multimedia subscription service for romance fans like you!

Read, Watch and Play.

Experience the easiest way to get the romance content you crave.

Start your **FREE 7 DAY TRIAL** at <u>www.harlequinplus.com/freetrial</u>.

*By the book success story Alexandra Herrera's got it
all mapped out. But when her birth father leaves her
an unexpected inheritance, she impulsively walks away
from her entire life! And now that she's snowed in with
West Wright, she learns that lightning really can strike
twice. So much, in fact, that the sparks between them
could melt any ice storm...if only they'd let them!*

Read on for a sneak peek at
The Christmas Cottage,
the latest in the Wild Rose Sisters series
by New York Times *bestselling author Christine Rimmer!*

So that was an option, just to say that she needed her alone
time and West would intrude on that. Everyone would
understand. But then he would stay at the Heartwood Inn
and that really wasn't right...

And what about just telling everyone that it would be
awkward because she and West had shared a one-night
stand? There was nothing unacceptable about what she
and West had done. No one here would judge her. Alex
and West were both adults, both single. It was nobody's
business that they'd had sex on a cold winter night when
he'd needed a friend and she was the only one around
to hold out a hand. It was one of those things that just
happen sometimes.

It would be weird, though, to share that information
with the family. Weird and awkward. And Alex still
hoped she would never have to go there.

"Alex?" Weston spoke again, his voice so smooth and deep and way too sexy.

"Hmm?"

"You ever plan on answering my question?"

"Absolutely." It came out sounding aggressive, almost angry. She made herself speak more cordially. "Yes. Honestly. There's plenty of room here. You're staying in the cottage. It's settled."

"You're so bossy…" He said that kind of slowly—slowly and also naughtily—and she sincerely hoped her cheeks weren't cherry red.

"Weston." She said his name sternly as a rebuke.

"Alexandra," he mocked.

"That's a yes, right?" Now she made her voice pleasant, even a little too sweet. "You'll take the second bedroom."

"Yes, I will. And it's good to talk to you, Alex. At last." Did he really have to be so…ironic? It wasn't like she hadn't thought more than once of reaching out to him, checking in with him to see how he was holding up. But back in January, when they'd said goodbye, he'd seemed totally on board with cutting it clean. "Alex? You still there?"

"Uh, yes. Great."

"See you day after tomorrow. I'll be flying down with Easton."

"Perfect. See you then." She heard the click as he disconnected the call.

Don't miss
The Christmas Cottage *by Christine Rimmer,*
available November 2022 wherever
Harlequin Special Edition books and ebooks are sold.

Harlequin.com

Love Harlequin romance?

DISCOVER.

Be the first to find out about promotions,
news and exclusive content!

- Facebook.com/HarlequinBooks
- Twitter.com/HarlequinBooks
- Instagram.com/HarlequinBooks
- Pinterest.com/HarlequinBooks
- YouTube.com/HarlequinBooks

ReaderService.com

EXPLORE.

Sign up for the Harlequin e-newsletter and
download a free book from any series at
TryHarlequin.com

CONNECT.

Join our Harlequin community to
share your thoughts and connect
with other romance readers!
Facebook.com/groups/HarlequinConnection

HSOCIAL2021

HARLEQUIN

Heartfelt or thrilling, passionate or uplifting—Harlequin is more than just happily-ever-after.

With twelve different series to choose from and new books available every month, you are sure to find stories that will move you, uplift you, inspire and delight you.